D0545048

THE ZENO EFFECT

ANDREW TUDOR

Matador
9 Priory Business Park,
Wistow Road, Kibworth Beauchamp,
Leicestershire. LE8 0RX
Tel: 0116 279 2299
Email: books@troubador.co.uk
Web: www.troubador.co.uk/matador
Twitter: @matadorbooks

ISBN 978 1789017 311

British Library Cataloguing in Publication Data.
A catalogue record for this book is available from the British Library.

Printed and bound in Great Britain by 4edge Limited
Typeset in 11pt Adobe Jenson Pro by Troubador Publishing Ltd, Leicester, UK

Matador is an imprint of Troubador Publishing Ltd

For Freya
In the hope that the world in which she grows up turns out better than the one portrayed here

PROLOGUE

The man in the white coat stood up and stretched. Bending over a microscope was particularly uncomfortable for someone so tall, and he felt the click of bones moving back into position as he lifted his arms and arched his back to ease the stiffness. The bench in front of him was busy with equipment: racks of glassware, a computer, implements of various kinds, a thermal cycler, as well as the microscope. His was but one bench in a large open-plan laboratory, presently filled with late summer light from windows that looked out onto the Wiltshire countryside. Or, at least, that part of it that could be seen beyond the high fencing that wound away in either direction. Other than him, the lab was empty. It was Friday and his co-workers had embarked on their weekends some time earlier. Pleading a pressing set of tests to finish he had remained behind, though truth be told he had no reason to get home early and there were things to do which were best done when he was alone.

Retrieving a sealed container from an iris-authenticated secure store, he carried it across the lab to a glovebox and placed it inside along with a needle syringe and a small blue-labelled bottle. Then, closing the cabinet, he eased his hands into its gloves and taking great care not to spill any of its contents, he opened the container. With the syringe he transferred a small quantity of clear liquid from container to bottle, resealing both when he had finished. Retrieving his kit from the glovebox, he dumped the syringe in the secure waste bag, returned the container to storage, and slipped the bottle into his pocket. The whole process had taken only a few minutes but, he thought with a private smile, its ramifications would rumble on for years.

His business complete, he hung the white coat on his peg, replaced it with a nondescript jacket, collected his briefcase and left the lab. There was a security barrier at the entrance foyer to the building, manned by a uniformed guard and equipped with surveillance cameras and X-ray screening.

"You're the last out, Dr Livermore," the guard said, running the briefcase through his equipment as Livermore emptied his pockets into a tray. "Still getting the hay fever then?" the guard added, seeing the small bottle among the other bits and pieces.

"Yes, it's not good at the moment, but" – Livermore pointed at the bottle – "that stuff helps with the eyes. Just as well really, having to work with screens and a microscope."

"That's you through. Enjoy your weekend. Any special plans?"

"A few things that need doing, but not much. See you next week, Graham."

With that, Livermore reclaimed his possessions and headed out to his car, one of only three remaining in the car park. Once it was disconnected from the charging post, he set the car's auto-destination and was on his way home. A matter of twenty minutes or so to his house in the little village of Pitton.

At home he sat for a while absent-mindedly staring through the window at his small garden. What to do next? Perhaps he would walk up to the Silver Plough and eat there. It was still a little too early for the evening rush when the shuttles from Salisbury would deposit their weekend revellers, so he would be able to find a quiet corner. Yes, that was a good idea. He deserved not to labour in his own kitchen on this evening of all evenings. Besides, the few minutes' walk to the pub would be a pleasant diversion in such splendid weather.

As he expected, the pub had only a scattered handful of customers.

"Evening, Charles," the barman greeted him. "A half is it?"

"No, a pint tonight I think, and I'd like to order some food."

"A special occasion?" asked the barman with a wry grin – Charles was not known for excessive or even moderate drinking.

"Not really. Just that kind of mood, I guess. I'll have the rabbit casserole and a side salad."

"Right you are. Shouldn't be long while we're still quiet."

Charles found himself a table from where he could take in the whole pub and fell into a kind of reverie, looking at the other customers but without really seeing them. Odd to think that he would never come in here again after so many years, first with his father and then, after his parents died, on his own. It was a familiar place, pleasant enough in its own way even for somebody like Charles who wasn't much inclined towards sociability. Decent food too, he reminded himself as he set about his meal.

By the time he had finished eating the shuttle buses were arriving and the noise level was becoming uncomfortable. Waving to the barman, he made his way out through the crowds, his now vacant table instantly occupied by a partying group who were commandeering chairs to put around it almost before he had got up to go. Definitely time for home, he thought, and to prepare for tomorrow.

Back in the house, he dragged a cardboard box from the depths of the under-stairs cupboard and carefully arranged its contents on the dining table: a pair of rubber gloves, a mask and protective goggles, a syringe, and three anonymous-looking 100ml spray bottles. From a drawer he took a dozen or so small blue-labelled eye-drop containers identical to the one already in his pocket, and these too were placed in an orderly group on the table top. Then, wearing gloves, mask and goggles, for each of the eye-drop containers he reversed the procedure that he had followed in the lab earlier that evening until the spray bottles were partly filled. Not too full, he told himself; best that they look ordinary and well used.

What a mixed blessing it had been to be brought up to be so meticulous, he reflected, as he returned the now empty eye-drop containers to the drawer and the other bits and pieces to the cupboard, leaving only the three spray bottles neatly lined up on the table. He sat looking at them for some time, fascinated by the ordinariness of their appearance and the extraordinariness of their contents, then, shaking his head as if to clear it, he crossed the room to switch on the television.

The main evening news had just begun, a familiar recitation of the troubles of the world which could serve only to stiffen his resolve. Or so he hoped. The presenter, blandly charming as always, was in the midst of explaining the latest diplomatic tensions between the determinedly independent Scotland and the surviving UK, a relationship fed half by mutual recrimination and half by the geographical and economic necessity of co-operation between two governments of such dramatically different political persuasions. Charles paid scant attention to the details; as far as he was concerned they would soon be of no significance.

When the bulletin turned to international matters, however, he focused on the screen almost voraciously. "Water levels are rising faster than expected," announced a reporter, behind whom the ocean was lapping against beachfront bars and cafés which had clearly once hosted the holidaymakers who could be seen beyond them on higher ground. "Representatives of the Confederation of Low-lying Communities are appealing to the United Nations to provide further practical and economic support." A graphic showing the rate of reduction of Antarctic ice was matched by another showing the flooding of islands across the world. "Even on the major continental landmasses settlements are now at risk," the reporter added, leading into a montage of shots of coastal cities in a number of countries where rising levels were all too apparent.

Its allocated five minutes complete, the televised disasters of climate change gave way to the even more visually dramatic disasters of warfare, terrorism, poverty and social disorder. "Going to hell in a handcart," Charles muttered, a phrase of which his father had been unduly fond and which Charles had come to appreciate more and more. "Enough," he said out loud, as much to the larger world as to the television, and switching it off he took a final look at the three bottles in their neat row on the table. They were ready. He was ready. Tomorrow was the day.

He was up early the next morning, determined to catch the first shuttle bus into Salisbury. He could have driven – his government authority to use a personal car extended to that – but it would have been unusual and he did not want to attract attention. Packing the three bottles into a small backpack, he added a thin fleece, a bottle of water, a couple of granola bars, his work-issue CommsTab, and a travellers' medical kit. From the bookcase he selected a single volume from a row of uniformly bound old-looking books. He checked around the living room and kitchen. All was as it should be, neat and tidy, windows shut, power sockets switched off. Locking the front door behind him, he set off up the hill to the shuttle stop without a backward look, waved his card at the ticket machine, and took one of the single seats near the front of the vehicle. There was plenty of room. The shopping rush would not come until later.

Arriving in town, he had only half an hour to fill before catching the early tourist shuttle to Stonehenge. This one was busy. Stonehenge attracted large numbers of visitors at the weekends, especially in weather like this, and Charles was surrounded by excited children in company with their already frazzled parents, as well as guided tour groups of various nationalities. Good, he thought, these people will be heading off in every direction after their day out.

At the newly expanded Visitor Centre, Charles joined the queue for admission to what was now a considerable complex of outlets and attractions. He recalled his parents bringing him here when the whole thing was much smaller, though even then you could no longer actually enter the ring of stones and his father always took great pride in reminding everyone that as a child he had wandered at will among the megaliths. But Charles was not greatly interested in Stonehenge itself today, nor in thinking too much about his father, so after a desultory stroll around the perimeter for the sake of appearances he headed for the café and the shops. It was there, among people, that he really needed to be.

First the café. Buying an espresso and a muffin, he carried them over to a table with a bench seat against the wall from whence he could survey the entire area. Crowds were building up, and although patrolling security guards were occasionally visible they stayed out of the café itself. Charles's backpack lay on the bench beside him, from which he extracted his CommsTab and, switching to a newsfeed, began to read. Or, at least, to look as if he was reading. As he did so he reached into the bag and removed one of the spray bottles along with his fleece, laying the bottle on the seat between his thigh and the pack then concealing it with the fleece.

No one was yet seated at the tables adjacent to his, so after a careful look around he drew the spray bottle from its hiding place and, holding it beneath the level of the table, fired three or four sprays in a semicircle. Not ideal, he thought, but he could hardly spray its contents high in the air without attracting unwanted attention. It would still do the job. Now for the rest of the building. He planned out a route. Inevitably the Visitor Centre was constructed to maximise income, so the shuttles deposited customers at one end of a long building through which they passed on the way to the stone circle itself. The café was next to that exit, partly because of the view it afforded across to the main attraction, but also to lure in visitors whether they were going out or coming back. Running from the café to the shuttle exit was a corridor of sales outlets of various kinds – everything from souvenir bric-a-brac to expensive scale models of Stonehenge – and at the far end were the toilets. Charles mused on the commercial opportunism involved in that placing of facilities. To visit the toilets from the café required you to twice run the gauntlet of the tourist shops. Well, he would stroll along that route browsing the goods as anybody might be expected to do, spraying from beneath the fleece whenever it was safe.

Finally he arrived at the toilets. He had only a little liquid left in the first bottle, so in the hope that he could finish it off more discreetly he headed into the gents. Doors stood ajar on the row of cubicles and there was no one in the open spaces in front of the washbasins and urinals. Charles caught a glimpse of himself in the mirror. He looked very ordinary, he thought, perhaps a little sad and dowdy, but nothing for anyone to notice. Still eyeing his reflection, he lifted the bottle and swept the spray around above his head. As he did so, one of the half-open doors swung fully open and a young boy emerged, perhaps ten years old. The boy stopped, surprised at the odd sight which greeted him.

He eyed the bottle in Charles's hand: "What's that?"

"Just some stuff to stop the smells."

"Oh." The boy did not look entirely convinced. "I can't smell it," he added, elaborately sniffing the air.

"It doesn't work like that – it's a special kind of air freshener."

"Oh, right. Cool." And, clearly not entirely sure that he should be having this conversation, he ran past Charles and out of the door.

Once more Charles turned to the mirror, to his now even more unprepossessing reflection. The boy was so young and so full of curiosity, as he himself had once been. And what was that boy's future now? For the first time today Charles felt a stab of doubt, a tiny fissure in his unwavering sense of purpose. Who was he to take on the problems of the world? What gave him the right to alter for ever the future of that young boy, in all probability to cut off his life before he had any chance even to experience it? Charles had answers to these questions, he knew he had, they had occupied his thoughts for years now. But confronted with the boy, with his vitality, the force and clarity of those answers was obscured in a swirl of ambiguity and doubt.

Such thoughts were vertiginous and, close to collapse, Charles stumbled into the nearest cubicle. Seated on the edge of the toilet bowl he lowered his head into his hands and stared vacantly at the tiled floor between his feet. How had he got here? He had been so positive once, so optimistic. When researching his PhD he had believed in a future in which he would do good things, in which he would 'make a contribution' as the academic cliché had it. Well, he was certainly going to do that, but not quite in the way that he had envisaged all those years ago. It was the right thing to do, he reminded himself, whatever the cost, and slowly his determination returned, his scientific rationality – as he liked to think of it – quelling the flood of emotions that the encounter with the young boy had precipitated.

After a few more minutes of steady slow breathing he was able to get back to his feet. Discarding the now empty bottle in the nearest bin he walked out towards the Salisbury shuttles. One was full and about to leave, but a second stood empty not due to depart for another thirty minutes. Here was a chance both to recover from his crisis and to begin phase two of his plan. Retrieving another spray bottle from his bag and holding it at waist level, he climbed aboard the vehicle, flashed his card at the ticket machine, collected his receipt, and walked slowly down the bus spraying as he went. Settling in a seat about two-thirds of the way along, he closed his eyes and tried to relax.

After a while the bus began to fill up, and what was initially a murmur of conversation became a hubbub of different tongues. Charles opened his eyes and looked around, pleased to see how many nationalities were in evidence. Only five minutes until departure. Having got this far, all he wanted now was to get back into Salisbury to complete the third and final phase of his mission. He settled back into his seat and, just as he was about to close his eyes once more, he saw the boy from their earlier encounter. In company with two adults and another child – a sister perhaps – he was coming down the bus in search of seats. Charles saw his look of recognition as he drew nearer, saw him tug at his mother's arm and say something to her, saw her quizzical glance as they passed. Charles froze, his earlier panic returning. He couldn't stay here, he thought, he couldn't bear it. Clutching his possessions to his chest and only just resisting the temptation to run, he made for the exit. The shuttle supervisor was standing by the door ready to set the vehicle in motion. Charles pushed past him, muttering as he went.

"I've just realised I've left something in the café."

"We're about to go," the supervisor replied with some irritation. "You won't have time to get there and come back and I can't refund your fare."

"Never mind," said Charles, "it's my fault. I'll catch the next shuttle."

As he turned towards the main entrance he caught a final glimpse of the boy and his mother. They were looking at him curiously, their faces pale discs receding as the shuttle swung out onto the main road. Charles turned and walked slowly down the aisle of shops, made a show of looking around the area where he had been sitting in the café, then returned the way he had come to occupy a bench outside the main entrance. Perhaps this wasn't so bad, he thought; now he had a chance to work on a second shuttle. He would wait for the next one and ensure that he was the first person to board.

Once the newly arrived vehicle had disgorged its occupants, Charles followed the same procedure as he had on the previous occasion, finally seating himself midway down the bus and closing his eyes. This time, although the passengers proved just as noisy as before, he kept his eyes firmly closed for the entire trip, opening them only when it was clear that they were arriving at the Salisbury terminal. It was now mid afternoon of a hot August day and the narrow streets around the cathedral were busy with Saturday shoppers as well as with tourists. After discarding his now empty bottle in a bin, Charles slowly worked his way towards the Cathedral Close, a route which he had followed so often over the years. He stopped briefly outside the restaurant which now occupied the site of Beaches Bookshop, recalling how he and his father would poke about in search of bargains among its extraordinary collection of second-hand books. One of those volumes was in his rucksack right now, part of a 1920s Macmillan Pocket Edition set of Thomas Hardy novels which had taken years of assiduous searching to assemble and of which his father had been very proud. Given that personal history he felt doubly sad that Beaches had closed, although hardly surprised. It was, Charles reflected, just another small example of where the world had gone wrong.

Turning away from these troubling memories, Charles made for his final destination of the day. Salisbury Cathedral remained his favourite of such buildings. Not, perhaps, as historically evocative as Winchester or as monumental as Durham or York, but so elegant, its magnificent spire reaching for the heavens. Constable had caught its splendour well in his famous painting of the view from the meadows, a print of which was hanging on Charles's bedroom wall. He stood for a while and allowed his gaze to travel along the building and, finally, up and up that spire. His father had always borrowed Orson Welles's description of Chartres Cathedral when confronted with Salisbury – 'a grand, choiring shout of affirmation' – and the phrase had stayed with Charles. Affirmation indeed, he thought. When they built this it was still possible to affirm, to celebrate humanity's relationship with its god. But now god was dead and humanity was busy destroying the world and leaving little worthy of celebration.

With that melancholy thought Charles gave the spire one last appraising look and then walked swiftly towards the main entrance. Coming in from the bright sunshine made the interior seem all the more cool and dark, the narrow nave with its high-vaulted roof appearing to stretch away into time itself. Although he had no religious beliefs, a kind of peace came over Charles as he wandered through the ancient building. The creators of the cathedral had wanted to celebrate the glory of their god and, less altruistically if more pragmatically, ensure their ultimate entry into heaven. He felt it entirely appropriate that this was where the day of judgment would arrive, both for him personally and, more important, in bringing to fruition the judgment that he was making on the world. Was that hubris? Perhaps it was, he thought, but necessarily so if humanity was ever to recover anything like the noble aspirations that had motivated this building. Had he done a terrible wrong? The cathedral's builders would certainly have thought so, but unlike them he was not a believer except perhaps in Nature and now, with his help, in the capacity of the Earth to survive humanity's worst depredations.

In this newly recovered state of quietude Charles took out the third bottle and, as a tourist might, wandered among the tombs, chapels and hidden corners of the cathedral, spraying as he went. At last the bottle was empty, and after dropping it in a rubbish bin near the main entrance, he found a deeply shadowed seat tight up against one of the pillars. His mission was accomplished. Events would take their own course now with no need for further intervention from him. He sat for a while listening to the organ music which seemed to float in the huge spaces around him. Was it recorded? Was it the real organist at rehearsal? He couldn't tell, but whichever it was it sounded beautiful. Now it was time. From his bag he removed the travellers' medical kit from which he extracted a hypodermic. First checking that no one was in his immediate vicinity, he filled the hypodermic from a small vial and injected himself in the muscle of his left arm. Then, returning the hypodermic and vial to the bag, he drew out his book, searched for a particular page and sat quietly reading.

z z z

To any of the tourists who passed by that corner of the cathedral as the late afternoon transformed into evening, there was nothing unusual to attract their attention. A man asleep in the deepening darkness, his head leaning to one side against the pillar by which he sat, open on his lap the book that he had been reading before sleep overtook him. Had they approached nearer, they might have wondered how he could remain asleep with his head at that uncomfortable angle, and nearer still they could have seen that his mouth was open in an oddly disturbing way and that he did not appear to be breathing. But no one came that close. If they had done so, they might have seen also that the book was an old-fashioned looking edition of Thomas Hardy's *Jude the Obscure*, and that it was open at the passage describing the deaths of Jude's two younger children at the hands of their elder brother, who then hangs himself. In the midst of the page, in italic and separated from the text around it, was the message left in a note by the older child.

'Done because we are too menny.'

PART 1

INCUBATION

1

The city smelled hot to Alison MacGregor as she picked her way along a busy pavement on her way to work. It was an oddly compelling mixture of scorched rubber, grilled food and dust, which she only ever encountered here in central London. Her home town of Edinburgh smelled quite different, washed, as it was, with sea-flavoured winds that blew in from the Firth of Forth. Even in these days of temperature extremes, Edinburgh never seemed to turn into this kind of cooking pot where the simple act of walking along was like pushing your way through an invisible wall of heat. It was a relief to see ahead the pillared portico of Dover House, once the home of the Scotland Office and now given over to the Scottish Liaison Executive, albeit reluctantly on the part of the residual UK government.

Once into the building and past security, air conditioning ensured that the temperature dropped considerably, though how long such energy use could be sustained was an increasingly divisive topic in the monthly staff meetings. The SLE retained the same attachment to democratic debate as the Scottish government itself, making meetings lively affairs if not always with conclusive outcomes. In marked contrast, Alison's encounters with the UK science administrators, with whom it was her job to liaise, were usually tame occasions in which deference to the established hierarchy was the main distinguishing feature. Happily, she had no such meetings today, and since she was due to return to Edinburgh to report at the end of the week, would have none for some time to come.

She settled into the lengthy and rather dull process of dealing with routine emails and circulated notifications. This was the price to be paid for what was otherwise engaging and often challenging work. As a Scientific Liaison Officer she was responsible for ensuring the flow of information between English and Scottish scientific communities – not always easy when there were layers of bureaucracy to negotiate, even where the scientists themselves were more than willing to talk to, or at least at, each other. After graduating in physics, her PhD specialism had been in philosophy of science, but it had soon become clear to her that her real talent lay in organising other scientists – herding cats, as her colleagues were fond of describing it – and mediating between constitutionally incommunicative experts in obscure fields of study.

It was a job that she enjoyed and one at which she had proved exceptionally good, aided by scrupulous attention to detail and a remarkable ability to remember verbatim whole pages of information with little or no effort. At twenty-nine she was the youngest full Liaison Officer in the Executive. With some of the male scientists she knew that it also helped that she was an attractive woman. Long dark hair, a clear complexion, and vivid green eyes had earned her the soubriquet 'The Selkie' among her student contemporaries, and she wasn't averse to turning on some of that magical charm when it would push things along.

She was well through the accumulation of emails when her CommsTab audibly demanded her attention. 'V-call from Irene Johnson,' the machine murmured. Calls from Irene were definitely to be taken, partly because she was a very senior scientific adviser to the UK government, but also because Alison had known her since childhood. Irene's daughter, Sarah, remained Alison's best friend.

"Hello Irene, how are you?"

"Fine Ali, fine. Could you meet me for lunch today? I know you're off north tomorrow and I've got a present for little Charlotte I'd like you to drop off when you visit Sarah."

"Yes, of course, but..."

Ali was about to add that she wasn't actually going until the end of the week and that she hadn't expected to stop off in York to visit Sarah and Hugh, but Irene gave her no chance.

"Great. Great. Let's meet in the National Gallery café at one o'clock. See you then."

And she was gone, leaving Ali open-mouthed, intending also to point out that she had told Irene of her travel plans only a couple of days ago. What was going on? Although Irene was in her sixties, she was as sharp as ever and had hitherto shown no signs of failing memory. She had been so quick to cut Ali off in mid sentence, almost as if she knew what Ali was about to say and didn't want it said. Oh well, Ali thought, maybe she's just having a bad morning at work. Too many people demanding too much of her time. That wouldn't be unusual.

By a quarter to one, Ali was walking into a crowded Trafalgar Square, the sunshine drawing a mixture of tourists, office workers on lunch break, and the scavenging pigeons that had been restored to their former location in the square as tourist attractions. She struggled to find somewhere to sit, finally settling on the steps of the National Gallery from where she would be able to see Irene approaching. The heat was soporific, and it was through half-closed eyes that she at last spotted her friend coming across the square, carrying a gift-shop bag and looking to left and right as she approached. Ali stood up so that Irene could better see her, and, when they made eye contact, walked forward to meet her. To her surprise, Irene enfolded her in a hug of greeting and, her mouth close to Ali's ear, whispered:

"Go along with whatever I say. We could be overheard."

Irene then linked her arm through Ali's and walked her into the building's Sainsbury Wing, chattering about the weather and the crowds as they went. Ali listened mutely, taken aback both by the uncharacteristically effusive greeting and, even more, by the unexpected instruction. Now she was really worried about Irene's state of mind.

They found their way to the café and, after queuing for a while, carried their food to a table which was fortuitously vacated by a man and a woman just as they turned to look for somewhere to sit. Irene fixed the departing couple with a suspicious stare until they had left the café, and then, after handing over the bag containing Charlotte's present, embarked on a torrent of talk which she kept up throughout the meal. About Sarah, about granddaughter Charlotte's upcoming sixth birthday, about Ali's work, about anything other than the reason for that whispered demand. Ali nodded her way through it all, speaking when Irene eyed her expecting a response, and becoming more puzzled by the minute.

At last the meal was over, and it was with some relief that she followed the still voluble Irene back out into Trafalgar Square. Taking her arm once more, Irene drew Ali towards an area particularly crowded with tourists where she stopped and announced that she had a little shopping to do so Ali should continue down Whitehall on her own. Then, just as she had earlier, she drew Ali into an embrace and murmured into her ear.

"When you have Sarah on her own tomorrow, give her this message. Zeno is in the wild. Just that. Zeno is in the wild. She'll understand. On her own, remember. It's urgent and very important."

And with that she disappeared into the crowd.

Ali returned to work but, unsurprisingly, found it impossible to concentrate. She could make no sense of Irene's behaviour except that it was clearly vital to her that Ali did as she asked. Well, Ali thought, there was no real reason why she shouldn't leave tomorrow and stay overnight in York before continuing on to Edinburgh. Having convinced herself of that, she called the Office Manager to make the arrangements.

"Moira, something's come up and I'll need to go north tomorrow instead of Friday, but stopping off in York on the way. I have to talk to a researcher in their Medical School. Could you rebook me on the eleven o'clock train but with a stopover. I'm really sorry about the last-minute change."

Moira, too, sounded sorry at being thus inconvenienced, but Ali comforted herself with the thought that at least her excuse was partly true. Sarah was an immunotherapy systems researcher in the Centre for Immunology and Infection, and it was part of Ali's job to keep in touch with researchers in different regions of the country.

Having taken the decision, Ali felt a little less ill at ease. She was still worried about Irene and puzzled by the strange message, but she and

Sarah could sort that out together. Pushing such concerns to the back of her mind, she emailed Sarah to say that she was coming and then returned to the work remaining from the morning. It would have to be dealt with before she left, a task which would certainly occupy the rest of the afternoon.

Just as she was nearing the last few bits and pieces her CommsTab sprang to life with the information that Richard Osborne was calling. This was not entirely welcome. Ali had an on–off relationship with Richard, one which she did not fully understand and which she was not certain that she wanted. They had met a few months previously at an official reception – Richard was a civil servant in some unspecified financial area of government – and he had proposed that they go out to dinner after the event had ended. He was pleasant company, and Ali found herself falling into a pattern of periodic social outings followed by sleeping together, usually at his flat since her SLE accommodation was altogether more spartan. She quite enjoyed the companionship, and the sex was welcome, but there was nothing there that spoke to her of a longer-term relationship. Still, she didn't feel able to simply ignore his call.

"Hello Richard."

"Ali. Glad to catch you. How about dinner tonight?"

"I've got a lot of work to get through, Richard. I'm still at the office now. I really ought to finish it off and then I've things to do at home."

"Oh come on. We can eat quite late and I'd love to see you. It seems like a long time since we went out and with you going away it's the last chance we'll get for a while."

The exchange continued for a minute or two with Richard in this rather wheedling vein until, as much as anything as the easiest way of ending the conversation, Ali agreed to meet him in a favourite Thai restaurant quite near to where he lived. Perhaps it would take her mind off the day's odd events, she thought, and she had to eat anyway. Cooking herself a solitary meal was even less appealing than usual today.

Another half-hour saw the remnants of office work finished and Ali on her way home. The impersonal official apartment was hardly welcoming and she began to feel a little more enthusiastic about meeting

Richard. Enough, anyway, to take some care about getting ready, having first packed her suitcase and left it along with Charlotte's present ready for the next day's journey.

Dinner turned out to be more entertaining than Ali had expected, mostly since Richard was going out of his way to be charming, keeping her amused with stories of the bureaucratic inaction and obfuscation which seemed to characterise the government circles in which he moved. As he talked, she found herself reflecting on the increasingly marked differences between the tone of politics and governance in her own country and that which prevailed in England.

"OK Richard," she said, interrupting his flow of humorous anecdotes. "It's all very well for us to laugh at this kind of behaviour, but why is it like that? I go to meetings with officials down here and there's no real discussion. A policy is announced and people go along with it. Sometimes I think they're just sitting there looking for ways to agree."

"Maybe it's because they do agree."

"No, you're missing the point. Yes, perhaps they do agree – though surely all of them can't all of the time – but it's more like they're unwilling to actually discuss anything."

Richard leaned across the table towards her as if to impart an important confidence. "Well, after all you are an alien in their midst, a representative from a neighbouring country with whom we have an uneasy relationship. Someone who is not to be trusted. Has it occurred to you that it's a show for your benefit?" He leaned back in his chair with the smug look of a chess player who has just made a compelling move.

Ali bristled at the condescension. "Yes, of course it bloody has. But at every meeting? Even on issues of no significance at all? Besides, all the stories you've been telling me reflect that same passivity, the same constant deferring to authority. And you're not dealing with dangerous aliens like me. I think it's something else. I think you're all so used to taking the lead from higher up that you've become terrified of disagreeing."

"That's not true."

The irritation was clear in Richard's voice, but Ali was on a personal hobby horse now and his discomfort wasn't going to stop her.

"Don't you understand?" she continued. "This is why we left the UK. Year after year we could see governments becoming increasingly authoritarian, brooking no disagreement on policy in spite of contrary evidence, favouring the rich and powerful, even bringing them into government as ministers who had been elected by nobody. For pity's sake, you've now even got military commanders as permanent members of Cabinet."

Richard seemed taken aback at the force with which she levelled this accusation, and, truth be told, she was a little surprised herself.

"It's because strong leadership is important," he said, "without it we wouldn't be able to hold our own in the world. The people want leaders to decide things for them, and for that to work the rest of us need to get into line. You can't go round querying policies all the time. It would make the system unworkable."

"But you have to do exactly that," Ali retorted. "It's by arguing things through that you work out what are the best options. Just playing follow-my-leader confirms for those in positions of power that they have every right to be there, and pretty soon they become *de facto* dictators, convinced that they always know best and that everyone else should simply do what they say. And you know where that leads? To massive control over all aspects of people's lives whether they want it or not. Just think of..."

"No, no," he interrupted her. "We have traditions, checks and balances that stop that happening. It's part of the whole English heritage. We like to have strong leaders to push us forward. Think of Churchill or Thatcher or Blair."

"Every single one of whom," Ali shot back, "whatever good they may have done, also did things which had terrible consequences, and which they were able to do only because of this foolish belief that the great leader knows best."

That said, Ali felt a little calmer, recognising that Richard's litany of heroes was so far from reflecting anything that she believed in that she couldn't hope to persuade him otherwise. He would never understand that it was the culture of blind deference in which he put his faith that had led, little by little, to severe restrictions on people's freedom. But to him that was the inevitable price to be paid for stability and social order, for peace and safety.

He was looking at her quizzically now, uncertain what to say next.

"Oh, what the hell," she said, "it's your country. As long as you leave Scotland alone I guess I can live with it." She smiled, half to herself at the uncharacteristic act of backing down, half at Richard as a kind of peace offering. He looked relieved.

"It's not worth us fighting about," he said. "Let's go home."

Back at his flat they sat down to a nightcap and some gentle music on the sound system, talking of trivial things and both working hard to avoid topics which might reopen the argument. Ali would have quite liked to go home, but it was late and she was too tired to make the effort, so when Richard suggested that they go to bed she was happy enough to comply.

They lay for a while without touching, as if there was now a border between them as clear and real as that between Scotland and England. Ali turned away from him to switch off her bedside light and remained in that position. But after a few uncomfortable minutes he cuddled up to her back and, slipping his arms around her, cupped one of her breasts. She could feel his erection as he pressed against her. She turned to face him. Oh well, she comforted herself as she reached for his cock, this won't take long and it's definitely going to be the last time.

2

After a cursory goodbye to Richard, Ali was on her way early next morning, snatching a cup of coffee and a croissant from a stall in the Underground. It was only a three-stop ride – had she not been in a hurry she would have walked – but there was packing to finish and a train to catch. She raced around the flat, adding a small backpack to the suitcase and filling it with the items she might want on the journey, including Irene's package. Then, as she picked up the suitcase, she noticed a scrap of the colourful wrapping paper on the floor behind it. Had she damaged the parcel? Taking it out of the backpack she turned it over in her hands, examining all sides. It was intact. She looked more closely at the paper fragment and saw that it had a curve drawn in black marker pen on it. Part of Charlotte's name which, characteristically, Irene had scrawled right across one side of the packaging. But on the parcel itself the name was complete. How strange. Perhaps, then, Irene had made a mess of the original wrapping, rewrapped the gift, but left a fragment of the original in the bag. Of course, that was it, and shaking her head at her own obtuseness Ali picked up her baggage and went on her way.

Kings Cross was quiet when she arrived. This was not unusual in Ali's experience, although it always struck her as strange. She remembered the excitement of first visiting London with her parents some twenty years earlier when Kings Cross seemed like the busiest place she had ever seen. Queues of people in all directions, a constant stream of announcements coming over the public address system, busy shops, cafés and bars. Now the arrival and departure board listed only half a dozen trains, while the great open area which used to be packed with travellers had just a few people wandering across it. And everywhere she looked there were armed and uniformed security guards.

Since her train was already boarding, Ali joined the small queue waiting to pass through security. The guards at the gate were running luggage through their X-ray machines and carefully examining documents, electronic pass-cards, and biometric ID details, a process which took some time and over which they were in no hurry. They appeared to quite enjoy this small exercise of power, especially when the prospective passenger proved to be a Scot. Tourists, who were mostly in closely marshalled groups, were waved through much more speedily than those bearing Scottish IDs, a process which would no doubt be defended in terms of the economic need to encourage tourism, but which was clearly also a reflection of the low-level ill will informing so much of officialdom's attitude to the disagreeably independent Scots. Accustomed though she was to such barbed inconveniences, they remained enough of an irritant to ensure that she didn't smile back at the young guard who favoured her with an openly appraising look, and who then took twice as long to check her biometrics.

But at last she was through and, finding her seat, settled in for the two-hour journey. The carriage was nowhere near full and she was one of only a handful of domestic travellers. Most of the passengers were foreign tourists, largely from Asian countries, travelling to York to admire the Minster and the Walls, and to be toured around the city where they would be parted from their money. Ali put in her ear-buds, chose a recording of Bach Partitas for solo violin, and absently watched the English countryside fly past the window as she lost herself in the music. She had just listened to the famous Chaconne from the second Partita when her concentration was disrupted by a thought nagging at the back of her mind. What was it? She switched off the music and focused on recovering the thought. It was something Richard had said. Suddenly it came to her. When he had been trying to persuade her to go out to dinner he had said that they wouldn't get another chance for a while since she would be away. But she was certain that she had not told him that she was due back in Scotland that week, let alone that she was now travelling on the very next day. How had he known?

Set off by that one puzzling question, her mind raced as odd fragments of information began to link up. There was Irene's strange behaviour: her pretence that Ali was due to travel north two days earlier than had been her declared intention; her conviction that they were being listened to; her watchfulness during their lunch; and the enigmatic message that she had given Ali to convey privately to Sarah. Then, on top of all that, Richard's unusually insistent demand that she dined out with him on the evening following the odd encounter with Irene. In fact, now that she gave it more thought, the general peculiarity of her whole relationship with Richard which, she now recognised, had been entirely driven by him. Seen in this context the fragment of wrapping paper took on new significance. Of course Irene couldn't have rewrapped the parcel. She had brought it directly from the gift shop who had surely wrapped it for her. Someone had been into Ali's flat while she was out with Richard, checked the contents of the gift, and rewrapped the parcel with identical paper. Improbable though it sounded, it was the only explanation that she could come up with.

The more she thought about it the more convincing it became. Irene clearly believed herself to be under surveillance, and if that were so then surely it would also be true of Ali. As Richard had been at pains to point out, she was an alien intruder from a problematic country. When she had been first appointed to the SLE, their training had involved warnings about the various UK intelligence agencies and their willingness to use all sorts of methods to acquire information and, thereby, keep control of Scottish/UK relations. Was Richard a part of that? She didn't want to believe so, if only out of reluctance to admit her own gullibility, but, ever the scientist, she had to concede that the hypothesis was disturbingly plausible.

She was still mentally testing all the possibilities when the train arrived in York. After calling Sarah to say that she would be at the university soon, she boarded one of the frequent shuttles and tried to calm herself by watching the old city go by. As ever, the Minster looked splendid in the sunshine while the Walls were peopled by continuous streams of tourists. Soon the shuttle arrived at University Road and from the campus central drop-off point she walked up to the Medical School and presented herself at Reception.

"Alison MacGregor to see Dr Sarah Johnson," she said. The receptionist checked her proffered ID in a rather more desultory fashion than she had experienced at Kings Cross, made a call, and announced that Sarah was on her way down. Minutes later she emerged from the lift and flinging her arms around her friend said, "Ali my lovely, it's always great to see you. Let me look at you. You look good. You must be enjoying London. Shall we go up to the lab? You can leave your suitcase down here and we'll pick it up on the way home."

Ali, who now wanted nothing more than to get Sarah on her own to give her Irene's message and so find out what it was all about, proposed that since she had been stuck on a train all morning it would be good to first take a walk in the fresh air. "You know how much I enjoy the lake," she added, knowing that Sarah, too, delighted in the waterways that meandered through the centre of campus. Leaving her baggage at Reception, the two women walked down the hill to the lakeside, picked their way through a gaggle of geese, and set out to circumnavigate the tree-lined water.

Now that she had reached the nub of her visit Ali suddenly felt reluctant. "Irene asked me to give you a message," she ventured finally, "she insisted that it was for you alone."

"Oh, what's got into my mother now? Why couldn't she just call?"

"She was very firm that I kept it just between us. I got the impression she thought she might be under some kind of surveillance."

Sarah stopped walking and turned to face Ali. "Surveillance? Really? That's not like Mum. She's not generally paranoid. So what was this important message?"

"I don't understand it at all," Ali replied, "but she said I was to say 'Zeno is in the wild'. Just that. She said you would know what it meant."

Sarah's eyes widened and she looked at Ali in palpable disbelief. Ali nodded. "Zeno is in the wild," she said again. "That's exactly it."

Sarah was silent for a minute then half shook her head and said "Oh shit!" And again, this time more vehemently: "Oh shit!"

Grabbing Ali by the arm she pulled her towards a nearby bench overlooking the water. "Come and sit down – I need to think for a minute."

Spotting the two women approaching the bench, a flock of ducks rushed over quacking as they came. They were accustomed to being fed from here but when, after some pestering, Sarah and Ali showed no signs of producing food they waddled off in search of other benefactors. Sarah remained silent for several minutes then, turning to Ali, said, "I guess my mum expects me to tell you what the message means otherwise she would have found some other way to let me know. How much do you know about virology?"

"What most people know, I suppose. The study of viruses, how they relate to disease, and so on. I've met a few researchers in the area."

"Well, you'll know that in this century there have been huge advances in applying genetic engineering techniques to viruses, a lot of it aimed at eliminating diseases and developing vaccines to promote immunity. Some of my work involves that."

Ali nodded. "Yes, you've told me about it."

"But that isn't the only way in which genetic manipulation can be used," Sarah continued, "there are much less benevolent approaches to messing with viruses. Because of that, governments have for years been worried that terrorist groups could weaponise disease, use it as a much more frightening threat than bombs. So most countries with the scientific know-how have secretly funded research into viral warfare – how we can combat it with vaccines and treatments, of course, but also how to create the engineered viruses in the first place. That's the scary thing about researching vaccines – you need to have samples of the nasty bugs so as to design ways of defending against them."

She paused and took a deep breath. "What I'm going to tell you now is a very well-kept secret. I only know because of Mum and because I put two and two together and made about a thousand. At the Porton Down Microbiological Research Centre they've developed a new technique for manipulating the genetic structure of viruses. It depends on something called the Zeno effect. Do you remember Zeno's paradoxes from school?"

"Yes," Ali replied, trying hard to recall. "Achilles and the tortoise. Achilles is chasing the tortoise, and each time he halves the distance between them but at the same time the tortoise has moved forward a little so Achilles never catches up."

"Yeah, more or less. It'll do anyway. You know about genetic drift, the fact that viruses mutate naturally over many generations?"

"Yes, it's why we get different strains of flu and have to change our vaccines regularly."

"OK. Imagine that you could engineer a virus so that it mutates more quickly. Much more quickly. Then our vaccines would be like Achilles and never catch up, because by the time they got near, the virus would already have mutated into some other strain. That's it: the Zeno effect."

Ali looked at Sarah in horror. "What viruses have they been experimenting with?"

"I don't know for sure, but an educated guess would be all the obvious ones since they would assume that the terrorists would be prepared to try anything."

She counted them off on her fingers.

"Smallpox for certain. In theory it's been eliminated since the late 1970s, and although in some countries there are stockpiles of vaccine it would be a hell of a killer if it was reintroduced, even in its ordinary form let alone as a Zeno variant. Ebola, I suppose. Its symptoms are well known to be horrific and, like smallpox, it would generate massive panic. Lassa fever perhaps, and a whole load of other haemorrhagic fevers too, as well as coronaviruses such as the one that causes SARS. And, of course, ordinary, familiar old flu, which can do enormous damage even if it's not as dramatic and panic-inducing as smallpox or Ebola. The H1 strain that created the 1918 pandemic is estimated to have infected at least five hundred million people and killed somewhere between fifty and a hundred million of them." She paused for a moment, staring blankly into space. "I'm afraid there's an awful lot of choice."

"So your mum's message – Zeno is in the wild – means that a Zeno-engineered virus has escaped?"

"Yes," Sarah replied with a deep sigh. "I'm afraid that's exactly what it means."

The two women sat in silence for a long time, looking out across the placid surface of the lake, past the trees and shrubs and flowers, past the familiar buildings. Finally Ali asked her friend, "How bad could it be?"

"It's hard to say without knowing precisely what the virus is and the circumstances that led to it escaping. If it's a small-scale accident and quickly discovered then, with the right precautions, its spread might be contained. But if it's larger scale and not detected until some way into its development, then it could quickly reach epidemic proportions. If it spreads out of its immediate area to other countries and continents, then you would have a pandemic. And with a Zeno-engineered virus that most likely means worldwide chaos. But, as I say, a lot depends on which virus it is."

"But if your mum knows about it now they must already be trying to limit its effects."

"Yes, they must. What worries me is that she went to all the trouble of sending a message by this devious route through you. That makes me think that it must be really serious. If it was already contained, she wouldn't have taken the risk."

Ali nodded her agreement. "Especially if she believes she's under surveillance."

"And it's not just me she's sent the message to," Sarah added. "Her choosing you to carry it can't be accidental. She knows you're going on home to Scotland. I think she expects you to warn your government. And so you should. If there's any chance of a pandemic then Scotland is right in the immediate firing line. You have to tell them so that they can make contingency plans. They might have some chance of controlling cross-border movement before it's too late."

"That would be only if they believed me," Ali replied. "I have no evidence. I'm just a junior civil servant bearing an ambiguous message. But yes, I guess I have to try."

Sarah was firm. "Yes, you do, however long the odds. It's too serious not to. You need to be on that first train tomorrow." As if to emphasise the point she stood up. "Come on then. Hugh will be collecting Charlotte from school and she's looking forward to seeing Auntie Ali. Let's pick up your things and go home. Don't mention any of this in front of Charlotte. We'll explain it to Hugh after she's gone to bed." She shook her head. "What a terrible mess this might turn out to be."

3

At the very moment that Ali and Sarah were talking about her in York, Irene was preparing for a high-level meeting at the Department of Health. She scanned through the documents on her CommsTab, not really paying them much attention since she was all too familiar with their contents, and wondered, as she did so often these days, why she was doing this work at all. When she had first agreed to become a scientific advisor to the government she had believed that it was her chance to do some good. But over the years she had discovered that to be much harder than she had expected. There was an inertial tendency which pervaded the administration of science policy and, she was beginning to understand, ran throughout government itself. Diktats were handed down the chain of command and to challenge them, as she had on occasion, was deemed at best inappropriate and, at worst, verging on insubordination. She was not, therefore, looking forward to this meeting for she knew very well that she would find herself in a vanishingly small minority. Her boss, Graham Ball, the Chief Scientific Advisor, would support her as far as he could, but as for the rest they would mostly toe the official line whatever that turned out to be.

Right on cue Graham arrived at her desk. "It's time, Irene," he said, clearly wishing that it wasn't. "Shall we go?"

"OK. If we must," she replied, collecting her bits and pieces. "Have you heard any more about the breach?"

"No. I'm assuming that we'll get a full update today so we'll have to figure out our position on the hop. Not ideal, but I guess there's no alternative."

Irene grimaced. "Whatever new information we get we'll still need to press for urgent action. Zeno demands it."

"You know I agree with you, Irene, but there will be those with vested interests who will take a different view."

"I know, I know," Irene muttered. "Come on then. Richmond House is calling."

The ornately wood-panelled meeting room was filling up when they arrived, its impressive oak conference table equipped with place markers, glasses and bottles of water. The Secretary of State and his officials were already seated, as were a uniformed Army General and the Home Secretary, both accompanied by aides. In a huddle with his assistants in a corner of the room was the Director of Porton Down, James Curbishley. He contrived to ignore Graham and Irene as they walked past to take their seats, hardly a surprise since he and Irene had clashed more than once. Then, just as Big Ben began to strike the hour at which the meeting was due to start, a woman and two men unknown to Irene came in and sat down together at unlabelled places directly opposite the Secretary of State. He smiled a greeting to them and opened proceedings.

"Right, we're all here now so let's begin. I'm sure I've no need to remind you that what is said here today is highly confidential, and, because the matter is potentially so serious, I've invited the heads of our three main security agencies." He gestured toward the three late arrivals. "Carol Singleton, MI5; Howard Beck, MI6; and Jonathan Hart, Domestic Security Division." The three nodded their acknowledgment and the Secretary of State continued. "I think everybody here has seen the earlier reports about the Porton Down security breach, but I understand that we now have rather more detailed information." He turned towards Curbishley. "James, perhaps you could briefly reprise what we already know and bring us up to date on subsequent developments."

Shifting uneasily in his seat the Porton Down Director took a deep breath and began.

"Last Saturday evening a man was found dead in Salisbury Cathedral. He turned out to be one of ours, Dr Charles Livermore, a long-standing researcher who had been working on the Zeno project. I think you have all been briefed as to what that is?"

He looked round the table seeking confirmation and, there being no dissent, he continued. "In the event of anything like this happening to one of our workers there is a specific set of procedures to be followed. As soon as the police informed us of his identity on Sunday morning, our security team went to his home – Dr Livermore lived alone – and checked for any suspicious circumstances. They found some laboratory equipment – protective masks, gloves, syringes, and the like – and an unusually large number of empty bottles labelled as hay fever treatment. Dr Livermore was known to suffer from hay fever, but the quantity seemed surprising so, as a precautionary measure, they brought the bottles and the equipment back to our labs for examination."

The Secretary of State interrupted. "Do we have any confirmed results from that examination?"

"Up to a point, yes, but if you will allow me I shall get to that in due course. When the local police searched Livermore's body they found a hypodermic and an unlabelled vial, and there was a puncture wound on his arm. They immediately suspected suicide, of course, but could find no note or other indication of intent. I pressed them to accelerate their investigation and, in particular, to conduct a post mortem as soon as possible. After calling on the Secretary of State's office to apply some pressure, I also required them to give us the vial and hypodermic so that we could make tests. I was concerned that it might be something from our labs. As it turns out it was, but not anything that would constitute a danger to anyone other than Livermore who simply used it to kill himself. The more pressing concern lay elsewhere, with the lab equipment and bottles found at his home. Examination of those suggested the strong possibility that they had contained products of the Zeno project lab, although identifying precisely which products would take some time. Meanwhile, the police had traced Livermore's movements on his last day of life. He had visited Stonehenge and the café there, from whence he had got on a Salisbury shuttle then got off again before it departed. The supervisor remembered him getting off and said that he seemed disturbed. He then joined a later shuttle and finally found his way to the cathedral."

The Director stopped to take a sip of water. He was clearly feeling the strain.

"By Monday morning we were becoming extremely concerned, and my security staff persuaded the police that, as discreetly as possible, they should conduct a joint search of both the cathedral and the Visitor Centre at Stonehenge in case Livermore had planted something there. In the cathedral rubbish, which had not yet been collected, they found an unlabelled spray bottle which was brought back to our labs for testing. They found nothing at Stonehenge, but their refuse had been removed earlier that day. The bottle from the cathedral did indeed show traces of a Zeno-engineered virus, which we have now identified as a strain of influenza."

Again the Secretary of State interrupted. "Is it a particularly virulent strain?"

"That depends on how you measure virulence," the Director replied, a little testily. "It's a mutated derivative of the previously eliminated H1N1 strain, some variations of which have proved rather lethal."

"Killing many millions of people in the Spanish Flu pandemic of 1918," Irene interjected.

"Indeed," said Curbishley, favouring her with a look of disdain. "Although far fewer in outbreaks later in the twentieth century when treated with modern medical science."

To cut short this incipient confrontation the Secretary of State raised his voice a little. "We'll return to the matter of the virus itself in due course. First I would like to know what else is known about Livermore and his actions last Saturday. Mr Hart, I believe you have some additional information for us."

"Yes, I do sir. The DSD was called in on Monday, effectively taking over the investigation from the local police and suppressing any flow of information that might reach the media. We were concerned to establish a comprehensive portrait of Dr Livermore and, in particular, a motive for his behaviour."

"Why is that relevant?" asked the General. "We know what the man has done. Why he did it is surely beside the point. We need to move on to consider what action to take."

Hart glanced briefly in the General's direction. "Ah yes. But the problem is that we don't actually know what the man has done. The bottle in the cathedral suggests that he may have released the influenza virus there, but has he also done so elsewhere? More important, has he released other Zeno project materials that we don't know about? Understanding him and establishing a motive will help us make an informed judgment about the extent of the threat that he intended. And that in turn will impact on any decision as to what action to take."

Meeting no further objection, Hart continued. "Examination of the files on Livermore, as well as a thorough search of his home, has given us some material to work with. In particular, we discovered that over the last few years he had become especially interested in environmental problems and in demography. There's no evidence that he was involved with any environmental activist groups – as you know they have anyway been severely curtailed in recent years – but he had assembled a great deal of material documenting human destruction of the environment and linking that to population growth. Furthermore, much of that was in paper form rather than stored on CommsTab servers, so he would appear to have known that his newfound interest would have attracted attention from Security had it been detected. He kept it secret."

Hart paused for a moment, allowing time for his audience to comprehend the gravity of this new information.

"Given all this, our view is that he has acted out of a desire to curtail human impact on the natural world and to do so by releasing a Zeno virus that would, over time at least, radically slow or reverse population growth. This proposition received further confirmation from an unlikely source when we interviewed the policeman who was first on the scene when the body was discovered. It seems that Dr Livermore had a book open on his lap – Hardy's *Jude the Obscure*. The policeman, himself a Hardy fan, noted that it was open at what I am sure you will agree is a significant page. It's the point in the story when Jude's eldest son kills his siblings and himself and leaves a note which reads 'done because we are too many'. This, I believe, was Livermore's suicide note and his justification for whatever he has done."

Hart stopped speaking, clasping his hands together on the table in front of him. The assembly remained silent until finally the Home Secretary asked: "You said there was no evidence of him being associated with any activist groups. Can we be certain of that? If he was, he may have supplied others and there may be similar threats in the offing."

"No," Hart replied, "we are convinced that he was working alone. He was a solitary person, the kind that might be described as a loner, so psychologically it seems very unlikely that he would have joined a group, however strong his convictions. And, as I said, there's absolutely no evidence to suggest it."

The Secretary of State leaned forward across the table and addressed Hart directly. "In the light of what you have learned about Livermore, what do you conclude about his behaviour on Saturday before he reached the cathedral?"

"Well, another feature of Livermore's character that quickly became apparent is that he was a very systematic and meticulous person. Obsessively so, you might say. It's one of the things that made him a good laboratory scientist. This is speculation, of course, but it seems likely that someone having those personality traits, who was set upon a course of action such as this, would plan very carefully and would want to ensure maximum exposure to the virus."

"So you believe that he will have released the virus at the Stonehenge locations as well?" the Secretary of State enquired.

"I do sir. His odd behaviour there hints at it. The business with the two shuttles, his reportedly disturbed demeanour. This suggests someone who is not simply on a pleasant outing to a famous attraction."

For a while Curbishley had been looking increasingly impatient with the DSD man's account and, at this point, he could no longer contain himself. "I don't see that at all. You're leaping to all sorts of conclusions based on very tenuous evidence. This was a man about to commit suicide.

You might expect him to behave oddly. He grew up in this area. Maybe he wanted to make one last sentimental visit to Stonehenge."

Hart was unmoved by the Director's ire. "Possibly so," he said, "but we do know for a fact that a bottle contaminated with a Zeno virus from your institution found its way to the cathedral, so we have to at least entertain the possibility that the virus may have been released at Stonehenge as well. Besides, if Livermore was aiming to kill off large numbers of the human population by infecting a few who would then go on to infect the many, where would he go?"

Hart paused and, with some deliberation, looked around the table.

"He would go somewhere where he could find people who were in transit, who would be able to carry the infection away in all directions. I remind you that Stonehenge attracts visitors not just from the UK but from all over the world. Where better to plant the seeds of destruction?"

His audience were stunned. Suddenly what had appeared to be a potentially containable local problem had become one of much larger proportions. After a long pause, the Home Secretary, seeming to address himself as much as anyone else, said: "I suppose we should be able to trace the foreign tourists who had visited Stonehenge via the Tourist Agency databases?"

"Yes, we are investigating that right now." This response came from the MI5 director who added ruefully, "But I have to say that our first enquiries have had mixed success. It would appear that the tour organisers are not as efficient as they ought to be at monitoring those overseas visitors who book with them. We will be able to identify some of them and, of course, UK visitors can be traced through the cards that they use to pay for the shuttles. But it will take time, and some will undoubtedly slip through the net."

At this news the various groupings around the table resolved themselves into murmuring huddles until, having consulted his own aides, they were interrupted by the Secretary of State. "Can I have some order here, please. I don't see how we can take that issue any further until we have more information, at which point I shall clearly need to bring the Foreign Secretary into the discussion. But now I'd like us to return to what we know about the specific influenza virus that has been identified. James, earlier I understood you to be suggesting that the threat posed by this breach was not as serious as it might have been. Is that right?"

"Yes, Minister, I do believe that to be the case." Curbishley's tone was confident. "First of all, given the range of possibilities available to Livermore, influenza falls at the relatively benign end of the scale. Imagine if we had been dealing with an engineered variation of smallpox."

"We don't yet know that we are not," Graham Ball interjected. "Until you have made all the tests and checked your lab records we can't tell, so we need to keep the possibility in mind."

Hart raised a hand. "If I may, sir, although Professor Ball is quite correct, given what we have established about Livermore's character I think we can allocate a low probability to that. I believe he has chosen influenza because, as he saw it, firstly it will do the job that he required but will not involve the truly horrific suffering that would be experienced with smallpox or some of the haemorrhagic fevers, and secondly, it will not therefore immediately generate the extreme panic and public disorder that would follow when people witnessed such frightening symptoms at first hand. In that respect, at least, Livermore has been humane in his choice."

"I'm not sure I would describe him as humane," the Secretary of State observed drily, "but I take your point. Anyway, until we have information to the contrary we should focus on what we actually know. You were saying, James."

Curbishley, relieved not to have to pursue the possibility of other viruses, returned to his theme with renewed confidence. "As I was saying earlier, unlike less aggressive strains of flu, H1N1 will certainly cause fatalities, and not only among the young, the old and the otherwise unwell. As my colleague was so eager to point out," – gesturing towards Irene – "the Spanish Flu variant in 1918 killed at least fifty million people. However, other later strains like H2N2, known popularly as Asian Flu, had a much lower mortality rate – perhaps two million worldwide."

"And this particular strain?" enquired one of the Department of Health officials.

"We have no way of knowing quite how virulent this one is," Curbishley replied, "it's hardly something that can be tested in the lab."

The official persisted: "But it has been engineered for that?"

"Yes, it is a new variant, and a Zeno one at that."

"What's your view of this, Graham?" asked the Secretary of State, turning to look at Graham and Irene.

"Irene is our expert in this area, sir. I suggest we consult her."

The Secretary of State inclined his head towards Irene. "Professor Johnson, the floor is yours."

Irene paused to collect her thoughts before replying. "Dr Curbishley is absolutely correct to say that we cannot assess the virulence of this particular strain until it actually begins to spread."

Curbishley nodded self-importantly.

"However," Irene continued, "the geneticists who engineered it were aiming to do two things. One was indeed to try to make it as virulent as possible in as much as the current state of scientific knowledge allowed them to do so. The other – more important in the long run – was to use the Zeno techniques to massively accelerate the pace at which the virus will mutate. On the first count, Dr Livermore has ensured that the real world is now the laboratory in which the virus's efficacy will be tested. We shall see. But it's the second feature that most concerns me. A Zeno-engineered virus is an extremely dangerous unknown quantity."

Curbishley was becoming increasingly agitated as Irene got into her stride, and at this point he interrupted her. "Mrs Johnson," he said, emphasising the prefix as if to underline his determination to deny her the academic honorifics of Dr or Professor. "Your opposition to the Zeno project, however misguided, is well known, and there is really no need for you to rehearse it here."

"Oh but there is, Dr Curbishley," she responded mildly. "It's precisely the Zeno element which should be of most concern to us." She turned towards the Secretary of State. "May I continue?"

"Yes, Professor Johnson, please do. But concisely if you will."

"I shall be as brief as possible, sir. The problem with Zeno is that the features that make it so desirable as a potential weapon are precisely the same features that make it so uncontrollably dangerous. In the case of an ordinary virus, however infectious, there is a very good chance that with a massive application of skills and resources a vaccine will be found quickly enough to prevent total disaster. In a matter of months, say. But with a Zeno-engineered virus, the mutations are well placed to stay one or more steps ahead of our attempts to resist them, and a super-pandemic is then on the cards."

Curbishley interrupted again. "But a random mutation is just as likely to be less virulent as more so."

"True enough," Irene replied, "and if that happens the virus will be able to lurk in its hosts without arousing suspicion that it is anything more than a mild infection, and then, after a Zeno-generated antigenic shift, flare up into a full-blown epidemic. And so on. The 1918 pandemic managed three waves, and that was without the benefit of Zeno modifications. Unless we can actually wipe it out completely, the Zeno engineering ensures that the threat continues into the foreseeable future."

"And could we wipe it out completely?" one of the minister's aides enquired.

Irene shook her head. "Not in our present state of knowledge," she replied, "and in all probability never, given the rate at which the virus keeps mutating. We eliminated smallpox for all practical purposes but only because the virus remained relatively unchanged and so the worldwide vaccination programme was able to do its job. The whole point of the Zeno engineering is to exclude that possibility and so create the ultimate biological weapon, and therefore, it was thought, the ultimate deterrent. A non-nuclear variation on the doctrine of Mutually Assured Destruction."

"But how could you use such a weapon if its consequences would inevitably run out of control?" the aide asked.

"A question that I raised back when the Zeno project was first mooted," Irene replied, "and I was told that alongside the Zeno engineering we would also develop an antidote which would protect our own population if the weapon was ever used. I expressed considerable doubt about that being a practical possibility with Zeno viruses, but I was overruled and the project went ahead. As far as I'm aware no antidote has been produced to counter the viruses that Porton Down has engineered."

The Secretary of State turned to Curbishley. "Is that the case, James?"

"Yes, I'm afraid it is. We continue to work on the possibility of course, but with no success as yet." The Director peered around the table in search of support but succeeded only in looking like a small animal cornered by carnivores. "As you know, Minister," he blustered, "our funding has been cut in real terms over the past few years. We haven't had sufficient resources."

Irene couldn't resist the opening. "But you've still remained pretty well funded, have you not, James? Surely this would have been something to prioritise given the known dangers of Zeno?"

"Enough, Professor Johnson." The Secretary of State was clearly becoming impatient with the squabbling. "Mistakes may have been made but, as the Americans are fond of saying, we are where we are. Thank you for making the dangers clear to us. I am going to have to consult with the PM and other senior colleagues as to what action we should take, but I would be pleased to receive any advice on that from this group."

Irene was unsurprised by the silence that followed, but rather taken aback when the Secretary of State turned to her once more. "I would be interested to hear your views Professor Johnson, but specifically on the future rather than on past mistakes."

In for a penny, in for a pound, she thought. "In the absence of a vaccine our policy would have to be one of containment. You may recall the Ebola epidemic in West Africa some years ago. That was finally ended by isolating and treating those who were infectious and, just as important, educating the population to avoid social activities that would expose them to the virus, such as their traditional funeral arrangements. Even so, there were upward of 11,000 deaths and untold misery among the survivors. With a virulent influenza virus this strategy would be much more difficult to implement. Ebola is transmitted via contact with bodily fluids. Influenza is airborne and so harder to quarantine effectively. The practical challenges would be considerable."

"If I understand you correctly, Professor Johnson," Hart said, "the implication of what you are saying is that the process of containment would have to start as soon as cases emerged if we were to have any chance at all of keeping things under control."

"Yes, that's right. We would need an immediate public health campaign to emphasise the seriousness of the disease and to ensure that cases were reported and then treated appropriately, isolated, and kept under quarantine conditions."

The Home Secretary looked aghast at this suggestion. "But wouldn't that risk all sorts of panic? People imagining they had the symptoms and overburdening medical facilities, scapegoating of those suspected of carrying the virus whether they were or not, and, if the source was ever revealed, political crisis and public disorder. Surely we couldn't possibly move to a campaign like this until we know that it's unavoidable."

Irene shrugged. "But then it might be too late."

"No! No!" Curbishley was almost shouting. "You're overstating the case. We've dealt with flu pandemics before when we were far less medically equipped to do so. Remember the Asian flu of the late 1950s. We got that under control."

"In the end, yes," Irene said, "but 14,000 people in Britain died and many millions more were ill. And that virus wasn't engineered."

"That will do," the Secretary of State intervened. "We are going over ground already covered. Professor Johnson, thank you for your views. They have been noted and I will ensure that they are brought to the attention of those who will make a decision. I'll convey all the information brought to this meeting to the PM and to whatever group he chooses to set up to deal with this issue. I think that we have done all that we can here today. Thank you for your contributions and, once more, I must stress that everything discussed here is absolutely confidential. There must be no leaks. Good afternoon."

Standing up to leave, Graham raised an eyebrow to Irene. "More or less as expected," he murmured as they headed for the door. "You did what you could but nothing concrete was ever going to come out of this meeting anyway. The real decisions will be taken elsewhere. We'll just have to wait and see." Outside in the corridor he added, "Hang on would you, Irene. I need a pee. Bloody prostate. I won't be a minute."

While she waited, Irene stood looking at an improbably dull Victorian portrait hanging on the wall, its gloom adding to her general sense of foreboding. How could they not grasp what was really at issue? The whole business made her both depressed and angry, furious at the idiocy of approving Zeno in the first place and in some despair at the disastrous consequences that now seemed all too likely. As she stared morosely at the picture, which seemed to her to stare morosely back, she sensed someone come up behind her.

"Not the most life-enhancing work of art, is it?" Hart joined her in apparently contemplating the picture. Speaking quietly he added, "I didn't say so in there, but I believe there may be another reason why Livermore chose influenza rather than something more obviously lethal. He recognised that flu was so familiar to us, so seemingly run-of-the-mill, that we would not feel obliged to act with the kind of alacrity that you very properly proposed, and that by the time we did it would be too late. I want you to know, Professor Johnson, that I found your position to be cogent and persuasive. But as I am sure you are aware there are always other interests at work, other voices that will be heard. They will not take kindly to what you have to say, however well founded it may be. I'd advise you to be careful, Professor Johnson, very careful indeed." And with that he was gone, striding off down the corridor in pursuit of his two intelligence agency colleagues.

When Graham returned, Irene was still standing in front of the painting, at a loss to understand the brief encounter with Hart. Was that a warning, she asked herself, or was that a threat?

ƶ ƶ ƶ

Later that evening, some thirty miles to the south-west in a pleasant semi-detached house in the Surrey town of Godalming, a ten-year-old boy put aside his recently acquired Stonehenge model and complained to his mother that he was feeling unwell. She laid her hand on his forehead, which was indeed hot to the touch. "Never mind," she said, "just a bit of a temperature. We'll get you to bed early and I'm sure you'll feel better in the morning."

4

Early the next morning Jonathan Hart was at his desk in the Soho Square building that housed his division. Not that there were any external signs to indicate the presence of the DSD. If one was to believe the brass plate on the door, the building was dedicated to the production and distribution of little-known documentary films. If you went inside, as hardly anyone did, you would be confronted with a receptionist who would politely advise you to get in touch via email since staff were out in the field with film-makers. Which was at least partly true, in as much as almost all DSD employees did indeed spend their time in the field, though not as film crew but as undercover agents adopting a variety of identities according to circumstance.

On this particular day the only company for Hart and the receptionist were the two duty technicians who attended to the impressive array of Comms and IT equipment that filled the entire upper floor of the building, a facility which, in conjunction with GCHQ, allowed the DSD to track, bug, and otherwise keep under surveillance anyone in the UK designated as a person of interest. In contrast to those facilities, Hart's own office was functional and unprepossessing. There was nothing personal on show to distinguish the room from any other anonymous workspace, making his occupation of it appear oddly transient. He could just as well be somewhere else. And certainly his mind was elsewhere that morning as he sat staring vacantly at the unadorned wall opposite.

Hart was thinking. Among the intelligence community he was known as a deep thinker. He was aware of this reputation but it was not a phrase that he would have used to describe himself. Deep thinkers were the likes of Albert Einstein or Immanuel Kant – both men much admired by Hart – and he was not inclined to believe that his capacity for thought was in the same class or even the same category as theirs. Hart understood his own talents well enough. He was a tactical thinker. Someone who understood people and who could work through and with them, rather as a chess player deploys pieces into pre-planned patterns to attain a specific goal. It was this playing of the game that fascinated him and at which he excelled. The final objective – the checkmate, if you will – had always been of less interest. He was happy enough to have it defined for him by those in power, those whose function it was, as Hart saw it, to articulate the will of the State and its citizens.

Today, however, his thoughts were carrying him to an uncomfortable place in which, perhaps for the first time, he found himself questioning the capacity of those State representatives to legitimately set his goals. The previous day's meeting had disturbed his customary equanimity enough to ensure a rare restless night and an early arrival at his desk. Less than an hour after that meeting, he and his fellow intelligence directors had been charged by the highest authority with ensuring that not a scrap of information about the Porton Down event found its way into the public domain. They were to 'take all practical steps to ensure this outcome', a directive which Hart knew meant that they could do whatever they felt was necessary, however extreme, without fear of retribution.

He also understood, therefore, that those authoritative figures on whom he had hitherto relied to set his goals were not under any circumstances prepared to consider an immediate public intervention. They intended simply to wait and see what might follow from the release of the Zeno virus and, when it became inevitable that they do so, deny all pre-knowledge of it. They were, in short, prepared to sacrifice thousands, perhaps millions of the citizens whom they represented and were expected to protect. Hart was not naïve. He knew as well as anyone that politicians were often driven as much by self-interest as by social altruism. But he considered this to be a step too far.

As he had lain awake in the early hours, his wife and child asleep and in ignorance of his growing anxiety, he had become steadily more convinced that to wait and see was the worst of all possible alternatives. Now, sitting alone in his office, he was systematically examining the situation that he faced, the key to which, he had concluded, was Irene Johnson. The DSD had been responsible for monitoring Irene for some considerable time, inevitably so because she had access to sensitive information in the biosciences. But her vaguely radical record, going back as far as her student activities during the Thatcher years, had flagged her up to the intelligence agencies as being of more than routine interest, and so both she and various of her contacts had been subjected to extensive surveillance. This had drawn Alison MacGregor into their net. As a representative of the Scottish government, however lowly, she would have been monitored anyway, but her multiple links to Irene through work and through Irene's daughter had ensured that she too was given special treatment.

Her precipitately arranged lunch with Irene had therefore been of particular interest, coming as it did almost immediately after Irene was informed of the Porton Down security breach. Both the DSD and MI5 were disappointed to learn nothing from their bug beneath that conveniently vacated table in the National Gallery café, but when routine eavesdropping on Scottish Liaison Executive communications revealed that Ali's previously established travel plans had been brought forward at the last minute to include a stop in York, where Sarah Johnson lived and worked, the gauge of suspicion rose by two or three notches. Given that both the Home Office and the other intelligence agencies had been immediately informed of this unusual behaviour, Hart knew that he would be expected to act speedily on the presumption that Alison MacGregor was a possible channel of communication to the Scottish government regarding the Zeno release.

With that in mind, he and Carol Singleton had arranged for the search of Ali's flat while she was diverted elsewhere. MI5 had taken responsibility for the break-in while DSD, in the person of Richard Osborne, had ensured her absence. As with the lunch, they had turned up nothing suspicious, although their now quite bulky file on Ali – mostly courtesy of Osborne – confirmed that she was markedly antagonistic to the UK state and would therefore be a likely courier for information contrary to UK interests should it come her way. Hart now had to act on the assumption that she was in possession of such information – not to do so would run counter to the 'all practical steps' order – but how could he make use of this situation to force the hand of a government that he now believed was espousing a profoundly mistaken and dangerous policy?

All the options were risky, but he was coming round to the view that detaining Ali should be his first move. At the very least that would cause the Scottish government to demand explanations, as well as access to her, and if he could time the DSD intervention for maximum impact their pressure would be immediate and considerable. Then he could seek a private alliance with Irene Johnson in which his good intentions would be underwritten by supplying her with information about Ali's detention and about her own and her daughter's surveillance. That would work, Hart thought, and would still leave him some room for manoeuvre. But Ali's rail booking from York to Edinburgh was for that very morning so he needed to act quickly. The only stop before the Scottish border was Newcastle and, although it might just be possible to intervene there, for a number of reasons Hart preferred the border itself which, on Scottish independence, had been redrawn at the river reaching the sea at Berwick-upon-Tweed. That would give him more time and would also serve to attract the immediate attention of the Scottish authorities.

The decision made, he first called Carol at MI5 to ensure her co-operation. As he expected she was initially resistant but, recognising that there was strong pressure on both of them from government and that he would be taking full responsibility, she agreed to arrange an urgent helicopter flight north for his agent and to provide support from those of her own people who were located with the military at Otterburn in Northumberland. The next call was to Richard Osborne who was, at that moment, inhabiting his cover identity in an obscure Whitehall finance office.

"Richard, I need you to pull out of there immediately and travel to Berwick to intercept Alison MacGregor before she crosses into Scotland. She'll be on the Edinburgh train arriving there mid afternoon."

"Berwick!" Richard's astonishment was clear. "Why? And how the hell do I get there by that time? And..."

"I'll send you all details electronically," Hart interrupted. "There's a car on its way to collect you now and you'll be flown to Otterburn where a couple of MI5 people will drive you to Berwick. The UK border guards at the station will be expecting you."

"Why send me? It'll undermine all the work we've put into establishing my cover."

"We're not going to need that any longer and you're much better positioned to identify her if she's not where we expect her to be on the train. Besides, before we interrogate her I want her to be as disoriented as possible by the whole experience. I want her to believe that we already know everything there is to know about her."

He did not add that he also wanted to give Ali a chance to create a public commotion, and that Richard's involvement should give her plenty of cause to do so. The more witnesses, the better.

"Is that clear, Richard? The car will be along to pick you up shortly and you'll have all necessary information and authorisations before you reach Northumberland. I'll see you when you get back. Any problems, get in touch. I'll be available throughout the operation."

"I guess so." Richard did not sound enthusiastic. "I'll sign myself out and wait for them downstairs."

"It's important, Richard. I can't stress how important. You'll be fully briefed in due course but at the moment I can't tell you any more. Good luck."

Hart broke the contact and sat back in his chair. The hounds were running. Now it only remained to see how the hare would react.

z z z

The last thing that Ali had said to Sarah before she set off for the station had been to encourage her friend to return to Scotland. Hugh, Sarah's partner, was a Scot, and both of them had expertise that would be more than welcome in his country.

"We need you, Sarah. I need you," she pleaded. "At least consider it. I'm certain there will be research posts for both of you and the way things are going I'm not at all sure that England is a good place to be."

Sarah had nodded, although Ali was not sure whether this was in agreement with the description of England or in response to the demand to consider moving. Both, she hoped, as she sat waiting for the train to depart and trying to put the experiences of the past days into some sort of order. At least she would be safe at home tonight and able to pass on the information about Zeno to the people who needed to know. She was tired, and not only because she, Hugh and Sarah had sat up late talking and drinking. The shock of the Zeno news had taken its toll, as had her flat being searched and her suspicions about Richard. But at last, lulled by the rhythmic passage of the seemingly endless green fields beyond the window, she dozed off.

She awoke to the hollow sound of their crossing the King Edward VII Bridge as they approached Newcastle station where a handful of passengers left the train while an even smaller handful joined it. Travel has become so delimited in England, Ali grumbled to herself, with only the favoured and the very affluent able to go other than where the designated shuttles would carry you. These limits were always laid at the door of environmental and energy considerations, but Scotland managed to allow much wider independent travel and still stay within its carbon targets. The truth was that restrictions in England had become part of the apparatus of repression, an environmentally legitimised method of maximising control over the population and ensuring that those in power could sustain their comfortable and mobile way of life.

This line of thought revived her previous day's anger at Richard's apparent duplicity. Of course, she couldn't be absolutely certain. It might all be coincidence. Perhaps she had mentioned to him that she was about to return to Scotland? Maybe she had been unduly affected by Irene's paranoia? But looking back over the history of their relationship didn't give her any confidence, particularly now that she recognised how very little she knew about Richard's background. She had met none of his friends and didn't even know in which Whitehall building he worked, let alone what he actually did. So troubled was she by these gloomy reflections that even looking out at the spectacular Northumberland coastline failed to give her spirits their customary boost, and as they passed the familiar landmark of Lindisfarne Castle she promised herself that if he had misled her so comprehensively she would make him regret it.

By the time they were approaching Berwick station Ali's anger was not just directed towards Richard but at the whole culture of secrecy and control that pervaded English life. Crossing high above the River Tweed came as a welcome relief, a reminder that her own country, just beyond the river, was for all its faults a much more open society. As the train slowed to a halt she leaned her head against the window and looked up the platform into Scotland. Although strictly speaking the river itself was now the border, for practical purposes the two governments had agreed to treat Berwick station as a kind of no-man's-land, a transition point policed by border guards from both sides. So looking from her vantage point in the last carriage Ali was hardly surprised to see a group of both Scottish and English border guards assembled on the platform at the head of the train. After some discussion and considerable waving of arms, they began to walk along the platform in her direction. Only then did Ali realise that behind the uniforms were three men in civilian suits and that – she turned away and looked again to convince herself – one of them was Richard Osborne.

Her mind raced through various possibilities and, given the events that she had been going over for most of the journey, she rapidly concluded that they were looking for her. They would surely know from the booking system which carriage and seat she was in and that was why they were coming down the platform rather than inside the train. So, if she was quick enough she could go the other way from carriage to carriage and hope to give them the slip. She grabbed her backpack and began to reach for her suitcase but then decided it would be better to leave it behind. It might buy her some time if they thought it implied that she would be returning to her seat.

Almost running, she worked her way towards the front of the train, stopping at the blind spots just before each exit to check that it was safe to proceed past the open door. At about the halfway point, as she paused by a toilet entrance, she heard a voice from outside.

"It would be the fucking last carriage, wouldn't it."

If there was a reply she didn't catch it as the guards continued out of earshot along the platform, but now, having had her suspicions confirmed, she hurried on in the knowledge that she no longer needed to stop between the carriages. When at last she reached the front of the train she risked a quick look back down the platform. It was clear. They must be inside looking for her. Directly opposite, across the platform, was a door bearing an old-fashioned decorative sign: 'Ladies Rest Room'. Berwick Station liked to indulge its tourist visitors in a kitsch kind of nostalgia. She remembered remarking on its curiosity value when she had been here with her uncle a year or so earlier, and, along with that memory, came a mental picture of its interior and another door labelled 'Staff Only'.

It was a chance. She crossed the platform at speed and threw herself through the entrance to the Rest Room. To her left were the toilet facilities, but straight ahead was the door that she had remembered. Please don't be locked, she pleaded, grabbing the handle and pushing the door. It didn't budge. Be calm, think, she told herself, and pressing the handle down as hard as she could and as far as it would go she leaned all her weight on the door. With a crack it came unstuck and she was through. Closing it behind her, she saw that it had a latch which she clicked into the locked position. That should delay them, she thought, and with any luck they won't realise that I've gone this way.

Turning round she was faced by a short corridor with rooms on either side. At the far end was an external door and she headed towards it, doing her best to look purposeful, as if she had every right to be there. No one came out of any of the rooms and Ali emerged into a fenced yard with a gate leading to the street. There was a small shelter by the gate, presumably for the use of a security guard, but it was unoccupied. Maybe he was otherwise engaged looking for her on the train. Or maybe they just didn't bother to staff the gate. Either way, in a couple of seconds she was through and onto the street outside, heading towards the shuttle terminus in the town centre.

Ali had often visited the area and knew that there was always a Border Towns shuttle scheduled to leave Berwick a quarter of an hour after the train from England arrived. It zigzagged cross-country, serving a number of the region's small towns – the likes of Duns, Coldstream, Kelso, Melrose, and Lauder, completing its roundabout journey in Edinburgh. It would be a great deal slower than the train, of course, but at least it would take her away from Berwick in directions unexpected by her pursuers and, ultimately, towards home. She boarded it with only minutes to spare, using her card to buy a ticket to Edinburgh and settling into a seat at the back as far from the windows as possible. She didn't want to take a chance that they might already be looking for her outside the station.

To her relief the shuttle left on time with no sign of any untoward activity on the streets of Berwick. For the first time since spotting Richard with the border guards she had a moment to stop and think. Surely she was safe now? Yet the fact that both English and Scottish guards had been looking for her was worrying. At the very least it meant that there had been sufficient authorisation to ensure cross-border co-operation; would that mean she could be followed into her own country? Ali simply didn't know the permissible extent of collaboration. She had done nothing wrong, so the UK authorities must have attributed some invented criminal offence to her in order to justify their actions. Even so, what would be sufficient at the border crossing itself would surely not justify actually breaching that border in pursuit of her. There were legal procedures to be followed and extradition applications to be made.

Nevertheless, Ali was uneasy. Although she knew very little about the technical details, she was aware that the English had sophisticated electronic techniques for tracking people. She had used her card to board the shuttle, information which she assumed was fed back to a central computing facility and which, therefore, could be hacked. And she was carrying a CommsTab which could always be used to trace her whereabouts, even, she recalled reading somewhere, when it was switched off. The small town of Duns came and went while she tried to think things through. She could risk a call to her office in Edinburgh, but even assuming that they took her seriously – which she doubted – there wasn't much they could do if she really was being followed. Somehow she had to throw her pursuers off the scent, if indeed they were on it, and as the shuttle approached its next destination in Coldstream she realised what she had to do.

When the shuttle came to a stop in the High Street she slipped her CommsTab under her seat, took her backpack and headed for the exit. The shuttle supervisor looked at her in surprise.

"You paid through to Edinburgh, didn't you?"

"Yes," Ali replied, looking as if she was exasperated at the inconvenience, "but I've had a message which means that I have to go back to England urgently and this is the nearest border crossing."

"Och, what a nuisance. You could maybe apply for a refund from central office if you register your card here."

Ali had no intention of digitally recording her departure from the shuttle. "It's OK," she said. "Not worth the trouble really, but thanks."

She rewarded the supervisor with a smile, hopped off the bus, and walked back down the High Street towards the bridge that crossed the Tweed into England. As soon as she was out of sight, she turned off to the north, reaching the farmland at the edge of town in a matter of minutes. An isolated cottage stood in several acres of land in which chickens, ducks, sheep, and a number of pigs appeared to wander at will. Ali knocked at the door, heard sounds from within, and after some fiddling with locks, the door opened.

"Hello, Uncle Bill," she said. "I really need your help."

z z z

Just then, on a London to Hong Kong flight some 40,000 feet over Kazakhstan, a middle-aged Chinese man was apologising to the stranger seated next to him. "I'm sorry. I seem to have got an English cough. Must be their weather." The stranger nodded politely, averting his head as the contrite Chinese was overtaken by yet another bout of coughing. Hours more trapped on a plane with this, the stranger thought. Just my luck.

5

Hart was becoming impatient. By now they should have picked up Ali MacGregor, he thought, as he absently drummed his fingers on the desk. But it was bad practice to interfere with an ongoing operation unless absolutely essential, so, irritating though it was, he had to wait until Richard Osborne reported in. At last the call came.

"We've...." Osborne paused uncertainly. "We seem to have lost her."

"How?" Hart almost shouted. "How could you? You knew where she was sitting, and even if she got off the train it's a closed station."

"I don't know. Her suitcase is there and the other passengers said that she got up and, they presumed, went to the toilet. But we've searched the entire train and the station – that's why we've taken so long. She isn't here. And the railway authorities are complaining bitterly about the delay."

"OK," Hart replied, rather more calmly. "Try to hold them a bit longer just in case you've missed her somewhere. I'll check with the techies upstairs who have a trace on her cards and CommsTab. Be back to you shortly."

Hart didn't wait for the lift but set off up the stairs like a man whose life depended on it.

"Drop everything else and bring up what we have on Alison MacGregor's current position," he called, as he was barely through the entrance to the Comms room. Both technicians bent immediately to their consoles. The Director was not often given to visiting their floor, let alone shouting instructions across it.

"She's used her card to buy a shuttle ticket from Berwick to Edinburgh, some time ago now. Just hold on and I'll try to get a live feed of her CommsTab's position."

Hart watched over the technician's shoulder as she rapidly typed in a series of codes. After what felt like an interminable wait, a map came up on the screen in the centre of which was a flashing arrow moving steadily along a road leading away from Coldstream.

Hart turned back to his CommsTab which was still connected to Osborne. "She's on a shuttle to Edinburgh, just leaving Coldstream now."

"Shit!" Osborne's voice carried a heavy weight of desperation. "How the fuck did she do that?"

"We'll worry about that later." Hart turned to the technician. "Where does that shuttle go next?" he asked.

Once more she typed into her keyboard. "Kelso next, then on to Edinburgh via Melrose, Lauder, Pathhead, and Dalkeith."

Hart was now back to his customary self. He had a decision to take and that always generated calmness in him, as if it switched on a circuit specifically designed for analytic thinking. What to do? He would still like to detain her if possible. She was important to the plan he had formulated that morning, and although it wouldn't entirely undermine his strategy if she got away to Edinburgh, he would have more pieces better placed on the board if he could bring her back to London. But UK agents couldn't simply chase off into the Scottish Borders without higher authorisation from Scotland, and they would have to be accompanied by the Scottish police if they were to stop and search a shuttle. He knew that the Scots were unlikely to give him that authority so it would have to somehow be contrived without their involvement. In this respect, the electronics were on his side. He had templates for a range of Scottish legal documents. One which appeared to emanate from a sufficiently high authority should allow Osborne to convince the Scottish border police to co-operate. Most of their work was dull routine. They would love a chance to pursue a shuttle across the countryside.

"Richard. You'll have to try to intercept her before Edinburgh. I'll arrange authorisation documents which I'll send to you shortly. You can use them to involve the Scottish border police. Probably best to aim to waylay the shuttle on the open road rather than in one of the towns. I'll send the documents as soon as I can set them up."

Cutting Richard off before he could complain, Hart returned to his office and to the task of high-level forgery. He settled on an authorisation form in the name of the Procurator Fiscal for Lothian and the Borders which required the pursuit and arrest of Alison MacGregor, as well as a memo from the same source naming Richard Osborne as the officer into whose custody she was to be given. It was some time before he was fully satisfied that the documents would pass scrutiny, then he sent them off to Richard and checked on Ali's whereabouts. She was well on the way to Melrose now, but the shuttle's route was sufficiently roundabout to still allow for an intervention with time to spare. Hart leaned back in his chair, if not with satisfaction then at least with the sense of having made a move which should partially rescue a difficult situation. All he could do now was wait and see.

z z z

Ali's Uncle Bill, as patient and attentive to her as ever, listened to her story of surveillance and pursuit without interruption. Although she always called him 'Uncle', he wasn't really a relative, but he was a lifelong close friend of her father's and had known her since she was a small child. She had been accustomed to using the title back then, and the habit had persisted into adulthood even though he regularly suggested that she could now reasonably address him by his proper name.

When she reached the end of her account, from which she had carefully omitted any details of the Zeno element, he whistled softly under his breath.

"That's some story," he said, "so what can I do to help?"

"Well, I need to get to Edinburgh as quickly as I can but I don't dare go on any public transport, so I wondered if you could get me there?"

"Yes, of course. I'm due to take the weekly delivery up to Jess in the shop tomorrow, but I can easily go today. The van is pretty much packed. We'd just need to load a bit more in and we'd be ready."

"That would be great," Ali said, with a sigh of relief. "And could I use your phone? I need to warn the office that I'm on my way and have to see the boss urgently, and I also need the technical people to make my CommsTab safe before somebody finds it."

"No problem. You do that and I'll finish loading up."

He passed her the battered old phone which, along with an equally ancient computer, was the cottage's only bow to modern technology. She called Ravi Panesar, with whom she shared an office, gave him an abbreviated version of events and asked him to try to arrange a meeting with the head of their department for that evening.

"Oh, and Rav," she added, "could you contact the duty technicians and get them to brick my CommsTab. Tell them it's been lost. I'm hoping to reach you before six so wait around for me please."

Ravi assured her that he would be there, and relieved to have finally made some progress by contacting Edinburgh, Ali went out in search of Uncle Bill. She found him just closing the rear doors of a grey hybrid van, on the side of which large green letters spelled out 'Turnbull Organic Border Produce' – the enterprise to which Bill and his partner Jess had turned when they retired from academic life.

"OK. It's done. I'll just call Jess, then lock up and we can be away."

Ali clambered into the van where she was greeted enthusiastically by Skye, Bill's Border Collie, who was already in her accustomed place behind the front seats and who planted her chin firmly on Ali's shoulder, snuffling happily.

"Hello Skye," Ali said, fondling the dog's ears and scratching her head. "You've no idea how pleased I am to see you."

"Och, I expect she knows very well. She assumes that everyone is pleased to see her. Even the sheep," Bill said as he joined her in the van. "Road will be quiet. We'll be there inside an hour, tractors and stray beasts permitting."

There proved to be neither tractors nor stray beasts to delay them, the journey remaining entirely uneventful until they joined the main A68 at Carfraemill and headed along the straight road towards the climb up Soutra Hill.

Bill tapped her shoulder. "Look up ahead, Alison. There's police cars and a shuttle at the side of the road. And the passengers are all out on the verge."

Ali, who had already seen them, sank deeper into her seat so that she was all but invisible from outside.

"Just follow the traffic normally." She was almost whispering. "They've no reason to stop us."

Once the van was past she risked a look in her wing mirror. The passengers were re-boarding the shuttle and, standing with the others by the police car, she caught a brief glimpse of Richard's figure as it receded to a dot in the mirror. They were safely through. In what seemed like an eternity to Ali, but was in fact no more than fifteen minutes, they came over the hills and could see Edinburgh laid out ahead. The Pentlands striding away to the left, the Firth of Forth shining in the afternoon sun behind the city, the hills of Fife beyond, and Arthur's Seat crouching protectively over her home. At last, she thought, taking a deep breath and leaning her head against Skye who nuzzled gently into her neck. Bill glanced across at her and smiled.

"Nearly there," he said.

z z z

At the luxurious Reebok Sports Club in Vila Olímpia, São Paulo, a young woman on a treadmill was struggling for breath. She had only just returned from an extended European holiday on the previous day and was determined to overcome her jetlag-induced lassitude by vigorous exercise. But instead of feeling better as she ran, she was feeling distinctly worse, and with a sudden lurch she grabbed for the machine's handrail, missed it, and tumbled hard to the ground. She lay there wheezing and coughing, desperately trying to catch her breath, as concerned gym users gathered around her in a doomed attempt to help.

6

Deep in dark dreams that featured Richard, betrayal and pursuit, Ali heard the knocking on her door as if from a great distance. It crossed her mind that it must be morning since even with her eyes closed much more light than usual was filtering into her bedroom. It's either very late or it's an exceptionally sunny day, she thought, as she tried to make sense of the continued knocking which was now supplemented by an insistently calling voice.

"Come on Ali. Out of there. We have business."

The voice mingled, merged, with Richard's voice in her dream. Suddenly she was terrified. Oh god no, he's here. He's followed me to Edinburgh. After all that effort to give them the slip, they've still caught up with me.

Overcome by a wave of panic she sat up in bed, opened her eyes, and, at last properly awake, realised that the room around her was not her own bedroom and the voice that she was hearing was not Richard's, it was Ravi's. Now she remembered. The previous night, after telling her story to the Chief Scientific Adviser and a security officer who had waited on her arrival, they had agreed that, although Richard would probably not dare to pursue her into the heart of Edinburgh, it might be safer for her not to stay alone in her flat that night. So she had gone home with Ravi, played computer games with his young son, dined with him and his partner Eleanor, and finally collapsed exhausted in their spare room.

"OK, I'm coming," she called. Ravi was right, they did have business that morning. The CSA was arranging a meeting for Ali with the minister for public health and with anyone else from the Scottish administration whom he thought would be useful and could be mustered at short notice on a Saturday morning.

"The Chief's been in touch," Ravi shouted back. "He's arranged a meeting with the health people for eleven o'clock so we need to get ourselves to St Andrew's House as soon as you've had some breakfast."

It was a pleasant enough walk along Leith Street and round Calton Hill in the sunshine, while Ravi did his best to divert her with the latest departmental gossip. By the time they arrived at the monumental government building sitting below the tourist attractions scattered on the hill, Ali felt more cheerful, sufficiently so even to take her customary pleasure in the strange combination of grey pomposity and art deco frivolity that distinguished St Andrew's House. She was always pleased to get back to Edinburgh from her London duties, and, in spite of the stresses of the past few days, she could feel her return home having a positive effect. For a moment she even forgot the seriousness of the Zeno threat, pretending to herself that it would be just another stupid self-imposed problem that would be overcome by humanity's seemingly limitless ingenuity.

The mood didn't last. Once she found herself in the minister's office and being quizzed in detail about what had happened, her anxiety returned.

"There was really no hint as to what family of viruses we might be dealing with here?" the minister asked for the second time.

"No, I'm sorry." Ali shrugged apologetically. "As I've said, Sarah suggested a list of possibilities and I'm sure that if Irene had known she would have told me. I suppose she might know more by now."

"Unless she's being deliberately kept out of the loop for security reasons. She obviously thought she was under surveillance so that might well be so."

This observation came from the same security officer who had heard Ali's account the night before and to whom Ali had not yet been introduced.

The minister gestured towards him. "Sorry, I should have explained about Douglas here. Douglas MacIntyre. He's our security liaison on this matter. Perhaps you could tell us what you've found out, Douglas?"

"Certainly." He looked first at Ali. "Naturally, we had to check the veracity of Dr MacGregor's somewhat improbable story."

Ali stiffened in her chair, but before she could say anything the CSA laid a restraining hand on her arm.

"It's all right, Dr MacGregor, nothing personal," the security officer continued, smiling in her direction. "We would do it for anybody. We've spoken with our own border police who confirm the details that you've given us about your pursuit. Interestingly, they were provided with electronic authorisation from the office of the Lothian and Borders Procurator Fiscal to apprehend you and to hand you over to a Mr Richard Osborne. However, when we checked with the Fiscal's office they had never heard of you or of Richard Osborne and had certainly never issued such an authorisation."

"Jesus!" The minister was clearly taken aback. "They actually went as far as to forge a Scottish legal document?"

"I'm afraid they did," Douglas replied. "Two forgeries in fact. Mind you, the border police should have cross-checked with the Fiscal before taking off across the countryside like gung-ho heroes in an action movie. We're issuing new standard instructions today and the officers in question will be disciplined. But the fact that whoever did this could produce the forgeries corroborates Dr MacGregor's story. The men with Osborne in Berwick had English Military Intelligence IDs. That they were willing to go to these politically risky lengths to stop her does suggest that they thought she was in possession of significant information. I think we have to take this Zeno business very seriously."

"We're doing that," the minister replied. "I spoke briefly with the first minister early this morning and we've set in train contingency planning in the event that we might have to quarantine ourselves by closing the border with England. But it's difficult to know what further action to take without knowing exactly what virus we're dealing with. Symptoms, incubation period, how it spreads, and so on."

"Shouldn't we approach the English government directly?" the CSA asked. "They've clearly breached all sorts of protocols, not to mention broken several laws, so we could pressure them for more information with the threat of going public about their actions."

The minister shook her head. "It's an option we're considering but we're not convinced that it would produce reliable information. They could spin us all sorts of stories and we'd have no way of checking. If it is such a serious breach it's unlikely that they would simply tell us the truth. Of course, we will raise objections through back channels about the forgeries and Dr MacGregor's pursuit, but they'll no doubt officially deny all knowledge."

Ali was becoming impatient. "But shouldn't we be making a public statement anyway? People need to be warned if there's a serious health risk."

"But what could we say? That we think there might be a dangerous virus around, though we don't know what it is or how best to protect against it? We'd just cause unnecessary panic." The minister rapped the table for emphasis. "No, we need much more information before we can make anything public."

"Perhaps, then, we need to contact Alison's two sources," the CSA suggested, "just in case they now know more. Is there any way that we can bypass whatever surveillance is in place?"

"Yes, I could probably fix that," Douglas said. "If Dr MacGregor could handwrite a note to each of them I can arrange for our agents in England to deliver the messages and collect any replies. It won't be easy, and it will take a little time, but it's probably the only line of communication that we can trust."

The minister nodded agreement. "Let's go for that then. In the meantime we'll do what we can to push along the contingency plans for dealing with an epidemic. Let's hope it doesn't come to that."

The meeting over, Ali was left alone with Douglas to write the letters to Irene and Sarah.

"Put something private in each that will confirm for them that the note is actually from you," he said, "and tell them that the person who delivers the note will arrange to collect a reply."

Ali took some time over the letter writing, encouraged by Douglas to include in each a graphic account of her experiences of the day before. His view was that those details would confirm for Irene and Sarah that they were under active surveillance and that the agencies responsible were to be feared. In Irene's case, in particular, he hoped that this affront to her sense of justice would make her more likely to provide the information that they needed.

"This isn't going to put them in danger, is it?" Ali asked, as she sealed the envelopes and handed them over.

"No more than they already are," came the reply. "Their security people will take what happened yesterday as confirmation that Professor Johnson really did pass information to you and that you have conveyed it to her daughter. Besides, all being well we'll get these letters to them without anybody knowing. But whatever you do, don't try to contact them directly. I'm sure all their standard communication systems will be bugged."

"I don't have a CommsTab any more anyway. You remember, I left it on the shuttle as a decoy."

"Ah yes," Douglas said. "That was a smart move. But..." He reached into his briefcase and, with a conjuror's flourish, drew out her CommsTab. "My people collected it from the Border Police last night. Luckily someone saw sense and didn't allow Osborne to take it away. It's still bricked of course, but if you give it to your techies they'll sort it out, set up a new CommsLink code and install some additional cryptographic software that we've passed on to them. Better than new and, for a while anyway, difficult for the English security people to track or bug." Looking pleased with himself, he gathered his things together and added, "We got your suitcase too. I'll have it sent over to your office. And Alison – I may call you Alison I hope – I thought that you did remarkably well yesterday."

With that he was gone, leaving Ali a little taken aback at the sudden compliment but also rather pleased. At least somebody appreciated her efforts, she thought, and he had given her a delightful smile. She sat for a while longer before leaving, mostly thinking about Irene and the risk that she had run in sending that message. If they had been prepared to chase

Ali halfway across the country, what might they do to Irene and Sarah? It was not a comforting thought.

ᴢᴢᴢ

In his Soho office that Saturday morning thoughts of Irene were also occupying Jonathan Hart. A disconsolate Richard Osborne had arrived back from the north and provided Hart with details of the previous day's events. Overnight Richard had convinced himself that Ali had to be something more than a Scientific Liaison Officer. How else could she have eluded them not once, but twice? His view – of which he tried to persuade his Director – was that she must be from Scottish intelligence, fully aware of their surveillance of her and double-bluffing them.

Hart could see that his erstwhile undercover agent was disturbed by the whole business, angry that he had apparently been taken in by this young woman. He had to believe that she too was an agent, otherwise yesterday's failure undermined his sense of his own professional identity. And beyond that, perhaps not fully recognised by Osborne himself who was not given to extensive self-analysis, there was a deeply felt affront to his masculinity. To be outmanoeuvred by a mere woman, one whom he had thought to have mastered by seducing her and drawing her into his own web of lies – that was utterly unacceptable.

Hart was quietly amused by Osborne's inability to see the irony of the situation: the deceiver deceived. Even if Ali was a Scottish intelligence officer – which Hart did not for a moment believe – she would only have been practising much the same deception as Osborne himself. But like many people with a strong sociopathic streak, Osborne lacked the empathy necessary to put himself in Ali's place or to see the situation from any kind of moral point of view. It was why he was a useful undercover agent, but also why he would never progress to a more responsible position in the intelligence world. Hart had sent him on his way with a "Never mind, these things happen," and then comforted himself with the thought that, when necessary, much of the blame for yesterday's fiasco could be deflected onto Osborne rather than finding its way to his own door.

Even so, if blame did not attach itself to him personally, it would be his organisation that had failed in the eyes of his government superiors and he would have to find ways of contending with that. This was why he had returned to thoughts of an alliance with Irene Johnson. Even leaving aside his agreement with her about the need for immediate action if there was to be any chance of limiting the spread of the Zeno virus, he knew that as the crisis developed – as it surely must – sides would be taken and nuances lost. For Hart there would be some longer-term benefits in lining up with the cross-departmental network of Scientific Advisers, especially when it emerged that their early advice had been rejected by the politicians. At the appropriate time he would be in a position to leak that information into the public domain independent of the government's formidable propaganda machine, something which the Scientific Advisers certainly could not manage on their own. If he could convince Irene that he genuinely agreed with her views on a Zeno strategy and, more important, that he was the only ally she had who was willing and able to do something about it, then in the long run his own position would be strengthened.

Timing is the key, he thought, if that's wrong then it all goes wrong. In pursuing and detaining Ali he had wanted to attract public attention from the Scots and thus put pressure on his own government. But now that she had reached Edinburgh, that was unlikely to work. She would certainly have told her superiors what she knew, but she couldn't know very much. She was on her way north before any details were shared other than the fact of the Zeno breach itself. In those circumstances the Scottish government was unlikely to act precipitately without having more solid information. They would make what the diplomats liked to call 'strong representations' to UK officials, but they would not yet do so in public.

Sooner rather than later, though, the story was going to get out, Hart was certain of that. Too many people knew that something unusual had happened connected to Porton Down, and although the security agencies had closed off most of the standard channels, somebody somewhere was bound to start asking questions. In these circumstances, Hart concluded, he had two lines of attack. He needed first to get Irene onside, and to do so he had to bypass her surveillance. MI5 remained in overall control of that, but given his familiarity with their procedures he could surely find a private way to make contact with her. This was something on which he could focus over the coming weekend. The other rather more speculative and difficult task was to find some gaps in the security clampdown through which he could feed selected snippets of information. That, unfortunately, was going to take time, and Hart was not at all sure that time was what he had.

z z z

Sitting among the hills and moors of the Derbyshire High Peak, the town of Buxton had known better days. Once a spa to be visited by those of the upper classes eager to take the waters, it still attracted a little tourism but not much else to keep its citizens employed. It retained a small hospital, however, and on that Saturday evening the generally quiet institution was facing something of a rush. Five members of the same family had been admitted, all running fevers and suffering from acute respiratory problems. The junior doctor on duty was puzzled. They looked like particularly bad cases of flu, but it was not yet the influenza season and there had been no notifications that a flu virus was abroad. Some kind of noxious-fumes leak in their home? He settled on a wait-and-see strategy. Ensure that they could breathe, monitor their condition over the weekend, and hand them over to his consultant on Monday morning. That decided, he leaned back further into his chair and tried to doze. It would be a long weekend.

7

The spire of Salisbury Cathedral reaches a startling 123 metres into the sky, a matter of some wonder to Julie Fenwick as she craned her neck to follow it upwards in its full medieval splendour. Her CommsTab announced that it was built in the early fourteenth century and was the tallest in England, cold facts which hardly captured its almost metaphysical weight looming over her. Julie was not easily impressed. As a young freelance journalist and vlogger she liked to cultivate a determinedly sceptical attitude, one that she felt was appropriate to her work, indeed, to what she secretly thought of as her calling. But the spire had done its business with her, as it had with so many others over the centuries, and she stood looking upwards in a state of awe.

Coming back to earth at last, she restored a sense of the mundane by wryly observing to herself that this was probably as good a place to die as you might find. For what had brought her here was not the architectural glory in front of her, but a puzzle. Earlier that week she had seen a brief news report that a man had been found dead in the cathedral. But since then, nothing. This had piqued Julie's professional curiosity. At the very least, surely, there was a human interest angle to be exploited and yet none of the normal outlets had pursued the story. It was as if it had never happened.

To Julie, who maintained a healthy belief in conspiracies, this complete news blackout was not just suspicious, it was a provocation. There must be a story to uncover and she was the one to uncover it. It might not be as consequential as the Watergate conspiracy – despite the film being over fifty years old, *All the President's Men* remained Julie's favourite – but aspiring investigative reporters had to start somewhere. In this case, she decided, after a desultory wander around the cathedral itself, in the shop and tea room. In her experience shop assistants and waiting-on staff were the most willing to gossip, and a recent death on the premises should be fair game.

She drew a blank in the tea room, but buying a souvenir mug in the shop started her chatting to a bored salesgirl. After the customary exchanges about the weather, the lack of customers that morning, and the beauty of both the town and the cathedral, Julie plunged in.

"I read somewhere that you had a death in the cathedral recently."

The salesgirl brightened visibly. "Ooh yes, it was amazing. One of the cleaners found him. She was ever so shocked. That was on the Saturday night and when I got into work on the Monday the place was full of police who were searching all over."

Her face took on an expression of distant contemplation, as if the event had been one of mystical significance. But then she refocused on her interrogator and, clearly disappointed to have missed out on the central exhibit, added: "But the body was gone."

"Was it a tourist?" Julie asked. "I don't think that the report I saw said anything about him, not even a name."

"No, we were never given a name either. But he wasn't a tourist. One of the policemen checking the shop told me that he was a local guy. From Pitton, he said, out in the sticks."

"I wonder what they were searching for."

"Dunno," the salesgirl replied. "The policeman I spoke to didn't seem too certain himself, but there were plainclothes people everywhere, detectives I suppose, who seemed to be in charge and looked as if they knew what they were doing."

"Sounds really exciting. Just like a cop show on TV," Julie said as she collected her purchase. "Did they find anything?"

"I don't think so, and we haven't heard anything about it since. I guess it was just a heart attack or something. Livened the place up for a day or two though," she added wistfully, looking as if she might enjoy a few more deaths in the cathedral if only to relieve the boredom.

Thanking her for the mug and the chat, Julie strolled out into the Cathedral Close where she found a bench, sat down, and opened her CommsTab. Pitton, she thought, where the hell is Pitton? A few seconds of searching established that Pitton was a small village about seven miles to the east and that, largely because of a very popular pub – the Silver Plough – there was a regular shuttle service, especially at weekends. Julie did some calculations. She had to get home to Southampton later that day, but given the frequency of the Saturday evening shuttles she ought to be able to make it out there, have a look round, and be back in Salisbury in time to get home.

Pitton in the afternoon sunshine turned out to be quite picturesque, a mixture of relatively modern housing and older but expensively refurbished cottages. Some of them even had thatched roofs. After being dropped close to the pub, Julie set out to explore and quickly came across a small cottage which had police blue and white 'No Entry' tapes across its garden gate and front door. She walked past slowly a couple of times, contriving to take a furtive photograph with her CommsTab while pretending to consult it. There was nothing much to see, however, and there was no way round to the back of the house without breaching the tapes, so Julie satisfied herself with the photograph and returned to the shuttle drop-off point.

The Silver Plough was open – in fact, it was rarely closed – so with plenty of time before she had to return to Salisbury, Julie went in. She found herself in a large bar area dominated by dark wooden beams which stood out against a white background on both walls and ceiling. It was very quiet, there being only a few customers scattered around the tables and a solitary barman filling the time by polishing glasses. Julie seated herself at the bar.

"Gin and tonic please."

"With lemon or lime?"

"Lime definitely. Much better that way."

"Yeah, I think so too, but you'd be surprised how many people prefer lemon."

The barman brought her drink. "You here on holiday?"

"Just for the day really. I was seeing the sights in Salisbury and came across a recommendation for this village and pub. So here I am."

Determined to keep the conversation going she smiled at the barman and added, "It's a pretty village and you don't see thatched cottages very often these days."

The barman rose to the bait. "No, they're much less common now. Skilled work, thatching, and not many left who can do it."

"I passed a cottage down the road with police tapes on it. Has something bad happened here? Not what you'd expect to come across in a quiet little village like this."

The barman leaned towards her conspiratorially.

"Biggest thing that's happened in the village in years," he said. "The guy who lived there was found dead in Salisbury Cathedral last Saturday and the police were crawling all over the place for a couple of days."

"Wow! That must have disturbed the rural peace a bit. So was the death suspicious for there to be that much police interest?"

"Well, he wasn't old, only in his fifties. Lived here for most of his life apart from when he was away at university. He was a scientist. Charles Livermore. Worked up at Porton Down. Maybe that's why the police were involved. They do secret stuff up there. The guys were going into the house wearing those protective suits."

"You mean the kind they wear for crime scenes?" Julie asked.

"No, more elaborate than that. Full masks, breathing kit and stuff."

"Oh right." Julie had to work hard to conceal her excitement. "I suppose he wasn't very old, was he? Poor man. Did they find out what happened?"

"Rumour is that he had a heart attack. Funnily enough, he was in here on the night before. Seemed fine. Had a meal and a pint. I remember thinking that he must be in a good mood since usually he only had a half. Bit of a loner, Charles, an oddity, though I quite liked him."

Her mind still processing the information about Porton Down and the protective suits, Julie turned the conversation onto other topics until the arrival of a shuttle was announced by a noisy group entering the bar.

"Here we go," said the barman. "Saturday madness begins."

"I'll leave you to it then," Julie smiled. "I can catch that shuttle back to Salisbury. Thanks for the company."

By the time she was back in the city she had decided that her next move would be a seemingly innocent call on Monday morning to the PR people at Porton Down. A pity about the delay, she thought, as she settled into the Southampton bus, but at least she could spend the rest of the weekend seeing what might be found online about Charles Livermore and his scientific specialism. It would be good preparation for the Monday call.

z z z

On a Sunday afternoon, weather permitting, Irene Johnson was in the habit of taking a walk on Tooting Common. It was not far from where she lived, and although she would never have admitted it, the fact that one of the roads crossing the Common was called Dr Johnson Avenue was a continuing source of mild amusement. Her late husband had always made poor jokes about it when they walked the park together. On this particular Sunday the weather did more than permit her stroll. It was positively encouraging: bright sunshine, blue skies, and a breeze just strong enough to moderate the heat to comfortable levels.

Irene was in need of pleasant diversion. It had been a stressful and disturbing week with the Zeno threat weighing heavily on her conscience. Although decisions had been taken to which she was bound by the terms of her contract as a Scientific Adviser, she remained convinced that the strategy of silence that the Ministry had adopted was profoundly misguided. Not just misguided, but deeply morally questionable. She had already partly broken that silence with the cryptic message that she had entrusted to Ali, but she was worried that she had not heard anything further from Ali and had only managed a prosaic CommsTab conversation with Sarah in which both were careful to avoid the subject.

She was uncertain as to what, if anything, she could or should do next. If – when – the spread of the Zeno virus reached epidemic proportions, containment would be much more difficult than it would be if action were taken immediately. But there was little prospect of that given a government determined to keep the Porton Down breach secret, and even if she felt ethically justified in going public it was not clear how she could do it with any hope of success. Most English communications channels had been brought under powerful central control in recent years, an insidious but highly effective process, and Irene had no idea how that control might be bypassed. If she took the desperate step of speaking out it was likely that nobody would hear, and even if they did the government propaganda machine would rapidly undermine her with slurs on her reputation and quite probably worse.

Overcome by the wretched impossibility of it all, Irene slumped onto a nearby bench and stared out across the usually comforting green parkland without really seeing any of it – the children at play, dogs in pursuit of tennis balls, people sitting in the sunshine entirely unaware of what lay in wait. Lost in distressing thoughts she barely noticed when someone sat down on the bench along from her.

"Good afternoon, Professor Johnson. A beautiful day, is it not?"

Jolted out of her gloomy ruminations, Irene turned towards the voice. It was Hart, Director of the DSD, issuer of warnings that might be threats or threats that might be warnings.

"What on earth are you doing here?" she asked. "Are you following me? I thought you had unscrupulous minions to do that sort of thing."

"Indeed we do," Hart replied with a wry smile, "but in your case they were not mine but from MI5 and they are altogether too busy elsewhere to trail around behind you at weekends."

Irene was astonished and not a little disarmed by this admission. She inclined her head towards him.

"I should be honoured then," she said, the obvious sarcasm somewhat undercut by her returning his smile. "To what do I owe the pleasure?"

"I think we might be on the same side, you and I, at least as far as Zeno policy is concerned. Neither of us agree with it but we're unlikely to have any impact through the customary channels."

Irene gave him a hard look. "It was obvious from last week's meeting where I stand but I don't recall you offering any vocal support."

"Yes, that's true. I didn't judge it to be appropriate at the time. Adding my voice to yours would not have made any difference to the outcome, and I felt that I could do more in other ways."

Irene shook her head. "I'd like to believe you," she said, "but given your official position that's really quite difficult."

"Of course." Hart moved along the bench closer to her and spoke quietly. "Perhaps if I give you some confidential information, that will help to persuade you?"

Irene remained silent and Hart continued.

"As you have surmised, you have been under surveillance for some time along with a number of your contacts. That includes both your daughter and her friend Alison MacGregor."

Although Irene had already come to believe as much, it was still a shock to hear it so bluntly stated and by someone who was in a position to know.

"As a result of your slightly odd behaviour earlier this week," Hart went on, "some of my colleagues came to the conclusion that you might have passed information about the Zeno breach to Dr MacGregor and, through her, to your daughter. This was confirmed for them when Dr MacGregor managed to evade an attempt to detain her on her way back to Scotland on Friday."

"Detain her! Is she OK?" Irene was horrified at the thought that she had put Ali, and perhaps Sarah, in danger.

"As far as my colleagues know she reached Edinburgh safely and is now out of their reach."

"And Sarah, have they done anything to her?"

"No. Not that I'm aware of." Hart was careful to leave the question open. "No doubt she is still under surveillance. I wouldn't necessarily know. But I can certainly tell you if I hear anything and perhaps help you to bypass surveillance to warn her."

Hart paused to allow Irene to think through the ramifications of what he had said. After a lengthy silence, she turned towards him with a resigned shrug.

"And what would you want from me?"

"Just co-operation really. An alliance. I'd like to know how much Alison MacGregor and your daughter know and, more important, I'd like your help in putting some obstacles in the way of government policy on Zeno."

"They don't know much," she replied. "Just that there's been a Zeno breach, but no information about the virus. When I spoke to Ali I didn't know what virus was involved."

"But they do know about the Zeno effect itself?"

"Sarah certainly understands it. It's her field after all. I assume she explained it to Ali."

"Yes, I suppose she would have." Hart looked into the distance for a moment. "That means that the Scottish authorities know enough about the breach to be concerned."

Irene saw where that might lead. "Surely they'll go public and that will force our government's hand."

"I'm not so sure," Hart demurred, "they don't know much and they would be wary of jumping the gun for lack of detail. I don't think we could rely on that to solve our problem, at least not in the immediate future."

Irene, noting the plural pronouns, felt that she had little choice but to go along with Hart's inclusion of her.

"What do you think we should do then?"

"We need to find a way of getting the information out there which bypasses the official media outlets. That's not easy. The intelligence agencies have national communications pretty much tied up. Trust me, I know." He looked rueful at this admission. "If I can establish a safe channel I would need you to provide the information, to be the contact. Nobody's better placed than you as an obviously reliable source for the facts."

Irene looked horrified at this suggestion.

"But then your colleagues would be onto me like a pack of wolves," she protested, "undermining anything I said and lord knows what else."

"No." Hart was adamant. "We can keep your identity out of it. As long as the channel sees you as reliable and independent it will work. They won't have to make your name known, just be convinced that the information you feed them is accurate. If you offer them a little at a time they'll have an investment in keeping you secret."

"And if I do this you'll help me keep Sarah safe?"

"Yes, I will. After all, we shall be allies, friends even, and friends must stick together."

Irene was not so sure that they could ever be friends, and certainly not convinced that Hart was entirely trustworthy, but his proposal did appear to be the only practical way forward. Reluctantly she nodded her agreement.

"OK. I'll go along with it, to begin with at least. How do we keep in touch?"

Hart reached into his pocket and passed her a tiny plastic object, most of the face of which was some kind of screen. It was rather like a much smaller version of the pagers Irene remembered from her youth.

"I can send short encrypted text messages to this device which won't be detected by the standard surveillance systems. There's a beep and a light which will flash when there's a message, and you press the key to read it. It's one-way only so any message I send will simply be a place and time to meet. You follow those instructions and we'll have an apparently accidental encounter. I'll contact you soon."

And with that he was on his way, a man strolling across the common in the sunshine and whistling quietly to himself, seemingly without a care in the world.

Irene remained seated for quite some time after Hart's departure, wondering if she had done the right thing by agreeing to his suggestion. She knew very well that you didn't rise so high in Hart's world without being skilled at duplicity, and she certainly didn't believe that he had her best interests at heart. He would have his own agenda and would not hesitate to sacrifice her if that served his purpose. But what choice did she have? At least this way she might get a chance to push the authorities towards positive action, and she did believe him when he claimed that this was also his goal. If he kept his promise to help protect Sarah then that would be a significant bonus. But the priority was to get information about Zeno into the open. That would ensure that proper contingency plans could be made to deal with the inevitable epidemic and, if Porton Down was forced to release the technical details of the virus, the full range of international scientific expertise could be brought to bear in the battle against it.

At last Irene rose from the bench and began her walk home. As she followed the familiar route across the park she looked with a different awareness at the families wandering in the sunshine, the children enjoying noisy and rambunctious games, people sitting on the grass deep in conversation or just taking pleasure in being out there in the open. How little they knew about the imminent fragility of their daily lives. Irene understood all too well that she was taking a considerable personal risk in allying herself with Hart, but that paled into insignificance compared to what might happen to so many of these people. Yes, she thought, she was doing the right thing, and with that resolve her pace quickened as she approached the edge of the park and set off homeward, looking neither to right nor left. Had she been doing so, she might have seen a rather ordinary looking man carrying a Support the Needy charity bag, who rose from his bench after she had passed and followed her out into the suburban streets. But, her mind now firmly focused on the challenges ahead, she did not, and he was able to follow her home entirely unnoticed.

z z z

On the bridge of the *MS Zeebrugge* its captain was staring blankly out into the darkness of the night-time Atlantic. The cruise ship was a day away from returning to port in Boston at the end of a lengthy USA/Europe round voyage and the captain was worried. In the last twenty-four hours a number of his passengers had come down with some kind of infection. The symptoms did not appear to be those of a norovirus – he had encountered that peril of cruise ship life before – but they were just as debilitating, if not more so. His medical staff were coping at the moment, but if, as seemed likely, more cases emerged tomorrow, then they would be pushed close to their limits. Still, he thought as he left the bridge for his cabin and sleep, we are nearly home. Then it will be someone else's problem.

8

A Sunday spent searching all the usual internet sources yielded Julie very little information about Charles Livermore. She found references to scientific papers on which he had been a co-author, mostly in areas of research so technical that they were entirely opaque to someone of Julie's humanities background. She found him on a couple of conference attendees lists and a brief mention on a university alumnus website. But that was it. No presence on social media. No biographical details. And nothing on the Porton Down website, which for security reasons did not anyway incorporate staff listings but might have been expected to make some commemorative reference to the death of a long-standing colleague.

All of which served only to feed Julie's conviction that there was something weird going on and that she would have to do her damnedest to find out just what it was. With that in mind she had v-called the Porton Down press office first thing on Monday morning with a polite enquiry about Dr Livermore's sad passing. She received an equally polite rejoinder to the effect that all relevant details were already in the public domain, and there was nothing that his former employers could add other than to confirm that he had been an outstanding researcher for them over a number of years. When pressed on the cause of his death the PR officer said that they understood it to have been a sudden heart attack, and when asked about Dr Livermore's research field he observed, regretfully, that such information was covered by the Official Secrets Act so he was not in a position to make any comment.

This was pretty much what Julie had expected and she resisted the temptation to enquire about the protective suits worn at the Pitton cottage and the extensive searches carried out at the cathedral. No point them knowing what she had already pieced together; so much better to save that information for the first instalment of the story. Even if she had asked, they would surely have done no more than to affirm that this was standard procedure in any such case. Clearly she was being stonewalled and she took that as confirmation that there was indeed something here worth investigating. She observed as much to the editor of *The Wessex Web*, an independent and somewhat unconventional news site covering the southern region, who retained Julie as a jobbing reporter.

"Well," he said, "not necessarily. Organisations like Porton Down are pretty paranoid at the best of times, let alone when they have a sudden death to deal with and a pushy reporter on the line."

"Even so," she insisted, counting off the points on her fingers. "The protective gear at his house; the extensive searches at the cathedral; the complete lack of public information about him; and the total news blackout on all of that."

Julie laid special emphasis on that last observation knowing full well that her editor would be unable to resist rushing in where other news sources feared to tread.

"OK, OK, I hear you," he said. "It's certainly worth pursuing. Write a punchy piece covering those topics. I'll look out some library pictures of Porton Down and the cathedral, and we'll use the shot you took of the guy's house. I'll give it some prominence and we'll see what that stirs up. If anything."

For the next hour Julie did as he suggested and then watched as he mounted the pictures and the story on the *Wessex Web* site, complete with her byline and under the unoriginal if attention-seeking headline, 'Porton Down Puzzler'.

"There you go, Julie. Another step on the long, hard road to a Pulitzer Prize. Except we don't have Pulitzers here so I'll buy you a drink instead. Come on."

zzz

Around the time that Julie was trying to persuade her editor that she was onto a significant story, Jonathan Hart received a v-call from the Head of Security at Porton Down.

"We've had a journalist asking about Livermore's death this morning, Mr Hart. She was quite persistent, wanting to know about his work, how he died, and so on. Of course, our press office took the agreed line but the person talking to her had the feeling that she might know more than she was letting on."

"What's her name and who does she work for?"

The security chief consulted a note on his desk. "Her name is Julie Fenwick and she said she was a freelance covering the southern region. Didn't give a specific news organisation."

Hart jotted down the name. "Leave it with me then. I'll get our people onto it and let you know if we find anything significant. Thanks for keeping us informed." And although he had no such intention, he added, "I'll pass the information on to the other agencies so you've no need to do anything more."

Hart stared at the name on his pad for several minutes. Perhaps this Julie Fenwick was just the person he was seeking. If she had become sufficiently interested to contact Porton Down in spite of the careful information blocks that the intelligence agencies had put in place, then she might be a good channel for his and Irene's leaks. He turned to his terminal, brought up the DSD's secure database and typed in her name.

Half an hour later he had all he needed. Julie Fenwick came originally from the Malvern area, the daughter of a farmer. She was twenty-four years old, single, and lived in a small apartment in Southampton. She had graduated with a respectable degree in English and had worked as a stringer and freelance journalist since then. There was nothing particularly distinctive in her confidential security records. She had edited a student news website at university, and while she had been outspoken on local student issues she did not appear to have espoused any more general political affiliations nor established a record of activism or dissent.

There was, however, one aspect of her biography that particularly attracted Hart's attention. On a number of occasions, both in print and on social networks, she had made a case for the importance of an independent fourth estate if those in power were to be held to account. Nothing especially radical – that would certainly have attracted the attention of the intelligence agencies – but clearly a strongly held belief which, presumably, informed her ambitions as a journalist. Ideal, then, for someone to be manipulated with carefully controlled leaks of confidential information.

He was confirmed in that view a little later in the day when the automated search algorithm that he had set up came back with a new internet item for Julie Fenwick. Hart read her article on *The Wessex Web* with growing interest. She was obviously persistent and also sharp enough to have fitted together some pieces of the jigsaw. A suitable person to be given one or two additional snippets then, and all the more so since *The Wessex Web* was probably sufficiently obscure to evade the prying eyes of the other agencies until it was too late. He would message her from an untraceable source and arrange for her to meet Irene as soon as he could safely bring them together.

z z z

It was with some distaste that Irene began her day by picking up the usual mess of circulars and charity come-ons that had dropped through her letterbox. How this archaic approach to marketing survived in an age of widespread digital communication remained one of the great unanswered questions as far as Irene was concerned, but survive it did, and on a daily basis she dumped the lot unread into her recycling bin. But on this particular morning her eye was caught by a leaflet and plastic return bag from an organisation called Support the Needy because prominently attached to it was an envelope addressed to her personally. Her curiosity piqued, she opened it to find a note and yet another envelope, this one also addressed to her and in what looked very much like Ali's handwriting. The cover note simply said: 'If you wish to respond to this letter securely you can do so by wrapping your reply in a donation of clothing, placing it in the plastic bag, and leaving the bag outside for collection tomorrow morning.' Irene opened the letter, which was indeed from Ali, and read its contents with growing astonishment.

Although Hart had told her of the attempt to waylay Ali en route to Edinburgh he had given her no details, and the lengths to which they had gone to detain her were nearly as startling to Irene as was Ali's ingenuity in escaping them. After recounting those events, Ali's letter went on to ask if there was any additional information about the Zeno breach, in particular about the specific virus involved, so that the Scottish government could be better prepared for an epidemic. Finally, she assured Irene that the person delivering the letter was to be trusted and warned her that she was undoubtedly under the kind of extensive surveillance that had been utilised in Ali's pursuit.

Irene laid the letter on the kitchen table in front of her, absent-mindedly flattening out its creases as she considered what to do. There was no question but that it really was from Ali. To confirm exactly that, the letter mentioned an event from Ali's and Sarah's past – involving boys, alcohol, and some money 'borrowed' from Irene's handbag – that could only be known to the three of them. So this was undoubtedly a channel of communication to the Scottish government, and if Irene told them what she knew it would not only break the terms of her employment as an English government adviser but it would also probably count as a treasonable act. Still, the security agencies already knew that she had given some information to Ali and they were not yet knocking on her door in the dark hours of the night. Would this really be any different to what she had already agreed to do at Hart's instigation? And how far would his promised protection of her reach? Not, she thought, as far as covering for her passing information to a foreign power. But she had already decided that there were serious limits on his commitment to her well-being so her deal with him could hardly be a factor in this decision. The real issues were the seriousness of the Zeno threat and the unacceptable behaviour of her government in refusing to warn its own citizens, as well as the rest of the world, about the terrible prospect of disease that they faced.

Irene was decided. She would tell Ali what she knew in the hope that the Scottish authorities would not only make their own preparations but would also ensure that the information about Zeno was made public. That way, even if Hart's strategy did not work there would be another route through which information could emerge. No doubt it would ultimately be traced back to her but Irene was already prepared for that as a consequence of the arrangement with Hart. What did she have to lose? Every day brought the potential disaster nearer and, compared to that, Irene's career and even her liberty were no longer matters of huge importance.

When she reached that conclusion it was as if a shadow had lifted from her mind. Now she could see clearly what had to be done for all their sakes. She would spend the coming day at work assembling everything she could about the virus, the breach, and probable consequences. Then she would incorporate that material into a letter to Ali and, in the morning, consign it to the care of the anonymous collector of charitable donations.

It was a relief to have made a decision at last and she felt energised by it. Whistling tunelessly under her breath, she got up from the table and prepared herself for the working day. It was going to be one of the more interesting ones.

z z z

In Edinburgh, Alison MacGregor's day was proving to be rather less than interesting. Since she was now *persona non grata* in England there was no way she could continue as a Scientific Liaison Officer and nobody had quite got round to deciding how she should now be employed. The Chief Scientific Adviser suggested that she take a few days off to recover from her ordeal, after which they could sort out a new role for her. Ali jibbed at this proposal, as much as anything because she didn't want to be sitting around with no work to distract her from thoughts of the impending Zeno crisis. They finally agreed on her completing all the reports due from her last posting in London and then accepting the offer of holiday time. As a result, she was now sitting in the office extending those tasks for as long as she possibly could. It was not compelling work, and repeatedly she realised with a start that her mind was wandering off unbidden.

At one point she found herself thinking of Richard, trembling with fury and frustration at the comprehensiveness of his betrayal. While it was never a particularly serious involvement on her part, it had been an ostensibly intimate relationship and she felt soiled by the ways in which he had taken advantage of her and of her desires. She sat at the desk physically hunched into herself at the memory of their sexual encounters, pleasurable enough at the time but, in retrospect, rendered grubby by the scale of his deception. She counted herself fortunate that the whole thing had been relatively short-lived. Imagine what it must be like – and she knew that there were cases of just this – to discover that a long-term relationship had always been a masquerade played out in the cause of state security.

Ali shivered at the thought, staring fixedly at her screen trying to refocus on the tasks in hand. This was no time to be upsetting herself with regrets about the past. What was likely to follow in consequence of Zeno was much more important. Yet again she reviewed what she knew. It was really pitifully little, and until Irene replied to her letter, assuming that she did reply, there was not much more that Ali could do. On top of that, she was becoming increasingly apprehensive about the Zeno effect itself, regardless of what specific virus had actually been released. From what Sarah had told her about the accelerated process of mutation she knew that they were not just facing a short-term epidemic, however disastrous that might be, but also a much more frightening long-term risk from a virus which would and could change its form unpredictably. She wasn't convinced that her superiors in the Scottish Science and Health Executives had quite grasped the magnitude of this threat, or had understood that it meant being caught up in a constant losing game of catch-up in the struggle against disease.

To her surprise and dismay, she was beginning to think that Scottish governance wasn't quite as distinctively transparent and democratic as she had always believed. It certainly wasn't as authoritarian and closed to debate and disagreement as were the English government circles with whom she had been accustomed to dealing, but the health minister's insistence on making no immediate public statement still rankled with her. Early containment was vital in controlling the spread of epidemic disease so they could at least have required notification from Scottish GPs and hospitals of any unusual viral episodes, even in advance of identification of the virus itself. Still, the real test would come when they got the additional information from Irene. Then, surely, officialdom would have to act. Doing her best to comfort herself with that thought, Ali returned to the distraction of writing reports. We'll see soon enough, she said to herself, and then no doubt things will really start to happen.

z z z

At Patchway Primary School in a north-west suburb of Bristol, a teacher paused outside the door of his first class of the day. He took a deep breath, listened fruitlessly for the customary sounds of lively behaviour from his fifth-year charges, opened the door and stopped dead on the threshold. Instead of the usual twenty-plus children there were only two. One of them, clearly relishing his teacher's surprise, announced: "It's a bug, sir. My sister's got it and so have lots of kids on the estate. There was even an ambulance around this morning. Are classes cancelled?" As he wondered what to reply the teacher became aware that two of his colleagues were emerging from their classrooms further down the corridor. They exchanged similarly nonplussed looks and then, as one, made their way towards the head teacher's office.

9

A few days later Irene and Julie found themselves unexpectedly in possession of tickets for adjacent seats in a small art-house cinema in East Dulwich. In Irene's case the source of the ticket was all too clear. Late one afternoon Jonathan Hart had arrived in her office unannounced, clutching a book.

"Professor Johnson, forgive me for interrupting but I knew I was coming this way and I recalled that you had asked me about the workings of the intelligence community."

Irene had done no such thing, but before she could say anything Hart hurried on.

"I've brought you this book. Originally I intended to give you an official history, but then I thought that fiction would be rather more entertaining. This is a classic. John Le Carré's *Tinker, Taylor, Soldier, Spy*. Well over fifty years old but still an excellent read and offers a vivid sense of the moral ambiguities of the intelligence world. I do hope that you enjoy it."

As he handed her the book Irene noticed the edge of a brown envelope just showing from among the pages. Of course. A means of passing a message without attracting the attention of whatever surveillance might be in place.

"Thank you so much. I think I did read it many years ago but I expect I've forgotten all the details by now." She raised a conspiratorial eyebrow. "If I remember rightly, it is a rather complicated story involving much deception and betrayal."

"Indeed it is." Hart's smile in response to her ironic tone was a little forced, giving him the look of an improbably benevolent shark. "We must discuss that when you have had a chance to think about it."

And with that he was gone, leaving Irene wondering whether she dared to check the envelope now. Probably not, she thought, putting the book in her bag to be examined later.

Julie's ticket, by contrast, had arrived digitally and anonymously. So anonymous, in fact, that when she ran some illicit software which was designed to reveal the true source from which the email had been sent, an error message informed her that it had, in effect, come from nowhere. Along with the ticket came a note suggesting that if she wished to know further facts about the death of Dr Charles Livermore she should ensure that she was occupying the seat detailed in the ticket at least ten minutes before the screening was due to start. Her informant – a middle-aged woman – would sit next to her, and they should strike up a conversation as if this were an accidental encounter.

Later in the day when Irene was finally able to examine her message safely, it proved to be similar except that it provided rather more information about her prospective cinema-going companion and suggested that she did not reveal her own identity. The journalist would surely figure it out in due course, it went on, but there was no point in making the task too easy. It also advised that she held back any information about the Zeno effect itself, while offering to provide more intelligence at a later date. This would keep the journalist committed to protecting her source in the hope of further such details. The facts of the Porton Down security breach, Livermore's suicide, and the spreading of a genetically engineered flu virus at the cathedral and at Stonehenge would be more than enough for this first meeting.

So it was that in the late afternoon of the next day Julie was in her seat a good fifteen minutes before the scheduled screening of an obscure Chinese film. The cinema was very thinly populated – Chinese art-movies, even well reviewed ones such as this, did not have huge drawing power – and Julie's section of seating was completely unoccupied. A combination of excitement and nervousness made her fidgety, and several times she half turned to check the auditorium entrance only to stop with the thought that she should not be drawing attention to herself at what was, after all, a secret assignation.

A couple of minutes passed extremely slowly. Maybe this woman won't turn up, Julie thought, maybe I'm being set up in some way. That possibility added to her anxiety and she was on the point of retreating to the toilets when an ordinary-looking woman in her sixties took the seat next to her. Leaning down to place her bag on the floor between her feet, she turned towards Julie as if to apologise for the inconvenience.

"Hello Julie," she murmured. "We'll have to be quick to get through this before the show begins. We've got about ten minutes."

It turned out to be a packed ten minutes in which Julie listened with growing astonishment to Irene's whispered chronicle, interrupting only a couple of times to clarify a point. Cynical though Julie was about politicians and their like, even she was taken aback at their determination to cover up something which would have such a terrible impact on so many of those whose interests they were meant to protect. It was only when Irene at last fell silent that Julie recovered some of her carefully cultivated journalistic scepticism. Perhaps she really was being set up. If she published wild claims such as these they might easily be refuted, whereupon the original story would also be discredited. But then again, why would they want to manipulate her in this way unless she really was onto something? She turned towards Irene and fixed her with a steady look.

"How do you know all this? How do I know that I can believe you?"

"I'm an official in the government's science division with access to this kind of information." Irene grimaced. "Believe me, I wouldn't be telling you any of it if I thought there was another way in which I could force the government's hand. As to why you should believe me, well, I'm sure we'll start getting serious flu cases soon enough. We probably have already, but not yet on a scale that's been worth reporting. Why don't you check with clinics and hospitals around Salisbury? Cases might show up there more quickly than anywhere else."

"I'll do that. How can I get in touch with you?"

Irene shook her head. "You can't. I'm under surveillance and you would be too if you tried to reach me. I'll contact you when I know more."

Then, as the auditorium lights dimmed for the start of the show, she added hastily, "We mustn't be seen leaving together. I'll sit through the whole film. You wait until part way through and leave as if you weren't enjoying it. You probably won't be anyway. I'm sure I won't."

As Irene predicted, Julie found the film interminably dull and was relieved to make her escape well before the end. She was staying overnight with friends in Clapham, and as she made her way there her thoughts were tumultuous. The story was potentially huge. It was her Watergate opportunity, even down to now having a 'Deep Throat' all of her own. But it was risky too. If the authorities were as eager to cover things up as her source insisted, they would think nothing of blocking anything she wrote, even, perhaps, detaining her. Like most citizens of England in the later 2020s she had become adept at suppressing her own awareness of how authoritarian the regime had become. It was easier and safer that way. Now, however, she was right up against it, considering whether to put herself at serious risk in the cause of the independent press ideals that she had so often espoused. If Deep Throat had been able to find her, presumably via the *Wessex Web* piece, then the intelligence agencies could certainly do so too. So if she was to publish she would have to do it quickly, via the website again, but also through other channels to ensure that the story was spread as widely as possible. That could give her some protection. The government, eager to deny any charges of running a police state, might not feel able to detain her when she was irreversibly in the public eye.

But if she was to go ahead she didn't have much time. The new piece would have to be drafted that night and consigned to her editor through one of several encrypted messaging systems to which he subscribed. Early in the morning she would travel home via Salisbury where she could make enquiries about a 'rumoured upsurge in flu cases', adding to the ongoing story any information that she gleaned. As soon as *The Wessex Web* had the report up – for his constant support she owed her editor the right to be first – she would pass it on to all the national news sites and vlog it herself across social media. With any luck this saturation would put her at the eye of an internet news storm, making it very hard for someone to arrange for her disappearance. Yes, it was a workable approach, she thought. Not much of one, admittedly, but in the circumstances better than just remaining silent. Her heroes, Woodward and Bernstein, would have wished for no less.

Early the following day Julie was on the first shuttle to the south-west in a state of considerable anxiety. She had worked late into the night, first of all hunting down her informant's identity. It hadn't taken long since the Science Ministry website conveniently carried photographs of its various advisory staff. Satisfied that her Deep Throat was genuine, she had then written and sent off the article and, that morning, had received a terse message from her editor: "Received. Going with it." Ever since then, oblivious to the scenic countryside of Surrey and Hampshire rolling past the shuttle windows, she had been repeatedly checking the *Wessex Web* on her tablet. At last the article appeared, blazoned with a huge headline and adorned with pictures of the various locations. He had done her proud, she thought gratefully as she reread the piece. Now she could post links to it on social media sites, cut and paste a blog here and there, record some vlogs, and lastly send links to the full set of national news organisations. Some of them would assuredly pick it up.

By the time the shuttle reached Salisbury that was mostly done, and it was with a mixture of elation, foreboding and urgency that she sat down to figure out a route around the city's various medical centres and hospitals.

z z z

In Edinburgh, Ali sat staring at her screen with glazed eyes. The tedium of writing endless and probably futile reports had reduced her to what felt like a state of terminal exhaustion. Even so, the fact that she was nearing completion of those tasks offered only temporary respite since actually finishing the job would then confront her with enforced holiday time. She had no wish to be cut off from the latest news on Zeno at such a sensitive moment, so she was determined to stretch things out at least until Irene had replied to her letter. She never doubted that Irene would reply, assuming that she could, nor that she would provide the information that Ali had requested. It was just a matter of time, but for Ali time was in shorter and shorter supply.

As if on cue her CommsTab sprang to life, its screen filled with the rubicund face of her boss, the Chief Scientific Adviser. She touched the response icon and the frozen face came to life.

"Ali, I know you're busy but could you spare me a few moments?"

Busy, Ali thought, you must be joking, and hiding her pleasure at being interrupted she replied, "Yes, of course. I'll be along immediately."

Arriving in the Chief's office, she found that he was not alone and his visitor stood to greet her with a smile.

"You remember Douglas MacIntyre, Ali, from security?" her Chief asked.

"Yes, of course. Hello Douglas, good to see you. Have we had a reply from Irene?"

"Um, yes," the Chief interjected before Douglas had a chance to respond. "But before you see it you'll have to give me your word that you'll keep its contents entirely confidential."

Although momentarily taken aback at this demand, Ali knew that she had little choice but to agree if she wanted to know what Irene had written. "Of course," she said, "no problem."

Douglas handed her an official-looking red folder containing an already opened envelope addressed to her as well as several handwritten pages.

"We've no reason to doubt it, but I assume that you can confirm that this is Professor Johnson's handwriting?" Douglas asked.

Concealing her irritation that a letter meant for her had already been opened and read by who knew how many others, she confirmed that it was indeed Irene's writing. While the two men waited she read carefully through Irene's account of the Zeno breach and of the subsequent decisions made by the English authorities.

"How could they decide to keep this secret?" she demanded, appalled by what she saw as extraordinary bad faith on the part of the English government.

"Like us, they're probably worried about causing a panic," the Chief replied, "and the fact that the virus is influenza, and not one of the truly horrific ones like smallpox or Ebola, has persuaded them that it can be contained."

"But it's not just an ordinary influenza virus," Ali pointed out, "it's been engineered for virulence. And anyway, even if it was mild, there's always the Zeno element to consider. It will mutate and keep mutating such that we won't be able to keep up even if we can develop effective vaccines."

Douglas nodded. "Yes, I agree, Alison. In the longer run the Zeno factor is crucial. But there's no point in making that public at this stage when nothing practical can be done. It would certainly cause unhelpful panic. What's needed is time for research, time to develop some way of stopping it in its tracks."

Realising that, beyond a belief in the innate virtues of government transparency, she had no real answer to that argument, Ali turned to the Chief.

"But something can surely be done to minimise the impact of the flu?" she asked.

"Yes, the health people are going to issue a warning that there's a new flu strain on the loose and they're going to make all cases notifiable. They'll do what they can to provide quarantine facilities and as soon as they have a sample of the virus to work with they'll supply it to researchers. They're making all sorts of contingency plans right now."

"And the researchers will know about the Zeno element?" Ali asked.

"Only some of them," the Chief replied, "it will depend on appropriate security clearances and so on. We're not yet sure how many researchers we have who are competent in this area, but it's bound to be fewer than they have in England."

Ali lapsed into silence, awed by the scale of the challenge facing them. The two men sat waiting for her. Finally she roused herself. "So we won't be making public that the source of the virus was Porton Down?"

"No," said Douglas. "We see no purpose in alienating the English at this point. If anything, we need to collaborate with them, not publicly condemn them for their irresponsibility. We'll make sure they understand that we know what happened so we'll always have that card to play, but we won't play it until it's unavoidable."

"So that's it, Ali," the Chief intervened in a tone that suggested their meeting was now over. "You're up to date on developments and we really are very grateful for what you have done. Now I think you should take that holiday. In fact, I insist. Where are you going to go?"

"I thought I might visit my dad in Argyll for a few days," she said. "Walk the hills with the dog."

"That sounds excellent. Just the thing to take your mind off all these troubling matters. You do that. But please remember, everything we have said here today is absolutely confidential. Now off you go."

Although irritated at being spoken to as if she were an errant schoolgirl, Ali nodded goodbye to Douglas and returned to her desk.

Once she was gone, the Chief turned to Douglas.

"Do you think she'll keep quiet?" he asked.

Douglas thought for a moment.

"Yes, I think so," he said, "for now at least. We'll be keeping an eye on her anyway. Unfortunate but necessary, I'm afraid."

z z z

As was his daily custom, the elderly man sat looking out of his fourth-floor apartment window. It was a fine vantage point and he could see across much of the Florida retirement community in which he lived, even as far as the golf course at its distant edge. Normally there was not a lot going on. A few people strolling in the almost constant sunshine, the occasional vehicle abiding by the rigorously enforced speed limit, colourfully dressed figures scattered across the bright green of the golf course. But today was different. On three separate occasions so far that morning the peace had been interrupted by the sound of sirens as ambulances sped to different parts of the complex. And now, most remarkably, streams of people were hastening towards the heart of the development where a building housed the administration, a few shops and restaurants, a gym, and the medical centre. Something's happened, the man thought as he settled back into his chair to watch the show. I guess I'll find out what it is soon enough.

PART 2

ONSET

1

Although the newsfeeds were increasingly depressing, Hart found himself drawn back to them several times a day. There was, he thought, a morbid fascination to seeing life unravelling in so many parts of the world, all triggered by Charles Livermore's self-appointed day of reckoning just four months earlier. The WHO was not yet officially willing to describe the spread of influenza as a pandemic, but pandemic it undoubtedly was and one for which, although they had tried to deny it, the English were by now widely blamed – quite fairly so in Hart's view.

The leak to Julie Fenwick had done its job, not simply in forcing the English authorities to act, but also in spreading the word across the globe. There were now documented cases of the flu on every continent except Antarctica where the fortunate handful of scientists had been cut off by weather conditions for several months. In some places – those that were poor, overcrowded, and with limited medical facilities – the epidemic was already running completely out of control. Death rates there were appallingly high and remained very considerable even in richer and better equipped countries. The English Flu, as it had come to be named, turned out to be unusually capable of adapting to changing circumstances.

Much to Hart's surprise the reason for the virus's facility at adaptation remained officially unknown. There had been speculation, of course, especially when two different mutations had been detected, a particularly virulent one in India and another milder variant in Chile. It was unheard of for a virus to mutate that quickly so a plethora of conspiracy theories had flooded the internet. Some were hugely popular if patently far-fetched, often relying on the familiar tropes of alien invasion or end-of-days mysticism. Others, invoking the twenty-first century's extraordinary advances in genetics, were much closer to the truth but were submerged amid the constantly shifting currents of opinion that flowed across global social networks. Hart had no doubt that governments and scientists around the world suspected that they were dealing with a virus deliberately engineered for rapid mutation. But none of them had an interest in making that public for fear of causing escalating levels of panic among populations by now on tenterhooks.

There had already been some social unrest, not least in England where demonstrators converged on Porton Down in the immediate aftermath of the *Wessex Web* revelations. At first such events were quite easily suppressed. Under the guise of environmental considerations, travel within England had for several years been limited to officially sanctioned routes and vehicles, thus ensuring that there was little difficulty in constraining the demonstrators' ability to reach rural Wiltshire in any numbers. Furthermore, the intelligence agencies – including Hart's own – instantly descended on the organisers and provocateurs of such actions. The *Wessex Web* had been temporarily closed down and the DSD had detained and interrogated Julie Fenwick for several days. It was with a certain ironic satisfaction that Hart noted her determination not to give up her 'Deep Throat'. He had chosen her well.

As time passed, however, and the sickness and mortality rates climbed precipitously, rumblings of dissent grew louder to be greeted by an increasing presence of armed police and military on the streets of English cities. For the most part this very public show of force – or 'safety maintenance' as the official euphemism had it – did its job in keeping order, although Hart believed that the stability it achieved was at best superficial. Too many essential functions were teetering on the edge of failure as illness deprived them of the skills and labour necessary to keep them running. To walk around London, as Hart did regularly, was to witness a city deserted by many of its inhabitants, while those who were prepared to take the risk wore surgical masks or respirators and carefully avoided any contact with each other.

It was a strange sight, this thinly populated metropolis, its ghost-like figures unrecognisable behind their masks, passing by without so much as a look. Restaurants and bars were mostly closed, theatres and cinemas dark, offices and businesses staffed by skeleton crews if they were staffed at all. Hospitals were overloaded, and anyway incapable of doing much other than alleviating some of the worst symptoms of their all too frequently dying patients. The government had with great fanfare extended the customary seasonal offer of mass flu vaccination beyond its normal range of recipients. But this was more a public relations exercise than a preventive intervention since they knew full well that the vaccine would have little or no effect on Livermore's original strain, let alone on its proclivity for sudden mutation.

All this, Hart recognised, was taking a severe toll on the tolerance of the population. Families fearful of infection confined themselves to home – schools and other educational institutions had been closed for some weeks – venturing out only to buy food at those supermarkets designated to hold the ever-decreasing and, therefore, rationed supplies. The economy was tumbling further and further into recession, faced with travel and trade embargoes from former international allies as well as a rapid decline in domestic production and consumption. The City of London, past keystone of the English economy and much vaunted provider of international financial services, had proved helpless in the face of worldwide economic crises. Basic infrastructure provision was just about holding up; there was still power, water, and waste disposal. But how long that could continue remained a matter for constant speculation in the newsfeeds, speculation which itself bolstered the spreading sense of imminent catastrophe.

It would not take much for all this to tip people over the edge into... what? Hart simply did not know. There were long-standing divisions and inequalities in English society which had hitherto been papered over by a combination of ideological manipulation and carefully concealed repressive measures, processes in which the DSD had played its full part. A crisis of this kind, which affected huge swathes of the population, could well feed into those underlying social tensions and generate a pressure which would ultimately find public expression.

Almost twenty years earlier Hart had been a young undercover officer at the time of the London riots. He remembered vividly how quickly they developed, how generally peaceful people had become caught up in street violence, looting and arson. It had simply needed the right catalyst to set things going, in this case the shooting by police of a young black man and a subsequent protest march. Within days there were similar actions in other English cities, although none reached the pitch achieved in London, and then the disturbances died away almost as quickly as they had arisen.

It was a pattern that Hart had recognised at the time. As a student he had written a dissertation on the causes and trajectories of just this kind of collective behaviour, and he could see now that all the preconditions for such an upsurge were in place. It might be, of course, that people's fear of infection and their retreat into their homes would minimise the risk. But Hart was not convinced. The sheer scale of the influenza outbreak was unprecedented in the modern era, as was the desperation that it engendered in people who witnessed sickness and death among their friends and relations. Not since the fourteenth century's Black Death had an illness spread so swiftly across continents, a rapidity matched by the pace at which social networks documented and amplified its progress. It was a truly terrifying prospect for most people who, uniquely in their experience, were being forced to confront not only the premature mortality of their loved ones but also the increasing probability of their own.

It was his growing awareness that social order was balanced on a razor's edge that had prevented Hart from taking the next step in his planned sequence of leaks – detailing the Zeno effect itself. In principle, the channel through Irene and Julie was still available to him. After the worldwide publicity that followed her revelations about the source of the flu, Julie had gained considerable freedom of operation. While she wasn't exactly untouchable, any attempt to muzzle her, whether by detention or even assassination, would now attract adverse international and domestic interest of a kind that the government was eager to avoid. Several transnational newsfeeds had retained her both as a vlogger and as an analyst of the English situation, installing her in a London apartment and providing her with protection, contacts, and secure communication systems. Of course, the intelligence agencies were still watching her, although as time passed and the health crisis intensified they found themselves lacking the resources necessary for full surveillance of anybody. They, too, had lost staff to the virus, and these limitations meant that Hart's channel to Julie remained open and secure.

Yet he had baulked at using it. It seemed to him that there was no longer much to be gained by exposing the full details of the Zeno effect and of the government cover-up. No one had the means to arrest the accelerated mutation rate of the virus so, Hart reasoned, the risks of much intensified panic far outweighed the likely positive consequences. True, forcing the authorities into publishing technical details of the Porton Down work would allow for international collaboration in the search for a solution. But that would be a very long-term gamble which, again, was probably not worth the risk. Hart sighed. He was going round in circles, he told himself, and there was no point to it. Better to get on with the more immediate job of maintaining some semblance of order in England. He was, after all, director of an agency committed to defending domestic security and that had to remain his first priority.

He turned his attention back to his CommsTab where an international newsfeed was currently spreading even more gloom. The fortress state of North Korea, in the person of its latest Great Leader, was, as ever, busy laying the blame for its own flu epidemic at the door of its southern neighbours and their allies, against whom it threatened unspecified retaliation. Hart was indulging a half smile at the familiar madness of statements from the improbably named Democratic People's Republic, which was neither democratic nor belonging to the people, when a pop-up on his screen signalled a v-call from Jill, his wife. He disliked being interrupted at work – Hart's life was carefully constructed into mutually exclusive compartments – so his response was brisk.

"Yes Jill, what is it? I'm busy."

Only then did he look properly at the screen and take in the fact that his wife appeared to be distressed.

"I'm sorry, Jonathan, but I think it might be a good idea if you came home. Rosie is running a rather high temperature and not breathing very easily at all."

Rosie – Rosemary as he preferred it – was their nine-year-old daughter, much adored by her father who was not otherwise given to close emotional ties.

"She seemed fine this morning when I left."

"Yes, it came on very suddenly during the day. Could you come home soon? I think we might need to get her to your government treatment centre. I don't want to risk the local hospital."

"Absolutely," he said, picking up his possessions from the desk as he did so. "Keep away from the hospital – it's a death trap. I'll arrange for the treatment centre on my way. Stay with her. She'll be OK. I'll make sure of that."

z z z

Alison MacGregor was distracted. She was all too aware that her attention was wandering after almost three hours in a seemingly endless meeting of the recently created Scottish Virology Research Group, of which she had been made secretary and facilitator. The Group was known to her more facetious science administration colleagues as the Baby Bug Hunters, a designation which had stuck in spite of its patent inaccuracy. Though they were indeed small, viruses could hardly be counted as bugs, nor was the Group in the job of hunting them. The SVRG was an attempt to bring together Scotland's leading expertise in areas germane to dealing with the flu. Its members were drawn from several universities and from the Scottish Health Service, and it was chaired by a very senior professor from the University of Glasgow. He had, Ali knew, a formidable scientific reputation, but as a chairman he lacked any inclination to direct discussion into practical areas. For the last twenty minutes two members of the Group had been engaged in an arcane disagreement about an obscure aspect of genetics and the Chairman, who appeared to be enjoying the debate, was showing no sign of returning them to the more pressing topics in hand.

Hence Ali's impatience, which was shared by several others around the table as she could see from their fidgeting.

At last the two men fell into a mutually recriminatory silence whereupon everyone else looked hopefully towards the Chair.

"Um, yes. Thank you, gentlemen. Most enlightening. Anything else we need to consider, Alison?"

Ali, who was determined that the already over-extended meeting should not continue for a moment longer, ignored a couple of other items on her own Any Other Business list and offered relief to all.

"No, Chair, I think we've probably covered everything for this week."

"Excellent. Well, thank you all for coming. See you next week when we meet… um?"

"In Stirling," Ali supplied.

"Ah yes. Stirling. Till next week then, when we can continue that interesting discussion."

This was the signal for an immediate rush to the door leaving Ali to retrieve any papers left lying around the room. Some of them highly confidential, she reminded herself as she prepared to go.

"Do you have a moment, Alison?"

It was a recently retired Professor of Genetics, Michael Lang, whom she had known vaguely when he had been Sarah Johnson's PhD supervisor.

"Of course, Michael. What can I do for you?"

"Well, you could organise a new chairman," he replied with a mischievous grin, "but I don't suppose that's really possible. No, I wanted a word about Sarah and Hugh. Both of them could be very useful to us in this work and I wondered if you knew how settled they were in York. I've been given funds to set up a secret unit focusing specifically on Zeno so I could find them decent research jobs. I'm not at all sure that England is a good place for them to be right now."

Ali nodded. "I agree about them being in England. In fact, I made that very point to Sarah last time I saw her and things have got much worse since then. But isn't the border pretty much closed now?"

"I'm told that exceptions can be made in special circumstances, although that still doesn't mean that they could get through the English side of the fence even if we were willing to accept them. But I've been speaking to someone else I think you know – Douglas MacIntyre – and he seems to believe that if there are people I want to recruit from England then there are ways and means. He didn't elaborate though."

"No, I bet he didn't," Ali said with a smile. "But he does seem to get things done. He can certainly contact Sarah privately, as he probably told you."

"Mmmmn, he did." Michael looked at her quizzically. "He thinks highly of you. In fact, he suggested that I had this conversation. He seemed to think you might be an ideal go-between. Would you?"

"I'd certainly like to get them up here if it's possible. What do you suggest?"

"I'll get back to Douglas and ask him to contact you directly, and I'll let you know what exactly I can offer them. Then you and Douglas can do whatever is necessary. Best if I don't know the details, I think."

Ali and Michael parted ways outside the Summerhall Virology Building. Eager to recover from the torpor induced by the meeting, she decided to cheer herself up by not returning to the office and instead walking home across The Meadows. As a child she had spent many hours playing in the park on what had then looked to her like a vast plain of green set down in the midst of Edinburgh's grey buildings. Today, in spite of the fact that it was a mild afternoon even for twenty-first century winter warmth, there were only a few people around, most of them walking dogs, and some of them, she noted, wearing protective masks.

As a result of the information that she had secured from Irene, the Scottish government had been able to act early enough to slow the spread of flu, though certainly not to stem it. Still, there were more than enough cases to be frightening, and, as everywhere, people were becoming less willing to venture out unless absolutely necessary. This fearfulness had not been helped by the decision to close the border with England to all but approved traffic. While this did have some small effect on limiting the passage of the virus into Scotland, it also served publicly to underline quite how serious was the threat. Hitherto the border had been viewed by Scots as an essentially xenophobic construction by the English who had fenced it a couple of years earlier in response to yet another scare about illegal migrants arriving via Scottish routes. Now, though, it had taken on the mantle of a last-ditch Scots defence against incoming disease.

As she left the main park and wandered slowly along Middle Meadow Walk, Ali mused on the parlous state of their resistance to the spreading virus. Of course, they were doing what they could – witness the frustrating meeting that she had just attended – but it was clear that this was not going to be sufficient. Unless someone could crack the Zeno code the world would face wave after wave of flu of varying degrees of virulence. Some people would undoubtedly be immune, others might develop resistance, but the death toll would still be fearsome. The reports that she had seen from England were shocking and, although her own country had put in place treatment and quarantine procedures very early, Scottish cities were beginning to follow a similar pattern to those south of the border. Containment was not going to be enough.

Worried by all this, she had called her father just yesterday to check on his health and he had told her that, although there were not yet any reported cases in his isolated corner of rural Argyll, the small tourist towns of the Highlands were suffering. In the likes of Oban and Ullapool, which carried ferry traffic to the Western Isles, or Fort William, which was something of a tourism gateway, the flu had arrived with travellers, and their medical facilities were now fighting losing battles. Bill and Jess, he added, had been forced to close the shop in Edinburgh when customers all but disappeared, and they were now permanently back in Coldstream. According to Bill the atmosphere in the town was extremely tense, sitting right on the border as it did, with armed guards and defensive blockades posted at each side of the bridge across the Tweed. Here, too, panic about the flu was spreading, not helped by unverified rumours that boats had been seen crossing the river in the dead of night.

These unhappy thoughts accompanied Ali all the way home, so it was with some relief that she climbed the stairs to her top-floor flat. In the years since she had moved to Forrest Road she had come to love her building's combination of history and newly acquired modern reconstruction. Once it had been a staircase of respectable and quite large apartments – the kind that had brass bell-pulls at the street entrance which residents took turns to polish – but in the later twentieth century it had become rather dingy, split into student accommodation, poorly maintained, and with graffiti on its once imposing front door. Recent work on improving Edinburgh's older housing had, however, led to external cleaning and internal refurbishment. Each of the original apartments was now divided into two smaller modern units aimed at single occupants, although the staircase was still constructed of the same unforgiving stone, and the bow windows overlooking the street were still in the traditional Edinburgh style. Ali's kitchen, her invariable first destination on arriving home, looked out across the rooftops towards Edinburgh Castle. It was a fine vantage point from which to view the firing of the one o'clock gun, something that had fascinated little Charlotte because of the time-gap between seeing the puff of smoke and then hearing the detonation. Now, admiring the castle as she stood waiting for her espresso machine to complete its cycle, this reminder of Charlotte returned Ali's thoughts to Sarah and to the suggestion that she and her family might be brought to Scotland.

She carried her coffee through to the living area and sat staring vacantly at the blank wall-mounted TV screen. Would Sarah be persuaded? And even if she could be, reaching Scotland was no longer simply a question of obtaining permits and getting on a train. Travel within England was heavily restricted, and that was before you got anywhere near the border. And on top of that there was no chance that either Sarah or Hugh would be allowed to leave. They were too valuable a resource. So how could it be done?

As if in response to her unspoken question her CommsTab sprang to life. 'V-call from Douglas MacIntyre' it announced. Ali touched the accept icon and, before Douglas could say a word, smiled at the screen.

"Well," she said, "that was quick."

He laughed. "Michael Lang just called me and said that you had agreed, so now seemed as good a time as any. We'll need to move soon given how fast things seem to be falling apart in England."

"Is it really that bad?"

"Yes, I'm afraid so. They spent too long denying everything when, if they had been honest, they could have been preparing people to deal with it."

"Should we meet tomorrow then?"

"Mmmmn, we could," Douglas paused and then added tentatively, "but I'm free this evening if you are. Perhaps we could have dinner? Just down the hill from you in the Grassmarket there's a rather good Italian restaurant, L'Avventura, which is still open and relatively safe. They have a scanner to test customers' temperatures and they won't let anybody in who is running any kind of fever."

"Yes, I read about that on one of the city newsfeeds. But does it work?"

"There's no reason why it shouldn't. The fever is a very early sign of the flu – you're not generally infectious until later. Or so I'm told."

Ali hesitated. Apart from a couple of evenings with Ravi and Eleanor she hadn't been out for dinner since that last time with Richard. The diversion would be welcome and Douglas seemed like a decent enough person. Quite good-looking too, she caught herself thinking.

"OK. Let's do it. What time?"

"Can we meet there in an hour?"

"I think I can manage that," she said. "See you there."

There was just about time for a shower and a change of clothes, she calculated, but not long enough to wash and dry her hair. She would put it in a ponytail – people always said how much that suited her. She giggled a little at this thought. After all the distress she had been through with Richard, here she was thinking about looking attractive for yet another intelligence agent. Still, at least she knew about this one's work in advance.

Douglas was waiting outside for her when she arrived at the restaurant. They were greeted just inside the entrance by a woman who briefly pointed a small scanner an inch or so from their foreheads, consulted a screen, and then waved them through. True to its name, the dining area was decorated with enormous black-and-white frame enlargements from Antonioni's classic film. Not perhaps the most encouraging décor for romantic diners, Ali reflected, given how bleak were the images and, indeed, the whole tenor of the film. Still, few customers would recognise the reference. Ali only did so because of her father's determined attempts to educate her in the history of the cinema.

Once seated, Ali realised that the place was completely full.

"It's really busy, isn't it. How did you manage to book a table at such short notice?"

Douglas looked a little sheepish. "Well," he said, "I actually booked it yesterday when Michael told me he would be seeing you today."

Ali arched an eyebrow. "So I'm that predictable, am I? You knew that I'd agree about Sarah and would be willing to go out to dinner with you? Must be the intelligence training."

"No, no, of course not." Douglas was flustered. "I just took a gamble. Seemed to be worth it. And it turns out that it was, because here we are."

"So we are," Ali agreed, "and I'm suitably impressed with your forward planning. Now, what are we going to eat?"

Having won this preliminary skirmish, at least in her own eyes, Ali settled in to enjoy her evening. And enjoy it she did. After sorting out the case that she would make in her letter to Sarah, they agreed that she would write it tomorrow, add the details of Michael's offer, and then Douglas would arrange for its delivery. Official business thus transacted, and the main course yet to arrive, they were free to talk of other things. To Ali's delight Douglas proved to be an entertaining dinner companion, and, as the evening progressed, for the first time in weeks she began to relax. For a while the horror of Zeno receded into the background.

All too soon the meal was over and the restaurant rapidly emptying of customers. Despite Douglas's protestations, Ali insisted on splitting the bill – she had her standards she told him – and they took themselves out into a now dark and deserted Grassmarket.

"If I can't buy you dinner at least let me walk you home," Douglas insisted.

"Fair enough," she said, and slipped her arm through his as they set off up the hill.

Passing the statue of Greyfriars Bobby she found herself telling Douglas how, as a child, she had loved visiting this little dog and had as a result always wanted a Skye Terrier of her own. But work commitments meant that she had never been in a position to properly look after a pet, so she had to be satisfied with the succession of rescue dogs that shared life with her father.

By the time she had finished extolling the virtues of his present canine companion – a Lurcher called Pike – they had arrived at her front door.

"Thank you," she said. "That was a lovely evening."

He smiled. "Good. I certainly enjoyed it, so thank you for coming. We'll have to do it again sometime soon."

"I'd like that. Perhaps I could cook you dinner. I can cook, you know."

Then, as much to her own surprise as his, she reached up and kissed him fleetingly on the lips, turned away, and with a hand raised in farewell disappeared into the building.

z z z

Syntagma Square in Athens had seen many demonstrations over the years, but few quite as explosive as this one. The square was filled to overflowing, thousands upon thousands of chanting protesters, many wearing roughly fabricated face masks, and all eager to find someone to blame for the rapidly rising death rate. A section of the crowd closest to the parliament building was confronted by black-clad rows of riot police, their faces concealed behind masks, their weapons and shields at the ready. As more people entered the square the sheer pressure of numbers squeezed the protesters up against the police lines until, whether from orders or from panic, a shot was fired. A kind of groan rolled through the crowd and with it a ripple of movement that threatened to flood over the riot police. Suddenly there were more shots as tear-gas canisters rained down on increasingly panicked people. Now the ripple became a tidal wave, spreading in all directions.

Fighting broke out, some between protesters and police, some between different elements in the crowd as they sought desperately to escape the fumes. One splinter group, led by radicalised former KKE members, smashed their way into the luxurious foyer of the five-star Hotel Grande Bretagne, while others, from various of the right wing anti-immigrant parties, spilled into the surrounding streets in search of non-Greek shops and cafés to attack. As the chaos grew, the rumble of heavy vehicles heralded the arrival of army reinforcements and the sound of gunshots became a continuous barrage. Wherever you looked, people were dying, whether trampled by the mob or hit by bullets that ricocheted crazily around the square. And right across the sprawling city of Athens the virus continued to do its work.

2

One of the many benefits of Jonathan Hart's position as DSD director was that at a time of severely restricted travel he had unlimited use of a chauffeur-driven official car. A second perk of the job, and in the present circumstances an even more important one, was access to one of the secretive government Treatment Centres specifically reserved for members of the ruling elite and their families. So it was that Hart, along with his wife and child, were being driven at speed into central London to the King Edward VII's Hospital in Marylebone. The hospital had been chosen to house a Treatment Centre in part because it had a history of association with the military going back to the Boer War, a connection reflected in the fact that throughout the twentieth century its official designation had even included the revealing addendum 'for Officers'. It also had an excellent reputation in expensive healthcare, encouraging an increasingly worried Hart to harbour at least some hope for his daughter's recovery.

Rosemary was clearly suffering from a severe case of the flu. Even in the relatively short time it had taken him to get home she had, Jill said, deteriorated significantly. Her temperature was now worryingly high and her breathing increasingly laboured. She lay across the back seat of the car with her head in Hart's lap, pale-faced but still conscious, struggling for breath and looking up at him with the kind of implicit trust that perhaps only a nine-year-old child might have in her father. He would surely protect her, as he always had. Hart hoped against hope that this would turn out to be true. In rushing her to the hospital he was ensuring that she would get the best care available, but, as he of all people knew, the virus was no respecter of medical expertise. They could only aim to keep her alive in the expectation that her own immune system would ultimately do its job.

The next couple of hours went by in a flurry of activity. After Hart had carried her into the hospital, the medical system took over. Rosemary was installed in a large family room which also included beds for her parents. She was connected to a plethora of monitors and drips, as well as to a mask supplying oxygen, and, for a while at least, her breathing was less laboured. With a weather eye to Hart's official position, the hospital administration ensured that a very senior consultant arrived to examine Rosemary inside half an hour and she confirmed that the symptoms were indeed those of the current flu strain. Tests would be carried out to check but she had little doubt about the diagnosis. They would do everything possible to make the patient comfortable, give her some medication to boost her immune system, but beyond that it was just a question of wait and see.

This was no more than Hart had expected. Wearing surgical masks, he and Jill settled themselves into chairs on either side of the bed. Hart felt oddly lulled by the continuous beep of the monitor, and looking down at his now sedated daughter he reflected on the sequence of events that had brought them here. For him it had begun with the discovery of Charles Livermore's body in the cathedral, although his awareness of impending disaster had only started to take proper shape at that crisis meeting in the Department of Health. It was then that he had learned the full scope of the Zeno experiments and, although he had said nothing at the time, he had been aghast that Porton Down and Curbishley had been allowed to pursue such a foolhardy course of action. Irene Johnson's objections, which she had obviously made from the very beginning, were irrefutable. Yet the powers that be had overridden her protests and allowed Curbishley free rein to develop what was clearly an uncontainable biological weapon.

How was that possible? How could intelligent and presumably sane people allow such a project to go ahead? His best guess was that

Curbishley had convinced them that his scientists would develop some kind of antidote or vaccination in tandem with the engineered virus, and that the prospect of possessing such a weapon had inclined them to believe him despite the absence of any plausible evidence to support his case. In Hart's experience people in power were easily beguiled when offered something that they thought would give them even more power, especially so in an England that, as far as the governing elite were concerned, now wielded much less international influence than once it had. The prospect of standing proud on what they liked to speak of as 'the world stage' all too often proved irresistible. The fact that this was no longer practical, or even desirable, appeared to escape them, although it was clear enough to Hart. Certainly he did not see such misguided ambitions as any kind of justification for embarking on an enterprise as hazardous as the Zeno project.

But then, as he had always believed, it was not for him to take such decisions. He was a servant of the state. However ill-advised a government might be, if the people saw fit to elect it then it was Hart's job to implement those aspects of its policies that required his particular kinds of expertise. He had no delusions about the ethical pitfalls of that commitment. His was a world in which, by and large, the ends justified the means, and if that required dubious morality – sending Osborne to inveigle himself into the life of Alison MacGregor, for example – then so be it. While he was not naïve enough to think that there were no limits at all on his actions, he was clear that the moral restraints that ordinary people might expect in their own lives did not apply to the inevitably murky activities of the intelligence world.

Thus far in his work he had not been obliged to confront directly what he considered to be a really serious ethical dilemma, although he liked to think that he would recognise that point should he reach it and would behave accordingly. In fact, until this Zeno business he had generally been untroubled by such concerns. But he was troubled now, and no longer just in the abstract. Looking down at his unconscious daughter while gently stroking her hand in the hope that she might be aware of his presence, powerful emotions were affecting what he always thought of as primarily rational calculations. Now, suddenly and uniquely in his experience, the administrative and the political were becoming deeply personal.

zzz

Writing to Sarah took longer than Ali had expected. She had spent a whole morning drafting and redrafting a letter and she was still not satisfied with the result. The problem was that, as she well knew, Sarah was happy where she was. She enjoyed her work, Charlotte had many friends, and Hugh had been content to go along with things even though, as one Scot to another, he had often told Ali that he would like to return home in the fullness of time. In the present much more precarious circumstances Ali was sure that she could convince Hugh of the need to move, but she was less certain about Sarah. Her friend could be very stubborn – 'determined' was how Sarah preferred to describe it – and, although she had studied in Scotland, moving there now was something she would be likely to resist.

Still, Ali knew that she had to make the effort. She was convinced that things were going to get a great deal worse as the epidemic spread, especially in England where the disease had established its first foothold and where the government seemed incapable or unwilling to propose any kind of coherent strategy to combat it. Decades of underfunding of the National Health Service, in combination with forbiddingly expensive private health insurance, meant that adequate medical treatment was out of the reach of many people. At least in Scotland they were pledging massive resources to the task, a very public commitment which, whatever its likely medical efficacy, had so far served to minimise unrest. Although England had not yet descended into the extreme protests and social disorder that were reported from some parts of the world, there were clear signs of growing and vocal dissatisfaction which was being met with increasingly repressive measures. In her time working there Ali had been dismayed to discover quite how authoritarian English society had become, with its constantly paraded nationalism and widespread insistence that others – outsiders, ethnic minorities, so-called scroungers – were always to blame when anything went wrong. Even now, after Livermore's and Porton Down's responsibility had been widely publicised, there were many who insisted that foreigners were behind it all, whether immigrants or terrorists, a belief that the authorities were more than happy to encourage.

All this looked like a highly combustible mix and Ali had done her best to summarise her forebodings in the letter. But as she reread it yet again she worried that Sarah would dismiss her claims as unnecessary panic since, by virtue of her professional expertise, Sarah was more inclined to focus on the biomedical dynamics of the disease than on its social consequences.

It was so difficult for Ali to argue her case at a distance like this. If only they could speak safely via CommsTab without the risk of being eavesdropped upon by the English intelligence agencies. But Douglas had been very firm about not doing that, insisting that this correspondence was the only safe way that they could communicate, and Ali certainly didn't want to put her friends at risk. Yet more than anything she wanted to get them up to Scotland, not just for their own good – although definitely that – but also because she really needed her best friend. They had been through so much together since childhood, providing each other with unfailing support. If things were going to get as bad as seemed likely then she wanted to be with Sarah, facing whatever had to be faced.

With a sigh she set the letter aside. As her father had always advised her, when having trouble writing something complicated turn your attention to some other task until you feel able to revisit the original. He should know, she thought, he had written more books than she cared to count. Besides, Douglas should be coming soon with the job offer details and he might be able to help. The thought of seeing Douglas cheered her up a little. Dinner the previous evening had been an entertaining diversion, and, lying in bed later that night, she had admitted to herself that she found him more than a little attractive. Older than her, certainly, but only by ten years or so, and as he had told her, currently single after separating from a long-standing partner.

Her mind half occupied with these pleasant speculations she turned her attention to writing up the minutes of the last SVRG meeting, a torpor-inducing task if ever there was one. Sufficiently so that when Douglas did arrive mid afternoon he was doubly welcome.

"Thank god you've come," she said. "Writing minutes is reducing me to an automaton."

"I know the feeling," he replied. "I used to have to do it myself before I escaped into the field. Now other apprentice agents are stuck with it while I dally with charming scientific liaison officers."

This last observation was accompanied by a self-deprecating look that somewhat defused its overt flirtatiousness. Even so, Ali felt the need to scrabble through the papers on her desk to cover her pleasure at the compliment, finally extracting a printout of her draft letter.

"I'm having a lot of trouble writing this," she said, waving it in front of him. "Have you got the job details?"

"Yes, they're here. They're in a formal letter which we can include in the delivery. But what's your problem?"

"I can't anticipate all Sarah's objections so it just gets longer and more confused the more I try to second-guess her. It would be so much easier if we could talk face to face."

Douglas shook his head. "Impractical, I'm afraid. You need to do the best you can in writing. Do you want me to go through it with you?"

"Yes, that would be good. Pull up a chair and we'll work on screen."

For the remainder of the afternoon they sat side by side and juggled Ali's arguments until it became clear that they weren't going to make any further improvements. Douglas slid his chair back from the desk.

"This is going to have to do," he said, in a tone that brooked no disagreement. "I really need to get this stuff into our system today. I won't have another courier until next week."

"Yes, I suppose you're right. It's probably as good as we'll get it but I really don't think it will work," Ali replied, then added: "it's all getting very depressing, Douglas. When the Zeno effect kicks in properly new mutations will spread and everything will get much worse. I'm worried, not just about Sarah, but about what this could do to our whole way of life. Everything could so easily collapse once basic resources can't be maintained."

"I know," Douglas said. "I've been thinking about it too. We need to develop contingency plans. I don't just mean the government, though I know they're trying. I mean us, ordinary people. We have to figure out what we are going to do if – when – things start to fall apart. We need to be prepared."

Ali looked at him wide-eyed. "What, you mean like those American survivalists? Cellars full of canned food and water and a whole armoury to protect it with?"

"Up to a point, yes. It may well get bad enough to require weapons, and food supplies are obviously vital. But that's essentially short-term stuff. If you get a real breakdown of social order then, in the longer run, we'd need something more sustainable. We'd have to produce food, maintain energy resources, defend ourselves from others who might want to steal what we have."

Douglas stood up and gazed out of the window across the Edinburgh skyline. "In those circumstances I don't think it would be wise to stay here," he continued. "The city would become very dangerous, a dog-eat-dog world with far too many people crammed into too small a space. I would head north into the Highlands. Try to establish a safe haven as far from cities as possible."

"You've really been thinking about it, haven't you?" Ali said. "You believe it may well come to that?"

"Yes, I suppose I do," he replied, looking none too happy about it. "Sorry to sound so downbeat but best to be realistic about these things."

Ali joined him at the window, resting a comforting hand on his arm. "Yes, true enough. I haven't really faced up to the possibilities yet. Not in that kind of detail anyway. It's a depressing prospect, isn't it?"

"It is, it really is." He put his hand over hers and squeezed it gently, then, disengaging himself, added: "Still, there are immediate things to do. I'd best get this letter sent off. We can talk about the rest some other time."

After Douglas left, Ali remained standing at the window thinking about the conversation they had just had. Edinburgh looked peaceful enough in the winter sunshine, as if nothing could ever disturb its serenity. But of course Douglas was right. When the epidemic did get worse its focus would be in the cities where people lived cheek by jowl and infection could spread rapidly, so it was in the cities that trouble would first arise. Her most likely refuge when that happened would be with her father in the mountains of northern Argyll. If he hadn't done so already – and knowing him he probably had – she should warn him to stock up on non-perishable food. It could be a long winter, she thought, as she gathered her things to go home. A very long winter.

By the time she reached the flat Ali was sunk even further in gloom. Her only positive thought was to visit her father over the coming weekend and discuss plans with him, but beyond that she was uncertain what else she could do. In an attempt to cheer herself up she drank her customary cup of coffee and then spent an inordinately long time under a hot shower. Such taken-for-granted pleasures might well disappear within months, she told herself, so make the most of them while you can. After drying her hair she dressed in what she thought of as her 'slouching about' clothes – an old scoop-neck top and a pair of loose cotton trousers – then, streaming what she hoped would be some comforting music, she curled up on the sofa and closed her eyes.

More than an hour later she awoke with a start. The music had ended and her doorbell was ringing. Still only half-awake, she opened the door to find a smiling Douglas carrying a bottle of wine.

"After our talk this afternoon I thought you might need cheering up," he said, thrusting the bottle into her hands. "Maybe we could share this."

"Right. Yes. Come in," Ali said, still not fully awake. "How did you get through the main door?"

"An elderly lady on her way out let me in when I said I was visiting you. She seemed pleased that you had a caller."

"Oh, that would be Bessie. She's determined to marry me off. Doesn't think it's right that I should be living on my own. As far as she's concerned that's for old ladies like her, not young women, so now she'll have you down as a potential suitor. She means well though and I'm very fond of her."

Ali fetched wine glasses from the kitchen, opened the bottle, and joined Douglas on the sofa.

"Here you go," she said, handing him a glass and pouring wine into it. "Have you eaten yet?"

"No, I thought maybe we could order a pizza. Though we might have to wait a bit. The delivery services are working overtime now that people are reluctant to go out."

"We could," she said, sipping her wine. "But I was going to cook some pasta and sauce anyway and that would be easy enough to make for two."

"OK, if you're sure. That would be even better. Can I help?"

"Yes, you can make a salad and talk to me while I cook. Come on, let's get started before we drink our way through the entire bottle on empty stomachs."

Half an hour of companionable activity in the kitchen saw them seated at the table and ready to eat.

"Thanks for this, Alison. It's a while since anyone has cooked for me."

"It's a pleasure. I'm relieved not to be on my own tonight." She paused for a minute, then asked: "One thing though. Why do you keep calling me Alison when everybody else uses Ali?"

"Ah. Well, I have this funny preference for full names not diminutives. It's – oh dear, this is embarrassing – it's because at school I used to get called Dougie, only pronounced the Scottish way, Doogie. I hated it. I still do. So I've got this obsessive thing about proper names. Do you mind?"

"No, no. I quite like to be called Alison. It sounds special. And you certainly don't look like a Doogie to me so I'll stick with Douglas. It's a deal. Now eat. Suddenly I'm starving."

They followed the pasta with cheese and fruit then sat finishing the wine and chatting of this and that until, out of the blue, Douglas suddenly announced, "You do look very lovely, you know."

"What, in these clothes? Surely not," Ali replied, looking down at her clothing and only then realising that her scoop-neck top was displaying rather more cleavage than usual and remembering that she had not bothered to put on a bra when she came out of the shower. "Ah, I see," she added, with a knowing smile.

"So do I," he said, his eyes dropping deliberately to her breasts. She was aware that her nipples were hardening under his look and, without the bra, were clearly visible through the thin fabric. She looked at him enquiringly.

"Do you mind?" he asked, reaching across and running his fingers down her cheek and then across the uncovered slope of her breasts. Ali took an involuntary breath.

"No. It's good," she said, and encouraged by her response he allowed his fingers to slip inside the neckline of her top, gently stroking her now hardened nipples. With a little groan Ali bit on her bottom lip and, looking him directly in the eye, grabbed his straying hand.

"I think perhaps we should go to bed," she said, and still holding his hand she led the way to the bedroom.

z z z

In the early hours of that December morning tanks and armoured vehicles emerged onto the streets of Istanbul, barricading both the Bosphorus and the Fatih Sultan Mehmet bridges. Fighter jets and helicopters patrolled the skies above the city while a group of military special forces captured the President and leading figures in his administration. The ostensible reason given for the military coup was that the government had failed entirely to halt the rampant spread of influenza and to sustain essential services. There had been public unrest and some violent demonstrations which, it was claimed, now required military intervention and martial law. It was widely agreed among commentators that the flu epidemic, although real enough and extremely serious, had provided opposition groupings with a convenient excuse to take power, and that they were unlikely to be any more successful in combating the disease than had been their predecessors. Beyond Turkey, in international diplomatic circles, there was much concern that this might not be the only coup precipitated by the English flu.

3

In spite of the hospital's bustle all around them, sounds from elsewhere barely penetrated the Hart's family room. Occasionally they could hear the rumble of a trolley being wheeled past the door, perhaps accompanied by the odd indistinguishable word or two. Even less frequently there might be the distant chiming of an over-loud nurse's alarm call, or, given that hospital employees were required to wear rubber-soled shoes, the distinctive click of a visitor's heels in the corridor. But other than the regular arrival of medical staff to monitor Rosemary's condition and the delivery of food for her parents, to all intents and purposes the room was a private, closed space. This almost hermetic insulation from the world outside was beginning to play on Hart's mind. He was exhausted anyway, unable to sleep even in the bed provided, preferring to remain seated next to his now mortally ill daughter.

To his growing horror her decline had taken little more than three days. First her breathing had become increasingly laboured and she had required intubation and connection to a ventilator. Then, much concerned about these respiratory problems, the consultant diagnosed viral pneumonia on top of the already deeply debilitating flu. Liquid was accumulating in her chest cavity and required to be drained, leaving her connected to yet another piece of life-preserving equipment. To Hart's despairing eyes she now resembled a butterfly trapped at the centre of an elaborate web of tubes and cables, waiting only for the spider to arrive. It was a measure of his state of mind that however hard he tried to dispel it, this image kept returning to him.

Hart himself had been hospitalised only once, a minor procedure which kept him in for just a few days. Yet he remembered vividly the sense of claustrophobic entrapment that he had felt when confined to the ward and the extraordinary relief on being released from what he had experienced as involuntary captivity. Unconscious as she was, Rosemary could hardly be having such feelings, but he felt as if he was reliving them on her behalf. When he had been discharged from hospital the first thing he had done was to seek out a tree that he had been able to see from the ward window and run his hand along its rain-dampened bark. The exquisite roughness of that profoundly physical sensation, confirming his return to the outside world, had stayed with him ever since, and it was now an experience that he desired desperately for his daughter.

Hospitals, Hart concluded, were paradoxical places. When you are ill you are relieved and grateful that they are there to look after you, but as the days grind by you want nothing more than to escape their pervasive embrace. Like all total institutions, however well intentioned, they inevitably undermine your sense of identity, shaping it to their own distinctive requirements. You have to become 'a patient,' ready to accept and live up to the everyday expectations of that role as it is defined for you. If, like Rosemary, you are seriously ill, that matters little. But if you still have your wits about you then, bit by bit, your autonomy is undermined and you become a marionette endlessly dancing to their tune. Of course, in a hospital they are trying to help you, but in other institutions – and not just total ones like prisons or care homes – they may well be trying to help themselves at your expense.

Hart had endlessly rehearsed this line of thought as he sat beside Rosemary's unresponsive form, and each time it had led him to the same disturbing place. Had he not spent his life in the intelligence world living up to precisely what was expected of him? And, in order to do so, had he not suspended his own judgment, his own sense of independent identity, his own evaluations of the objectives set for him by the governing elite known traditionally to their administrative servants as 'our masters'?

What a phrase that was – 'our masters' – capturing in just two words a whole universe of tacitly masculine authority and deference. If he had been less ensnared in that world, less cautious at that fateful meeting about the Zeno breach, if he had only spoken out as Irene Johnson had, then he might not now be seated helplessly by his daughter. At least they could have been making preparations for the epidemic, slowing its spread, developing a strategy of containment. But he had not done so, and now he felt that he was directly confronted with the consequences.

Assailed by these dark thoughts Hart dozed fitfully until a voice cut sharply through them.

"Jonathan, Jonathan. Wake up," Jill was calling. "It's Rosie. Something's badly wrong. I've pressed the emergency button."

Hart sat up, shaking his head as if to empty it of unwanted echoes of his dreams. His daughter was thrashing about on the bed, a thick green discharge flowing from her nose and mouth. She was staring up at him, though without any sign of recognition, while the violence of her desperate struggle for breath disrupted and broke the web of tubes and cables in which she was contained. He took hold of her shoulders in a forlorn attempt to control her convulsions but she continued to writhe beneath his hands, the force of her movement finally weakening as the effort of breathing became too much. Just as the door burst open with the arrival of two nurses and a doctor, Hart thought he saw a look of recognition and appeal as her eyes locked onto his, but then they went blank and lifeless and her body seemed to collapse in on itself.

"No, no," he moaned, as the medical staff forcibly pushed him aside and set about the challenge of reviving their patient. Hart sat hunched on a chair in the farthest corner of the room, Jill beside him, both helpless in the face of the terrible sight of Rosemary being subjected to CPR and defibrillation. Hart could not tell how long the frantic treatment continued – it seemed an eternity – but finally the doctor turned away from the task with a shake of his head.

"I'm sorry," he said to them. "There's nothing more we can do. She's gone. We'll leave you with her for a few minutes then I'll send in someone to talk to you about making arrangements."

Alone with the inert body of their child they mutely held on to each other. The steady hum of the ventilator and monitors that had for days accompanied their vigil was now gone, its absence feeling to Hart like a reproach. How could he have let this happen? His whole adult life spent protecting the state and yet he could not manage to protect his own daughter from something which, ultimately, should be laid at the door of that very state. In less desolate circumstances he might have appreciated the irony, but instead he simply felt his grief and guilt turning to anger.

"They won't get away with it," he muttered, more to himself than to Jill who by now was standing over Rosemary, holding the child's hand and weeping silently.

"What?" she said. "What was that?"

"Nothing," he replied, joining her beside the bed. "Just something I have to do."

z z z

Somewhere an alarm was bleeping. Not very loudly but definitely bleeping, and persistently so. Irene Johnson stood in her hallway peering hopefully at the Home Control app on her CommsTab. Everything was working satisfactorily, it told her, no malfunctions anywhere. So why this warning signal? Shaking her head at the unreliability of computerised household systems, she resigned herself to searching out the source of the sound. No doubt it was a glitch, but far too irritating to ignore. It seemed to be emanating from her study and, sure enough, when she opened the door the bleep became louder. Perhaps it was coming from her ancient computer – Irene had never become entirely accustomed to doing everything on a CommsTab and remained attached to her old technology – but no, that wasn't the source. The noise was coming from inside her desk and, opening a drawer, she saw the flashing red light on the long-forgotten paging device that Jonathan Hart had given her several months earlier. This was the first time it had shown any sign of life.

Irene looked at the unremarkable piece of plastic for a moment then picked it up. The flashing light was clearly an invitation to depress the small button on which it was located and, somewhat warily, she did so. The tiny screen illuminated with the briefest of messages: 'same bench 2pm today'. Irene was nonplussed. Why would Hart want to see her now, so long after that carefully arranged encounter with the reporter, Julie Fenwick? She hadn't heard from either of them since then, though she had of course seen the reporter's name strewn across innumerable internet news items about the source of the flu. What could have happened to cause Hart to make contact, and by this roundabout route?

Well, she thought, there's only one way to find out, so a little before 2pm she was strolling across Tooting Common as she generally did anyway on a weekend afternoon. The bench where she and Hart had conversed previously was unoccupied – the Common was hardly busy on a cold winter's day – and pulling her coat more closely around her, Irene sat down and prepared to wait. She would give him twenty minutes, she decided. If he hadn't shown up by then she would simply continue her walk. In the event Irene only had to wait half that time before she saw Hart approaching from the same direction that she had arrived. On reaching the bench he nodded a greeting and sat down.

"I'm sorry to have kept you waiting," he said. "I wanted to check that you weren't being followed. I didn't really think that you would be. The intelligence agencies are getting far too short-staffed to pursue anything but the most serious cases, but I like to make sure."

"I'm pleased to know that I'm no longer a serious case," Irene replied with a frown, adding, "whatever that might be in present circumstances."

This effort at sarcasm produced a weak smile from Hart. "Yes," he said, "the agencies are not always very good judges about what counts as serious."

Irene gave him a sceptical look. "Including yours?" she asked.

"Yes. In its time, I'm afraid so. But not any more. I'm a great deal clearer about priorities now than I was when we last met."

Irene turned to him again, this time more attentively. He was obviously serious in this unexpected claim and, Irene realised now that she looked at him properly, he appeared haggard and anxious.

"What's brought about that change?"

"Oh, events. Things have happened," he said with a shrug, then, as if eager to change the subject, he stood up. "Let's walk," he proposed. "It's getting cold sitting still."

Hart remained silent as they wandered towards Tooting Common Lake until, becoming impatient, Irene asked: "So, what is it that you wanted to see me about?"

"I'm afraid that I've done something which will likely have repercussions for you, so I wanted to warn you."

Irene halted and turned towards him to protest, but before she could say anything he raised his hand to stop her.

"I know, I know. You think that I should at least have consulted you first. Well, perhaps I should have. I'm sorry. I felt that I had pressing reasons to go ahead."

He looked apologetic, dejected even, but then his expression hardened into something resembling the ruthless Jonathan Hart with whom she was familiar. "I assure you that it was necessary," he said. "Anyway, it's done now so we should move things on from there."

With that they resumed walking and Hart continued his explanation.

"I've given a great deal more information to Julie Fenwick. She doesn't know that it's come from me. I've provided it electronically in a way that she will find entirely untraceable. But, given your previous contact with her she will almost certainly assume that it has come through you. And given what it is, I think she'll try to contact you."

Irene frowned. "But she doesn't know who I am. We simply met in that cinema and I gave her certain information. In her reports she gives no details. She even described me as her Deep Throat."

"True, but she's not stupid and she's very resourceful. I'm sure that she long ago figured out who you are. She has seen you, remember, even in a dimly lit cinema, and she would know that you had to be placed somewhere in government science circles to have the kind of information that you gave her. It wouldn't be difficult to find photographs of you online. What's more, she's thoroughly resourced now, mostly from international organisations. She has 'researchers' who are, in effect, private security. I'll bet that she knows exactly where you live."

Irene took a deep breath and followed it with an irritated exhalation. "You'd better tell me what you've told her then."

Once more Hart stopped walking, turning to face her. "Pretty well everything. The history of the Zeno project. The fact that the flu is a Zeno variation. Who was responsible. Who was in charge." He was mentally counting them off. "And some stuff that you don't know about, like the specifics of the cover-up, how high the decision-making went, and so on. Everything I had access to really."

Irene's expression must have told him how horrified she was because he hastily looked away across the park to where a couple of children and their parents were playing chasing games with a dog. When at last he turned back, she saw to her astonishment that there were tears in his eyes.

"I really had to do it," he said.

"But I thought we'd agreed that it would be too risky to release the Zeno information, too likely to provoke unrest and panic. And probably even more so now with the flu taking so many lives."

"Yes," he said. "That's precisely the point. I've concluded that it's time for drastic measures. We've been servants of a deeply irresponsible government, and the people, its victims, need to know what has been done without their knowledge. Perhaps then things will change."

"But at what cost?" Irene asked.

"A high cost probably, yes. But at the moment a high cost is being paid anyway and almost entirely by ordinary people. This way, at least those who have been really responsible may get held to account, pay a price that they are not paying at the moment. That's all I want."

Irene thought for a minute. "You're sure that she'll use the information and that the news sites will carry it?"

"Of course. Why wouldn't they?" he replied. "But I think she's likely to check it out with you first. You gave her reliable information before. She trusts you, in as much as she trusts anybody. That's why I've come to warn you. Of course you could deny it, which might stall her for a while. But in the end she'll use it anyway. The material I've given her is too convincing for her to ignore. It is, after all, a huge story."

"What if I told her that it came from you?"

Hart half smiled at the suggestion. "She would certainly use that. Just think of the headlines. 'DSD Director Reveals Conspiracy' and such like. I could deny it, of course. But I'd be out of a job inside twenty-four hours, and probably worse. It's up to you really. I'm hoping that you won't so that we can maintain our alliance."

"Alliance?" Irene spat out the word. "It's not been much of that so far. More like you using me as a convenient front."

"OK, I admit that. I'm sorry. But as I said before, things have changed. I regret not openly siding with you earlier but now I think differently. When it all becomes public, working together we could still be in a position to influence whatever policy decisions get made. It won't make up for the fact that you were ignored before, but we might just be able to do some good."

Irene shook her head. "I think it's too late for that. They're not likely to listen to me now even if they do regret not doing so back at the beginning."

"Maybe." Hart shrugged. "But assuming that you don't give me away, they'll be more inclined to listen to me. And remember, there will be big changes in government circles. People will be sacrificed. There'll be a vacuum to fill and I should be in a position to influence decisions about who is brought in to deal with the crisis."

Irene stared out across the park, not really taking anything in, wondering how far she could trust Hart and whether releasing full information about Zeno would prove to be a positive step in the longer run.

"I'll think about it," she said finally. "And if Julie Fenwick does show up, I'll let you know what I've done. How can I contact you?"

He rummaged in an inside pocket of his coat and produced what looked like an old-fashioned mobile phone. "This will find me. It's preprogrammed. Just press the Call button. If I can answer, I will. If not, I'll call back when I can. Don't give any details or names when we do speak. Just say whether she's been in touch and whether you involved me."

They stood in silence for a minute or two, watching the children throwing a ball back and forth while the increasingly frantic dog ran between them. Were it not for the surgical masks that the children were wearing, it could be an ordinary weekend scene in the park. Didn't these people have a right to know the truth, Irene thought, however terrible it might be? Even if knowing would make things that much worse, raising anxiety levels and, quite possibly, causing public unrest? But then, it was hardly her decision now. Hart had rather pre-empted her there. Whatever she said to Julie Fenwick, even if she denied all of it, the story would surely get published. And how could she deny it? As Hart said, Curbishley and all the others whose hubris and sheer stupidity had led to this disaster should be made to answer for what they had done.

She turned to Hart. "I think I'll go home now. I'll let you know if Julie gets in touch." And then, almost in spite of herself she added: "Take care. You're not looking well."

Hart nodded. "No, I'm not, am I? Still, that's how it is. You take care too."

Irene raised a hand in farewell then set off by the route that she had come. After a minute or so she looked back and saw that Hart was still standing there, watching the children at play.

z z z

From the Jemaa el Fnaa square in Marrakesh it is possible to glimpse the distant, snow-capped Atlas Mountains. But on this particular late afternoon none of the many thousands of people packing the square were interested in the view. Instead, they were focused intently on one man, an Imam, who was addressing them from a temporary platform behind which towered the red sandstone minaret of the Koutoubia Mosque. They roared approval as, in no uncertain terms, he condemned 'the Infidel' for bringing down this pestilential disease upon them all. He called on the faithful to carry out jihad against those responsible and to strive for a return to the world of the Great Caliphate. His audience were stirred. They called for more. And in response the preacher wound them into something close to frenzy.

Scattered around the periphery of the square were armed police in twos and threes, clearly helpless in the face of the vast crowd. They looked at each other and at the scene before them, then without any apparent signal they slipped away into the narrow streets and alleys of the city, abandoning the square to the monstrous creation that was coming into being. At that moment, perfectly on cue, the lights illuminating the minaret sprang to life, its shape towering over the Imam and his devotees, while the repeated cries of "Allahu Akbar" rolled across the city and rose into the darkening sky.

4

Julie Fenwick became increasingly excited as she worked her way through the collection of files that had arrived unbidden from the digital ether. The internet news world was full of conspiracies, invented facts and downright lunacy, but this was surely the real thing. The details of the tale told by the leaked documents fitted neatly into what she already knew, and if they were genuine – Julie was trying hard to maintain a sceptical view on that – this would be even bigger than her previous Porton Down story. Of course, there was always a risk that she was being misled. There were powerful people who would be only too pleased to see her destroyed by reporting a controversial story that could then be proved false. It would undermine her credibility with the less gullible sections of her audience and, perhaps more important, damage her relationship with the organisations that now protected her and funded her work. She had to be careful.

Even so, she could barely resist cheering out loud when she arrived at a set of minutes, marked Top Secret, that recorded a decision not to release any information about Zeno, a decision that had ultimately been taken at prime ministerial level. No public statements were to be made, not even about the flu let alone about the apparently more serious threat posed by the genetic modifications. As Julie juggled back and forth among the files it became clear that there was a whole sequence of precisely documented actions here, revealing a cover-up on a monumental scale. This was a story that would shake the foundations of the English government, matching any of the famous leaks of the past – the Panama Papers, Wikileaks, the Trump Tapes, the Denizovich Documents. It all made sense, fitting in with some odd rumours that she had picked up over the past few months but had never been able to confirm. But where had the material come from? None of her tracing software could identify a source, and given that her technology was provided by some extremely well-equipped organisations this meant that, for all practical purposes, it was untraceable.

She needed at least some degree of corroboration if she was to take the risk of publishing the story. Maybe Deep Throat could provide that. In fact, maybe Deep Throat was actually the source. The message inviting her to that meeting in the cinema had also been mysteriously untraceable. Julie smiled to herself at the fact that she continued to think of Irene Johnson as 'Deep Throat' although she had long since identified her. Julie's attachment to *All the President's Men* remained strong, especially so now that she was even better known to modern audiences than Bernstein and Woodward were in their time. But this new story, this one would be quite extraordinary, which made it all the more important that she tried to confirm it with Irene.

She located a contact on her CommsTab and touched the v-call icon. A man's face appeared on the screen.

"Dennis, hello. We need to make a visit this evening. Can you pick me up at around six?"

"Yes, no problem. Where are we going?"

"South London, Streatham Hill area. There's someone I have to see and I'll need you to ensure that we're not followed and, if you can, confirm that the person we visit isn't being watched."

Dennis frowned. "You're not giving me very long to do that," he said.

"I know," Julie replied, favouring him with her most appealing smile. "But you've checked her out before – Irene Johnson. Anyway, have a look, and if you don't think it's possible let me know and we'll delay it. OK?"

"Yes, I guess so. I'll spend all day on it and call you around five o'clock to tell you what I think. Better get started. Bye."

The screen blanked and Julie gave herself a metaphorical pat on the back for persuading Dennis to be a little less wary than usual. He was her chief minder, a function that he carried out exceptionally well, but by her somewhat impulsive standards he erred too much on the side of caution. That was hardly surprising. Although he treated her as his boss, in fact, of course, she wasn't. He was employed by the shadowy group of organisations who retained her journalistic services, and it was to them that he was actually answerable. No doubt he would be consulting his real employers at this very minute, informing them of her latest escapade. Julie wasn't overly concerned about that. They were aware that Irene was one of her sources and would certainly have no objections to her making contact.

Sure enough, when Dennis called back late in the afternoon it was to confirm that the visit was on. He was as certain as he could be in the time available that there was no surveillance in place, and so a little after 6pm Julie found herself crossing London in an electric City Car. The fact that the car was brand new and top of the range fed her new-found sense of her own importance which, when added to the excitement of setting off in pursuit of a big story, made her feel unusually pleased with herself. It was such a relief not to have to resort to public transport as most people were obliged to do, and gratifying to be driven. Well, not exactly driven – the car drove itself – but Dennis was in the driver's seat which allowed her to mentally transform him into her chauffeur. Nor would the car pass muster as a limousine. It was tiny, as required for the relatively few private vehicles that were permitted to drive in central London, but it still gave her a kick to see pedestrians enviously eyeing it and her.

Abruptly Dennis interrupted these pleasing daydreams.

"I trailed her home from work so let's hope she hasn't gone out again. Couldn't see anyone following her."

"That's good. When we get there I'll go in while you stay in the car and keep watch. Call me if you think anything's wrong."

"Right. Any idea how long you'll be?"

"Not really. She might just refuse to talk to me at all. But as long as she lets me in I think I have a reasonable chance of getting her to tell me what I need to know."

Dennis glanced across at her. "Same business as before, is it?"

"Connected certainly." Julie was never quite sure how much Dennis knew. Probably a lot, she admitted to herself in those occasional moments when she recognised that he was her minder in more senses than one. "I'll find out soon enough," she added, and lapsed into silence.

Twenty minutes later they were pulling up outside Irene's front gate.

"Here goes then," Julie murmured as she got out of the car, as much to herself as to Dennis. "Wish me luck."

The door was opened almost before she had finished ringing the doorbell.

"Hello Professor Johnson," she said. "Remember me?"

Irene replied with just a hint of a smile. "Yes. I do believe that I do, Julie. Come in."

Once seated, and offered a glass of wine from an already opened bottle, Julie began: "You don't seem surprised that I've been able to identify you."

"Well, I expected it really. I have a bit of a public profile so I assumed that someone with your journalistic curiosity wouldn't find it too hard."

"No, it wasn't difficult," Julie replied, then added, "I had a feeling when you opened the door just now that maybe you were expecting me."

"Expecting you? I don't think so. I gave you the information that I had and you made good use of it. Why would you need to see me again?"

Julie opened her shoulder bag and laid a folder of printed documents on the coffee table in front of Irene. "Have a look," she said. "I've received this material that relates to what you told me and goes a whole lot further."

Irene opened the file and gave the first few documents a cursory examination. "There's a bit much here for me to read now. Why don't you save me the trouble and tell me what you think you've learned from all this."

"So you didn't send them to me?"

"No." Irene shook her head firmly. "I've sent you nothing."

Julie looked unconvinced. "OK," she said at last, pulling the folder towards her. "I'll try to give you a summary."

For the next twenty minutes she worked her way through the pile of papers, piecing together a plausible story until, returning the last document to the folder with something of a flourish, she looked Irene straight in the eye and asked again: "So this hasn't come from you?"

"No. I already told you. But I am familiar with the information."

Julie straightened in her chair. "So you can confirm it?"

Irene sat looking thoughtfully at the folder for a moment as Julie waited expectantly. At last she raised her eyes to meet Julie's.

"Yes, I can confirm most of it. There are some decisions recorded there that I've not been privy to, but they sound convincing enough to me."

"Oh my god!" Julie's excitement was tangible. "I thought I might be being set up with a false story."

Irene smiled, if a little mirthlessly. "Perhaps you are. I could easily be party to it."

"No, no. I trust you. You were right before. And it was you who came to me. I can trust you." She paused and then added tentatively, "Can't I?"

"Yes, you can," Irene replied with a sigh. "In some ways I wish you couldn't. I wish that none of this was happening. But it is, and it needs to be faced."

"Oh it will be." Julie was animated again. "It's an amazing story. Such a comprehensive cover-up and one that leads right to the top. And I've got evidence for every stage of the conspiracy."

"Wait, Julie," Irene interrupted. "Stop and think. There's much more to it than the cover-up. You haven't really understood the Zeno effect, have you?"

"Yes, I think so. They manipulated the genetics of the flu virus to make it much worse than we thought."

"No, unfortunately it's rather more than that. Let me explain."

After Irene had finished describing the Zeno mechanism and its implications, Julie took a large gulp of her wine and replaced the glass on the table. "Could I have a little more?" she asked, her voice not much above a whisper.

"Of course," Irene replied, pouring wine for both of them.

"So, what that means…" Julie paused. "What that means is that instead of this one epidemic caused by one strain of the flu, we'll get different ones on into the foreseeable future?"

"Yes, that's right. Pandemics, to be more precise. The present strain has already spread worldwide and it will mutate worldwide as well."

"And..." Julie paused again. "Because of the speed of the mutations we'll not be able to develop vaccines to keep up?"

"Also right. For the past seventy years or so we've been able to isolate flu strains and make vaccines so that the next time that particular strain or a minor mutation came round we'd be much better protected. The Zeno effect changes all that. Even if, say, we develop a vaccine for the present strain – and as far as I know we haven't yet – the rapid rate of mutation will still leave us chasing shadows."

Julie was aghast. "How could they do that? How could they even think to make something so uncontrollable?"

Irene shrugged and bowed her head. "Quite," she said. "So now you know. What will you do?"

"I'll tell the story of course. People deserve to know, and maybe it will push governments into providing more resources for care and for research."

"Maybe. But I think it might also make people even more desperate than they already are. And who knows what they'll do then?"

The two women lapsed into silence contemplating that prospect. Then, at last, Julie finished her wine, stood up, and carefully replaced the folder of documents in her bag.

"We shall see then," she said. "I won't use your name. You can stay as Deep Throat. It's a much better name anyway."

Irene smiled. "Come on. I'll see you out. You be careful. There'll be a lot of powerful people looking for someone to blame."

"Yes, I know," Julie said as she stood up. "But I do have some protection." When they reached the door she turned and impulsively flung her arms around Irene, drawing her into a close embrace.

"I'll keep in touch," she whispered, then, opening the front door, walked down the path to Dennis and her car.

Irene returned to her kitchen table where the dregs of the wine awaited her. She sat for a long time staring into her now empty glass, then reached into a drawer and retrieved the odd-looking device that Hart had given to her. She pressed the call button and, after a short wait, all but whispered into it.

"She's been. I didn't mention you. God help us now."

ᶻᶻᶻ

"As you can see behind me…" The TV reporter glanced back over his shoulder, "… this huge crowd in Trafalgar Square is flowing, yes flowing is the only word for it, is flowing inexorably into the mouth of Whitehall where a phalanx of riot police await."

Ali and Douglas, seated next to each other in Douglas's New Town flat, stared in astonishment at the extraordinary images on the TV screen. The Square was indeed full to overflowing with demonstrators, and as the coverage cut to various other camera positions it was clear that many more were pouring in from the streets to the north.

"They won't be able to keep them out of Whitehall," Douglas said, "the pressure of numbers is just too much. There'll be trouble."

The front line of demonstrators were now face to face with the police at the entrance to Whitehall, squeezed up against the row of riot shields by the pressure of the crowd behind them. As the defensive line was slowly pushed back a female voiceover from the studio introduced a cut to an aerial shot.

"This is the view from our drone. You can see that there are police and military backup forces further down Whitehall. They're blocking Horse Guards Avenue as well as the entrance to the Ministry of Defence Main Building, and there are armoured military vehicles across the mouth of Downing Street. According to the well-known journalist and vlogger, Julie Fenwick, the organisers of the demonstration have said that it is their intention to besiege the Ministry of Defence until those responsible for the Zeno Project are brought to justice, and it's clear from the numbers of troops that have been mustered that the government has no intention of allowing any such protest." She paused, evidently listening to a voice in her earpiece. "Ah, thank you. I'm told that we can hear again from our reporter, John Wilkins, who is just behind the police line in Whitehall. What can you see, John?"

"The line is three deep, Miriam, and it's definitely being pushed back. Hang on, I can hear hooves. There must be mounted police moving up Whitehall to lend their support."

The studio voice interrupted him. "Yes, John, we have a drone shot of them."

The TV image showed, from above, a dozen or so mounted police milling around immediately behind the riot squad's human barricade.

"They can't be serious," Douglas said, turning towards Ali and waving at the screen. "If they really intend to stop that crowd they'll need to deploy armour, perhaps a couple of water cannon if they've got any. They've obviously been taken by surprise at the scale of the demonstration. Maybe they thought people would be too scared of infection to come out."

"They certainly should be scared," Ali replied. "When Sarah was telling me about the 1918 pandemic she mentioned this Spanish town where a much higher death rate was recorded. She said it was because the local Bishop kept summoning the people to public prayers, providing a perfect environment for transmitting the disease."

As she spoke the TV coverage was continuing with the aerial shot when, abruptly, Wilkins' voice cut over that from the studio. "They've opened a gap in the line to let the horses through. They're going to try to use the mounted police to disperse the front of the demonstration."

"Oh god no," Ali groaned. "This is madness."

As the first horses burst through people scattered to avoid the flying hooves. But there simply wasn't enough space for those at the front to retreat into, and several demonstrators fell and were trampled. Then, quite suddenly, one of the horses tumbled heavily to the ground, frantically kicking out and rolling over on its rider. And then another, and another.

Wilkins' voice returned, this time sounding panicked. "Someone's throwing ball bearings or marbles under the horses' hooves. It's an old trick. People and horses will get badly hurt. Now, in all this chaos, the line is bound to give."

And give it did, as the graphic TV images showed in the minutes that followed. The now overflowing crowd in Trafalgar Square poured into

Whitehall, trampling over police, horses, and demonstrators alike. In the studio Miriam's voice took on a note of near hysteria.

"These are extraordinary scenes the like of which we haven't experienced since the last century, perhaps since the Vietnam demonstrations of the 1960s. John, are you there? What can you see?"

Amid a concatenation of background noises Wilkins' voice was just audible.

"Yes, I'm here Miriam. I've lost my camera operator in the chaos. It's carnage just in front of me where the defensive line once stood. People are running further into Whitehall since they have nowhere else to go because of the pressure of the crowd behind them. I think I can hear the sound of motors further down the street, but I'm not certain and I'm pinned against a wall at the side of the road and can't see in that direction at all."

"We can see from the drone, John. Yes, there are military vehicles and soldiers moving up Whitehall. It looks as if they're aiming to hold a line north of Horse Guards Avenue to stop the demonstrators reaching the Ministry of Defence."

"I'll see if I can move down with the crowd, Miriam."

To Ali and Douglas, secure in Edinburgh, the aerial images lent a strange sense of distance to what was happening, as if they were witnessing some kind of computer game. The crowd moving down Whitehall, although clearly composed of people, seemed more like a single entity, a kind of giant snake with individuals only distinguishable at its head. Meanwhile, seen from directly above, the vehicles advancing towards them looked like toys or graphic renderings of armoured cars and lorries. The seeming artificiality of these images was accentuated by the fact that there was no synchronised sound, only some general background noise, presumably in a feed from Wilkins' microphone.

"I'm being carried forward by the mob, Miriam." Wilkins sounded frightened. "I can't move in any direction other than along Whitehall and I can't see any further than the people immediately around me."

Miriam's voice-over responded: "The army have parked vehicles as a barricade across the road, John. They're taking cover behind them. It won't be long before the head of the demonstration reaches them." She paused. "It's hard to see clearly from the drone, but I think someone is standing on one of the armoured cars and speaking into a microphone. Can you hear anything?"

"Yes, maybe the sound of an amplified voice but I can't make out any of the words. I'll try to hold my mic up in the air to see if it will pick up anything for you."

The volume of background noise increased briefly, but none of it individually distinguishable other than the occasional louder cry of pain or fear. Then, through it all came the sound of an explosion and the TV screen, which had been carrying the drone images, suddenly went blank.

"What's happened?" Ali asked.

"I don't know," Douglas replied. "Something's interrupted the feed from the drone."

After a few seconds the blank screen resolved itself into a head and shoulders shot of Miriam in the studio.

"John, we've lost the drone images. We have no pictures from Whitehall. What can you tell us?"

"Not much, Miriam. The crowd's movement has slowed and now I can just about hear that there's an amplified voice up ahead somewhere, but I can't really tell what's being said. I presume it's some kind of warning from the military at the barricade. Maybe you can hear it if I hold the mic up again."

As the volume of the sound feed rose Miriam cocked her head to one side in what was almost a parody of someone listening.

"Yes, you're right, there's definitely a voice and also a lot of shouting, but none of it is very clear. We're trying to reconnect to the drone but the operator has reported that she's getting no response from the controls. She thinks it must have gone down, and we've had an unconfirmed report from someone on the Victoria Embankment that it was hit by something and exploded in mid-air. Can you get any nearer to the front…".

Her question remained incomplete and unanswered, interrupted by the unmistakable sound of shots. Nor were they only single shots, loosed perhaps as warnings. This was the terrible rattle of automatic weapons.

Ali and Douglas looked at each other in horror. "Oh shit," Douglas murmured.

"Did you hear that?" Wilkins was shouting. "Someone's opened fire. The crowd around me is in panic. They're trying to turn back but it's impossible. People are falling and being trampled. And I think there may be tear gas among them, away to my right."

The gunfire continued only to be joined by the sound of a couple of small explosions.

"I can smell petrol, Miriam, and there's dark smoke rising from the direction of the barricade. Something's definitely on fire. There's a low wall here. I think I can climb up onto it and see over the heads of the crowd."

Wilkins fell silent for a moment as the gunfire continued and then his voice returned.

"Yes, I can just about see. One of the military vehicles is on fire and there's a line of troops advancing ahead of it, shooting into the crowd. Not above them, but actually into the people."

Just then there was the noise of another small explosion.

"Someone's just thrown some kind of bomb in front of the advancing troops," Wilkins continued. "Maybe something like a Molotov cocktail. It's certainly spreading burning liquid across the surface of the road. I'm going to have to move before the soldiers reach my position. I'll call in again as soon as I'm safe."

"Yes, do that, John." Miriam looked and sounded as if she was in shock. "Be careful."

The TV images then began to cycle through a series of camera positions in Trafalgar Square, all of them revealing an ocean of people sweeping this way and that as some tried to flee while others pressed on towards Whitehall.

Miriam's voice returned, sounding calmer now.

"One of our units in Trafalgar Square has got hold of Julie Fenwick, the reporter who broke the initial Porton Down story and, last week, the Zeno story that is the focus for today's demonstration. I think we can speak to her. Julie, can you hear me?"

The sequence of shots of Trafalgar Square gave way to a head-and-shoulders of Julie Fenwick, wearing a headset and speaking into a microphone held by someone off-screen. She nodded. "Yes, I hear you, Miriam."

The camera stayed with Julie as Miriam continued.

"Julie, you're the only reporter to have spoken with the organisers of this demonstration. Is this chaos what they were aiming for?"

"No, of course not. Their intention was to have a peaceful demonstration and to establish an occupation around the Ministry of Defence to make clear the strength of public feeling about the Zeno conspiracy. From what I can gather from my contacts here, it's the authorities who have panicked and turned it into a riot. I've had a call from one of the organisers who is somewhere in Whitehall. He says that there are people dead and dying, indiscriminately fired upon by the military."

"But we've seen violence from both sides, Julie. The horses were brought down by people hurling objects under their hooves and our reporter in Whitehall saw some kind of fire bomb thrown at the soldiers. That's hardly peaceful demonstrating."

Julie shook her head vigorously. "But you have to ask yourself, who escalated this into violence? The demonstrators are only responding to being attacked."

"But Julie, people must have brought the fire bombs with them, intending violence."

"Yes, that's true," Julie conceded. "But all demonstrations attract some people like that. The organisers that I spoke with definitely wouldn't have behaved in that way. I'm absolutely certain. But once someone starts the violence, then it takes on a life of its own."

As if to confirm this claim, just then there was a much louder explosion which echoed back and forth among the buildings surrounding the square, followed by the sound of a helicopter evidently hovering close by. A man leaned into the TV shot and whispered something into Julie's ear.

"I have to go now, Miriam. I'm told that we're not safe here." As she spoke, Julie was removing her headphones and handing them to someone out of shot. She turned away from the camera and, led by a powerful-looking man who forced a passage for her, disappeared into the crowd.

The TV image cut back to Miriam in the studio. "That was Julie Fenwick, arguably the individual most responsible for precipitating today's events. She was heavily criticised by government figures earlier this week for, they claimed, stealing and publishing secret documents, and forging some others. After today, no doubt they will be even more concerned."

Just then Wilkins' voice returned.

"Miriam, it's terrible here. There have been several explosions and a couple of buildings are on fire. People have found alternative routes into Whitehall via Great Scotland Yard and Whitehall Place and there appears to be a pitched battle going on near the Household Cavalry Museum. I've never seen anything like it. And I can hear helicopters approaching. There's one almost overhead, and another..."

Wilkins' voice disappeared mid sentence, drowned out by the sound of a large explosion. Then, nothing.

"John, John, are you still there? Can you hear me? What's happening?"

But there was no reply and no background noise from his microphone. Only the sound from Trafalgar Square where the crowd's growing fury was all too apparent. Then, one by one, the TV units scattered about the square were overwhelmed, unable to hold their positions as they were struck by wave upon wave of desperate people. At last, all contact was lost, leaving only a shocked Miriam seemingly alone in the studio. After a moment of silence, she nodded and spoke to camera.

"I'm told that video shot by demonstrators in Whitehall is finding its way onto internet sites. We can show you some of it now. I should warn you that these are distressing images, so much so that we can't screen all of them. But there's no doubt that many people have died and that several fires are raging at various points along Whitehall. There appears to be no sign of the violence abating. In fact, it all seems entirely out of control."

A final shot of Miriam revealed her shaking her head at someone off-screen and repeatedly mouthing what looked like "fuck, fuck, fuck," an image that quickly gave way to the compilation of uploaded video from the street.

Ali and Douglas sat in silence, holding on to each other, unable to find words to respond to the mayhem playing out in front of them. At last the terrible images ceased and, as if there was nothing that could possibly be allowed to follow them, the screen simply went blank.

Douglas turned to Ali.

"It's begun," he said. And again, shaking his head in despair: "It's begun."

z z z

Even at the best of times, in freezing winter weather the late-night streets of Helsinki would not be teeming with people. But with flu raging through the city virtually nobody was to be seen. As the official Night Recovery Vehicle trundled slowly down towards the harbour and the frozen Baltic sea, lamps mounted on its roof swung in 180° arcs illuminating the darkened doorways and alleys as it passed. Suddenly it came to a halt, one of the lamps shining into a shop entrance. Two figures emerged from the vehicle, clad in full isolation suits and masks. They walked to the now illuminated alcove and one knelt down and examined an indistinct form lying in the doorway. After a moment he looked up at his colleague and shook his head. Then, between them, they lifted the object, which once fully in the light revealed itself to be a body, and gently added it to the accumulating pile in the back of their vehicle. Only a year ago they would have been searching for drunks or the homeless with a good chance of finding them alive and carrying them to safety before they froze to death. Now their business was almost entirely with corpses, those overtaken by illness and by drink and by the winter's cold. Climbing back on board they continued on their sombre way, the constantly swinging lights receding into the icy darkness.

5

Hart found himself taking a certain morbid pleasure in observing how rapidly things fell apart. While, like most people, he had been shocked at the loss of life at that first big Zeno demonstration, he had noted with some satisfaction the inadequacy of the government response both to the demonstration itself and in their subsequent actions. They had even managed to alienate the normally deferential BBC by shooting down their drone and, whether by accident or design, killing one of their reporters. None of this particularly surprised Hart who had spent sufficient time close to the politically powerful to have grasped the manifest truth that they were as capable of profound errors as anyone else. Perhaps, indeed, more capable, given their propensity for hubris and their willingness to believe their own deceits.

In the immediate aftermath of the Whitehall Massacre – not a designation accepted by the government but in common use by almost everyone else – the intelligence agencies had been instructed to 'solve the problem' by detaining or otherwise disabling the presumed leaders of the protest. Some had been eliminated, but with little impact on the actions that followed across the country. Because members of the government routinely saw themselves as an elite skilled at leadership, they presumed that any apparently organised mass activity had to be similarly dependent upon individual leaders. But in this they proved mistaken for, however hard they tried to lop off the head of the Zeno protest movement, it just kept on resurrecting itself.

The DSD had inevitably been a party to this misguided policy of repression, although Hart had done what he could to ameliorate its effects as far as his agency was concerned. Besides, the intelligence agencies and the police were seriously short-staffed and were increasingly required to focus their attention on the capital city. London was, after all, where most of the major government institutions were located, and the now rather frightened ruling elite was insistent on the need to prioritise their protection. This inevitably restricted resources elsewhere in England and it was clear, to Hart at least, that established order was fragmenting in the urban centres of the Midlands and the North. Vast reaches of the larger cities – Birmingham, Manchester, Leeds – were becoming no-go areas for anyone other than locals, their neighbourhoods annexed by the criminal gangs that had always operated among them.

By guaranteeing supplies of essentials, local bosses commanded the loyalty or, at least, the resigned acceptance of the population. They constructed and policed their own borders and effectively conducted themselves as warlords, excluding what remained of the regional police forces and maintaining fluid and fragile truces with neighbouring enclaves. So far this was only happening in some cities and in specific areas within them. Elsewhere a kind of normality coexisted with this quasi-tribalism, but Hart was uncertain as to how long that might continue. His shrinking band of agents around the country reported, when they could manage to report at all, that some smaller towns were entirely out of the control of recognised authorities and that even in areas retaining orderly structures there was constant dissatisfaction directed towards central government.

Not that all the emerging enclaves were fundamentally criminal in character. In communities which had long been segregated on ethnic grounds, usually in particular zones of the big cities, there were ready-made foundations on which to construct local systems of self-support. Many of them had always had their own lines of supply for their distinctive requirements, dietary and otherwise. Protecting these delivery routes had become the key challenge for them, especially if neighbouring enclaves were aggressive. To this end a number of ethnic communities had established their own modes of policing – again something that they had anyway been doing for some time to compensate for the inadequate protection that the state had offered them in the past.

Meanwhile, outside the urban areas, where rural communities were accustomed to rather more self-reliant ways of life, there was as yet less pressure to establish defended territories, although other distinctive responses to the growing crisis were becoming apparent. In East Anglia, for example, there had been an explosion of unusual religious groupings, perhaps not unexpected in a region that had in the past often played host to deviant religiosity. Cults, sects, Hart was uncertain how best to describe them, but he expected the phenomenon to spread as circumstances became more dire and people sought spiritual sustenance as well as material security.

All this had developed within a few months, surprising even Hart with the extent and pace of social disruption. Initially his 'masters' – he now used that term to himself with heavy irony – had believed that order would be restored quite quickly given application of appropriate sticks and carrots. They were now beginning to understand that their confidence was misplaced, that most people rejected their empty guarantees of safety and, anyway, were beyond the reach of the shrunken police forces ordered to discipline them.

A measure of quite how far things had gone was that over the past couple of days Hart had been required to attend two lengthy meetings of the Security Co-ordinating Committee, a small group charged with establishing detailed plans for Operation Homestead. The general objective of the operation was clear enough – to establish and protect the governing elite in a variety of secret underground sites around the country, though mostly concentrated in the South-East. This, it was hoped, would allow them to continue to govern securely in spite of growing instability. The detail, however, was much less clear. Who was to be housed in these various successors to the Regional Seats of Government, first established in response to Cold War fears of nuclear attack? How would their supply chains be maintained? Could military personnel be relied upon to protect them even though the soldiers themselves would be largely outside the complexes? These and many other questions were exercising the collective minds of the SCC, pushed along by the prime minister himself who had personally addressed them and emphasised the urgency of their task.

Hart, of course, would be among those provided with a place in one of these putative safe havens. And not just Hart. Immediate family members were permitted to accompany the notionally fortunate recipients of state protection, although Jill had scoffed at the very idea when he had raised it.

"If you think I'm going to be locked up with that load of shits," she had said, "you can think again."

Her response did not especially surprise him. Rather than binding them closer, Rosemary's death seemed to have pushed them further apart, and Hart suspected that as far as Jill was concerned he too was now one of 'that load of shits'. Although she certainly blamed the government for her daughter's fate and for the terrible havoc wrought upon the population at large, he was not at all sure that she would approve of his private plans for retribution and so he had not felt able to confide in her. But if Operation Homestead was implemented, as seemed increasingly likely, Hart knew that that he had to remain on the inside of government from whence he would be able to do the most damage. For as long as he was privy to high-level decision-making he would be in a position to pick precisely the right time to strike. How he would actually do so remained undecided, depending, as it did, on unpredictable circumstances. But strike he would, he was sure of that, and directly at the heart of those who had been responsible for taking away the one thing that he loved most in the world.

z z z

After yet another largely inconclusive meeting of the SVRG – the Baby Bug Hunters were not having much success in their hunt – Ali was on the train from Glasgow to Edinburgh. She generally quite enjoyed the hour of peace that this afforded her, but today she was seated next to Michael Lang who was eager to engage her in conversation.

"I'm afraid that my group isn't making much progress," was his opening somewhat cheerless gambit. "It would still be a big help to have Sarah and Hugh on the team. I gather that you had an inconclusive reply to your letter with my offer." This last observation was conveyed in what Ali thought to be an entirely unmerited tone of reproach.

"Yes," she said, reluctantly turning towards him, "as ever, Hugh is willing but Sarah wants to stay where she is."

"Even in the present circumstances? Things sound to be getting pretty bad in England. Or at least, so Douglas told me when I asked him if there had been any progress."

"They surely are," Ali said, shaking her head ruefully, "but as well as everything else Sarah wants to stay in reach of her mother. I'm positive that Irene would advise her to move but she won't know about the offer and Sarah won't have told her. They have to be careful what they say on CommsTab links."

"But there is a secure line of communication to Professor Johnson is there not? Maybe you and Douglas could set something up."

Ali thought for a moment and then nodded: "I'll speak to Douglas about it." She did not add that she and Douglas had already talked their way through most of the obvious options and could see no immediate course of action. But perhaps if they could engage Irene's support? At least it would be worth a try.

Arriving at Waverley station Ali and Michael parted ways, Michael to his home in Corstorphine and Ali to walk up The Mound to her flat. There had been some unexpected late-winter snowfall during the previous night, and it had just begun to snow again. Since the latest Zeno revelations fewer people were to be found on the streets of Edinburgh, and that plus the snow meant that Ali seemed to have the white-clad city almost entirely to herself. As she walked she looked across to the castle, still partially illuminated in spite of the power rationing, and reminded herself how fortunate she was to live in such a beautiful place.

The footpaths and lawns of Princes Street Gardens now had a fair covering of snow, the park's lamps creating intermittent pools of brightly reflected light. But for all the pleasure these sights afforded her, at heart Ali felt despondent. Was this all going to fade into nothing as more and more people became victims of the virus? Douglas was convinced that social order would collapse in the cities sooner rather than later, and reports from England appeared to confirm his pessimism. How could she bear to see her lovely birthplace descend into such chaos and decay?

The answer was, of course, that she couldn't, and, what's more, she was determined that she wouldn't. At Douglas's behest they had thoroughly discussed this possibility and she knew that if it came to such desperate straits they would have to leave. Douglas was already making detailed plans, accumulating supplies and even weapons, plotting out places to go and considering long-term survival strategies. In the light of this, Ali had spoken at length with her father who was now acting as a kind of storekeeper, receiving the equipment and provisions that Douglas organised and adding them to the resources that he had already assembled on his own account. Their plan was to head to his house in Argyll when Edinburgh became too dangerous and, if necessary, to move further north after that, although this last proposal was something of a sore point with her father who was determined to stay where he was.

"I retired here intending to be carried out feet first," he told Ali. "I shan't be moving again whatever the circumstances. Besides, I'm too old for all that survival crap. I'd just be a liability."

Ali still retained some hope of persuading him otherwise, but not much. Her father could be exceedingly stubborn, a trait that she knew very well since she had inherited it. Anyway, she thought, they would deal with him if and when things became that bad. Her hope was that they would never face such a predicament, although in her heart of hearts she knew otherwise.

These ruminations had occupied her all the way home and it was with some surprise that she realised that she was in Forrest Road. Taking a last look at the snow-covered streets, she climbed the stairs, unlocked her front door, and, after switching on the coffee machine, slumped into a kitchen chair. The remnants of her breakfast were scattered across the table; she had been in too much of a hurry that morning to clear things away. I must sort this out, she thought, and in a surge of last-gasp energy she put dishes in the washer, wiped the table clean, drew an espresso from the machine and carried it through to the living room. A few sips of coffee later and she felt revived enough to v-call Douglas.

"Hey," he said. "You look like it's been a tough day."

"Mmmmn. No more than usual with that lot. But I've had my ear bent by Michael Lang. He wonders if we could approach Sarah again by enlisting Irene's help."

"Yes, he had a go at me yesterday. What do you think? Might Irene sway it? Or would she want to keep Sarah and her grandchild in England?"

"Given the way England's going she might believe they'd be safer up here. Can you still get a letter to her?"

"Yes, just about," Douglas said, not looking entirely certain. "It's getting difficult for my people down there and we're thinking of pulling them out. We'd have to move quickly."

"OK. I'll draft something tonight and get it to you in the morning. I've nothing special on tomorrow."

"Lunchtime will do. I'm busy in the morning anyway. Let's eat at my flat. One o'clock?"

"Right," said Ali. "See you then."

Setting her CommsTab to Do Not Disturb, she called up some music on the sound system, leaned back on the sofa, and began to plan her letter.

z z z

Vasilis Kouklakis had lived his entire life in the same small village tucked into the foothills of the Lefka Ori, the White Mountains of Crete. He was an old man now, related by blood or marriage to many of the villagers, and well known to them all. On this particular evening he was sitting outside his house, wrapped up against the night-time chill and staring absently across the olive groves. All was quiet except for the call of a Scops owl somewhere out in the darkness.

Vasilis could barely comprehend what had happened. Over the past weeks the foreign disease that they had heard about on TV had overcome the village, and while some had fled north to the city of Chania in search of treatment, most had remained and died. Now Vasilis was alone with only the sounds of the night for company. All his life he had loved the call of the tiny Scops owl, mournful though it was, knowing it as part of the texture of the countryside in which he had been born, lived and worked. But today he could only hear its familiar melancholy as a desolate cry for the dead souls that surrounded him. Vasilis closed his eyes and listened and waited. What else was there to do?

6

The train from York to London was all but deserted. There were no more than half a dozen civilians in the carriage and as many soldiers playing a noisy card game in the section of seats next to Irene. That the train was thinly populated was hardly a surprise. The current crisis had precipitated a further clampdown on travel and, even for an official of Irene's status, it was difficult to obtain permits. She was only there courtesy of Jonathan Hart. She had reminded him of his long-ago promise that he would facilitate contact for her with Sarah and, a little to her surprise, he had come up with digital authorisations allowing her to visit her daughter. As far as she understood it, she was designated as one of his staff away in the field on DSD business, a status that quite appealed to her sense of the absurd.

Happy though she always was to see her family, the trip had inevitably turned out to be more business than pleasure. A few days earlier there had been a ring at her doorbell one evening and, on answering it, she found a figure on her doorstep wearing a shoulder bag marked with the familiar 'Support the Needy' insignia. From the bag he drew a bundle of leaflets and thrust them into her hand.

"I'll be back around this time next week," he said, beaming at her. "You donated last time so I hope you'll be able to do so again."

"Yes," she replied, returning his smile. "I'm sure I'll have something for you. See you then."

Sifting through the leaflets she found, as expected, a letter from Ali, but this time not seeking information but asking for help in persuading

Sarah of the need to move to Scotland. Initially Irene was aghast at the suggestion, but after reading the whole letter and thinking it through at some length she saw the sense in Ali's proposal. England was fast becoming disturbingly unstable – Hart made that very observation to her when she saw him later about the travel arrangements – and it was likely that her daughter and granddaughter would have a better chance of survival north of the border. Survival. That was what it had come to, Irene thought, sheer survival.

So it was that she now found herself sitting on a train after two days of intense discussion with Sarah and Hugh. Hugh had been no problem. He was already convinced that they would be best served by returning to his home country. But about Sarah she was less certain. Irene had tried to make it very clear to her daughter that she would not see their departure as in any way abandoning her. Quite the opposite, she argued. It would be a great comfort for her to know that they were out of immediate harm's way, and, what's more, they would be well placed to receive her if and when she felt it impossible to remain in England. Not that she had any idea how she might reach them in that event, but at least it absolved Sarah from some of her concerns. In the end, though, her daughter remained undecided, if less determinedly so than she had been before Irene's visit. Now, as Irene sat staring out of the train window looking back over their conversations, she felt that she had done her best. All that was left to do was to let Ali know and encourage her to apply even more pressure.

This line of thought was interrupted suddenly by some overheard talk among the soldiers, who mercifully had at last given up on their boisterous game of cards.

"Anybody been to this place we're going to be stationed at? What's its name? Northwood?" a soldier enquired of the group. Several shook their heads or shrugged until one responded: "Nah, not been there, but I know somebody who has. He says it's a cushy number, guarding a big underground control centre. In the suburbs south of Watford."

"Wonder why they're dragging us down there all the way from Catterick? There must be plenty of specialist units a lot nearer than us."

The man with the information nodded.

"Yeah, I wondered that too. Rumour is it's something to do with a big national op – Operation Homestead. Seems there's a lot of people on the move."

"More training then. Let's hope it's cushy like your mate said. Can't be worse than what we've been doing."

The group then fell to chatting about other matters, and Irene, who had carefully avoided looking at them throughout this exchange, leaned back in her seat and closed her eyes. She knew that Northwood had long been a strategic military HQ and Control Centre, and according to civil service rumour had latterly been significantly expanded to include a considerable number of additional underground bunkers and residential quarters. The cost had been enormous, sums dwarfing the puny science budgets with which she was familiar, or so the rumours alleged, while the whole development had been shrouded in secrecy and nobody she asked had been able to come up with any reliable information. But now it appeared that they were drafting in additional troops, specialist ones of some kind if the conversation she had just eavesdropped upon was to be believed. She opened her eyes for a moment and looked again at the group. They were wearing military fatigues with no distinctive badges that she could see. She closed her eyes once more. Something's brewing, she thought.

A few days later, having safely dispatched her letter to Ali via the 'Support the Needy' courier, Irene was walking down a corridor in the Government Office for Science building. She was deep in thought and paying little attention to what was around her with the result that she all but collided with Jonathan Hart.

"Whoops! Sorry. Miles away," she said, then, on seeing who it was, added lamely, "Oh, it's you. What brings you here?"

"I've been visiting your Chief. But I did have something I wanted to speak to you about as well. Is there somewhere we can go? A quiet coffee perhaps."

It was clear from his tone that Hart wanted to talk away from prying ears, electronic or otherwise.

"There's an outdoor coffee kiosk just down the road," she suggested. "They've stayed open and they do good coffee. It's not too cold a day."

"Yes, that sounds fine. Let's go there."

Irene collected her coat and they headed out onto Victoria Street.

"Look at it," Irene said with a sigh. "This street used to be packed with people. Travellers to and from the station, tourists, folk going about their business. Now it's so quiet. Just those who absolutely have to be here."

As he prepared their drinks the proprietor of the kiosk also commented mournfully on the lack of passers-by. "Don't know how much longer I'll be able to stay open," he said, shaking his head, "and coffee's getting hard to find anyway."

Once they were standing at a drinks station where they could not be overheard, Irene got in first.

"Actually, there was something I wanted to ask you about. What's Operation Homestead?"

Hart looked at her in astonishment. "You've heard about that? It's why I wanted to see you. Where did you come across it?"

"I overheard a conversation among some soldiers on the train last week. They didn't seem to know much except that they were due to be part of it. But it made me wonder why soldiers were being brought down from the North when they're obviously needed up there."

"Yes, I'm sure they are. Though whether they could do much about what's happening in the northern cities is debateable." Hart paused for a moment. "It's a question of government priorities. That's what Operation Homestead is about. Establishing secure bases from which government can continue if – when – things get considerably worse."

"Ah, I see. That makes sense of something they said. The men on the train were going to Northwood and there have been a lot of rumours about hugely expensive developments out there. That's part of it then?"

"It is indeed. In fact, Northwood is the key location. It's where the government, senior officials, top military staff and so on, will be housed. That's why I wanted to see you. I'm part of the group organising the migration to Northwood and I just suggested to your Chief that you would be a good person to have along." Hart paused to let his revelation sink in. "He's agreeable, so I hope you'll consider it. When things get worse it will be the safest place to be. Defended, provisioned, with medical support and comfortable accommodation."

Irene looked at him doubtfully. "Why me? I don't have any skills that would be useful there. I'd be – what's the official phrase? – surplus to requirements."

"No," Hart replied, "I think you do have skills that will be important. You're much more willing to be critical of prevailing views than most of them, and it was you, after all, who tried to steer them away from the Zeno project."

"And failed completely," Irene interjected, "with the consequences that we now see around us. Don't you think I feel guilty about what's happened? How could I tuck myself away in a hole, safe from all this?" She gestured towards the almost deserted street. "Besides, they're no more likely to listen to me now than they were then."

"You could bring close family with you," Hart said hopefully. "You've got a daughter and granddaughter to think about."

Even more reason to get them to Scotland, Irene thought, then replied: "I wouldn't wish it on them. I'll take my chances out here and so will they."

Hart sighed. "I was afraid you might feel like that. At least promise me you'll think about it. To be completely honest with you, I would personally very much like to have you there. As I said before, I count on you as an ally and I'm going to need one if I'm to have any impact on what happens."

"OK. I'll give it some thought, but don't get your hopes up. It doesn't look like an attractive proposition to me."

"Good. That's something. But you haven't got long to decide. I think Homestead will swing into action quite soon. When it does you'll get an official notification that there's a place for you. It'll come via the Chief Scientific Advisor, not from me."

Irene gave him a hard look. "Do you really think it's a good idea?" she asked. "It sounds to me like you would be trapping yourself in a kind of cage with a collection of unsavoury and duplicitous people. Not how I'd like to see the world out."

"I can't say that I'm enthusiastic," Hart replied with a shrug, "but I don't see any viable alternative at the moment. Basic resources are already running short. At least this option should guarantee supplies longer than they'll be available on the outside."

"I suppose so," Irene said. "But even then I think I'd rather stay out here."

"It's up to you, of course. But one other thing you might want to bear in mind. Once Homestead is fully implemented the intention is to declare a State of Emergency. That will mean curfews, travel even more limited than it is now, severe rationing, restricted access to medical services. Surviving will be tough."

Irene spread her hands in a gesture of acceptance. "It will be tough anyway," she said. "But at least I'll be making my own choices. Good luck with it, Jonathan. And thank you for the offer."

Hart smiled. It was the first time she had called him Jonathan and, given how determined she appeared to be, it would probably be the last. "Fair enough," he said, turning to leave. "I'll try to keep in touch."

Irene watched him depart, not for the first time wondering what was going on in his head. He had seemed like a changed man when they had last met on the common. As if his life had become a chore, yet a chore that he absolutely had to complete. Clearly something significant had happened to him but what it was remained entirely opaque. Nor was she likely to find out now, she thought, as she dropped their coffee cups into the bin and set off back to her office.

z z z

In New Zealand, about as far away as you could get from the virus's birthplace, a huge queue snaked around Christchurch's Cathedral Square, winding back on itself and contained within a maze of roped walkways. Armed guards were posted every ten metres or so, sullenly eyeing the people waiting in line. Their goal, frustratingly visible to all as the queue edged forward, was a large marquee in front of which officials checked each person's documents and, if they met with approval, issued a bag of basic foodstuffs. To those caught in the outer reaches of the spiral their destination never appeared to get any nearer, and whenever the queue ground to a halt as officials queried a supplicant's status, a kind of low moan travelled along the line of people like a tidal bore flowing up a river. Otherwise the crowd remained remarkably silent, beaten into submission by disease, hunger, and an utterly dispiriting lack of hope. The restored cathedral, once destroyed by earthquake, loomed over them as a kind of rebuke to their despair. But for the most part they ignored it, shuffling forward looking only at their distant destination.

7

Once a day, usually in the morning, Julie worked her way through a carefully chosen set of internet news feeds. By now it had become a routine, the presumed bias of each site taken into account, their respective specialisms balanced one against the other. Of course, this procedure was no guarantee against false reports – all sites were subject to those, if only because the vast network of live sources was altogether too large to be properly monitored. But all the sites that Julie consulted were well aware of the fake news traps and of the associated risk that if something was repeated often enough it would become a self-fulfilling prophecy. The various editors did what they could to ameliorate the dangers of malicious fabrication, primarily by applying mutually agreed corroboration standards. That didn't mean that they got it right every time. There was simply too much information flowing across the system for that. But it did lower the failure rate, particularly where stories could be checked and cross-checked over a number of independent sites and sources.

On this particular day she was encountering the customary distressing reports of death and disorder, whole communities all but wiped out by the flu, especially where public health was already weakened by food shortages and ineffective hygiene. In the poorer and more populous areas of the world mortality rates were already high and continued to rise. Their health systems were unable to stem the tide of illness even where they sought to do so, and their citizens, undernourished and isolated, acquiesced to what they increasingly saw as an inescapable fate visited upon them by malevolent external forces. In the richer countries efforts to combat the disease were only marginally more effective, but here the people were more disposed to hold their governments to account, resorting in many cases to radical action and social disruption. All of which offered golden opportunities for the brutal and self-interested who could exploit the growing weakness of official forces of law and order and fill the power vacuums that they left behind.

It was this kind of confrontation that was of particular interest to Julie. As a result of her Zeno revelations she had become the communications channel of choice for the anti-Zeno movement in England, and their ongoing campaign was now the major focus of her reporting. Their organisation was fluid, as it had to be to evade government attempts to clamp down, but Julie had reliable lines of communication with the network and particular links with a couple who were key members of the Brixton Enclave. Although official sources denied it, Brixton was one of two London areas which had securely established themselves as effectively independent of state control. Aided by some strategically placed roadblocks, an uneasy peace allowed the Brixton Enclave to function as a self-supporting neighbourhood which therefore also served as a shelter for organisers of the Zeno campaign.

Today's survey of her sources was not yielding much directly to do with the Zeno protesters, but there was one item that virtually all sites were reporting prominently. Large numbers of soldiers – nobody had a reliable estimate of precisely how many – were arriving in and around the capital city, drawn, it would seem, from units right across the country. Speculation was rife as to what this might signify. Julie's first thought was that they were planning an attack on the Brixton Enclave and she was not alone in entertaining this possibility. But others had very different interpretations, ranging from the vaguely plausible suggestion that this was additional security for the all too often overwhelmed health facilities, to the rather more outlandish claim that it was a military rehearsal in case it became necessary to protect London from invasion by the Northern counties.

Julie was reflecting on some of the more credible suggestions when she was interrupted by a soft double knock on her door. Puzzled – visitors generally had to ring her bell from the closed entrance foyer so that she could give them access to the residential sections of the building – she consulted the door peephole app on her CommsTab. To her surprise she saw Dennis, her chief minder, who was holding up to the camera a piece of paper which read 'Laundry Room in 10 minutes.' He stood for a few seconds, nodded, then disappeared from view. Initially flummoxed by this odd behaviour, after a moment's thought Julie collected her laundry bag and took the lift to the basement. There was no sign of Dennis. Looking about her suspiciously, she loaded up one of the washing machines in the laundry room, set it going, and, seating herself in front of it, stared vacantly at her tumbling clothes. A movement in the shadows just outside the door caught her eye and resolved itself into Dennis who gestured her to come out into the corridor. Once she was there, he guided her into a small storeroom for cleaning equipment and closed the door.

"Sorry," he said. "I'm trying to keep us out of range of the security cameras and microphones. I don't suppose anybody's monitoring them, but you never know."

"What the fuck's going on, Dennis?"

"I've come to warn you," he replied. "I've been reassigned, taken off your security."

"So who have they given me?"

"That's the point. Nobody. And I've been told not to make contact with you or answer your calls."

Julie looked at him in astonishment. "What? Why?" She was almost shouting.

"Hush. Keep it down," he replied, holding up a hand to silence her. "I think it means they're cutting you loose. My new responsibility is for someone with links to the top levels of English government. They've obviously done some kind of deal and I'd guess that part of it involves withdrawing protection from you."

"Does that mean I'll lose the apartment as well?"

"I should think so. Best guess is that they'll serve you notice this month." He paused, looking at her with genuine concern. "My advice is get out as soon as possible. Don't wait for them to throw you out. If they really have done a deal it will expose you to the risks that we've been protecting you against. You've made a lot of enemies, Julie, and they won't be slow to try to silence you. You need to disappear from their radar right now."

"But where can I go? I've got nobody that I can depend on. You were my guarantee of safety."

"I know. I'm sorry. If there was any more that I could do to help, I would. But I can't. Even warning you like this is pretty risky." He put his hands on her shoulders and looked her seriously in the eye. "Do what I say, Julie. Get out while you can."

He turned away and opened the door. "Good luck," he said, and walked quickly off down the corridor leaving her standing forlornly in the midst of a grubby collection of vacuum cleaners, brushes, mops and buckets.

When she recovered her composure enough to find her way back to the laundry room she sat in front of her machine deep in thought. By the time it had finished its final drying cycle she had made up her mind. She would take Dennis's advice and get out immediately. She was going to miss the comfort and security that she had experienced over the past months, but she had no illusions about her erstwhile employers. They had been ruthless on her behalf and they would no doubt be equally so now that they no longer needed her. She had to try to stay at least one step ahead of the danger, which meant disappearing as effectively as she could. The only immediate possibility was to take refuge in the Brixton Enclave. She had friends there, and although it might be an obvious location for anyone searching for her, at least she would be surrounded by people who were out of sympathy with the authorities.

Wasting no further time she returned to the flat, packed a large backpack and a small wheeled suitcase, then took a final look around the rather luxurious accommodation that she had lately enjoyed. It was good while it lasted, she thought, but there's no room for sentiment now. Time to move on. Hoping that she was not under direct surveillance – she cursed herself for not asking Dennis if he knew whether she was – she left the building by its less prominent rear trade entrance and headed towards Victoria where she knew she could get a shuttle to Clapham.

After that it would be a question of working her way through side streets to Brixton and to the anti-Zeno campaigners' home on Brixton Hill. There she would be safe, at least for a while.

It was her good fortune to catch the Clapham shuttle just as it was about to depart, and from its terminus she set out to walk east, picking a route through a warren of residential streets while keeping away from the major roads. There were few people around, making Julie worryingly aware of the odd figure that she cut, laden with a backpack and dragging a suitcase along the pavement. To add to her self-consciousness, the nearer she got to Brixton the more she found herself subjected to curious glances as the only white person among a largely black population. Finally she arrived at one of the Enclave's checkpoints, a ramshackle shelter manned by a couple of young men. They didn't appear to be armed but Julie assumed that they would be and approached with caution.

"You comin' to stay?" one asked cheerfully, eyeing her luggage.

Julie returned his smile. "Yes, I hope so. I have friends living on Brixton Hill – Albert and Rosa of the Campaign. You maybe know them?"

"Surely do. You've not far to go now then. Follow this road along for a way, then turn right down the Hill. But first we have to check your bags. Sorry 'bout that. You'd be surprised what people have tried to smuggle in."

Julie handed over her bags. As he was checking them she became aware that the second guard – she supposed that they should be called guards although they had nothing to distinguish them from any other young men on the street – was eyeing her curiously. Suddenly his face lit up.

"Yeah," he said with satisfaction. "Knew I'd seen you somewhere. You that vlogger and journo. Julie somebody. The one that told the Zeno story. Ain't that right?"

"Yes I am," Julie conceded. "But I'd be grateful if you didn't spread it around. There are people I need to hide from."

"Nah, don't worry," he said with a grin. "Plenty of folk moving into Brixton who don't want to be found. We can keep secrets."

By now the baggage search was complete and she was waved through. "Keep doing the work," one of them called after her. "We need it."

Oddly pleased at this encouragement, Julie waved goodbye and strode on into Brixton with more confidence than she had felt all day. By the time she reached her goal she was feeling quite cheerful in spite of everything that had brought her there, and all the more so when Rosa answered the door and embraced her with a cry of joy.

"Ah, Julie," – Rosa, who was Afro-Ecuadorian by origin, pronounced 'Julie' with an extended soft J which invariably charmed its recipient – "what are you doing here? So good to see you."

"I've come to stay if that's OK with you. There are people after me and this is the safest place that I could think of. But if it's a problem I'm sure I can find somewhere else."

"Don't be crazy! Of course you can stay. We want you as our guest. Albert will be so happy to have you here. Come in, come in. You must tell me all about it."

Whereupon Julie found herself propelled into the house, settled into a chair, plied with coffee, and required to give every detail of her day's adventure. At last I feel safe, she thought, pushing to the back of her mind what she knew all too well. That in these terrible times, nobody was safe.

z z z

Ali and Douglas had been at odds with each other for several days. After receiving Irene's reply to her letter, Ali had concluded that the only way to persuade Sarah to move was to talk to her face to face. She had put it to Douglas, knowing that he had routes into England, but he insisted that it was far too dangerous. She pointed out that he was constantly sending agents back and forth across the border and none of them had yet been caught. He responded that they were trained for precisely that exigency, while she was a rank amateur in such matters. She reminded him of her successful escape in Berwick and of the fact that he had complimented her on it; he suggested that it was down to luck as much as judgment; she accused him of being overprotective, patriarchal even; he took offence at the accusation; and so it went on. Now they were barely speaking to each other, and certainly not sharing a bed. It had turned into a stalemate which both of them found intolerable.

In the end, and after yet another intervention from Michael Lang who was increasingly desperate to reinforce his research group, Douglas was first to break.

"All right," he said, with the resigned air of someone reluctant to admit that he is beaten. "Let's say I can get you in and out of York. If we're to do it then I'm coming with you."

"That's not necessary," Ali grumbled, "you're needed here," though in truth she was grateful for the offer. As well as feeling safer with Douglas along, she knew he would be able to add extra weight to her attempt to persuade Sarah. Irene had already made her views clear, Hugh had always been in favour, so surely their case would prove all the more forceful with the addition of Douglas's assessment of what was likely to happen in the near future. Ali hoped so anyway, not because she wanted to reinforce Lang's research group – she was convinced that there was now neither the time nor the capacity to find anything resembling a fix for Zeno – but because she wanted Sarah and family with her when she was obliged by circumstance to escape to the Highlands.

It took a few days to organise fake documents for Ali. Asked to choose a name, she semi-facetiously came up with Heather Burns on the improbable grounds that this was exactly what happened, disgracefully in her view, across the 'sporting' moors of Scotland and northern England. Douglas insisted that she keep her own forename – this made giveaway naming errors less likely – so, for purposes of the trip, she became one Alison Heather Burns. A Scottish enough name, she thought, for a secret invasion of England.

The invasion itself, such as it was, involved a goods lorry with a hidden compartment between the cab and the carrying space. In the event they did not need the compartment on the journey south. There was still a fair amount of trade across the Scottish/English border and the guards on both sides were accustomed to simply waving through familiar vehicles. Even the post-Zeno tensions had not caused much change to the flow, no doubt aided by the fact that regular payments found their way into the guards' pockets from the firms and individuals involved. The lorry in which Ali and Douglas travelled had long masqueraded as the property of a fictional but well-documented Edinburgh transport company rejoicing in the name Wm. MacDougall & Son, and regularly providing additional income to those manning the border. Their driver, a cheery Glaswegian called Jimmy, could not recall ever being asked even to open the rear doors of his vehicle. Once safely across the border, the drive down to York also proved to be trouble-free although they were at pains to avoid the Newcastle area where hijacks were not unknown.

As a precaution they were dropped a couple of hundred metres from Sarah and Hugh's house in Heworth, a residential suburb of the city, Jimmy waiting and watching while they walked cautiously down the street. It was after nine at night leaving much of their route in darkness – energy conservation had reduced street lighting to every third lamp. Although Sarah had been warned by note that Ali was coming on this particular day, they had not put a precise time on their arrival so when she opened the door at their knock her excitement was evident. She drew Ali into a hug, lifting her off her feet and spinning her around as if in some demented waltz.

"Ali, Ali, I'm so glad to see you. I've been driving Hugh mad for the last two hours, unable to sit still for more than five minutes at a time."

A smiling Hugh emerged from the room behind Sarah, nodding agreement. "Yes, she's been impossible," he said, "even worse than Charlotte, and she's been bad enough."

When Ali finally managed to untangle herself from her friend's embrace, she gestured to her companion. "This is Douglas. He's from Scottish Intelligence and arranged all this."

Sarah turned to him. "Thank you, Douglas. You don't know how much this means to me."

"I'm beginning to get an idea," Douglas replied, shaking hands first with Sarah and then Hugh.

Just then a sleepy voice interrupted them from upstairs. "Is that Auntie Ali? Please say it is."

Sarah grabbed Ali's hand and urged her up the stairs. "Yes it is. We're coming."

For the next fifteen minutes Ali and Sarah sat on the side of Charlotte's bed while she gave Ali a detailed account of how excited she had been and how impossible it was to go to sleep. This turned out to be not quite true since, bit by bit, Charlotte's eyes first drooped and then closed as, holding firmly onto Ali's hand, she finally did fall asleep.

"Let's sit for a minute to make sure she's properly gone," Sarah whispered. "Then you can have something to eat and we'll sort out somewhere for Douglas to sleep. He'll be best in my study, I think. There's a decent inflatable bed he can have."

"No need," Ali whispered back with a sheepish look. "He can share with me."

"Mmmmn! I see. You've kept that quiet." Sarah gave her a grin. "How long has this been going on?"

"I'll tell you all about it tomorrow. We can have a long chat. Right now, that meal sounds wonderful."

Sarah made a wry face. "Don't get too excited," she said, "it's only a bits-and-pieces casserole. Been sitting on the hob waiting for you. You'll have to eat off your laps, I'm afraid. Ever since we were discouraged from going into work as too much of an infection risk, we've converted the dining room into a lab. There's all sorts of equipment in there."

They crept downstairs and joined the two men who were already deep in conversation.

"Hugh's just been telling me that he's actually had the flu and recovered from it," Douglas said to Ali.

"Yes," Hugh confirmed. "It wasn't a lot of fun, but I didn't suffer from the really terrible respiratory problems that have caused so many deaths."

"We were treating him with some experimental drugs that we've been developing," Sarah added, "some general antiviral ones that stimulate the immune system and a specific one that's aimed at the release phase of the flu virus. Maybe they helped. We really don't know. It could be that Hugh has some natural resistance. Some of us clearly do since not everyone is getting the flu and there are people like Hugh who become ill but then recover."

"So does that mean that your research has made progress?" Ali asked.

Sarah frowned. "Perhaps a little in relation to the current strain, but nowhere at all as far as the Zeno effect is concerned."

Ali saw her opportunity. "That's what Michael Lang's group are focusing on. You really should join them. He's desperate to have you both."

"I know, I know." Sarah shook her head. "Can we talk about all that tomorrow? I'd really like just to have a pleasant evening with friends tonight, try to forget about the bloody virus for a while. Pretend things are normal."

The four of them looked at each other for a long moment then, simultaneously, they nodded agreement.

"Aye," Douglas said. "Why not?"

z z z

The End Days Witnesses had for some years occupied a compound on the western Patagonian steppe, close to the wooded foothills of the southern Andes. Here they sought to cut themselves off and live a life at odds with the social and sexual mores of the world outside. But it was materially necessary to maintain some contact with people beyond their walls, so they had not been spared the flu. Significant numbers of the community had died over the past months and their leader – a ruthless sociopath believed by his acolytes to be divinely inspired – had concluded that the real end of days was finally upon them and that it was time for him to abscond with the cult's accumulated resources. After making careful preparations aided by a close confidant, he summoned the entire group to their central meeting hall, adults and children alike. Leading them in frenzied supplication he announced that the Rapture foretold had arrived whereupon, at a prearranged signal, his assistant detonated a chain of firebombs all around the walls of the building. The dry timber flared into terrifying life and, as the divine leader slipped out of a private door behind his pulpit, the singing and praying transmuted into shrieks of agony. For the Witnesses, if not for their leader, Zeno had indeed brought about the End of Days.

8

When at last it came, the announcement was brief and to the point. All licensed newsfeeds carried it live, while many of the independents picked it up within minutes. The setting was sober, a carefully constructed expression of dignified seriousness. The English prime minister seated at a desk in front of a dark panelled wall. Unsmiling, he looked directly into camera and began.

"My fellow citizens. Over the past several months we have all suffered greatly. Your government has sought to alleviate that suffering wherever it has been able to do so, but the scale of the epidemic has been such as to limit what could be done. Our Health Services have performed magnificently in the face of these challenges. Inevitably, however, they have been unable to deal with every case and all of us – I emphasise the 'all' – have lost loved ones, friends and neighbours to the disease. You have faced these travails with the fortitude that we have come to expect from the English when confronted with hardship, and on behalf of the government I would like to thank you for that. But there have been elements among you who have taken advantage of the situation to pursue their own antisocial agendas. This cannot be allowed. It undermines our ability to function as a democracy and to ensure that we continue to provide you with the basic needs of water, food, and energy. Accordingly, after consultation with my senior colleagues and with the Privy Council, his Majesty the King has authorised the declaration of a State of Emergency.

"This will have three immediate consequences for you. First, you will experience a much greater presence of armed soldiers and police on our streets. They will be empowered to deal firmly with any antisocial behaviour, including, where necessary, by use of weapons. Second, a strict curfew will be imposed from 8pm until 7am on a daily basis. Certain workers will be free of these limits so that they can fulfil essential functions. They will be informed at their places of work within the next twenty-four hours and issued with the appropriate authorisation documents. After that period of grace, anyone breaching the terms of the curfew, other than those designated as essential workers, will be dealt with summarily. Third, rationing of food and other resources will be extended. This is necessary to ensure that we continue to maintain acceptable living standards across the entire population. Anyone seeking to undermine or evade the rationing regulations will be detained. It is of course to be regretted that this has become necessary but I am sure you will agree that it is for the general good. Thank you."

Julie, watching the broadcast while curled up in an armchair in Albert and Rosa's living room, turned off the audio leaving only a succession of silent talking heads. She had no wish to hear the speculation dominating the news sites after the PM's broadcast, although it was diverting to idly watch their increasingly frantic dumbshow. Julie needed the distraction. She was not at all certain about the implications of the State of Emergency for her. She didn't doubt that her erstwhile employers had received advance warning of the announcement and that her loss of protection was a consequence of them feeling it necessary to strike a deal with the government in the light of what was about to happen. This was not a cheerful thought. Now she felt even more exposed than when she had first fled to Brixton. Part of the State of Emergency would surely involve what the government liked to call the 'pacification of illegal enclaves' and those in London would be high on the list, Brixton all the more so in that it was known to shelter a number of leading anti-Zeno activists.

She was turning all this over in her mind, wondering where she might find a safe hiding place, when she heard someone running in the yard and the sound of the back door opening. Then a voice calling out.

"Julie, Julie, where are you?"

It was her hosts' twelve-year-old son, Marcus.

"I'm in here, the living room."

"Good. There you are. Mum sent me. There are soldiers, lots of them, at the north end of the Enclave. It looks like they're going to try to take us over. She says you should be ready to run. They'll know whose house this is."

"But where's your mum and dad? What are they going to do?"

"They're with a big crowd up near the Town Hall. They're going to try to stop the soldiers coming down the hill." Marcus looked disappointed. "They wouldn't let me stay. All the kids are to shelter in the school."

"Quite right too," Julie said. "You'll be a lot safer there than out on the street. I'll walk you to the school then go up and join them at the Town Hall."

Marcus grinned. "Mum said you'd say that. But you're not to join them, she said. You'd be too obvious if they're looking for you. She said to go south."

Julie saw the sense in that. She would stick out like a sore thumb in the sea of largely black faces. She'd be an obvious target even if they weren't specifically looking for her.

"OK. I guess she's right. You get off to the school and I'll figure out what to do. Tell your mum and dad thank you. I'll try to keep in touch."

After Marcus's departure Julie stuffed as many of her possessions as she could into her backpack. It wouldn't take everything, but she knew that hauling the wheeled suitcase would both slow her down and draw unwanted attention. With a final regretful look around, and contrary to Rosa's instructions, she set off up Brixton Hill. Just a quick check on the situation, she told herself; I am a journalist after all. As she walked, however, she began to feel a little more doubtful. Almost all the people on the street were going in the opposite direction, most of them in great haste. After five minutes or so of struggling against the flow she almost collided with a couple pushing a child in a baby buggy.

"Julie," the woman said, "where do you think you're going?"

It was someone she had met through Rosa, part of a mutual support group for young mothers.

"You mustn't go up there," the woman continued, pointing back the way they had come. "It's really bad. There are an awful lot of soldiers and they look as if they're up for it. They'll be coming down the Hill soon. You don't want to be in their way when they do."

The couple hurried on while Julie stood contemplating her next move. Then, as if to reinforce the warning, there came the dull thud of a distant explosion followed by the unmistakable sound of gunfire. Perhaps it's not such a good idea, Julie thought, journalistic curiosity notwithstanding, and admitting to herself that she was frightened she turned around and joined the growing stream of people fleeing south. But where was she to go? There were lodging houses and hotels scattered across south London where she could probably find refuge, but they were required to do a central check on the identity of new arrivals and that would make her immediately traceable by the authorities.

It was only as she neared Streatham Hill that it dawned on her that she was within easy reach of Irene Johnson's house. Of course. She could seek shelter there. Surely Irene would help. They had been on good terms last time they met. Turning off the Streatham High Road, Julie made her way through the maze of streets between there and Tooting Common until finally arriving at Irene's door. To her disappointment there were no signs of life and she rang the doorbell in vain. Not really expecting it to be open, she tried the door but it was locked. Maybe she could find somewhere to hide in the back garden in the hope that Irene would return soon? There was a gate and a path along the side of the building and, to her relief, the gate was on a simple latch. This led her into a small garden area, neatly laid out with lawn and shrubs but lacking any shelter in which she could escape the late afternoon chill. There was a garage but it was firmly locked, so with no real hope of success she tried the back door. To her surprise it opened and in seconds she found herself in the relative safety of Irene's kitchen.

Seated at the kitchen table Julie rested her head in her hands and breathed a long sigh of relief. At least she was no longer out on the streets where the soldiers were confronting the people of Brixton. Beginning to feel calmer, she concentrated on listening for the sounds of vehicles and gunfire. Were they getting any closer? Although she was no longer inside the boundaries of the Brixton Enclave it was always possible that the military would pursue people into adjacent areas. She could just about catch some street noise at the limit of her hearing even though the windows were closed, but then, as she concentrated all the more, she became aware of a different sound. A kind of soft wheezing which came and went, like an intermittent draught blowing through a crack in the door. Yet she had shut the door firmly behind her and the kitchen windows were all closed. Still nervous from the day's events, she walked cautiously into the hallway listening as she went. The sound was coming from upstairs. She wasn't alone. There was somebody – something – up there. Grabbing an umbrella which was propped up in a corner of the hall, she inched her way up the stairs holding the improbable weapon out in front of her. At the end of the first floor landing a door stood slightly ajar and as she approached it she realised that this was the source of the sound.

She nudged the door open and peered in. There, in bed, was Irene, her face an unhealthy blue-grey pallor with dark marks on her cheeks, clearly struggling for every breath. Julie rushed to her side.

"Professor Johnson. Irene. Can you hear me?"

There was no response other than the continued erratic wheezing.

She laid her palm on Irene's forehead. It was hot. Grey though she looked, she was evidently running a fever. It had to be the flu and perhaps worse, Julie thought. She pressed her ear against Irene's chest and could just about hear a faint bubbling sound. Julie knew that the flu could easily lead to pneumonia which, among the very old and the very young, was as often a cause of death as the flu itself. Irene obviously needed treatment but what could Julie do? She could hardly go out in search of help in the present circumstances.

Then she remembered. As part of her deal with them, her former protectors had supplied her with an extensive anti-flu kit which included a package of drugs, both antibiotics and newly developed antivirals, as well as some basic training in their use. That kit was in her backpack downstairs, although most of the drugs were capsules and the unconscious Irene was in no state to swallow anything. But, Julie recalled, there was a broad-spectrum antibiotic that was delivered by injection. Maybe that would help to alleviate some of the respiratory symptoms and restore Irene to consciousness.

After retrieving her bag and consulting the instructions in her medical kit, Julie succeeded in rolling Irene onto her side so that she could be injected in the buttock. She half expected her patient to shriek as she plunged what seemed like a frighteningly long needle into soft tissue, but Irene showed no sign that she had felt anything at all. Leaning her up against her pillows once more, Julie fetched a bowl of cold water and dampened a cloth which she held to Irene's temples. She wasn't at all sure that this would be of any benefit but could think of nothing else to do. And so she sat as it grew darker, periodically refreshing the cloth and talking softly to Irene in the hope that somehow she would be aware that she was not alone.

Julie was uncertain how long she continued in this way, or what time it was when she realised that rather than fall asleep in the chair she might just as well lie down on the bed. It was hard to judge, but she thought that Irene's breathing was a little less laboured than it had been when she arrived. She lay down, and although she expected sleep to be elusive given the stress of the day's events and Irene's continual wheezing, exhaustion overcame her quite quickly.

She was awakened by a voice, Irene's voice, murmuring "Sarah, Sarah." It was still dark so she leaned across the bed and turned on a bedside lamp.

"Irene," she said softly. "It's me, Julie."

Irene, still short of breath, turned her head with some difficulty and peered in Julie's direction.

"Julie? Where's Sarah? I thought Sarah was here."

"No, there's only me." Julie had no idea who Sarah was but didn't think now was the time to ask. "You've been very ill," she continued. "When I got here you were unconscious. But now you're awake you must drink something. You're dehydrated. Wait a minute and I'll get you some water."

Julie persuaded her patient to sip rather than gulp the water while she explained the circumstances that had brought her to Irene's bedside. She wasn't certain that Irene was taking in the full detail of the story, but her eyes remained open and she was sufficiently attentive to ask about the various pills that Julie prevailed upon her to swallow. In the end she slumped back onto her pillow, only her hand gripping Julie's showing that she was aware of her surroundings. It was still dark outside, so conscious that both of them were in desperate need of rest Julie turned out the light and lay down once more. She listened to Irene's breathing – it was definitely not as much of a struggle as before – and bit by bit it slowed down, its now regular rhythm lulling Julie into a kind of hypnotic trance until, at last, the two exhausted women fell asleep, hand in hand.

z z z

Ali, who believed that she was finally close to persuading Sarah, was yet again rehearsing the benefits of the Scotland move when Douglas burst in.

"Have you seen the broadcast?"

"What broadcast?" Ali replied. "We haven't had any Comms turned on. We've been sitting here talking."

"The English government has declared a State of Emergency and there'll be a curfew from tomorrow." Douglas, normally calm to the point of seeming disinterest, was clearly worried. "Alison, you and me have to get out while we can. We need to travel tonight so that we can get back over the border before the curfew comes into effect tomorrow. Sarah, you and Hugh have to decide whether you're coming with us. Declaring a State of Emergency means that they believe things have reached a point of no return, that the situation is going to get a whole lot worse. It's now or never, I'm afraid. After today I don't think I can get you to Scotland."

Sarah looked at Ali, then at Douglas, then back to Ali.

"Well, that's it then," she said with a shrug. "Better start packing." She turned to Douglas. "How much can we take?" she asked.

"There's quite a lot of storage space in the lorry. If you can pack stuff into bin bags, boxes, anything really, then we can put it into crates in the lorry that are already labelled as recycling waste. Loading it in will be the problem, especially since we'll need to set off tonight. When's Hugh back?"

"Today's one of the days that Charlotte's voluntary education group is running so he's picking her up from there at three. They'll be back by half past."

"We'd best get started then," said Ali, beaming with pleasure at Sarah's decision. Then, turning to Douglas, "When will you bring the lorry round?"

"It'll have to wait until after dark," Douglas replied. "We don't want to attract more attention than necessary. If you're definitely sure, Sarah, I'll go and sort it all out now."

Sarah nodded. "I'm sure. Between Hugh, my mum and Ali I was pretty convinced anyway, but the State of Emergency finally settles it."

"Right. You folk get started and I'll make the arrangements."

The next few hours involved frantic sorting and packing, various disagreements about what should and should not be taken, and, in Charlotte's case, much anxiety about the safety of her ever-growing list of favourite toys. Hugh stripped down the dining room laboratory, carefully packing the bits and pieces of equipment into boxes.

"No point leaving this lot behind," he told Ali. "It's really good kit and we can always make use of it on top of what Michael's got for us in Edinburgh."

When Douglas returned he surveyed the chaotic scene with the look of a man faced with impossible choices.

"I'm not sure we have enough crates to hide all this," he said. "You can take some small essentials with you in the concealed compartment, but nothing big. We'll see what works. The other thing to think about is money. Can you make transfers to Ali and me? That way we can get the money to Scotland before anybody has any idea that you've skipped out."

Hugh looked up from sifting paperwork into piles. "I've already partly dealt with that," he said. "I've always had a savings account at home and

I've been moving money into it ever since the Zeno crisis began. But yes, Sarah has English savings and we do have some other bits and pieces. I'll see what I can do about transfers."

"Leave it until the last minute," Douglas advised. "Then there'll be little chance of anybody picking up on it until it's too late and we're safe."

The last minute in question proved to be around 7pm when the familiar MacDougall & Son lorry arrived and backed into their drive. In a flurry of activity the packing was transferred to the empty crates which, once full, were shielded by another layer containing genuine recycling.

"If we do get stopped," Jimmy, their driver, explained, "they can check these crates all they like. Though I've never had anyone actually do it."

"Even so," Douglas said, "best to be safe. The State of Emergency may make a difference. And there have been reports of hijackings on some of the isolated sections of the northern roads. Local gangs taking control."

"Can't we avoid those areas?" Sarah asked.

Douglas shook his head. "Only up to a point. We have to keep away from the big urban concentrations like Newcastle anyway so we need to be on lonelier roads. We'll go from here up towards Darlington and then across onto the A68 route into Scotland. But we might have to take to the backroads in Northumberland. If the military are being moved around I'm a bit wary of going near the Otterburn camps. We'll see how it's looking. But let's get going now."

Sarah and Hugh took a final look around.

"Just as well it's rented," Hugh said. "I wouldn't want to be leaving my own house empty when things get worse. It's owned by a guy in London. He can worry about it."

Charlotte, Hugh and Sarah climbed into the concealed compartment and made themselves as comfortable as they could on cushions and bedding, while Ali remained in the cab on the middle seat which masked the entrance to their hidden space. They left the access panel open to allow at least some communication among them, although as time went by Charlotte fell asleep and the adults lapsed into silence. There was very little traffic or anything else to attract attention out in the darkness, so, lulled by the rhythm of movement, Ali found herself dozing off.

They were driving along a section of isolated high-level road well west of Newcastle when she was startled awake by a shout from Jimmy.

"Lights up ahead. And there's a van blocking the road."

"Slow down," Douglas told him. "It doesn't look like police or military. Could be hijackers."

"Shall I try to run the barricade?"

"No, too risky. Even if we got through they'd probably try to chase us down. Stop when we get there and we'll see what's what." Douglas turned to Ali. "Get down in the hole with the others and lock the panel in place behind you. Best if they don't see you. And keep quiet."

Ali did as instructed, but held the panel slightly open so that she could hear what was going on.

"They're armed," Jimmy muttered.

"Yes, I can see," Douglas replied. "I think there's only two of them. Can you spot any more? There's a car at the side of the road but I don't think there's anybody in it. Hard to tell in the dark."

The lorry came to a halt and the two hijackers, weapons visible, stationed themselves by the cab doors on either side. Jimmy opened his window.

"Got a problem, pal?" he said.

"No," came the reply, "but you have. What are you carrying?"

"Recycling stuff. Not of any value to speak of."

"I'll be the judge of that," the man said. "Both of you get down here and open the rear doors."

Jimmy glanced across at Douglas who gave him a meaningful look and, almost imperceptibly, moved his hand towards the inside of his jacket.

Jimmy nodded, and they both opened their doors and stepped down to the ground.

As they did so, Ali was carefully pushing the entrance panel back into place aware that Hugh was just behind her and Sarah had Charlotte in a hug with her hand over the little girl's mouth. Then, just as Ali was easing the latches closed, there was a loud double explosion followed by the sound of Douglas shouting.

"Get back in, Jimmy. I'll move the van out of the way."

Ali pulled the panel open and looked out in time to see Jimmy throw himself into the driving seat and start edging the lorry forward.

"Shit!" she heard Douglas call. "It won't start without the ignition remote. I'll search them."

"No, don't bother," Jimmy yelled back. "We don't have time. There may be others nearby. Get in. I'll push it out of the way with the wagon."

The passenger door opened and Douglas hauled himself into the cab.

"Will it work?" he asked.

Jimmy grinned. "Sure," he said. "This thing's got a low gear that would shift an elephant. Here we go."

There was a crunch of metal on metal and, its engine emitting a high-pitched whine, the lorry moved forward pushing the van towards the edge of the road where, with a final triumphant surge, it was tipped onto its side in the ditch.

"Go, go, go," Douglas cried. "Let's get the hell out of here."

The lorry jerked forward, speeding off down the road.

"What happened?" Ali asked. "I heard gunfire."

"We dealt with it. They were going to hijack us."

"You mean, you shot them?"

"Yes." Douglas turned to look at her. "If we didn't do it first, they would have done it to us."

Ali was distraught. "But you didn't know that," she said.

"No," Douglas replied. "But we couldn't afford to wait to find out. You're going to have to get used to it, Alison. This is how the world is going to be as things fall apart. This will be the only way to survive."

She looked at him uneasily, recognising the truth in what he said but not wanting to believe it. Two men had just been killed so that she and her friends could continue safely on their way. She sank back onto a cushion next to Sarah. How is it possible, she thought, how can the man I know as a gentle and considerate lover also be a ruthless killer? Is this where we're all going?

The lorry drove on into the night with its shocked passengers occupying themselves as best they could in the cramped space available to them. Charlotte slept next to Hugh while Ali and Sarah, after a whispered conversation about what had happened, leaned shoulder to shoulder against the bulkhead. They continued in this way until, with no warning, the vehicle came to a halt. Douglas's face appeared in the entrance to the compartment.

"Anyone need a pee? Now's the time to do it. We're in the middle of nowhere on a side road. Maybe worth stretching your legs for a few minutes even if you don't need anything else."

Obediently they clambered up into the cab and out onto the side of the road. It was dark, no light to be seen in any direction. Aided by a torch that Jimmy produced, Hugh took Charlotte to relieve herself in a nearby field.

"Where are we?" Sarah asked.

"We've had a change of plan," Douglas replied. "I've received warning messages reporting trouble at the main border crossings. New soldiers brought in are disrupting normal operations. So we've left the A68 and we're heading cross-country to join the road that finally reaches the border at Coldstream. We've got a secure hiding place for the lorry near there where it can be parked up for the night. Jimmy will stay with it and the rest of us will be picked up and taken across the Tweed by boat, well away from the official crossing points. Then tomorrow, when things should be easier in daylight, Jimmy will bring the lorry over the border and all your possessions with it. It means that the trip will take a bit longer tonight, I'm afraid. We can't go very fast on these little roads."

Once they had restarted and the others appeared to be dozing, Ali settled herself on some cushions in a corner of the compartment and tried to sleep. But sleep wouldn't come, her thoughts constantly returning to what had happened. Was Douglas right? Were they inevitably drifting into anarchy and violence? She had to admit that the evidence from England suggested as much. Even before Zeno there had been many years of growing unrest, fed by a widely held belief that those in power cared little for ordinary people and understood less, being only interested in maintaining their own comfortable world and their position within it. The flu epidemic had provided a focus for this deep-rooted discontent, buttressed by the realisation that it had been caused by the very people whose notional job it was to protect the population from such disasters.

And, of course, once the legitimacy of those in authority is constantly questioned, dissent finds its own channels in which to flow.

But did this necessarily lead to violence and disorder? This was the question that was exercising Ali. She wanted to believe that it was not so, that however terrible the circumstances people would always find ways of joining together in mutual support. But what if that proved impossible? Although she had studied science, and then philosophy of science as a graduate student, her father had always encouraged her in more general philosophical interests. So she was all too aware that there was a danger here of tumbling into Thomas Hobbes's infamous 'war of all against all', the condition that he had described in a famous passage which, eager to please her father, she had learned by heart in her teens. Now she recited it silently to herself.

> *In such condition there is no place for industry, because the fruit thereof is uncertain, and consequently no culture of the earth, no navigation nor the use of commodities that may be imported by sea, no commodious building, no instruments of moving and removing such things as require much force, no knowledge of the face of the earth, no account of time, no arts, no letters, no society, and which is worst of all, continual fear and danger of violent death, and the life of man, solitary, poor, nasty, brutish, and short.*

It was those last few words that everybody knew – solitary, poor, nasty, brutish, and short – but it was what came before them that was truly terrifying. If social order failed, then so too would our capacity to create, to produce, to survive as humans in any meaningful way. Was this what was happening now? The beginning of a war of all against all? What had hitherto been for Ali a rather distant piece of seventeenth-century philosophical rhetoric suddenly seemed all too real.

Haunted by such distressing thoughts she at last fell into a strange state of suspension, neither fully asleep nor awake, a condition in which she remained until they were all aroused by Douglas calling softly into the compartment.

"Wake up. We're near Cornhill, close to the border. Time to leave the lorry."

"What time is it?" asked a sleepy Sarah.

"Almost four o'clock. We need to get a move on and cross the Tweed before it begins to get light. Gather your things and let's go."

For Ali the next hour passed in a blur. First they were driven a short distance in a farm utility vehicle and dropped at the edge of some woodland. Then they were led through the woods by a shadowy, unidentified figure with a tiny torch, who, after giving a low whistle and hearing a response, left them crouching beside a wide pool in the river. A few minutes later a large rowboat appeared out of the darkness, and in no time at all they were deposited by the border fence on the far bank. From here yet another anonymous guide took them through a locked gate and, finally, to a road where a vehicle awaited them.

Dawn was edging over the eastern horizon as they were driven north from Coldstream, allowing Ali to recognise the familiar Borders countryside. At last, she thought, we're safely here in Scotland. To which a small insistent voice in the back of her mind added, but safe for how long?

z z z

The Llano de Chajnantor group of astronomical observatories sit at an altitude of around 5000m in Chile's Atacama desert, its dry unpolluted air ideal for peering out into the universe. On this particular night, as always, the sky was blazing with stars, but the observatories were all but deserted. The flu had taken its toll on the scientists and technicians. A solitary figure, Dr Esperanza Guzman, well wrapped up against the fierce cold, stood in the midst of the surreal forest of radio telescope dishes. She was staring up at the spectacle above, reminding herself, as she often did in such circumstances, that the light filling the sky came from deep in the past. On the timescale of the stars human beings were no more than the tiniest moment, yet they had built this remarkable shrine to their desire for knowledge of the universe. Perhaps, she thought, that tiny moment was over, and in consequence of its own arrogance and stupidity humanity was sinking back into a doomed struggle for survival. In the bone-dry air of the plateau the dishes would survive well beyond their creators, gravestones marking human ambition and human folly. Esperanza looked up at the night sky one last time, shedding tears which promptly froze on her cheek in the icy desert air.

9

In the weeks of Irene's convalescence she and Julie fell into an undisturbed domestic routine. Although she had recovered from the infections themselves, the after-effects of her illness rendered Irene extremely weak leaving Julie to take on all the tasks requiring physical effort. In particular, this meant scouring the local area for food. Since Julie didn't dare reveal her own presence by using her designated food rations, they both had to survive on Irene's allocation and on anything that Julie could find in the burgeoning black market. Fortunately, neither of them were huge eaters so they were getting by on a single main meal a day plus the occasional treat that Julie turned up on her foraging. Irene insisted on doing the cooking – one experience of Julie's culinary skills had been enough to ensure that division of labour – and otherwise they spent much of their time talking, reading, and listening to music. To their mutual surprise, they found that they shared a taste for string quartets and Irene had the necessary audio equipment, as well as a collection of scores, to allow them to indulge themselves in serious listening and in even more serious argument about which was the superior interpretation.

It was an idyll that could not last of course, they both knew that. The world outside their little retreat was riven with conflict, supplies were becoming increasingly unpredictable, and as winter came to a close there was no sign of the hoped for decline in the epidemic. They counted themselves fortunate to be living through their peaceful interregnum if only for a few weeks, so when it did come to an end one Thursday in mid

April it was not entirely unexpected. The event that changed things was the arrival of an unforeseen visitor. Irene was at home resting, though becoming a little stronger every day, while Julie was out hunting down whatever supplies she could find. After so long with no callers, Irene was taken aback when the doorbell rang and even more amazed when she found herself confronted by Jonathan Hart, smiling tentatively and carrying a large shopping bag.

"Hello Irene," he said. "May I come in?"

"Yes, of course," she replied, noting as she did so that he now looked even more pale and drawn than he had on the last occasion that they had met. Remembering that the kitchen table still bore the remnants of two breakfasts, she led him into the living room. No point drawing his DSD attention to the fact that she was not alone.

"So, to what do I owe the honour this time?" she asked.

"Well, I wondered how you were doing now that the Science Advisory Executive has closed down. You must have time on your hands."

Irene smiled at the thought. "Oh, I find plenty to do. But you're still busy I guess?"

"Yes, I suppose I am. Though I don't have many staff left. People have got ill or, in some cases I think, just given up on the job. Can't blame them really. Trying to maintain security is a thankless task right now and not likely to improve any time soon."

"Last time we met I recall that we spoke about Operation Homestead. Has that gone into action? I suppose it must have."

He nodded. "Yes, the government apparatchiks are tucked away in various safe havens. I could still get you into Northwood, you know. It's where I'm based."

"No thanks, Jonathan." She smiled and gestured to the room around her. "I'm really much more comfortable here than I would be in a confined space with all those career politicians and bureaucrats."

"Yes, well, I didn't really think you would have changed your mind." He paused, looking down at his hands which he was nervously clasping together in his lap. "There's something I ought to tell you. About why I'm here."

"OK, I'm listening."

"I've had an agent keeping an eye on you, off and on. Well, I say 'agent' but he's barely that. More of an office junior really." Seeing Irene's frown of dismay, Hart hurried on. "It was in your interest really. The government wanted you watched because of your opposition to the Zeno project – they thought you might be a source of the leaks – so I volunteered my agency. It was that or allow them to set MI5 on you, and you wouldn't have wanted that."

"Nor would you!" Irene's response was acid. "They might have turned up evidence of your involvement."

"That too," he said, doing his best to look suitably contrite. "Anyway, my guy didn't actually see much of you and he was only here now and then. Too many other jobs and too few staff. But he did report one interesting thing. A young woman was coming and going quite regularly. Initially I thought maybe it was your daughter, but then he got a photograph. Not a very good one – he really is an amateur – but good enough for me to recognise Julie Fenwick."

"Really," Irene said, ignoring Hart's expectant look. "I wonder what she was doing around here."

"Come on, Irene," Hart laughed. "He saw her coming out of your house." He held up his hands palms outwards in a gesture of surrender. "I assure you, I don't want to do her any harm. Quite the opposite in fact. I want to feed her some more information. But I've not been able to contact her. I know she was in Brixton, but since the pacification campaign she's been off the network. Not using her CommsTab, no public profile at all."

"I wouldn't call it pacification," Irene replied, her irritation obvious. "More like invasion from what I hear. But yes, Julie came here running from the soldiers. Just as well for me that she did since I was very ill. If she hadn't arrived you wouldn't be talking to me now."

Hart looked at her with concern. "You had the flu?" he asked.

"Yes, and probably pneumonia as well. When Julie found me I was unconscious and could barely breathe. She nursed me through it, so as you can imagine I feel quite protective of her."

Hart remained silent for some time. "Yes," he said at last, "I can understand that. But I really don't want to harm her. Apart from anything else, she's much more valuable to me if she's free to do her work. Because of her record people believe her, while they don't believe the official sources."

"But what is it that you're trying to do, Jonathan? What do you expect to achieve by giving her more information at this late stage?"

Hart sighed then looked her straight in the eye. "It's as I told you before, Irene, I want to hold them to account. I want them to answer for what they've done. The only way I can do that is by feeding public opinion, by telling people what's really happening."

"But won't that just cause more trouble, more unrest, lead to more deaths?"

"Maybe. But it could also clean out the Augean stables, give people a new start without the pernicious influence of these irresponsible bastards."

Irene looked doubtful. "Sounds pretty apocalyptic to me. Have you suddenly become a revolutionary?"

"No," he replied. "Unfortunately I'm too much a product of their world for that. But I think something drastic is needed or whatever's left of England will just get into a worse and worse mess. At least this way there might be a chance of recovery."

About to dispute his claim, Irene stopped when over his shoulder she saw that Julie was coming up the path.

"Well," she said, inclining her head towards the window behind him. "You can try to recruit her to your cause. She's here now."

"Hiya," Julie called as she came through the front door. Then, sounding pleased with herself: "I've found us four eggs. We can have omelette."

She carried her shopping into the kitchen and finding no one there shouted, "Where are you?"

"In here," Irene replied. "In the living room. We have a visitor."

"A visitor! That's a first," Julie said, entering the living room just as Jonathan got to his feet to greet her.

"This is Jonathan," Irene said, waving in his direction. "What you need to know is that he's your real Deep Throat."

Julie stopped in the midst of reaching to shake Jonathan's outstretched hand.

"What!" she said. "Really?"

The query was addressed directly to Jonathan who replied, "Yes, I'm afraid so. Not too much of a disappointment I hope."

Julie looked across at Irene for confirmation and the older woman nodded.

"Well, umm, no," Julie said. "I never expected to meet you at all so it could hardly be a disappointment." She smiled suddenly. "Though a dark underground car park might have been preferable to Irene's living room."

Jonathan looked puzzled.

"Ignore me," Julie said. "Just an image from a film."

Jonathan, still not understanding the reference, pressed on regardless.

"I've got some more information for you," he began, as he rummaged in his bag and produced an anonymous-looking CommsTab. "You'll find it all on here – documents, some bits and pieces of video, maps, all sorts."

Julie's eyes lit up. "That's great," she said, "but I'm out of contact with my usual sites. I haven't dared to use my CommsTab in case it was being tracked."

"I'm coming to that," he replied. "You're right not to use your CommsTab. There's certain to be a trace out on it. That's why I've brought you this modified one. I'll take yours away with me and get rid of it where it can never be connected back to here."

"So what's so distinctive about this one?" Irene asked.

"It's specially shielded," he said, holding it so that they could see the screen. "Unlike ordinary ones it has three modes. In Mode Zero, which it's in now, it's completely dead. Normal CommsTabs are never entirely that, even when you think you've switched them off. They keep some basic processes running and in principle they can be traced, though it can be rather difficult. But in Mode Zero this one is effectively an inert lump. The switch here turns it on," – he pointed to a small slider on the side which he moved – "and requires your identity. At the moment it's a passcode but we'll set it up to read your biometrics, Julie. And yours, Irene, if you're willing. This is Mode One. You can access data held on it, you can feed data to it, like record a vlog or create a document, all the usual stuff. But in this mode it doesn't connect to the Net – no signals emanate from it."

"So that means it's untraceable?" Julie asked.

"Not a hundred per cent, but near as dammit. Less traceable than an ordinary CommsTab would be even when completely switched off. It should be safe for all practical purposes."

"And Mode Two?" Irene and Julie chorused.

"Then it behaves like a normal CommsTab though a lot faster and more powerful, as well as using more elaborate encryption systems. You access Mode Two from this menu here and it always gives you a chance to pull out before it runs. In this mode you can download and send. What I suggest you do, Julie, is prepare your material in Mode One, then when it's ready to transmit put the tablet in Mode Zero and take it as far away from here as is practical, then put it into Mode Two, send the stuff, and then immediately switch back to Mode Zero. It won't take long to send and doing it this way will minimise any chance of tracing it to source. Clear?"

"Yes, seems straightforward enough." Julie looked at him curiously. "Where on earth do you get hold of something like this?"

"Oh, I have contacts in security and technology areas. Benefit of a lifetime working for the government," he added, glancing towards Irene to ensure that she understood he wanted to keep his DSD identity a secret.

Julie, however, had caught the glance, and knew that whatever Jonathan was holding back she could find out from Irene later. "OK," she said, "shall we sort out the biometrics and then I'll make us all a cup of coffee – or whatever it is that passes for coffee at the moment."

"Ah, that reminds me," said Jonathan, handing his shopping bag to Julie. "I brought this for you. It's food of various kinds. The government safe havens are rather well provided for. You'll find some proper coffee in there. Drink first, biometrics after."

Julie peered into the bag and beamed. "You're not joking are you? Right, I'll make the coffee."

Once Julie was in the kitchen Irene spoke quietly to Hart. "You do realise, don't you, that I shall have to tell her who and what you are."

"Yes, I supposed as much," he said with a sigh. "But at least this way I'll be spared her interrogating me about DSD today. I don't think I could deal with that right now."

"I'll make sure that she doesn't use your name. She has no need to anyway and from her point of view it will be better to keep you as a secure source."

"True enough." He thought for a moment. "Have you still got that little Comms device I gave you?"

Irene nodded.

"Get in touch if anything goes wrong. Not just about my identity but anything at all. You never know, I may be able to help."

Irene just had time to nod her assent before Julie returned, and once coffee was taken and the technology dealt with, Hart departed carrying Julie's old tablet in the now empty shopping bag.

"Right Irene," Julie said when they were alone. "Out with it. Who is he? I saw that little exchange of glances."

"He's in intelligence. Director of the Domestic Security Division."

Julie gave a low whistle. "That is something. But why is he passing information to me?"

"I'm not sure now. Back at the beginning it was because he wanted to force the government to act in the hope that they could mitigate some of the effects of the flu. But now?" Irene frowned. "Something's happened. He's changed. He says he wants to hold them to account, but to me it's more as if he wants to punish them."

They sat in silence for a minute lost in their different thoughts, then Julie picked up the new CommsTab.

"What the hell!" she said. "Let's see what we've got stored on here."

z z z

The cluster of gas rigs looked from the distance like a strange copse of artificial trees struggling to hold their own on the rolling surface of the Pacific Ocean. As the helicopter closed in on one of them, easing carefully down towards its landing pad, it was apparent to those on board that almost all the structures were abandoned, left dark and lifeless. This one, however, was still functioning, and they had received a desperate emergency call from it that morning. Clad in anti-contamination suits, they disembarked from the chopper and spread out through the rig. They found its skeleton crew in various states of illness or death, victims of a particularly aggressive mutation of the flu virus. At last, in its control room, they came upon the author of the emergency call, the rig's cook, slumped in a swivel chair and surrounded by screens. He was alive but unconscious. To anyone qualified to read them, the screens told a terrible story of malfunction and growing pressure. Unfortunately, the person who first reached the control room was a medic not an engineer, so when it did come the explosion was entirely unexpected, its massive fireball visible from the coast some forty miles away.

10

April had given way to May by the time Julie's third vlog appeared. Hart had been waiting for it, checking the newsfeeds compulsively every day. She was smart, he thought, drip-feeding her audience, keeping them waiting for the next instalment of her revelations, encouraging them to imagine her out there investigating on their behalf. The first vlog had been a straightforward report on the retreat of the government to unidentified safe havens. The second had singled out Northwood as a key location and named many of the prominent figures now housed there. Hart was pleased to note that this list included James Curbishley, former Director of Porton Down, whom Julie identified as the person principally responsible for developing Zeno. The third was even more explosive, revealing the relative luxury in which politicians and officials were living in the Northwood Homestead, detailing their facilities and food supplies even down to the range of wines and spirits with which they could comfort themselves. To a population reduced to bare essentials, and little enough of those, this was more than sufficient to encourage anger and yet further unrest.

So it was time, Hart decided. Time to put into practice the riskiest and most unpredictable part of his plan. There was already a permanent encampment of protestors outside the Northwood perimeter, one that the authorities had allowed to remain, despite the curfew, for fear of worse consequences if they were forcibly removed. But after the detailed revelations of Julie's third vlog, pressure was building for a much larger demonstration to be mounted at the end of the following week with most dissident groups across London and the South-East mobilising their supporters. Direct co-operation among them would be difficult, Hart knew, since they covered every shade of political opinion from liberal hand-wringing to permanent revolution. But he did have a tenuous link to a leading figure in one of the groups, the English Revolutionary Anarchists, a link which he was hoping to exploit.

No point visiting the ERA dressed like a government bureaucrat, he thought, changing out of his customary suit and into a battered pair of jeans and a nondescript jacket. As one of the most senior intelligence officers in the Northwood Homestead he was free to come and go at will, even provided with his own transport. The little City Car was housed in a lock-up close to one of the Homestead's emergency exits, an exit which was itself outside the perimeter and effectively disguised as a shed in the back garden of a safe house. It was guarded both inside and out, but Hart was its most regular user and therefore well known to the guards who waved him through that morning with a cheerful greeting.

Emerging from the shed, he disconnected the car from its charging point in the lock-up and drove east through the seemingly endless suburbs of north London, finally coming to a halt in a street of large houses in the Harrow area. Leaving the car parked some way from his destination, he walked down the street to a house with an unkempt front garden and in need of some decoration. I don't suppose that's popular with the neighbours, Hart thought, assessing the house as he rang its doorbell. It took three rings before the door was finally opened by a young woman.

"Yes?" she said, looking at Hart with complete disinterest.

"I'd like to speak with Jerry Rowlands. Is he in?"

"No one of that name lives here," she replied, making to shut the door.

Hart blocked the closing door with his foot and leaned in until his face was inches away from hers.

"I'll tell you what I'll do," he said coldly. "I'll walk down the road to that little green area down there and I'll find somewhere to sit enjoying the sunshine. Meanwhile, you'll tell Jerry that Jonathan Hart is here to see him. Tell him that I have information that he might find very useful. If he doesn't meet me down there I'll come back in half an hour." He leaned a little closer. "Got that? Jonathan Hart."

The woman nodded nervously, closing the door as soon as Hart released it. Smiling to himself at his little show of melodrama, Hart strolled down the road and settled on a low wall just inside the entrance to a children's play area. While he waited he rehearsed the history that had brought him to this spot. He had first met Jerry Rowlands on arriving as a rather nervous first-year student at Oxford. Jerry had been a year ahead of him, already a flamboyant figure in college and much given to dramatic political gestures. At a time when students were relatively depoliticised, Jerry stood out as a kind of throwback to an earlier age. Although it made him cringe now, Hart had rather hero-worshipped Jerry for much of the two years that their paths had crossed at university and had found himself drawn into what was for him an entirely unfamiliar world of dissident political discourse. They had certainly become friends, if a somewhat lopsided friendship, the one a confident, larger-than-life product of an affluent background, the other a diffident, even shy child of the lower-middle classes. It was, Hart thought, the old cliché of a leader–follower relationship among young men, but it had meant a lot to him at the time and their mutual affection had seemed genuine enough.

Jerry had graduated a year before him, by which time Hart had begun to assert some independence from his friend, both politically and personally. They hadn't exactly drifted apart but it had become apparent to both of them that Hart's developing sense of his own identity was leading him in a different direction. After graduation Jerry had moved away, first to his family home in Surrey, and then into London where he survived on a trust fund and various inheritances, and where, charismatic as ever, he gathered around himself a group of like-minded dissenters.

Meanwhile, during his third year Hart had been subjected to the infamous 'tap on the shoulder' which had for so long been the mode of recruiting Oxbridge students into the intelligence services. To his surprise he found himself quite at home in this role, using his contacts with the remaining radical students in Oxford to feed information to his handlers. They had been sufficiently impressed by their new recruit to offer him a full-time job on graduation, the beginning of what had become a formidable career. But in all those years he had never tried to cash in on his links with Jerry, even when Jerry's group had become of interest to the police and intelligence services. Residual sentiment perhaps, he thought, a desire not to betray what had after all been a formative relationship for him.

These reflections were interrupted by the arrival of the man himself, the tall smiling figure of Rowlands still a striking presence in spite of the passage of time.

"Well, well. Jonny Hart has come to visit after all these years. How long has it been?"

Hart grimaced at the forgotten diminutive of his forename. "Must be about ten years, Jerry. That college reunion. You didn't stay long."

Rowlands sat down on the wall next to Hart and draped a companionable arm over his shoulders.

"Oh yes, I remember. The college trying to screw money out of us. Cheeky really, considering how much land they own." Rowlands shook his head. "I only went to say hello to old friends. Like you. You still working for the government? Which department was it?"

Hart had not told him that he was in intelligence though he rather thought that Jerry may have suspected as much.

"Oh, different parts of the system at one time or another," he replied with deliberate vagueness. "We bureaucrats get shuttled around."

Hart's evasion produced a knowing smile from the other man. "Of course. It's all very complicated isn't it." Rowland's face hardened into what on somebody else might have been an unfriendly expression. "Jean said that you claimed to have useful information for me. So what's that all about?"

"Maybe a bit more than just information," Hart said. "This big demonstration that's being planned near Northwood next week. You're part of the umbrella group of organisers aren't you?"

Rowlands nodded. "No secret about that. All the organising participants have been made public so as to encourage the widest possible range of support."

"Right. But it must be pretty difficult getting all those groups to act in unison. A lot of jockeying for position?"

Rowlands grinned. "If you mean there's a lot of the old People's Front of Judea stuff, well yes, of course there is. You remember what it used to be like back in Oxford days."

Hart smiled at the memory and at Rowlands' invocation of the famous Monty Python routine from *Life of Brian*. They used to recite it to each other whenever they were involved in the internecine feuding of student leftist groups.

"Yes, I do remember," he said. "Frustrating and counterproductive…"

Rowlands interrupted him. "But all an entertaining part of the game, though I don't think you ever really grasped how significant those sectarian distinctions were for keeping things going and ensuring people's involvement."

Hart thought about that for a moment. "No, maybe I didn't. I never properly understood the psychology of political posturing about minor ideological disagreements. What was Freud's phrase? 'The narcissism of small differences', wasn't it. Still, I do have a bit better grasp now, which is why I've come to see you."

"OK. I'm listening."

"If you could make a big splash at the demonstration, pull off something really striking, then you'd be in a prime position in the movement, wouldn't you?"

Rowlands looked doubtful. "Maybe," he said. "It would depend a lot on what it was."

"What if I could give you somebody important, somebody you could parade as a captive, proof of your effectiveness as a revolutionary group?"

"Again, maybe. Have you someone in mind?"

"Yes, as a matter of fact I do." Hart paused for effect. "You've heard of James Curbishley?"

"Curbishley! The Porton Down guy who ran the Zeno project. You can produce him? How the fuck do you propose to do that?"

"I'm well placed to convince him that he's in danger and bring him to you under the guise of taking him to somewhere safe. You don't need the details but, believe me, I can do it. I would deliver him to you on the night before the demonstration. Then it would be up to you how you make use of him."

Rowlands looked at him curiously. "I don't understand, Jonny. It's been, what? Twenty years, more, since we were political allies. Then suddenly you appear out of nowhere and make me this unlikely offer. Why would you do that?"

"Oh, personal reasons, Jerry. It's too long a story for now. Besides, you don't have to do anything except agree to receive Curbishley."

Rowlands snorted in disbelief. "Sounds awfully like a trap to me, Jonny."

"No, it's really not a trap. Why would the authorities want to trap you in this way? If I can find out where you live then they surely know, so if they wanted rid of you they could have made you disappear by now. Frankly, it's because they've never thought it worth the bother. Your group is just too small and too little known." Hart paused to let that sink in. "But do this and you'll become the best-known radical group in the country, at least for a while. It'll be up to you to find ways of building on that. Of course, they'll be interested in you then and you'll have to take measures to protect yourselves. But I'm sure you can do that, especially with all the new supporters that you'll get if you play it right."

"I don't know," Rowlands said, leaning back and staring up into the blue sky as if the answer might be found there. "I'll have to think about it."

"Fair enough. But don't think too long. I'll need to get things set up if we're going ahead." Hart paused for a moment, appearing to calculate. "I'll come back here at the beginning of next week, Monday afternoon, about this time. You can tell me your decision then. OK?"

"Can't I just call you?"

"No. You never know, they may well have a bug on your CommsTab. Best if we meet."

Rowlands shrugged. "Right, Monday it is. See you then." And with that he set off back up the road, head down, deep in thought.

Hart smiled to himself. The bait had been offered and he was certain that Jerry would take it. He was much too attached to the pleasures of the grand political gesture not to do so, a character flaw on which Hart had relied, recalling it only too well from their student days. Yes, he said to himself, I think we're definitely in business.

So it proved when they met on the following Monday and settled the details for delivering Curbishley into the hands of the ERA. Somewhat to Hart's surprise Rowlands made no enquiry as to what position Hart held that allowed him access to information, transport and, indeed, to Curbishley himself. But then, he thought, perhaps that wasn't so surprising given that the only way he could have such access was by virtue of security clearance and a senior position. Rowlands had evidently decided that the likely rewards merited the risks involved, even if he wasn't entirely convinced of Hart's trustworthiness. Maybe their joint history had carried some weight after all – Hart was oddly pleased to think so.

Whatever the truth of that supposition, at 7pm on the evening before the big demonstration Hart was knocking on the door of Curbishley's Homestead room.

"Good evening, Dr Curbishley," he said when the door was opened, careful to appear deferential and to use Curbishley's formal title. "May I come in? It's a rather urgent matter."

"If it's urgent then I suppose so, though I am rather busy," Curbishley replied, in the tone of a man interrupted while engaged in serious work.

"I imagine that you know, Dr Curbishley, that for reasons of security most members of the Cabinet and their senior administrators were moved to an alternative safe location earlier this week."

"I certainly do," Curbishley spluttered, "and I'm at a loss to know why I wasn't included in that move. After all, my presence here is publicly known and I am a well-established senior figure in the scientific administration."

Hart nodded agreement. "I'm afraid I wasn't party to that decision, but I do agree that you should also have been moved. An oversight by somebody I suspect. So, given the imminence of a big demonstration nearby tomorrow, we've arranged to get you out of here tonight and to a DSD safe house. From there you will join the other senior officials at their new location in due course. Because of the earlier error, and given your importance to the government, I shall be taking you personally. I hope that will be satisfactory."

Curbishley visibly inflated with self-importance. "I should hope so," he said, "and not before time, Hart. I'll have to pack up my stuff."

"No need, sir." Hart was struggling to maintain his obsequious manner. "We have people who will do that for you and transfer all your belongings directly to the new Homestead. You'll just require an overnight bag for the safe house. Perhaps you could pack that now. We have to be on our way as soon as possible."

Hart had to cajole Curbishley into speeding up the packing process as he hemmed and hawed about what he would need, but at last he was ready. As he went to pick up his CommsTab, Hart stopped him.

"Best to leave that behind, sir. These dissidents are pretty well equipped now. They will certainly have tracing devices which can pin down the location of your CommsTab. We'll leave it here so they'll have no reason to think that you're anywhere else. I've arranged for a new one to be waiting for you at the safe house."

Curbishley complied, albeit reluctantly, and Hart led him out of the residential area to his usual emergency exit. Fortunately they met no one along the way and, although Hart had prepared papers to allow Curbishley free passage, on recognising that it was Hart, the guards simply waved them through. Soon they were in the car retracing the same route across north London that he had followed twice in the past ten days. They were not delayed by any curfew checks, which was just as well as Hart grew increasingly irritated with his passenger, a man whose pomposity knew no bounds and who kept up a constant stream of criticism levelled at all with whom he had to deal. At last a relieved Hart came to a halt outside the ERA house. The front door opened – they had arranged that a watch would be kept – and Rowlands, accompanied by a second man, came down the path. Hart got out and opened the passenger door for Curbishley.

"Here we are, Dr Curbishley. These gentlemen will be looking after you now."

Hart glanced at Jerry who gave him a half-smile.

"Indeed we shall, sir," said Rowlands. "Indeed we shall."

"Goodbye then, Curbishley." Hart's tone was suddenly no longer deferential. "I shall be off to visit my wife now. She's not too well I'm afraid. Our daughter died, you know. Of the flu."

At that, Jerry looked in some surprise at Hart, then nodded. "Goodbye, Mr Hart. We'll certainly take excellent care of Dr Curbishley for you."

As Hart drove away he glanced back to see Curbishley struggling ineffectually as the two men, one on either side, half guided and half dragged him into the house. For a minute he wished that he really was going to visit Jill to tell her about his revenge, but she was no longer in their family home. She had left to stay with her sister shortly after he had failed to persuade her to move into the safe haven, and they had barely spoken since. So it was an empty, unwelcoming house at which he arrived some forty minutes later, a place haunted by memories of his wife and daughter. He promised himself that he would not – could not – stay there a moment longer than necessary, but since he could hardly now return to the Northwood Homestead he had little immediate choice. He would stay in London only long enough to witness Curbishley's public humiliation. Beyond that, it mattered little to him where he went.

After a restless night dozing on a sofa in the living room – he couldn't face going upstairs past Rosemary's bedroom which had remained untouched since her death – he assembled various items that he thought he might need when he left the city, including two handguns with ammunition and a considerable quantity of cash. The bare essentials crammed into a backpack, he loaded the car with such food as there was in the house and readied himself to leave. He would use the car until its charge ran out then abandon it, he decided. It would get him well out of the city before he was obliged to continue on foot. By midday he was ready, setting off towards north London. He parked the car some distance from his final destination at Ruislip Common where the demonstration was to be held, walking the remainder of the way. There were large numbers of people on the approach roads and already a massive audience was gathered around a dais that had been erected on the common itself. Hart squeezed his way through the crowd until he was close to the front of the platform. There was a large wooden letter Z mounted prominently on it, perhaps two metres high, its horizontals painted red and its central strut black. The traditional anarchist colours, Hart noted, wondering if this was Rowlands' doing.

As the waiting crowd swelled there was a growing sense of anticipation. Quite what they were expecting was not clear to Hart nor, indeed, to the crowd itself. But there was certainly something in the air, a desire for action, a need to insist on their significance in the face of uncaring and seemingly untouchable authorities. Finally, when the tension was stretched close to breaking point, there was some movement by the steps at the side of the dais and several people clambered up and arrayed themselves across the stage in front of the giant Z. Hart could see Jerry among them, standing at the back, his height making him visible to all. But there was no sign of Curbishley. One of the group came to the microphone, introducing herself as Rosa, co-ordinator of a well-known Zeno protest organisation and the facilitator for today's speakers. She listed the assorted groups who were represented on stage and summoned the first of them to speak. By the time she called Jerry, the crowd had been subjected to several variously ineffective harangues from a variety of political perspectives and they were becoming restless. Cries of "Get on with it" and, more aggressively, "Let's march on Northwood" were increasingly heard, meeting with a growing volume of vocal support.

Rowlands was clearly in his element. He was anyway an imposing physical figure and, unlike several of those who had preceded him, a powerful and lucid public speaker. His particular brand of generic anti-authoritarianism resonated well with the mood of many in the crowd who had by now lost interest in the pedantic political divisions being played out before them. Rowlands wound them up, used humour to discharge the tension that he himself had created, and then wound them up again. Hart was impressed. Jerry had always been an effective performer, but here he was really rising to the occasion and the crowd were rising to him, roaring their approval. Then, at a particularly climactic point, he raised his hands in the air to call them to silence. There was a hush while the huge array of faces looked towards him expectantly. He slowly lowered his arms to the horizontal, as if to take them all into an embrace, then spoke deliberately and quietly.

"My friends, the English Revolutionary Anarchists have a gift for you today."

He half turned towards the side of the stage, arms still outstretched. The vast audience seemed frozen in place until the terrified figure of Curbishley, his hands tied behind his back, was pushed up the steps and escorted across the stage to stand next to Rowlands, who put an arm around his shoulders as if to greet a friend.

"Let me introduce our guest," he continued. "This unappealing specimen is Dr James Curbishley."

At this, a sound resembling a low growl emanated from sections of the crowd.

"I see that some of you recognise the name. For those who may not, this, my friends, is the one-time Director of the Porton Down Centre, the man who initiated and pushed forward the Zeno project. This..." he gripped Curbishley with one hand at the back of his collar, hauling him almost off his feet, "this is the man more than anyone else responsible for the terrible plight in which we find ourselves, for the illness, death and misery which has afflicted us all."

Curbishley stared around in terror as the crowd howled its hatred, his eyes darting from side to side as if he expected someone to come to his aid.

"What shall we do with him?" Rowlands asked.

"String him up," came a shout from a woman close to where Hart was standing, a cry taken up by others here and there among the mass of people.

"I know," Rowlands said. "Let's remind him of why he's here, of why we're all here."

Continuing to hold Curbishley by the collar while carrying the microphone in his other hand, Rowlands gestured the group of speakers out of his path and made his way towards the red-and-black Z at the back of the dais. When he reached it he was joined by two men who took hold of Curbishley. Rowlands turned once more to the audience and raised the microphone to his lips.

"Z," he said. "What does Z stand for Dr Curbishley?"

Unsurprisingly there was no reply.

"Don't know? I'll tell you then. It stands for everything evil that you and people like you have done in the name of the state. It stands for the unfettered desire for power. It stands for the utter disrespect in which you hold your fellow human beings. It stands for the disease that you created and loosed upon us, for death, the destroyer of worlds. It stands for Zeno."

By now the entire crowd was screaming its approval. Rowlands nodded to his two comrades. They untied Curbishley's hands and pressed his back up against the wooden Z. Only then did Hart see that there were cuffs mounted on the two cross-beams and realise what Rowlands intended. Curbishley's wrists and ankles were swiftly fitted into the restraints and, when the two men stepped back, the crowd could see the results of their handiwork. Curbishley was spread like an X across the wooden Z. Rowlands spoke again.

"We reject you, Curbishley, we cross you out and everyone like you. Today we sacrifice you on the mark of your own terrible creation. On Zeno."

By now there was near riot, those further back pressing forward to get a better view of the spectacle.

Then, out of the crowd came a frenzied shout: "Nail him up. Nail the bastard up," which was quickly echoed by others until it seemed as if the entire throng was chorusing "Nail him up. Nail him up."

For the first time in his performance Rowlands looked discomfited. This was not quite what he had intended, but now it was clear that the hatred called forth by his oratory was out of his control. Deciding that he had little choice, he leaned down and from behind the giant Z retrieved the toolbox that had been used in its construction. He took out a hammer and a handful of long nails, then turning to face Curbishley reached up to his left hand, placed a nail at the juncture of wrist and palm, lifted the hammer and drove the nail home. Curbishley shrieked as a wet patch spread down the front of his trousers and urine pooled on the platform below him. Rowlands turned his attention to the right hand and then to the feet, while the sound of Curbishley's agony was lost in a great rumbling thunder of approval from the mob. Hart was close enough to see the victim's eyes cloud over as he began to lose consciousness, and he thought that there was a brief moment when their gazes locked and Curbishley recognised him. But then it was gone, and Hart turned and slipped away through the tumult of people, both horrified and fulfilled at what he had just witnessed.

z z z

The tiny Chinese fishing boat was slowly making its way north in the Yellow Sea, some miles off the coast of South Korea. The area was pretty well fished out, had been for many years, but food was now in such short supply that the skipper had decided to give it a try. Maybe by now some stocks had regenerated. At that moment they weren't actually fishing – the grounds for which they were aiming were a little further north – so while the skipper steered, his two surviving crew were taking it easy, sitting on deck and listening to a Chinese radio station.

All day the music had been interrupted by newsflashes recounting the latest developments in the rising crisis between North and South Korea. The Republic's Supreme Leader had become increasingly aggressive over recent weeks, blaming South Korea and its allies for the especially virulent epidemic that had been sweeping his country. Today, if the newsflashes were to be believed, the level of threat and counter-threat had escalated wildly. Then, suddenly, away to the east in the direction of Seoul, the sky lit up. The two crewmen were blinded by the flash, but the skipper, who was facing the other way, only caught its reflection in the metal along the side of his bridge. He turned around in time to see a vast mushroom cloud ascending into the sky and, what seemed like ages later, to hear a deep explosive rumble. In the distance a dark line was just visible on the horizon and as the minutes passed he realised that it was growing larger as it sped towards them across the water. In desperation he swung the boat around to head west, away from the blast front and its attendant tsunami, but in his heart of hearts he knew that he could never outrun it.

PART 3

FEVER

1

From the welcome safety of Edinburgh, Ali witnessed the rapid collapse of social order in England. Much later she would recall it as a series of *tableaux vivants*, frozen moments representing a succession of terrible events, but at the time it was like watching someone sliding inexorably to their death down an icy mountainside. The images that reached the news sites were so compelling that it was impossible to look away from them, yet all too often Ali couldn't bear it and was to be found peering childlike through her fingers. It was one such occasion that, in retrospect at least, appeared to precipitate the whole sequence: the nailing up of James Curbishley at the behest of what she could only think of as a ravening mob. It was an image that she could not expunge from her memory, coming to stand for the whole Northwood Riot that followed. The 'Northwood Riot' – that was the name given to the day's events by the government-controlled propaganda machine – but 'riot' hardly captured it. It was more like a pitched battle and one that the government lost.

As far as she could work out from the confusion of reports and video fragments, a large section of the crowd broke away from the demonstration and marched on the Northwood Homestead. This was despite attempts to restrain them by the demonstration's co-ordinator who called vainly for all to remain at the peaceful protest on the common. Along with the familiar anti-Zeno placards, the red-and-black banners of the ERA were prominent among the breakaway group, and several of those filming zoomed in on the distinctive figure of Jerry Rowlands. On arrival at the Northwood gates they were met with a small military force. When it became clear that by sheer weight of numbers the crowd was intent on breaching the Northwood periphery, the soldiers were ordered to use their weapons, which they did, although with some reluctance as a number of observers noted. Rumours spread that several had declined to open fire on their fellow citizens and that their NCOs had been ordered to threaten and even to shoot them if they continued to refuse.

The truth of this was never established, either at the time or subsequently, but the allegations spread like wildfire serving to further enrage the crowd who stormed the gates and, in spite of fatalities, overwhelmed the military defenders. Making their way to the underground complex's main entrance, they routed the skeleton crew of guards and invaded the Homestead itself. Information was scarce as to what happened once they gained entry. Explosions were heard and there were certainly deaths and injuries on both sides. After an hour or so there was no more gunfire and, as smoke began billowing from the entrance and from ventilation ducts, the demonstrators emerged and could be seen carrying loot of various kinds: weapons, food and drink, even some small items of furniture. The Homestead continued to burn for several days, deemed impossible to contain by the short-staffed fire services, and a huge pall of smoke loomed threateningly over the north of the capital city.

Widespread dissemination of images, vlogs and news reports of these events then served to precipitate actions elsewhere across England. Where government safe havens were known to exist – and many were identified by local workers who had been involved in their construction and fitting out – they attracted massive demonstrations and variously successful attempts to emulate the Northwood assault. The already stretched forces of law and order proved incapable of exerting control over these large crowds, and in many regions, already fragmented by the emergence of independent local enclaves, the official authorities simply gave up and fled.

During all this, central government continued to issue pronouncements, condemnations, and fruitless appeals for calm. Somehow the location of the PM and the cabinet remained secret – it emerged later that they were concealed in a Homestead in deepest East Anglia – but that was not sufficient to keep them in power. After a month of continuous unrest and violence a group of high-ranking military officers took over the reins of government in a coup, although they insisted that this was approved by the elected administration and was only a temporary measure. Their first act was to declare a state of martial law.

The existing curfew was extended, travel even more restricted, and public assembly forbidden on pain of death, a policy which began to have some effect after a heavily publicised series of summary executions. The impact of the declaration across the breadth of the country was limited, however, since the military focused its entire resources on London and the home counties. Of course, the military junta continued to claim to be the legitimate government of the whole of England, but in practice everywhere outside the South-East became prey to local fiefdoms and varying degrees of chaos. Material infrastructure quickly disintegrated, leaving large areas without electricity or potable water and with limited food supplies. In both the established and newly emerging fiefdoms, those aspiring leaders who could find ways to satisfy their population's basic needs gained a degree of legitimacy, some of them by preying upon weaker neighbours, others by attempting to construct and defend local facilities. The net result of all this was that England collapsed into variously warring groups whose activities were overlaid upon unstable regional alliances. The dark ages had returned.

The rapidity of this decline in just a few months shocked Ali to the core, and in spite of her government's best efforts, as she looked around at her own country on this late August day she was registering similar warning signs. Only the week before in Dundee, which had been ravaged by a particularly aggressive strain of flu, there had been a near riot when it emerged that their local health services had been starved of drugs and funds in favour of support in other cities, most notably Edinburgh. This blatant inequality of treatment horrified Ali, though it no longer surprised her as it once would have done. Her faith in the government for whom she worked had taken a considerable battering since the first Zeno revelations.

So far, though, other than that one occasion in Dundee, there had not been massive shows of violent dissent of the kind now commonplace in England. In part this was because Scotland had put in place public health initiatives very early on in the crisis, which, however limited their effect in restricting the flu's spread, had at least demonstrated that the government was willing to do what it could. As well as this intervention, Scotland was not yet facing the scale of shortages that were feeding radical action south of the border. Although there were some constraints on energy consumption in the large cities, the now long-standing Scottish commitment to renewables meant that there had as yet been no sustained power cuts. Water supply was not a problem and unlikely to be so given Scottish rainfall, only provided that sufficient of the industry's workers remained healthy. Inevitably there were limitations on food since a significant proportion was still imported. This had not yet led to rationing other than by price, but the available range of foods was steadily decreasing and, Ali's father told her, in the Highlands the clandestine taking of red deer was on the rise. Since the deer population was much larger than ideal this was not really a problem, except for those landowners accustomed to treating deerstalking as a significant source of income and status. But as so many of their clients had historically been from the affluent English, this market had anyway collapsed – a fact that gave her father considerable satisfaction.

Nevertheless, Ali knew that sooner or later food shortages would intensify in Scotland even allowing for the fact that, at a little less than six million, her country's population was only a tenth of that of their southern neighbour. Though not yet self-sufficient, the Scottish authorities had for some years prior to independence sought ways of enhancing food security and minimising reliance on imports for basic foodstuffs. That process was by no means complete, but it had been sufficiently effective to ensure adequate provision thus far, even where the spread of flu had interrupted the supply chains.

There was an unintended consequence of this limited success, however, as Douglas had pointed out when Ali questioned the scale on which they were stockpiling food with her father. In the border regions it had become all too apparent to those on the English side that, unlike them, the Scots were as yet neither rationed nor suffering serious shortages. In consequence, as law and order failed in northern England, raiders increasingly crossed into Scotland and were soon identified as a new generation of Border Reivers, although unlike their historical namesakes they invaded only from south to north. It was just a matter of time and of growing desperation, Douglas suggested, before the Reivers would form larger alliances and venture as far as the Central Belt or perhaps even further. Scotland would once more face invasion from the south.

This was, Ali believed, a distant prospect, but one which she supposed that she should take seriously. Given the terrible things that were already happening in England, marauders from across the border seemed as likely as anything else. Even Sarah, who retained a residual loyalty to her country of birth, conceded that when faced with starvation otherwise decent people would resort to desperate measures. She had said as much that very evening when she and Ali had been setting up their regular CommsTab v-call to her mother – remarkably, the Comms infrastructure was still functioning, largely because it was internationally implemented and, apart from isolated areas where booster stations were required, ran direct via satellites.

For weeks now Sarah had been concerned that her mother looked very worn out and, under pressure from her daughter, Irene finally admitted that she had been laid low by a bad case of the flu and was still not fully recovered.

"Why didn't you tell me before?" a frantic Sarah asked.

"I didn't want to worry you unnecessarily," Irene replied. "And I'm much better now."

"But how did you manage on your own? When Hugh had the flu he couldn't even get out of bed."

"Oh, a friend came and nursed me through it. She's still here organising food and stuff."

"Who's that?"

"No one you know, Sarah, but she's been a great help. The food situation in London is getting difficult, that's true, although we're doing OK at the moment so we'll try to stick it out together."

Ali turned the CommsTab so that Irene could see her face. "Why don't you both try to make it up to here? You were a senior civil servant. Couldn't you use your influence to swing some travel arrangements?"

"No Ali, I don't think you grasp quite how bad things have got. It's pretty well impossible to travel anywhere, whoever you are. Martial law isn't much of a respecter of persons, even harmless unemployed old ladies. We'll just have to do our best here. But I'm really happy that you're all safe and especially that my lovely granddaughter will have a better chance of a future."

With that, they could see tears welling up in Irene's eyes and she hastily brought the call to an end. Sarah and Ali looked at each other in shared misery.

"Can't Douglas arrange something? Like he did with us," Sarah asked.

"No, I don't think so." Ali was despondent. "He's had to pull all his people out of England, and even the goods lorries aren't crossing the border now. It's too dangerous. If Irene can't fix anything I'm afraid there's not much we can do from this end."

"I'm scared, Ali," Sarah said, after a long pause. "Not just for mum but for us too. Things keep getting worse, and I'm afraid that just like we did in York we'll lose all this." She gestured around the room in which they were sitting. "It's a good apartment, Bruntsfield is a nice area, Charlotte's made new friends, and we can walk to work at the virology unit. But how long can it continue like this? And then what?"

"Maybe it won't get as bad as it is in England," Ali said, though not with any great conviction. "Perhaps someone will come up with a medical solution. There must be so much money and expertise being thrown at the Zeno problem now, right across the world."

"Well, it sure as hell won't be happening here." Sarah frowned. "Our research group are getting nowhere at all, just going round in circles. And from what we hear from researchers elsewhere that's par for the course. If a breakthrough is to happen, it will have to come from some completely unexpected line of inquiry. Don't hold your breath."

z z z

Irene and Julie sat at their kitchen table looking mournfully at the meagre supplies assembled in front of them.

"The rations are so low now that there's hardly enough for one person, let alone two," Irene complained. "Look at you, Julie. You were never fat but now you're skinny enough to be a supermodel. It's not healthy. We can't go on like this."

Julie nodded her agreement. "I'll just have to use my card and hope that they're not looking for me any more. Otherwise we're going to get weak and then we'll have no resistance to any infection that comes along."

"You can't do that," Irene said firmly. "We're under martial law. They're sure to be still looking for you after all the trouble your reporting caused. Come on, you've seen what's happened to some of the Zeno campaigners. Simply disappeared. No trace at all."

Julie knew that Irene was right. Rumours had reached her that both Rosa and Albert had not been seen since shortly after the Northwood demonstration, along with several other prominent figures in the anti-Zeno movement.

"I know, I know," she said, "but what else can we do?"

"I've been thinking about that. How about we try to pass you off as Sarah? We can go to the local Authentication Office and tell them that you're my daughter and that you managed to get all the way down here from York to look after me, but along the way you were robbed of your possessions, including identity documents. If we approach it right I think we can get them to issue you with authorisation for food rations."

Julie looked uncertain. "Do you really think they'll buy that? It doesn't sound too plausible. And won't their central computer records have a picture of Sarah on file?"

"If we cut your hair and give you an old pair of her glasses we might get away with it," Irene said. "Besides, the local systems are so rickety now that they may not even be able to check the central records. And anyway," she added mysteriously, "I think I know just what to do to make this work."

So it was that the very next day, with Julie's once long hair newly cut, they were to be found waiting patiently for attention in the Authentication Office on Streatham High Road. Irene had warned Julie to say as little as possible and to follow her lead. When it was finally their turn with the solitary Authentication Officer, Irene introduced herself as a retired Professor and Scientific Adviser, then immediately launched into a vivid account of her daughter's valiant struggle to reach her ill mother and the terrible travails that she had suffered along the way. The official did not look overly impressed with her story – no doubt he was accustomed to hearing much more fanciful appeals – but, grumbling about the lack of a computerised application system, he gave her a folder of forms to complete while he attended to another applicant. When they returned to his desk with the completed documents, he looked them over carefully.

"Hmmmn. Yes, that seems to deal with most things," he murmured, then, giving Irene a meaningful look, he handed the folder back to her and added, "I think I need one or two more details."

"Ah, I see," Irene said, and to Julie's astonishment withdrew several twenty-pound notes from her bag and surreptitiously slipped them into the folder before handing it back.

"Will that cover it?" she asked.

The official made a show of once more examining the contents of the folder. "Not quite," he said, returning it to Irene. "I think perhaps just a couple more details are needed."

Irene slid two more notes out of her bag and passed them over hidden in the folder.

The official smiled, albeit mirthlessly. "Yes, that does it I think. Just hold on while I sort out the card." He turned to Julie and told her to look into the lens of the camera mounted on his desk, pressed a key to take her picture, then disappeared into the back regions of the office.

"Oh god, he's going to report us," Julie whispered.

"No, I don't think so," Irene replied, looking unconcerned. "We're home clear."

After a minute or two the official returned and made a show of presenting Julie with her card.

"That will serve for identification as well," he told her. "The military are trying to streamline the process by having one card to serve all purposes, so keep it safe Miss… um… Johnson. That's right, isn't it." He nodded to Irene. "Good day, Professor," he said, waving them towards the door.

When they got outside Julie let out a huge sigh of relief.

"How did you know that would work?" she asked Irene. "We could both have ended up under arrest."

"Not at all," Irene replied. "You have to understand that when things get as bad as they are now, self-important bureaucrats, people who have been accustomed to exerting petty power, they realise that they have an opportunity to lord it even more and to improve their own situation at the same time. It's a recipe for corruption. They see that those further up the ladder have been making the most of it so they want their share too. That's why I went out of my way to use my title – to make the guy feel even more potent because he was in charge of me, a well-paid senior civil servant and professor. This is what happens when legitimate social order collapses. Everyday ethics go out the window and then self-interest rules."

"I never thought of you as so Machiavellian," Julie said, looking at Irene with new eyes.

"I'm not really," Irene replied, "but I did spend a lifetime in university and government circles so I had plenty of opportunity to see how it's done." She looked into the distance and smiled at this thought. "At least I learned something," she added, then, turning to Julie, took her by the arm and set off down the street.

"Let's go buy things," she said, as if the world was as it always had been and they were embarked on a mother–daughter shopping spree.

z z z

They brought him breakfast at 7am. A piece of mouldy cheese, some stale bread, and a bowl of what was described as coffee but bore little resemblance to it. He didn't deserve this, Georges thought, all he had wanted to do was feed his surviving children. He had lost his wife and his youngest son to the flu, he was out of work, and there was no food in the house. He had stolen just a little and he hadn't meant to hurt the shopkeeper. But only last month France had introduced the death penalty for food theft in a desperate attempt to halt the descent into chaos in provincial towns. Georges was the first to be sentenced in Lille. They had offered him the services of a priest, which he had refused. What comfort was there in a god who permitted all this misery? When they came for him at 8am he could think only of his children. What would happen to them now?

2

Although it was dusk there was no sign of light or life in the house. Hart was gliding from the shadow of one tree to the next, working his way around the garden fence while studying the building. Nothing moved. All was quiet apart from a blackbird offering up its final song of the day. Still Hart waited, watching patiently as the darkness deepened and silence enveloped him. Then, at last, he slipped through the rear garden gate and made his way up the path to the back door. Its flimsy lock did not delay him for long, giving access to a large kitchen. Now safely indoors, he switched on his head torch and set out to explore.

The downstairs rooms were exceptionally tidy, lived in yet not lived-in, as if someone had just completed the housework and had been called away. Slowly, stepping softly in case of creaking treads, he made his way up the stairs. Opening off a central landing there were four bedrooms, a bathroom, and a toilet. The door was closed on the third bedroom so he edged it open as quietly as he could. Immediately he was met by the smell of decay, foul enough to require him to control an impulse to retch. Holding a handkerchief over his nose and mouth he peered into the room. Lying on the bed, their hands intertwined, were two inert figures who on closer inspection revealed themselves to be the corpses of a man and a woman in the early stages of decomposition. On the bedside table lay a hypodermic and a small bottle.

Hart backed out, relieved to close the bedroom door on the sights and smells within. He stood for a minute at the top of the stairs recovering his composure then made his way back down to the kitchen. Systematically working his way through the storage cupboards he found a variety of dried and canned foods which he assembled on the work surface. If I'm careful there's enough here for several days, he thought. His food supplies had all but run out so discovering this source of both sustenance and shelter was more than welcome. He had been moving around on foot for the past couple of weeks, erratically working his way south, here and there breaking into deserted houses in search of food, though not always with this much success.

His journey had begun near Nottingham where his wife was staying with her sister. After the Northwood business he had been uncertain what to do, finally deciding to seek out Jill although not sure quite what he expected from her or, indeed, from himself. His car had carried him almost to Leicester before its charge had run out, leaving him no choice but to abandon it and cover the rest of the way on foot. He found this solitary wandering peculiarly satisfying and took his time working his way towards his destination via back roads and open countryside. On arrival he had received what might best be described as a qualified welcome. Jill was pleased to know that he was alive but the chasm that had opened between them after Rosemary's death was still there, a haunting from the past that neither of them could overcome.

He had stayed for several weeks, finally managing to tell her about his part in Curbishley's terrible fate. She showed little emotion at his revelation, murmuring only that Curbishley and people like him had brought it on themselves. Whether or not she approved of his actions was unclear. He suspected that she did not since, although she blamed the scientists and government for the death of her daughter and for the terrible plight now faced by so many innocent people, unlike Hart himself she was not by nature given to the corrupting pleasures of revenge. She was, he told himself, a fundamentally generous spirit, quite in contrast to his more calculating egotism. Perhaps it really was the case that opposites attract, or so he had often thought since he could find no other explanation for their relationship lasting as long as it had. But now that it was clearly over, and although neither Jill nor her sister made him feel especially unwelcome, he knew that it was time to move on. The truth was that stranded there in the Midlands he felt useless. He needed to be much closer to the centre of things, to be in a position to have some influence over events, however limited that might be.

His final departure was precipitated by a story picked up on one of the surviving underground newsfeeds, a report that the ERA and their now widely recognised leader, Jerry Rowlands, had established what was to all intents and purposes a large, semi-militarised commune on the 600-acre site of the former Whipsnade Zoo. This became the ultimate objective of his southward journey and was why he was now somewhere in the county of Bedfordshire, although he was not quite sure of his precise location. That was not navigational incompetence on his part. He had been content to drift cross-country just as long as he was heading broadly in the right direction. Now though, he thought, given this opportunity to stock up on food, perhaps it was time to make a final push towards his destination.

While considering this possibility he occupied himself in searching the remainder of the ground floor. From the neatly organised contents of a roll-top desk he learned the identities of the two bodies upstairs. They had both been doctors, recently retired, with a son, also a doctor, who had emigrated to Australia. He had emailed his parents regularly, messages which, touchingly, they had printed out and preserved in a binder. The last one was dated several weeks earlier and reported his increasingly desperate attempts to combat a serious flu epidemic in his practice in Melbourne. After that there were no more messages, perhaps from a failure of internet services or, more likely Hart surmised, because the son himself had succumbed to the virus. Yet more lives destroyed by state-sponsored hubris.

Depressed at this thought, and even more so at his previous complicity with the state in its steady promotion of incremental tyranny, Hart poured himself a large whisky from a bottle that he found in a kitchen cupboard. The same source yielded a box of candles, three of which, when distributed across a coffee table in the lounge, gave a more pleasant light than his head torch. He sank back into an armchair trying not to think about the bodies in the room above his head, and nursed the whisky while contemplating his next move. Jerry Rowlands' commune – if that was what it really was – would provide more permanent shelter and, he hoped, a context within which he could feel that he still had some purpose in life.

Exactly what that purpose might be was as yet unclear to him, but he was sure that he would not find it in his present solitary, peripatetic existence. Inspired by this renewed sense of commitment, he extracted a map and a small GPS unit from his bag. It was a more laborious mode of navigation than his CommsTab would provide but he needed to preserve the tablet's power until he could ensure a reliable source for recharging. As he had expected there was no electricity supply reaching the house. A few minutes' work gave him his present location which, he was pleased to discover from the map, was at most only a couple of days' walk from Whipsnade. He would rest here the next day, then push on to the ERA's stronghold. That decision taken, and unwilling to spend the night upstairs in company with the dead, he arranged his sleeping bag on the settee, blew out the candles, and settled down.

The following day passed quickly enough. Avoiding the bedroom with the corpses, Hart examined the entire house in search of anything that might prove useful. His most significant discovery was a cache of medical equipment and drugs, the latter of which he carefully sorted, retaining those that could be useful as trade goods as well as any medication that he might need to call upon personally. By now medical supplies must be running low, he reasoned, and even everyday drugs like standard analgesics could come to play a role in bartering. He also found a considerable sum in cash. Worth much less now, of course, given the ballooning inflation rate and the use of local currencies in some areas of the country, but still welcome. After being on the road for so long he would like to have taken a shower, or, better still, a bath, but he couldn't face immersing himself in cold water. A superficial wash would have to do. It was not as if he was likely to find himself in polite company any time soon. As evening and darkness approached he heated some soup on his camping stove and followed it with a can of baked beans. Then, intending to be up at first light, he retired to the settee and his sleeping bag.

He was on his way early next morning, heading broadly south-east towards Whipsnade but zigzagging across the countryside to avoid major settlements. He was in no hurry and it was fully two days before he arrived at the gates of the former zoo. Just outside the main entrance, where once there had stood a large red Whipsnade Zoo sign mounted on a plinth, there was now an even larger black-and-red Z with a white X superimposed upon it. Rowlands was ever the man for a symbolic gesture, Hart reflected, and with this one he had excelled himself, invoking both Curbishley's much publicised fate and a generalised desire to negate Zeno.

Hart approached the entrance cautiously. The former turnstiles and ticket booths had been replaced by a single closed access point with two guards posted outside and a CCTV camera above. As he neared them they levelled weapons in his direction.

"Just stop there," one of them called. "What do you want?"

Hart stopped as instructed and raised both hands, palms facing the guards. "I'm a friend of Jerry Rowlands," he said. "Please let him know that I'm here. My name is Jonathan Hart."

One of the guards nodded to the other who disappeared into a small booth by the door.

"You can lower your arms. But stay where you are," said the first guard, keeping his weapon directed at Hart. "Watch the birdie," he added, glancing up towards the camera.

After several minutes the other guard emerged. "We're to let him in. There's someone inside who'll escort him to the Chief."

Hart smiled to himself as he was admitted. Jerry's become a Chief now, he thought. There's yet another departure from anarchist principles. A woman waiting for him inside the entrance introduced herself as Jerry's PA and walked Hart to a house set on its own in a pleasantly wooded area. Standing at the door was Rowlands himself, beaming a welcome.

"Well, well. Jonny Hart shows up again just like the proverbial bad penny," he called out as Hart approached. "What have you brought for me this time?"

"Just myself I'm afraid," Hart replied, as Rowlands dismissed the woman with a "Thank you, Sylvia" and guided Hart into a comfortably equipped office-cum-lounge.

"Have a seat, Jonny," he said, gesturing towards an armchair. "Fancy a cuppa?"

"Tea would be good if you have it. It's been a long walk."

Rowlands busied himself making tea while talking to Hart over his shoulder. "Where have you come from?" he asked.

"Initially from Nottingham. I'd been up there to see my wife who's staying with her sister. But it's been a circuitous route since then."

"Here you are," Rowlands said, handing him a cup. "There's sugar and milk – the milk's from our dairy cattle. Make the most of the sugar though. I don't think it's going to last much longer." He sat down opposite Hart. "So, if you haven't got another gift for me what is it that brings you here?"

"I thought I might be useful to you in this enterprise." Hart gestured to take in the room and the Whipsnade parkland visible through the window. "I saw online that you had got a community going and thought I might have helpful skills."

Rowlands laughed. "You're looking for a job? No longer Director of DSD then? Curbishley told me all about you before he came to that sticky end. He wasn't very complimentary."

"I can imagine," said Hart, pulling a face. "No, I knew better than to try returning to the DSD after giving him to you. I'd burned my boats. But I've got a lot of information in here." He tapped his forehead. "I know how the security services work and a great deal about the army people who are running the South-East. You're bound to have confrontations with them sooner or later. After all, it can't be far from here to their northern boundary. I could do a job on your security."

Rowlands nodded. "Yes, I suppose that's true. You know they've started calling their controlled area the Homeland. It covers London, Kent and Surrey, plus a few odd fingers stretching out into the countryside. They claim to be governing it in the name of the King, for Christ's sake. They get the poor bugger to do broadcasts from the palace to encourage his starving subjects."

"That's a lot of people," Hart said, pausing to calculate. "Even allowing for flu deaths they must have at least ten million mouths to feed. Sounds like a potentially unstable situation."

"I've only got a few hundred here," Rowlands observed ruefully, "and they're hard enough to keep fed and happy. Still, at least they're committed to the project."

"So what exactly is the project?" enquired Hart.

"Initially it was just to create a defendable community and to ensure lines of supply. But now..." Rowlands paused, looking thoughtful.

"Now...?" Hart encouraged him.

"Well, there are differing views. You have to understand that we're only self-sustaining up to a point so we depend on maintaining good relations with the people living around us. So far that's worked out OK. So far. But in the longer run we're going to be threatened on two sides. To the east there's an evangelical preacher who is gaining massive support across Essex. They're calling themselves the Peculiar People, though they don't have much in common with the original nineteenth-century sect. The old Peculiar People were pacifists but this lot are aggressive and see it as their god-given destiny to convert all us sinners by force of arms. And to the south, of course, we have the Homeland. So far they've left us alone – they've got their work cut out simply maintaining what they have – but they still claim to be England's legitimate rulers so they may yet get to be expansionist."

Hart frowned. "And they both have access to seaborne trade and resources, while you're landlocked. You could easily be starved out in the end."

"Yeah," Rowlands replied. "So now I've got militants who think that we should take the fight to the enemy. That we should be actively recruiting discontented people. In effect, forming an army of our own. One group want to focus on the Homeland, fight a guerrilla war on its edges, a war of attrition. Another lot, who are even less realistic, think that we just have to get out there and the people will spontaneously rise up and join us in revolution. So far neither group have got much in the way of wider support among the Whipsnade folk, but as things get worse, who knows?"

Hart smiled. "Strikes me that you do need someone with my intelligence experience just to keep tabs on your own people let alone to track what's going on beyond your boundaries."

"You may be right. And I could certainly do with a person who is independent of those cliques and who can keep a calm head." Rowlands smiled wryly. "Bit like old times in Oxford."

"Though rather more at stake now," Hart said, returning the smile. "So, I can stay?"

"Yes, why not? I'd quite enjoy having an intelligence agent working for rather than against me. It would make a change. We'll find you some living space and see how it goes."

And then, with what was to Hart an all too familiar mischievous grin, Rowlands held out his arms and announced: "Welcome to the revolution!"

z z z

St Peter's Square was packed to overflowing. The new Pope, Gregory XVII, stood at his apartment window and offered up a prayer which echoed from the speakers surrounding the throng. His predecessor had died from the flu, as had many in the Holy City, and his election had been rather hastily pursued in an attempt to shore up the commitment of an increasingly sceptical worldwide congregation. When he reached the point in his prayer where he sought deliverance for the faithful from the terrible pestilence now afflicting the world, there came a loud explosion from somewhere in among the colonnades and a large banner was unfurled along that edge of the crowd. It had a simple message, offered in both Italian and English: 'God is Dead'. Those of the faithful near enough to do so turned on the demonstrators, tearing down their banner and trampling it and them into the cobbles. But even as they did so, fireworks exploded all around the colonnades while banners were undraped offering up that same message in most of the world's main languages. Pope Gregory quickly retreated into his apartment as behind him the square erupted into ungodly chaos.

3

In Scotland that winter was widely agreed to be a harsh one. This was not because of particularly inclement weather, although there was significantly more snow than there had been in recent years. It reflected, rather, the death of so many from a rampant epidemic of the flu. With the arrival of the first stirrings of spring the rate of infection eased, but by then recorded deaths for the winter months had passed the 400,000 mark. Nor were these deaths confined to the most vulnerable. The virus was indiscriminate in taking the old, the young, and those whose general health and fitness might hitherto have been thought to make them least likely to succumb. As well as leaving survivors mourning the loss of friends and family, this surge in wholesale mortality had a devastating psychological impact. However inadvisably, many had comforted themselves with the thought that the flu predominantly took the weakest. Now they had to face the fact that Zeno was capricious and that all were insecure in its path.

Of course, this had already become clear in many other parts of the world, not least to Scotland's immediate south, but thus far the Scots themselves had proved uncharacteristically positive in the face of the crisis. Ali had often wondered about that. The stereotypical Scot was not perceived as a congenital optimist; indeed, the adjective 'dour' had historically been all too common in application to her co-nationals. But finally achieving independence from the Auld Enemy, as her football-supporting father liked to describe the English, seemed to have brought about something of a cultural change. The perhaps illusory sense of now having control of their own fate had created a mood of optimism altogether unjustified in such a globalised world, a belief that things could and would be made much better. Increasingly Ali had come to think that this faith was misplaced, especially since serious levels of deprivation were still to be found all over the country. In the estates that surrounded her city, for example, in the likes of Craigmillar, Niddrie or Wester Hailles, there was as much poverty as there ever had been.

Such thoughts were preoccupying her now because in the past few weeks trouble had erupted in and around the estates. Their often disaffected young men and women had always been potential recruits for the criminal gangs that had in the past marred Edinburgh's respectable image, but now they had been joined in their sense of grievance by whole families, both old and young. This had been precipitated by the fact that people were starving. There was no other way to put it now that widespread food shortages had pushed up prices. For those who could afford it, that was still just about manageable, but the poor had no way of feeding themselves and neither the state nor charities were in a position to provide for them. At first, violence and theft had been largely confined to the estates, all the more so since Police Scotland had given up on a presence within their boundaries. But it was not long before desperate people, whether singly or in gangs, invaded more affluent neighbouring areas, looting such shops as were still open and terrorising residents into yielding up their supplies.

This was just what Douglas had predicted, Ali thought morosely, precisely the situation in preparation for which they had been transferring resources to her father's Argyll home. If events continued after this fashion they would soon have to implement their plan and flee the city. It was for this reason that she was now sitting staring vacantly out of the window in Douglas's New Town apartment in company with Sarah, Hugh and Charlotte, as well as Ravi, Eleanor, and their son Iain. They were waiting for Douglas to bring the latest intelligence so that they could decide the best way forward, but he was already over thirty minutes late.

Suddenly Ravi's voice interrupted Ali's ruminations. "Isn't that right, Ali?" he said.

"Sorry, I was miles away. Isn't what right?"

"I was just telling Hugh about the chaos in the Department and the fact that, in effect, we're all on notice to quit."

"Yes, it's a weird situation. They're still paying us but they've nothing for us to do, and they don't want us going into the office in case we spread infection." Ali half smiled. "At least there are no more Baby Bug Hunter meetings to drive me crazy," she added, then, nodding towards Hugh and Sarah, "it's only your group who are continuing work."

"And we're not really getting anywhere," Hugh replied. "Still running up against a brick wall. Zeno is not giving up its secrets at all easily."

"But it is worth continuing," Sarah interjected, half paying attention to the adults and half focusing on the old-fashioned board game, Ludo, which she was playing with the two children. "We know more than we did at the start even if it's not directly relevant to a cure or a vaccination. You never know. There might be a breakthrough."

Ali smiled at her. "Ever the optimist," she said, "that's why I need you around. Without you I'd tumble into the slough of despond."

Charlotte gave her a puzzled look. "What's the slough of despond, Auntie Ali?"

"Well," Ali began, looking around at the others for help and finding that none was forthcoming.

"Yes Auntie Ali," said Hugh, "what is one of those?"

Just then, much to Ali's relief, they heard the apartment's front door open and a shout from Douglas.

"Sorry we're late. Unavoidably delayed."

He entered the room followed by two men, one of whom was Jimmy, their driver from the border crossing, while the other was new to them all.

"You remember Jimmy," Douglas said, adding for Jimmy's benefit, "that's Eleanor and Ravi and wee Iain." Then, gesturing to the other man, "This is Jimmy's partner, Kenny. I've invited them along to join us."

Introductions complete, Douglas sat down beside Ali, looked around at the waiting company and began counting off points.

"I've got various bits and pieces of news for you, gleaned from all sorts of sources but reliable I think. First, the trouble in the Edinburgh estates is getting worse. The looting seems to be more organised now, presumably by the gangs, and violence is spreading further into the city. Nor is it only here. Glasgow, where Jimmy comes from, has even worse problems, and there are similar situations in Aberdeen and Dundee. Second, the disturbances in the Borders are spreading further north. Bands of Reivers have plundered towns like Kelso and Melrose and Peebles…"

"And Coldstream?" Ali interrupted, concerned for Uncle Bill and Jess.

"Yes, I'm afraid so," Douglas replied. "Most of the towns down there have suffered and there have been claims of isolated incidents as far north as Pathhead. That's getting pretty close to Edinburgh. There have been raiders over on the west side too – I've seen reports from Ayrshire and some of the smaller towns south of Glasgow."

He paused for a moment taking in their gloomy faces.

"Third," he continued, "this is still a bit vague, but it looks as if something like a war has broken out between various nations' fishing fleets in the North Sea and the Atlantic. If that's true then another significant source of food in Scotland will soon become even more curtailed."

Once more he stopped to survey the group until finally and firmly announcing: "I think it's time to take action. We're still safe here right now but it can't last much longer."

Ali listened but said very little as possibilities were tossed to and fro until, after half an hour or so, they arrived at broad agreement on a timetable. In ten days' time the three no-longer-working adults would move to Argyll, taking with them the two children whose schools had long since closed. Shuttles were still running into the Highlands so they ought to be able to travel without difficulty. Once there, they would help her father make ready the house next door for the arrival of the rest of the group. This house had been a holiday rental owned by the London-based daughter of the original occupants and for several years she had paid Ali's father a token sum to look after it. Nothing had been heard from her since early in the epidemic, nor had there been any take-up from holidaymakers, so for all practical purposes the house was in their hands. The others, whose jobs would no doubt disappear soon enough, would join them when that happened or when the situation in Edinburgh became too dangerous. They would use the lorry to travel and to carry everyone's possessions, as well as bringing additional supplies.

Once the details had been agreed the visitors dispersed in their various directions leaving Ali and Douglas alone.

"What's the matter, Alison?" Douglas asked. "You've been unusually quiet and you're looking very pissed off."

"Well, yes I am," she conceded.

"But why? We've settled on a workable plan. This was bound to happen sooner or later. We always knew we would have to move in the end."

"I know. It's not that. It's Jimmy and Kenny. God, those names, they sound like they're a fifth-rate Scottish comedy duo."

Douglas looked at her quizzically. "What about them? They're decent guys and I've known Jimmy for years." He paused. "Do you have a problem with them being gay?"

"What?" Ali exploded. "No, of course not. It's you I've got the fucking problem with. You bring two more people into the group without consulting any of us, without so much as even mentioning it to me. You should have discussed it with us all first."

Douglas, taken aback at the intensity of Ali's fury, held up his hands in capitulation. "I'm sorry," he said, "but they'll be very useful. They've got practical skills that the rest of us may not have. You've seen it with Jimmy and the lorry already, and Kenny's a hands-on engineer – one of those folk who can fix broken stuff and make anything work."

"That's not the point," Ali sighed, exasperated. "You really don't get it, do you? You can't just take decisions as serious as that and expect everyone to fall into line. That's the kind of shit managerialism that led to Zeno in the first place. We've got to get away from this behaviour – I suppose you'd call it strong leadership – or we'll just end up making the same mistakes again."

Douglas gave her a hard stare. "But you chose all the people who were here today," he insisted. "I didn't have a say in that. They're all your friends."

"But you knew them too and we talked about it way back at the beginning." Ali stood up and began gathering her things together. "I can't help it if you didn't have any friends to suggest – that's your problem," she added acidly, regretting the insult even as she said it, but too angry to bring herself to take it back.

"That's not fair, Alison, and you know it. I was happy to go along with your suggestions. Now I come up with a couple of useful people and you take exception."

Ali shook her head. "I already told you – it's not the people, it's the way of doing it. But this isn't getting us anywhere, Douglas. I'm going home. I'll see you later in the week."

As she made her way along Princes Street, Ali felt her anger slowly subside only to be replaced by feelings of guilt. She was right in principle, she knew, but she shouldn't have lost her temper. Douglas was doing his best to help them all and there would have been much better ways to make her point. The stress was getting to her, she told herself, you can't watch your world falling apart without it taking its toll. She'd once had so many hopes for her life, for her country, for a good future, and now they were all in ruins. Well, maybe not entirely in ruins. She had Douglas, or at least she hoped she still had him despite the way that she had treated him today.

Dusk was beginning to slip into night as she turned up The Mound. The Princes Street Gardens away to her right were completely dark now, as was the castle above them. Winter had brought energy-saving measures and they had not yet been lifted. Perhaps now they never would be, Ali supposed. Yet another small step along the road to social disintegration. Moving into the warren-like Old Town she became aware of just how dark it was, with only the occasional lamp illuminating its immediate surrounds. The streets were deserted. What on earth was she doing walking alone at night in this now deeply troubled city? Her nerves were jangling and she grew increasingly convinced that she was being followed, that there was someone in the darkness behind her. Unbidden, Coleridge's famous lines came to mind, a passage that she knew very well and had first encountered in a short ghost story by M.R. James.

Like one, that on a lonely road
Doth walk in fear and dread,
And having once turned round walks on,
And turns no more his head;
Because he knows, a frightful fiend
Doth close behind him tread.

Defying the poem's advice she several times halted and looked back, seeing no one but becoming more and more uneasy. At last – it seemed to take for ever – she was in Forrest Road and at her door. Greatly relieved, with one final look behind her she retreated into the safety of the building, for a moment leaning up against the inside of the closed door breathing heavily. Fear was an insidious emotion, she reflected, but maybe it was something they would all have to learn to live with.

Some way back down Forrest Road a figure emerged from the shadows and stood for a moment looking at the closed door. That's her safe then, Douglas thought, as he turned around to make his own way home.

z z z

Irene was wandering along in a daydream when she ran into the soldiers. Her mind was occupied by memories of a particularly delightful holiday on the Greek island of Santorini back in her student days. She could still vividly recall the beauty of the light and how it set off the contrast between the white walls and blue domes of the tiny churches scattered across the island. Her musings were rudely interrupted, however, when she rounded a corner to see half a dozen camouflage-clad soldiers coming down either side of the street towards her, ducking in and out of doorways, weapons at the ready. The contrast with her memories could hardly have been more extreme. So it's come to this, she thought, in my old age I'm living in a military dictatorship as bad as any suffered in Greece.

She halted and moved to the side of the pavement to allow the soldiers free passage, turning her head away to avoid any confrontational eye contact. Then, as they came closer one of them called out.

"Hey, Granny J, how are you doing?"

There was only one person, Peter, who called her that. She had met him several months earlier when in a similar encounter with soldiers she had slipped on the icy pavement and he had caught her as she fell.

"Careful Granny," he had said, "you'll hurt yourself."

"I'm not your Granny," she had replied haughtily, irritated at her unsought need for his helping hand. "My name is Mrs Johnson and I'll thank you to call me that."

"OK," he said, "then I'll call you Granny J."

This was accompanied by such an infectious grin that Irene could do nothing other than smile back and, more gracefully now, thank him for his help. Ever since, whenever she encountered him with his patrol he hailed her with her new title and stopped to chat. Truth be told, she was now quite fond of the soubriquet, dubbing him Corporal Peter in return.

"So, Corporal Peter," she said, "I haven't seen you for weeks. Where have you been hiding? I've missed your refined conversation."

He laughed. "Good to know that my efforts are appreciated," he told her, signalling to his colleagues to wait. "We were transferred for a while, up near Loughton. The PeePees were pushing down through Essex and causing trouble so we were sent as reinforcements."

"PeePees?" Irene inquired.

"Sorry. The Peculiar People. The religious maniacs led by that mad Essex preacher. There's almost an army of them now. Anyway, we made them retreat with their tails between their legs and now we're back here to look after you." He paused, checking that the other soldiers were out of earshot, and then continued almost in a whisper. "Is your daughter still with you?"

Only just recalling that he thought Julie was her daughter, she managed to stop herself from saying that Sarah was in Scotland. "Yes," she said. "Why do you ask?"

"A warning. I hear that the Recruiters are coming into this area the week after next. While you might be safe – they don't generally take the over-sixties – she certainly won't be. Young and able-bodied is just what they're looking for. They'll know where the two of you live. If you can find a hiding place, then do it."

"Thanks, Peter," replied the now worried Irene. "We'll see what we can do."

"Great, great," he said, voice back to full volume. "We must get along. You take care Granny J. See you soon."

Irene walked slowly on towards home, disconcerted by Peter's warning. 'Recruiters' was a euphemism for what amounted to modern press gangs, introduced by the military government to provide labour for the Work Camps that they had set up in the Kent and Surrey countryside. Rumours abounded about the camps. Work was long and hard, and although workers were at least fed regularly – how else could they be kept working? – the rations were the absolute minimum. Most of the camps were processing agricultural products, planting, tending, harvesting and packaging basic foodstuffs, though some, it was said, were in the manufacturing business. Quite what they manufactured remained a matter for whispered speculation. It was unwise to be heard speaking of the camps and those who were recruited did not return. It was as if they had disappeared through a wormhole into an alternative universe, never to be seen again.

At home, after depositing the rather dismal fruits of her shopping expedition, Irene sought out Julie.

"I've bad news, Julie. I ran into Corporal Peter and he says that the Recruiters will be coming here in a couple of weeks."

Julie's eyes widened. "That *is* bad news," she said. "What can we do?"

"I don't know. Peter said that if we could find somewhere to hide then we should do that. You, in particular. He didn't seem to think that they'd be very interested in me. Too old and decrepit for the Work Camps."

"But where could we go?" Julie asked. "From what I've heard about the other areas that they've been to, they come in with dogs and thermal sensors and stuff so they can find anybody who is hiding. I don't see how we could escape them. And I certainly don't want to be sent to the camps. Just last week someone in the rations queue was telling me about a girl they'd heard of who'd escaped. She said that many of the younger women were taken to special R & R compounds for the soldiers. Brothels in all but name."

"Yes," Irene said, "I've heard that too. But we don't know if it's true. There are so many rumours going around."

Julie shook her head. "True or not," she said, "I wouldn't want to take the chance. Besides, I've no intention of being picked up for a Work Camp either. I could easily get recognised and arrested. After all, they were looking for me back when I first came here."

"You're right, Julie. We can't hide around here. We need to leave. Maybe get out of the Homeland altogether."

"Yes," Julie agreed. "Or at least I do. You'll be safe enough if you stay. Like Peter said, they don't send older people to the camps."

"Maybe not, but I've no intention of staying here without you. If we're going to run for it then we should do so together. The only question is where do we go? If I thought we could make it I'd try for Scotland and Sarah. They're expecting to move to Ali's father's place in Argyll when things get too bad in Edinburgh. But I don't think we'd have any chance of reaching them. It's too far and very lawless between here and there."

"Uh-huh, you're right about that." Julie stopped, lost in thought. "There is one possibility I've been thinking about. Remember I told you about my family being farmers over in the Malvern area?"

Irene nodded. "Yes, I remember. But you said that you didn't get on with them at all well. They disapproved of you taking off to become a journalist and even more so after you broke the Zeno stories."

"That was just my dad really – he's very reactionary. But I've kept in touch with my brother, as far as I could anyway. We used to be very close. He pretty much runs the farm now. That might be somewhere to go and it's a lot nearer than Scotland."

"True enough, but it's still a long way to walk. It's a shame there are no shuttles any more." Irene stared miserably out the window into the back garden until, suddenly, her face lit up.

"I've got it!" she exclaimed, and leaping to her feet she retrieved a bunch of keys from a kitchen drawer and headed for the back door. "Come with me."

Puzzled, Julie followed her down the garden where she unlocked the side door to the garage. Julie had never been in there and was surprised to see an ancient car standing on bricks. "We couldn't use that," she said, pointing at the vehicle.

"No, no, of course not. It hasn't run for years. It was Robin's pet restoration project. No, look here," she said, pointing at the wall behind them. There, mounted on hooks, were two touring bicycles, one red and one blue.

"The blue one's mine. The red one was Robin's. We did a lot of touring and camping with them until he got too ill." Irene paused at the memory. "Good times," she said, adding "we'd just need to lower the saddle a bit and that one would be fine for you. You can ride a bike can't you?"

"Yes, of course I can," Julie said, taking a closer look at the bikes. "They're good ones, aren't they?"

"Yes they are. Cost a fortune back then. And look here." Irene almost ran to a steel cupboard at the back of the garage, unlocked it and flung open the door. It was full of gear – panniers, helmets, toolkits, a tent, and a whole array of bicycle spare parts. "We can ride and camp," Irene said triumphantly. "That's how we'll do it."

She reached into the cupboard, pulled out a file of documents, then started thumbing through them. "Look," she said, thrusting one towards Julie. "This is a map of cycle route 57 – it goes to Cheltenham and then on to Malvern. It's about 130 miles. We can do that in a matter of days, unfit though we are."

Julie felt herself being drawn into Irene's infectious excitement. "Yes, I suppose we could," she said, trying hard to maintain a more sober tone. "But we'll still have to find a way past the Homeland borders. They must be guarded."

For a moment Irene looked crestfallen. "True," she said. Then, cheering up a little, "We'll need to do a bit of training during next week so we'll cycle out in that direction every day and see how it looks."

Julie smiled at Irene's refusal to be cowed and, wrapping her arms around the older woman, murmured in her ear, "You're right. We can do this, I know we can. We can get away."

z z z

Fayetteville, which sits close to the Ozarks in northwest Arkansas, had a reputation as a cultured city, largely because of the long-standing presence of the University of Arkansas and its many thousands of students. In recent months, however, it had been hit hard by successive waves of infection. The seeds of fear that this engendered had fallen onto fertile fundamentalist soil and given rise to an apocalyptic and deeply anti-science religious movement. On this particular day its Soldiers of God, as they liked to call themselves, surrounded the University's Department of Biomedical Engineering eager to take revenge on the sinners within. They burst into the building and swept through its laboratories and offices, dragging their occupants outside where they were paraded before the mob. Egged on by their evangelical leaders, the Soldiers tossed their captives one by one into the hysterical crowd where they simply disappeared, as if devoured by an inhuman creature that now roared its hatred into the blue Arkansas sky.

4

Hart walked a circuit of the Whipsnade grounds on a daily basis. In part that was to check on the security precautions that he had put in place, including a company of armed guards that he had recruited from the restless young men and women of the collective. He knew very well how bored they could get patrolling the perimeter so he hoped that his periodic presence would do something towards focusing their attention and sustaining their morale. But more important was the fact that he took an unexpected pleasure in wandering past the enclosures that had once served as homes for such a rich variety of animals. Hart had been taken to Whipsnade Zoo as a child and nurtured remarkably clear memories of the creatures that he had encountered there for the very first time. In his mind's eye he could see them still: in this section, the pair of tigers; over there the giraffes; down here the rhinos. He had always intended to bring Rosemary to Whipsnade in the hope of engendering in her the same wonder that had entranced him. But somehow he was always too busy, there was too much work to be done, so they had never managed the outing. And now it was too late.

Always quick to suppress such unwelcome reflections, on this day Hart was instead contemplating the fate of the once resident animals. Jerry Rowlands had told him that none of the more exotic beasts had remained when his group had forcibly taken over the site. As far as he knew they had either been removed to London Zoo quite early in the crisis, or else, as the capacity to feed them had declined, they had been killed. Some remained of course, notably those herbivores that could more or less look after themselves and would be a continuing source of sustenance for the human residents. There were still quite large numbers of fallow deer who contested the grazing with the sheep and cattle that the ERA community had seized from the surrounding farmland. There also remained a small group of yaks, often sought out by Hart who was fascinated by their extraordinary appearance, and there were large numbers of wallabies still bouncing around the parkland exhibiting little or no fear of the humans with whom they shared their home. Hart had not yet brought himself to sample their meat but was told that it was both succulent and high in protein.

Just then a wallaby unconcernedly crossed his path, such a captivating creature that he hoped never to be sufficiently desperate to resort to one for food. Today all he desired from the animal population was distraction and entertainment. The whole depressing morning had been taken up with one of the regular Collective Councils, enterprises meant to ensure everyone's active involvement in the group's business but more often than not characterised by fruitless squabbles among the different political persuasions. Today's meeting had been such an occasion, with the two main factions sniping at one another throughout. In private conversation with Hart, Rowlands had labelled these cliques with their own variations on the ERA's acronym. One group – the English Republican Army in Rowlands' designation – were committed to overthrowing the Homeland government and its monarch by guerrilla warfare, modelling themselves on a highly romanticised vision of the IRA's activities in the previous century. The other faction – the Existentially Radical Arseholes to Rowlands – seemed to believe that they had only to march out into the world and the oppressed peoples would immediately rally to their revolutionary summons. Fortunately neither of these views prevailed, but their mutual antagonism made all but impossible any semblance of rational discussion and coherent decision-making.

The net result was that most important decisions were taken by 'The Chief' as Rowlands had come to be known, to whom Hart was now effectively principal adviser and second in command. It was not a position that he had sought, nor particularly wanted, but his effectiveness in creating a security team, as well as his aloofness from the factional infighting, had made him indispensable to his former Oxford contemporary. So it was that, having almost completed his full circuit, it was to Rowlands' quarters that he was now headed for their daily meeting when he was stopped by a voice calling out from behind him.

"Jonathan. Jonathan Hart. Hang on!"

Turning round he saw a young woman jogging along the path towards him. This was Jennifer Connolly, one of three people whom Hart had singled out as having the skills necessary for special intelligence duties beyond the Whipsnade boundaries. Her task had been to infiltrate the Peculiar People and report back regularly on the Essex sect's intentions and activities, something which she had thus far managed very effectively. But she was not due to report for at least another two weeks so her presence did not bode well.

"Hello Jenny," he said when she had caught up with him. "I wasn't expecting you. What's happened?"

"They've been on the move," she panted, struggling to recover her breath, "and they may come this way."

This was a possibility that Hart had feared for some time. The PeePees, as they were now widely known to non-adherents, had an evangelical propensity to spread their word and to do so at the metaphorical and sometimes literal point of a gun. Sooner or later it had been inevitable that they would seek to expand out of their present territory in East Anglia, making Whipsnade a possible obstruction along the way.

"Oh bugger," Hart murmured to himself. Then, to Jenny, "I'm just on my way to see the Chief anyway. Best you come with me and give the details to both of us."

Jenny's account was not such as to offer Hart and Rowlands any comfort. She had managed to insinuate herself into one of the PeePees' more activist groupings, well looked upon by the leadership and, therefore, frequently favoured by the presence of the demagogue who had founded the sect – a charismatic figure sufficiently narcissistic to have unselfconsciously named himself 'The Chosen One' or, sometimes, 'The

Prophet'. Jenny's view was that he was clinically insane but to his followers he was seen as their and the world's only hope of salvation. In recent weeks he had been preaching in ever wilder terms, insisting that the time had come for his people to rise up against the sinners and, through sanctified violence, recapture the world for the faithful, so ensuring their entry to paradise on the coming day of judgment.

A large body of supporters, Jenny among them, had been prevailed upon to march south towards the Homeland's northern border which roughly followed the route of the old London orbital motorway. This they had crossed, overcoming limited resistance from the border guards, but then, close to the small town of Loughton, they had been confronted by a much larger force. A chaotic pitched battle ensued in which the PeePees had been outmanoeuvred and outgunned by the Homeland's military, whereupon they had retreated in some disorder. To Jenny's astonishment this bloody setback had not diminished the evangelical fervour of The Chosen One or his followers. They had, rather, seen it as a test of their faith, one to which they must respond with further expeditions. This was their divine mission, or so The Chosen One insisted. But they would not go south again. At Loughton the Lord had revealed to them the error of their ways. Instead they would go west, drawing ever more converts into their fold until they were such a multitude that the disciples of Satan in the Homeland would be overcome.

Jenny's account was followed by a lengthy silence. Then, at last, Rowlands exhaled heavily. "Well," he said, "I suppose we always knew this might happen sooner or later. Do you have any idea what route they're likely to take when they do decide to come this way?"

"No, nothing official," Jenny replied. "These decisions aren't discussed publicly. They get announced in the course of the Prophet's sermonising." She managed a wry smile. "*Ex Cathedra*, you might say."

"Any rumours even?" Hart asked.

"Gossip maybe," she replied. "Rumours would be a strong word for it, but there is a common belief that Luton would be a useful outpost to have. People seem to think that there is already some support for the PeePees there."

Hart nodded. "Yes, I think that might be true. Back when the Peculiar People were just getting going and I still had access to intelligence sources, it was reported that there were groups in Luton who were amenable to their message."

"That's what, about ten miles to the north-east?" Rowlands asked. "I suppose they might bypass us if they did go there. Jenny, have you ever heard any gossip about us?"

"No, neither Whipsnade nor ERA have ever been mentioned in my hearing. I think they probably don't even know that we're here."

Hart shook his head. "Once they're in this area they'll find out soon enough," he said. "We'll need warning of when they're on the move, whatever the route. Are you able to go back, Jenny? Say no if you think it's too dangerous."

"I don't think they suspect me of anything. They've no reason to. When I come here they think I'm visiting my sick mother. I don't see why I shouldn't go back."

"OK." Hart thought for a minute. "If you return to Essex tomorrow and keep your eyes and ears open, you can let us know when a move is imminent. In fact, as soon as anything seems remotely certain you should make yourself scarce and get back here as quickly as you can."

"Yes, it would be great if you could do that, Jenny," Rowlands added. "You've done magnificent work already. Thank you. Now you go and get some food, see your friends, have a peaceful night and go back in the morning."

Jenny, looking part embarrassed and part pleased at the compliment, got up and smiled a goodbye to both men.

"What do you think, Jonny?" Rowlands asked as soon as she was gone.

"I think we need to make some contingency plans. Even if they do head for Luton they might well send a reconnaissance party to check us out and we wouldn't want to have a confrontation with them. We might fight off a small recon group but that would probably bring them all down on us and we wouldn't stand a chance. We need to find a way of hiding our supplies and dispersing into the countryside until they've passed through. Time for some hard decisions, I'm afraid."

z z z

Julie's legs were aching. Her calf and thigh muscles felt as if they were on fire, and her bottom – well, she thought, it's so numb that I'm not even sure that it's there any more. She eased herself further back into the hot bath, closed her eyes and told her body to relax. They had just returned from their third day-long cycling trip, an experience that appeared to have had little or no physical impact on Irene but had left Julie painful and exhausted. Julie's problem, Irene insisted, lay in her failure to make proper use of the many gears on her bike. Faced with uphill slopes she simply increased the force applied to her pedals rather than changing gear and continuing in the same cadence, an error that unnecessarily stressed her hitherto little-used muscles. She would get it right tomorrow, Julie promised herself. She would have to soon since there was only a little time left before their journey started in earnest.

Over the three days they had reconnoitred various possible escape routes. Major roads to the west were barricaded and constantly manned by armed troops, even though they now carried little or no traffic. The backroads, however, were controlled only by patrols. If they could time it right it would be possible to slip through the notional Homeland border and into the countryside beyond. But they hadn't been able to agree on the best route or the best time to start their ride. The truth was that neither of them had any basis on which to make a sensible judgement and both were reluctant to impose a decision on the other. Julie sighed and lowered her head into the water. Perhaps she would feel better after washing her hair.

On breaking surface she realised that Irene was knocking on the door.

"Julie, can I come in? I've thought of what we might do."

"Yes, of course," Julie called. "It's not locked."

Looking pleased with herself, Irene perched on the toilet seat.

"Tomorrow you can have a rest from cycling," she said. "We'll see if we can waylay Corporal Peter's patrol. He can give us advice."

"Really? Can we trust him? He might report us."

Irene shook her head. "No, I don't think there's any chance of that. He's a good person, I'm certain. Besides, it was him that warned us about the Recruiters and told us to hide. I'm sure he'll help us if he can."

"OK, if you think so." Julie smiled. "If nothing else my bum and legs will be grateful for the respite."

"It's our best chance, Julie. Otherwise we'll just have to choose a route at random."

With that, Irene rolled up her sleeves. "Now pass me the shampoo and I'll wash your hair for you."

The next day, carrying shopping bags as an excuse for their outing, they wound their way around the area normally covered by Peter's patrol. By late morning they had found him and, to an accompaniment of gently raucous comments from his troops, Irene privately explained their problem.

"Ignore that lot," he said, nodding towards the soldiers. "They think I've got the hots for Sarah here and they can never resist taking the mickey." He smiled at Julie who returned the grin and said, "Tell them you have to watch out for my mum – she's very protective."

Turning back to Irene he spoke more quietly. "I'll see what I can find out. I'm off duty on Thursday night and I can get a Curfew Pass easy enough. I'll tell my mates that I've got a date with Sarah and come round to your house. About eight o'clock. That OK?"

"Yes, that's splendid," Irene replied. "You must stay for dinner. It won't be much I'm afraid but we'll do our best."

Meanwhile Julie, accompanied by cheers from the patrol, leaned forward and kissed him briefly on the cheek. "That should help with the excuse," she said, laughing at Peter's apparent embarrassment.

True to his promise he was at their door by eight on Thursday. "I've checked the area you want to go through," he said, as soon as he was seated. "There are various possible routes but I think one is better than the others." He handed them a sheet of paper. "I've marked it on this map for you. This should get you out close to where you can join the cycle route. Once there, put as much distance as you can between you and the city's edge. There'll be nobody enforcing a curfew out in the sticks so you can keep going as long as you like."

"That's wonderful, Peter. Thank you so much," Irene said, as both women pored over the map.

"I've got another suggestion," he continued. "The timing of patrols varies but on this coming Saturday afternoon there's a big London League football match. We're all allowed to watch it via TV links. In fact, we're encouraged to: they think it improves morale." Peter didn't look persuaded. "It means that there won't be any patrols between three and five, so if you can aim to get through during those two hours you should have a clear run."

The serious business out of the way, and aided by a bottle of wine that Irene had retrieved from her diminishing store, they spent an enjoyable evening chatting about this and that. For a while their predicament and the distressing state of the world retreated into the background. All too soon, however, it was time for Peter to go, both women giving him a hug as he went off into the night.

"Well, that was very pleasant," Irene observed as they closed the door behind him.

"Yes, wasn't it. Such a pity that we have to leave," Julie said, adding wistfully: "he's really nice."

Irene gave her an amused look. "Never mind," she said, "plenty of other fish in the sea." But even as she uttered that traditional comforting platitude she wondered if it were any longer true. After all, the sea was now a much less populous place.

Friday was spent in final preparations. They went out in search of as much food as they could find, whether from official sources or on the black market. They weren't hugely successful but calculated that it would be sufficient to see them to their destination. Then they packed and repacked the bicycle panniers until minimum weight was harmonised with maximum supplies. Irene, who was accustomed to cycling with a loaded bike, took the heavier items like the tent, cooking gear and repair kits, leaving Julie with a share of the food, her own clothing and a few personal possessions. Among the bits and pieces of equipment that Irene retrieved from the garage cupboard was a small solar charger and a bundle of connecting cables. She sorted through the cables until she found one that would fit the CommsTab that Hart had given them.

"We'll take this with us," she told Julie. "It's still connecting to whatever Comms infrastructure is working. We can pre-record messages for Sarah and for your brother telling them what we're aiming to do, and once we're on the road we'll transmit them. The charger will keep the CommsTab topped up while we travel."

When they were finally satisfied that everything was suitably packed there was nothing left to do other than to eat whatever food they were not going to carry and make the most of their last night of indoor comfort. They listened to music, drank what remained of the wine, and tried to distract each other from the dangers ahead. A restless night meant that they were up early the next morning, still nervous and having to find ways of occupying themselves until they were close to Peter's window of safety. Then it was time to go.

In the event everything went smoothly. As Peter had predicted, they encountered no soldiers or guards of any description and by the time that they stopped to transmit their messages Irene was sure that they were well into Buckinghamshire. The countryside appeared completely deserted, the roads and fields empty. They did pass one man working in his garden who looked up, clearly astonished to see a pair of baggage-laden cyclists, but then smiled and raised a hand in greeting as they pedalled past. They saw no livestock on the farmland other than a couple of grazing horses, an absence which confirmed the common rumour that the Homeland government had appropriated – stolen was probably a better word – all the cattle, sheep and pigs from the areas closest to London and taken them to be factory-farmed in the Kent and Surrey Work Camps.

Pushing on at a steady pace, Irene and Julie made good progress and by early evening were somewhere in the Chiltern Hills searching for a safe place to make camp. A copse a little way off the cycle route proved suitable, all the more so since it was close to a stream. The tent pitched and food eaten, they retreated to sleeping bags and made desultory conversation until sleep took them both.

To her surprise Julie slept quite well. Never having spent a night in a tent before she had not expected much rest, worrying that every little sound or movement outside would induce wakefulness. But that had not happened, and by the time she was properly conscious Irene was already up and preparing breakfast.

"Come on, sleepyhead," Irene called out cheerfully when she heard Julie stir. "It's a beautiful day."

Which it was, as Julie discovered on poking her head out of the tent. Blue sky in all directions and the sun already hot on her face.

"It'll be warm riding," Irene observed. "We should set off quite soon and rest up for a while in the middle of the day when it gets really hot."

Apart from the heat, the ride was much the same as the day before. The same quiet countryside even when they passed quite close to Oxford, and the same lack of other travellers, although once or twice they sighted distant figures on foot. For safety's sake they did not stop other than to rest in the shade of some trees during the hottest part of the day. Julie was more at ease on the bicycle now and by evening they were into the beautiful rolling countryside of the Cotswolds, looking for somewhere to spend the night. As the shadows grew longer they spotted what appeared to be a barn about a quarter of a mile from the road with a rough track leading up to it.

"Let's take a look," Irene suggested. "If nothing else we can camp out of sight by those trees on its far side. It'll be dark soon so we need to find somewhere."

On closer inspection the barn itself seemed ideal. It had evidently been used as a workshop of some kind and various tools were scattered across a couple of benches. Bits of farm equipment lay here and there but there was no sign of any recent activity. A layer of dust sat undisturbed on most surfaces. Happy to be relieved of the task of pitching the tent, they decided to sleep in the barn. It was going to be a very warm night anyway and the spacious building would be comfortably airier than the confining tent. After cooking an improbable stew of bits and pieces, accompanied by the contents of an aged packet of couscous, they settled down. It was far too warm to get into sleeping bags so they lay on their mats using the bags as loose covers, happily drifting off to the muffled sounds of the peaceful night outside. Julie's last thoughts before sleep were of gratitude for their two enjoyable days in the countryside, far away from the city's constant reminders of the Zeno catastrophe.

A few hours later she awoke suddenly in a panic, overwhelmed by the nightmare sensation of something heavy bearing down on her chest. In the dim light of early dawn she saw that it was a man straddling her, grubby and unshaven, flint-hard eyes staring down as he held a large knife to her throat.

"Stay quiet," he said "or I'll cut you another cunt."

She bit down on her lower lip, doing her best to control her desperate desire to scream. Where was Irene? Had he killed her?

The man grinned evilly at Julie and, moving the knife away from her throat, hooked her sweatshirt onto its point and tugged upwards.

"This. Take it off. Don't try anything or you're dead," he said, returning the knife close to her face and raising his weight off her enough to allow a little movement.

Her hands shaking she reached down and with some difficulty tugged the sweatshirt up and over her head. Beneath it she was wearing only a bra and, with evident relish, he slid the knife between its cups and cut the fabric. The bra fell away leaving her breasts exposed. He made an inhuman sound deep in his throat, reaching down with his free hand to fondle her.

"Get my cock out," he said, pressing the point of the knife into her throat until she felt it pierce the skin and draw blood.

Utterly terrified she reached trembling hands up to undo his belt and fly. She pulled down his trousers and pants, freeing his erection.

"Hold it. Play with it," he instructed her.

Making a huge effort to overcome her revulsion she did as he asked, taking his penis in both hands. Could she crush his balls and throw him off that way, she wondered, but rejected the thought in the face of the knife at her throat. Even if she hurt him his first act would surely be to plunge the knife home. If she did what he asked at least he would want to keep her alive. As she moved her hands on him, he groaned.

"Take it in your mouth now," he said, roughly pulling her head and shoulders up towards his body.

Seeing no alternative, she had opened her mouth to receive him when a ferocious shriek split the silence. The man jerked backwards in shock and then tumbled sideways from the force of a blow to his head. Irene stood over him clutching a lump hammer. Seeing that he was still conscious she knelt down and repeatedly swung the hammer onto his skull. The cracking of fractured bone was followed by a more liquid sound as the hammer penetrated the brain itself. Still Irene swung her weapon.

"Irene, Irene." Julie was shouting. "You can stop. He's dead."

She flung her arms around her friend and the human contact seemed to summon Irene back from wherever the terrible frenzy of violence had carried her. They clung to each other sobbing until, at last, they quietened and were able to survey the scene. The man lay on the ground, his head – or what remained of it – a pulpy mass, the hammer discarded beside it.

"Is he alone?" Julie asked, looking around fearfully as she rescued her sweatshirt.

"Yes, as far as I could tell," Irene replied. "I'd gone outside for a pee and it was such a lovely night I went for a walk in the woods. I didn't see anyone out there, just spotted his rucksack outside the door when I got back. After all this noise, if there was anybody else they'd surely be here by now."

"Still, perhaps we'd better get ready to move on as soon as we can. There may be others around."

"Yes, you're right," Irene said, standing up but still trembling. "You get packing our stuff and I'll bring in his bag. Maybe there's something useful in it."

When Irene returned with the bag Julie had managed to cover the body with an old tarpaulin that she had found in a corner of the barn. She had begun to gather their things together, but was now sitting on the floor with her head in her hands, rocking slowly back and forth. Irene sat down next to her and put an arm around her shoulders.

"I know Julie, I know," she whispered. "It's terrible to go through all that and then to see a man killed as well. But there was no choice. He would probably have killed you anyway after subjecting you to god knows what humiliation and pain. We both have to keep going. What else is there?"

Julie raised her tearstained face to Irene. "Yes," she said. "You're right, of course. It's shock. I'll get over it. It's just… oh, I don't know what it is."

Angrily she rubbed at her eyes as if wiping away the tears would expunge the memory. Then, gritting her teeth, she sat up straight and began piling their possessions into the panniers.

Irene turned away and emptied the dead man's bag onto the floor. Among the clothing there was a little food and, hitting the floor with a double thud, two heavy items covered in cloth. Irene unwrapped first one and then the other, revealing a semi-automatic pistol and a box of 9mm ammunition. She laid the gun on the floor between them and they both stared at it.

"Have you any idea how to use it?" Irene asked.

"Only what I've seen in films," Julie replied, picking the weapon up and, after a moment of fiddling, managing to release the magazine. "It's loaded," she said, showing Irene the column of bullets then slotting the magazine back into place.

Irene gave her the box of ammunition. "Best if you keep it, I think," she said. "You've got more idea than me."

She returned to rummaging through the contents of the bag and found a large wallet which, when opened, revealed a considerable sum in cash and an array of identity and banking cards.

"Jesus! Look at these, Julie. They're all for different people."

"Was he using aliases then?"

"No, I don't think so," Irene replied, examining the cards more closely. "There's both men and women here, some of them with the same family name and address. And all the addresses are across this area. I think…" She paused and looked grimly at Julie. "I think he stole them, perhaps killed these people."

With a gesture of disgust she dropped the wallet and money onto the ground. "I'm not even going to keep the money – probably taken from all those poor folk anyway. Now…"

"Hang on, Irene," Julie interrupted her. "Look. It's not just sterling. There are other notes."

She picked one up and turned it over in her hands. It was an English ten-pound note but overprinted with the words 'Bristol Scrip'. And then she found several which looked more like American currency, displaying the dollar sign next to a capital M.

"My god," Julie said, reading from the smaller print on the note, "it says 'Issued by the Malvern Estate Bank'. They've got their own money. I think we should take this. It might be useful for my brother, maybe even for us."

"OK," Irene agreed, though with some distaste. "We'll keep the money and the gun. Leave everything else with him. Now let's get out of here."

Once on the road progress was slow. Julie was falling behind even though Irene was not cycling at any great speed and kept stopping for her to catch up. The fourth time that this happened Julie was in tears.

"I'm sorry," she sobbed. "I just don't seem to have any energy."

"It's all right," Irene replied, doing what she could to comfort her stricken friend. "It's a reaction to last night. You can't help it, you're still in shock."

She studied the map which was clipped to the top of her handlebar bag. "At this rate we won't make it to Malvern today," she said, "but we're not too far from Cheltenham. I have an old friend, Eva, who lives there. I've not heard from her in a while but if she's still there we could ask her for shelter for the night. Can you manage a few more miles?"

Julie nodded. "Yes, I think so. But what will we do if she isn't there?"

"She lives quite near the edge of town so we wouldn't have to go into Cheltenham itself. I cycled there on a trip with Robin once. It's not too far. If she's not there we'll be able to head back into the countryside and find somewhere to camp."

Julie looked distressed at that possibility, but fortunately it did not prove necessary since Eva was at home. Her response to finding Irene on her doorstep was a mixture of amazement and happiness.

"Irene," she cried. "Heavens! Where have you popped up from?"

"It's a long story, Eva," Irene said, embracing her. "Julie here has been assaulted. Perhaps you could give us shelter for a day or two while she recovers?"

z z z

As he cruised along Mulholland Drive the young man knew that his car's batteries were almost discharged. The red flashing light on the dash told him so in no uncertain terms, the dulcet-voiced on-board computer counting down the minutes of power that remained. He would just about make it, he thought, and, as the count dropped below two, he turned off the road into a parking area overlooking the San Fernando Valley. He had been here often with his wife to admire the lights of Los Angeles spread out before them and to make love as they had done when they had first come here in their teens. Now she was gone, as were so many of his friends and family. Gone also was the familiar criss-cross pattern of street lights that had always so beguiled them. Instead, the valley was now lit by many hundreds of fires, some of them, even as he watched, joining with others into what he knew must be whole blocks of burning buildings. It was all too much, he thought, and inserting the muzzle of a pistol into his mouth he pulled the trigger. Unmoved by his despairing end, the fires burned on.

5

Ali had been in Argyll for almost four weeks when Douglas and the others arrived. She and Charlotte were sharing the house with her father, Duncan, while Ravi, Eleanor and Iain occupied the former holiday rental next door. They had spent their time sorting out various problems in the rental house, walking Pike the dog, and helping Duncan with his vegetable garden and his poultry. The hens had become favourites of the children, especially Charlotte, who took upon herself the daily task of scattering poultry pellets and chasing down straying chickens.

On the opposite side to the rental house Duncan's immediate neighbour was an elderly woman, Murdina, whose husband had died from flu complications a few months earlier. She was now living alone and making heavy weather of running the croft. All she had left was a small flock of sheep and a couple of Highland cattle with calves, but even that was proving too much. Duncan had been helping out since her husband's death and Ali now added her endeavours, but it was clear that Murdina would not be able to continue for long even with their support.

So it was that on their second evening after the latecomers' arrival the now complete group of refugees were assembled in Duncan's house, finishing off their evening meal and considering how they might best help Murdina. The discussion had meandered over various possible courses of action when, seemingly out of the blue, Duncan enquired of the adults how long they thought they could last.

"How do you mean, Dad?" Ali responded. "Last in what way exactly?"

He looked from face to face for a minute and then, retired professor that he was, began to lecture them. "OK, so let's look at the practicalities of our situation. Just think of all the things you've learned to take for granted. First of all, obviously, food."

He gestured at the empty plates in front of them.

"There's still some national food distribution, though that may well change soon, and we've got a fairly extensive supply of non-perishable goods stored away. We've still got electrical power to cook with, which should hold out for quite a long time given that we have local hydro and wind resources and, hopefully, people willing and able to keep them going. When winter comes we've plenty of wood to burn for heat even if power supplies do become erratic. We have medical kits and Eleanor is an experienced nurse, which is just as well since there's no doctor around here. We've got weapons to protect ourselves if and when that becomes necessary. We've plenty of fresh water coming off the mountains to replenish supplies if the taps run dry, and sewage from both houses runs to septic tanks which should continue working well enough provided that we manage to de-sludge them periodically."

He paused to let all this information sink in.

"Given that lot," he continued, "what timescale are we talking about? A few months? A year? More? We need to make a systematic assessment so that we can plan for the longer-term problems before they arise."

The company looked rather shaken at this blunt summary and remained silent for a moment. Then, mindful of her increasingly strained vegetarianism, Eleanor spoke up.

"You didn't mention your vegetable patch," she said. "Can't we make more of that? Expand it next door and maybe into Murdina's land? Grow stuff to ripen for different seasons?"

"Yes, well, that brings us to the first problem," Duncan replied. "Think about what you've seen around here so far, Eleanor. Not much in the way of vegetables growing, is there?"

"That's true," Eleanor replied. "But isn't that because people haven't bothered with gardening when veg has been so easy and cheap to get from the shops?"

"No, not entirely. Think again." He smiled at her. "It's because of where we are. Apart from the crofters there are three larger farms within five miles of where we're sitting but you haven't seen any fields of crops, have you? It's the soil and the climate. There's plenty of empty land but it's only good for rough grazing or forestry. My vegetables are growing in raised beds which are filled with soil that I bought in for the purpose. I'm not saying that you can't grow anything in the native soil. You can. But its productivity is very limited and only some crops will grow."

Kenny was nodding agreement. "Yes, that's dead right. It's a West Highlands problem isn't it? You'll find arable crops over in the east where there's better soil and conditions, even quite a long way north. Like the Black Isle just beyond Inverness, which is good for growing potatoes and cereals and stuff like that."

"Right," Duncan said. "And the Black Isle is on about the same latitude as Torridon over here in the west and there sure as hell isn't much arable farming there."

"Too true. I was brought up not far north of Torridon, near Poolewe," Kenny added. "My family has some land and stuff there. But it's only good for sheep and cattle and deer. Not for growing crops on any scale."

"But isn't that where those semitropical gardens are?" Sarah asked. "They certainly grow a lot of exotic plants. I went there years ago with my mum and dad."

"Aye," Kenny replied. "That's Inverewe Gardens. But it took a huge investment of energy, time and money back in the nineteenth century to get the land fit for it. And it takes an awful lot of work to keep it going."

"Still," Ali said, "we don't need that much land. Dad, couldn't we buy in some more soil to make a few more raised beds?"

"I guess that might still be possible," her father replied, "but I'm not certain. Apart from getting hold of the soil itself it's difficult keeping lorries fuelled and on the road now."

"Our hybrid wagon will run on all sorts," Jimmy pointed out. "Electricity and different fuel types depending on what you can get. If you could find a source for the soil maybe we could transport it in that."

"Certainly worth checking," Duncan replied. "I'll see if I can contact the people I dealt with before." He thought for a moment and then continued. "But growing vegetables is only one of the problems and probably not even the most pressing. I'm more worried about safety." He turned to Douglas and asked, "What's the situation with Reivers and marauding gangs to the south of us?"

"Not too good I'm afraid." Douglas looked gloomy. "As you know the Borders have been pretty well overrun, and the last I heard was that bigger and better organised groups had pushed up through the affluent suburbs to the north of Glasgow and on towards Loch Lomond."

"So it's only a matter of time before they get to us then?" Hugh enquired.

"Yes and no," Douglas replied. "Once they're into the southern Highlands the pickings are going to get slimmer. Settlements are more spread out and with much less worth stealing. I don't doubt that we'll get some small bands of scavengers up here but maybe not the really big gangs."

At this, Kenny exchanged glances with Jimmy and then nodded, whereupon Jimmy spoke up.

"Kenny and me have been thinking a bit about the risk of Reivers coming this way. Obviously the further north we can get the less likely they are to reach us. It just wouldn't be worth the effort for them. So we thought that if it got too dangerous here then we could all move to Kenny's family land up north. In fact, we thought that him and me might soon take a trip up there anyway, just to check things out and mebbe transport some emergency supplies and store them."

There was silence as the implications of all this sank in. At last, Ali spoke.

"So it's possible that staying here may be only very temporary. We might have to move again soon."

"I'm afraid so," Douglas replied. "When we left Edinburgh three days ago things were already getting really bad. As well as the city's own gangs there were Reivers who had worked their way up through the Borders, looting and killing as they came. If they haven't already, the central-belt cities and towns will collapse into chaos soon enough. Then it'll be a free-for-all. The further away we can get, the better it will be. Kenny's home in the far north-west sounds ideal to me. I doubt that the gangs would even think of travelling that far."

"And for good reason," Duncan interjected. "It's a hell of a long way to go without decent transport. It must be a couple of hundred miles from here. It would be a long trip for you all."

After that it was a somewhat subdued group of friends who retreated to their beds, Sarah and Hugh with Charlotte, Ali and Douglas in Duncan's house, Kenny and Jimmy with the others next door. After the evening's discussion, Ali was troubled and found sleep elusive. She lay next to Douglas, staring at the ceiling and lost in mournful thoughts.

"You knew about Kenny's family home when you invited them to join us, didn't you?" she said at last, turning to face him.

"Yes," he replied, a little sheepishly. "I thought it might give us another option when things got bad."

"And I got angry with you for inviting them. I'm sorry." She smiled at him. "Though you should have discussed it first."

Douglas laughed. "That's my Alison," he said. "Never knowingly without the last word."

They lay in silence for a while until Ali whispered with immense sadness, "You know my dad won't come with us, don't you? He's determined to see out his life here and I won't be able to persuade him."

"I thought that might be so from what he said about it being a long trip. But you never know. Maybe we'll be able to change his mind."

"I doubt it," she replied. And reaching out her arms added, "Come here. Just hold me please."

z z z

Eva insisted that the two women stayed with her until Julie was sufficiently recovered from her ordeal to travel. She also said that she could arrange a lift for them to a safe setting-off point for the final section of their route. Eva, it appeared, had influential friends, largely in consequence of having worked for many years as a computer scientist at GCHQ. As Irene told Julie, she had been an outstanding researcher much valued by her employers. But as the years went by she found it more and more difficult to make her daily activities compatible with her principles. She was, after all, working for a major surveillance agency, and as GCHQ became involved in what she saw as increasingly dubious monitoring of the domestic population she found her position becoming untenable. In the end she took early retirement but remained in Cheltenham and continued to give occasional technical advice to some of her former colleagues.

As it turned out, remaining in Cheltenham had proved to be a wise decision. In an irony that was not lost on Eva, the deepening Zeno crisis had made GCHQ into something of a saviour for the local population. The Homeland government, always paranoid about internal threats, had continued to fund the agency and had allocated a significant military force to protect it. Since so many of its workers lived in and around the town, that protection had been extended to the entire urban area. The soldiers had been ruthless in dealing with miscreants of any description with the result that those like Julie's assailant, seeking to rob, rape and terrorise, now gave Cheltenham itself a wide berth. How long this would continue remained to be seen, dependent as it was on the survival of the Homeland and the continuing flow of resources. But for the present Cheltenham was an oasis of relative tranquillity in the midst of burgeoning social disorder, and as a kind of semi-detached outpost of the Homeland it was much less authoritarian and oppressive than was the case back in London. It was this situation that enabled Eva to arrange transport and safe passage for them out to the Cheltenham boundary.

True to her promise, on the third morning of their stay a military van drew up outside the house and two soldiers loaded in their bikes and baggage. They were driven through the town, which did indeed look remarkably normal with people on the streets and a number of shops open. Then they headed north-west until, at a junction with the motorway, they reached a guarded military barricade. Waved through, the van took them a little further into the countryside and then came to a halt.

"This is as far as we go, ladies," one of the soldiers announced as he unloaded their bikes. "Show me your map and I'll tell you where you are. You can make your way cross-country from here. But keep an eye out for armed groups. There's a crooked guy running the Malvern area and he sends out occasional patrols."

Their position located on the map, the soldiers waved goodbye and disappeared back the way they had come. Irene and Julie looked at each other, shrugged, and mounted up. Accidents apart, they expected to reach their destination by mid afternoon. The Malvern Hills were visible from where they stood, dramatically rising up out of the flat countryside like a huge wall, the main ridge stretching ten miles from end to end.

"That's home," Julie said, nodding towards the distant view. "Fortunately we won't have to cycle all the way to the top."

"Right then, best get going," Irene replied, and pedalled off down the road with Julie struggling to keep up.

For an hour or so they made good if rather indirect progress, keeping to small backroads as much as possible and watching the distant hills slowly grow larger. Then, suddenly, something caught Julie's eye at the side of the road and she came to a precipitate halt, almost tumbling her bike in the process.

"Irene, wait," she shouted, and her friend stopped about thirty metres further on and turned round to look.

"What's wrong?" Irene called.

"I saw something," Julie said, wheeling her bike back down the road until, with a cry of dismay, she lowered it onto its side and plunged into the thick hedgerow.

Irene cycled back just in time to see her lifting a small figure out from below the hedge. It was a little girl, perhaps seven or eight years old, her clothes dirty and tattered.

"She's alive and conscious," Julie called as she cradled the child in her arms. "Bring some water and something to eat. Anything. She seems very weak."

Hastily Irene grabbed a water bottle and retrieved her precious supply of energy biscuits from her handlebar bag, then rushed them to Julie who was now seated at the side of the road supporting the girl and murmuring encouragement in her ear. After she had drunk some water and been persuaded to eat one of the biscuits, the child simply lay with her head in Julie's lap gazing big-eyed up at her rescuer. Julie stroked her hair which was matted and full of small twigs from the hedge.

"What's your name?" Julie asked, receiving only an uncomprehending stare in response. "Do you live near here?"

The girl slowly shook her head and then looked from one to the other of the two women as if searching for some sign of familiarity. Finally she whispered something unintelligible and then, when Julie leaned forward better to hear, she spoke more clearly.

"Lucy," she said. "I'm called Lucy."

"Hello Lucy," Julie replied. "I'm Julie and this is my friend Irene. Where's your mum and dad?"

A momentary shadow passed across the child's face. "Gone," she said. "They're gone."

"Gone where?" Irene asked.

"Just gone away." Her eyes filled with tears. "They got sick."

Julie and Irene exchanged looks.

"Have you got any uncles and aunts? Neighbours?" Julie asked. "People to look after you."

Once more the girl shook her head. "They all went away and left us. Travelling. That's what we was called. Travellers. But then they went one way and my dad said we had to go a different way. And then mum and dad got sick."

Exhausted by the effort of this lengthy speech she slumped back onto Julie's lap. "Could we heat up some of that soup?" Julie enquired of Irene, who nodded and busied herself with the stove while Julie cuddled the tiny figure. "If we can get some decent food into her so she's a bit more alert maybe we can figure out some way of carrying her on my bike."

After a while the combination of hot soup and the comfort of Julie's body warmth seemed to inject life into the child, and she sat up and paid more attention to her surroundings.

"You're riding bicycles," she said, with some semblance of enthusiasm. "I had a bike. It had a puncture and my dad was going to mend it for me. But he didn't."

"Would you like to ride on mine?" Julie asked, looking in Irene's direction in search of inspiration as to how they might manage such an arrangement. Irene nodded and turned away to rummage through her panniers.

"That would be good," Lucy said, with unexpected enthusiasm. "But where will I sit?"

"Aha!" Irene said triumphantly, pulling out a roll of strapping from the tent bag. "I've got an idea about that," she told Lucy. "If we fix this sit-pad on top of the pannier frame" – she demonstrated what she meant – "then you can sit on that and we can fasten you to the seat and to Julie with these straps so that you don't fall off."

Lucy clapped her hands. "Yes, yes," she cried, "I want to ride on the back."

Julie looked rather more sceptical, but in the absence of any alternative proposal agreed to give it a try.

"But where will her legs go?" she asked Irene. "The panniers are in the way."

"If we take as much out of yours as we can cram into mine then there'll be some space for her legs. It won't be ideal but she's quite small so it should be possible. I don't think there's any other way unless we walk, and that's not a good idea."

After considerable fiddling on Irene's part, and with enthusiastic if ineffectual help from Lucy, they at last had the seat rigged and the straps set up, the girl now firmly held in place.

"You have to hold on to me as well," Julie told her. "Put your arms around me and hang on tight."

Obediently she did so, and with the baggage rearranged and repacked they set off once more towards the now much closer hills.

The roads remained very quiet but the nearer they approached to their destination the more fields they encountered showing signs of cultivation. Occasionally they would see someone actually working on the land, and for the first time on their entire journey they saw cattle grazing freely. There was a general sense of orderliness which had not been apparent in the countryside bordering the Homeland, but they could see no direct evidence of how that order was sustained – no patrols, no road barriers, no sign of defensive emplacements. Were it not for the absence of vehicles, they could have been riding through a pre-Zeno landscape.

Now the hills were very close so Julie called a halt to check the map and decide on their most direct route to her family farm. Lucy, who had somehow managed to doze off on the back of the bike, awoke when they stopped moving and sleepily asked where they were.

"Not far now," Irene told her. "Just need to hold on a little bit longer then we'll be able to rest."

"Or so we hope," Julie murmured under her breath. Although they had sent a message to Brian, her brother, on the day that they left the Homeland, they had not received a reply so had no way of being certain of a welcome or that he and her parents would still be there when they arrived. Communications were so erratic now, even using Hart's special CommsTab, that they felt that they had little choice but to take the risk on the farm being a safe destination. Julie knew that her brother had still been there a few months earlier, and almost anywhere seemed preferable to remaining in London and facing the Work Camps. But now that their arrival was imminent, carefully suppressed doubts were beginning to surface. It wasn't as if it was only Julie at risk. In their different ways Irene and Lucy were dependent on her. Still, they would know soon enough, she thought, as they set off on those last few miles.

Twenty minutes later she began to recognise features of the countryside around her.

"Hold on, Irene," she called. "Let me go in front now. I know where we are."

Irene slowed down and allowed her to overtake, smiling encouragingly as Julie and Lucy rode past. They continued for another half-hour or so by which time they were very close to the edge of the Malverns. Finally, Julie turned off the road and along a roughly tarmacked track which led towards a group of buildings: a large farmhouse, a smaller bungalow, and an array of sheds and barns. But before they could reach the house there was a shout from away to their right and a man could be seen running towards them through a field of sheep.

"Julie! Is that you? Wait."

The two cyclists halted, a much relieved Julie turning towards the running figure and calling out to him.

"Yes, it's us, Brian. We've got here at last."

Her brother reached the field's gate and, unwilling even to stop to open it, vaulted over and flung his arms around his sister, almost knocking her, Lucy, and the bike to the ground.

"Careful," Julie laughed, "you'll have us down."

"Sorry, sorry. I've been so worried," Brian said breathlessly, releasing her from a hug. "I expected you a couple of days ago."

"You did get the message then?" Julie asked.

"Yes. I tried to send a reply but it bounced."

"Ah, right. We wondered if you'd even get it so that was something. This is Irene." She gestured in her friend's direction. "And this one on the back of the bike is Lucy. We collected her along the way."

"Hello Irene and Lucy," he said, smiling at both of them. "Come on up to the house. Jean and the boys are there. They'll be so pleased to see you. Here at last, safe and sound."

"Yes," Julie said, turning to grin at Irene. "I suppose we really are, aren't we?"

z z z

The township of West Point in Monrovia, the capital city of Liberia, had a deserved reputation as the most desperate slum in one of the world's poorest countries. Although by the 2030s it was partly inundated by rising sea levels, it remained home to over 100,000 people who lived in the most abject of circumstances. When the flu arrived it tore through the densely populated shanties, killing many in its first wave. Weakened by illness and poor diet, thousands more of the initial survivors fell victim to other diseases, including typhoid, which rapidly caught hold in circumstances of almost non-existent sanitation. Then on top of that came a second wave of flu, raising the death rate to a level hitherto never seen by the World Health Organization staff reporting on it. Corpses piled up in the streets and washed around in the ocean, while the smell of death and decay was everywhere. Neither the Liberian government nor the international authorities were willing or able to provide any meaningful response to disease on this scale. West Point and its godforsaken people were simply left to rot.

6

The mottled black-and-brown yak stood chewing the cud directly in front of the seated man. Then, with the relaxed confidence born of an oft-repeated action, she took a few steps forward until she was no more than a metre from the bench, her large shaggy head inclined purposefully in the man's direction. Hart smiled to himself and, slowly reaching forward, he scratched the animal between her formidable horns. The yak lifted her head a little, pressing into his fingers with every sign of enjoying the contact, letting out the occasional quiet grunt. If only humans were as easily pleased, Hart thought, grimacing at the memory of his day thus far. As if she could feel his discontent the yak once more raised her head and looked placidly into his face. Then, with a final sympathetic grunt, she turned away and continued her grass-eating progress across the Whipsnade pasture.

Hart watched her go with some regret. Of an evening he had fallen into the habit of sitting on this bench just as the yak had fallen into the habit of visiting him there, the two evidently enjoying each other's company. But today had been particularly frustrating and, as the beast had sensed, Hart was restless and irritated. The ERA commune – if an enterprise so lacking in communal spirit could be called that – was tumbling deeper and deeper into a hole of its own digging, disputatious cliques undermining its capacity to survive in the increasingly threatening world. Although Jerry Rowlands was making some efforts towards ensuring the safety of the group, usually by delegating tasks to Hart, it was also apparent that like the Jerry of their Oxford days he actually rather enjoyed the political squabbling among his fractious activists. Not so much a case of divide and rule, Hart thought, as one of divide and relish.

Today's discussion had in theory revolved around the plan to disperse and hide in the event of the PeePees confronting them. In practice, however, it had collapsed into violent disagreement about the most effective methods of guerrilla warfare, an activity in which none of them had any experience. The futility of all this was then further reinforced by stubbornly held differences of opinion as to who constituted the real enemy. One now quite substantial group was set upon ignoring the PeePees altogether in favour of waging a secret war of terror within the Homeland. They were already manufacturing improvised explosive devices and had decided that in the event of a direct threat from the PeePees they would return to the Homeland and foment revolution there. Another rather more amorphous group – Hart thought of them as uninformed latter-day hippies – insisted that, in spite of all evidence to the contrary, those that they liked to call 'real people' were essentially good. They fully expected the PeePees' evangelical army simply to embrace their doctrine of peace and love, a deeply naïve position from which they refused to budge. Hart's own expectation was that if faced with an ultimatum most of Whipsnade's occupants would allow themselves to be converted to the PeePees' cause, in his view an entirely justifiable position when the only alternative was death.

In spite of all the dissent and confusion, however, over the past few weeks Hart had at least managed to organise some transfer of resources to various hiding places. How long these caches would survive in the face of ruthless invaders remained to be seen, so he had taken additional precautions. Most of the stores were booby-trapped, and in company with only one of his most trusted security guards he had concealed a choice selection of supplies and arms in a couple of particularly well-hidden locations. If desperate measures became necessary, he and a small group, the membership of which he already had in mind, would draw upon these resources and evade the PeePees as best they could. Recalling how many empty houses he had encountered on his journey south from Nottingham, he was sure that they would be able to find shelter somewhere and hope to outlast the fundamentalist storm.

It would be a sad conclusion to the Whipsnade venture, but had he really expected any other outcome when he first made his way here? Hart thought not. He had known only too well what kind of enterprise Rowlands would be likely to create and he had also known that in due course England would inevitably fall into a state of profound social disarray. He had simply been curious, evincing a kind of anthropological interest in observing the devastation that Zeno would precipitate. Hart flinched mentally at the thought of Zeno and particularly at his own failure to take action when that was still possible. It would have been too late to stop the epidemic but it might have helped maintain order rather longer, perhaps even long enough to put precautionary measures in place. He simply did not know. What he did know was that he had not intervened directly and that this was an abrogation of responsibility for which he and others had paid too high a price.

Preoccupied by these dismal reflections, he walked slowly back towards his living quarters in one of Whipsnade's old Lookout Lodge chalets. Not for the first time he wondered what had happened to Irene and Julie, having heard nothing from them since that last occasion at Irene's home. Were they still stranded in the Homeland? Had they fled, as he would have advised them to do? Were they even still alive? He promised himself that when he got home he would try to contact them via the CommsTab that he had given to Julie. The Homeland authorities would undoubtedly be able to eavesdrop but he didn't suppose that they were bothering any more. They had much more important things to worry about.

Lost in such thoughts Hart was vaguely surprised to find that he had arrived at his front door. The chalet was tiny but it had become home to him, and at least he had it to himself. Always independent, since the onset of the crisis he had discovered that he valued his solitude more than ever. Once inside he looked around the interior with a critical eye and, after sending a message to Irene and Julie, set about tidying up the documents that had accumulated on his table. This was what the plan of resistance had come to, he thought, piles of paper of no interest to anyone except me. Just as he completed the tidying operation there came a knock at the door. This was unusual – Hart did not have visitors – so it was with some curiosity that he responded. There on the doorstep stood Jennifer Connolly, his undercover agent among the PeePees.

"Jenny!" he exclaimed. "I wasn't expecting you until the weekend. Come in. Is everything OK?"

"It's fine, Jonathan," she replied with a smile of greeting. "At the weekend there's a whole lot of motivational assemblies and crap like that which I daren't miss, so I thought I'd best come now while I could get away."

"So what's happening over there?"

"They're having a huge recruitment drive the length and breadth of East Anglia. I guess they've learnt their lesson from the Loughton fiasco and are going for much greater numbers. As far as I can tell they're not aiming to move yet. They're going to build up their army then head west with a front reaching from the Midlands down to here." She shook her head ruefully. "It will be pretty bad, I'm afraid."

"Seems hardly worth you going back then," Hart said. "We know it's coming and the precise timing probably won't matter – we'll hear all about it from the people who flee ahead of them."

"I'm not so sure about that. From what I gather there's a lot of disagreement among the people around The Prophet. Some want to avoid winter and wait until spring; others want to go as soon as they've got the biggest army possible even if it is winter; and he's crazy enough to claim divine inspiration and set out tomorrow. You'll get a lot more warning if I stay there until the decision's made and then make a run for it. I don't think anyone suspects me." She grinned and gestured towards him. "They know I'm visiting my sick mother."

Hart laughed. "And I'm failing in my motherly duties – have you had anything to eat? I've got some eggs and mushrooms. We could have omelette."

"Sounds good," Jenny said. "It's a long bike ride and I haven't had anything since morning."

Over the meal Hart brought her up to date on the intricacies of recent ERA politics, her unrestrained laughter at the foolishness of it all doing much to relieve his earlier black mood. He told her about the secret caches and that, if she were willing, she was to be one of his special group when they had to leave Whipsnade.

"Of course I'll come," she said, laying a hand on his arm and adding, "thank you, Jonathan."

A little discomfited at this unexpected show of affection, Hart stood up. "I've got some malt whisky. Would you like some?" he said, crossing to a cupboard from which he produced a bottle and two glasses. About to pour the drinks he suddenly became conscious of Jenny just behind him. When he turned around she drew him into an embrace and kissed him on the lips. Initially he froze – he had not expected this – but then the sensual pleasure of the contact, as well as the passion that Jenny brought to it, overcame his initial resistance and with growing intensity he returned her kiss. Enveloping her in his arms he pressed her body hard against his own. Encountering bare skin at the base of her back he slid his hand up inside her shirt and, finding no underwear to obstruct him, continued on around her body to caress her naked breast. She pulled away from him a little and looked into his eyes.

"That's lovely," she whispered, drawing him back to her.

When he came to think of those moments later what he would especially recall was her joyful giggles as they struggled to remove each other's clothing and then her smiling down at him, long fair hair now hanging loose about her face, as she straddled his hips and began moving her body against his.

In the morning he awoke to find her already up and dressing.

"I'm going to have to set off soon," she said apologetically. "I can't take the risk of being too late back."

"You know you don't really have to go," Hart replied as he rose from the bed. "Why not just stay here?"

"No, I should definitely finish the job. Then I'll be back." She smiled and kissed him lightly on the cheek. "Don't worry. I'll be OK. I've been doing this for months, remember."

Hart sighed. "If you say so," he said, resigning himself to her decision. "Jenny," he began, then paused. "Why? You know… last night?"

She took his hand in both her own and looked directly at him. "Because I like you, of course. A lot. And..." she paused, perhaps seeking the right words or wondering whether to say any more at all. "And... because you always look so sad."

After breakfast they walked together to the main entrance where Jenny had left her bike in the care of the guards. Reclaiming it, she and Hart stood chatting for a moment by the ERA sign and then, conscious of the watching men and their propensity to gossip, Hart hugged her briefly and whispered in her ear.

"Thank you, Jenny. Be careful."

She mounted up, and with a cheerful wave to the guards and a private blown kiss to Hart she set off down the road, at last vanishing from sight around the corner. Had Hart been able to see that far he might have observed a figure, also with a bicycle, who emerged from the woods at the side of the road just after Jenny had passed. But he did not, and nor did Jenny who cycled on knowing nothing of the man who followed her all the way back to the PeePees' Essex territory.

Hart spent much of that day in a haze, at times not even certain that what had happened was real. He tried to stop himself from wondering if anything might come of their encounter, convincing himself instead that it was a one-off, a passing in the night. But, as he realised to his considerable surprise, he really wanted there to be more. Not just more lovemaking, although that had been pleasurable enough, but more of their simply being together. Although he was maybe twenty years Jenny's senior that had not seemed to bother her, so perhaps when she came back they might pick up from where they had left off. He wished now that he had insisted on her not returning to the PeePees, that he had been firm enough to keep her with him. But committed to her task as she was, she would surely have found that to be an unacceptable use of his official authority. No, he would just have to wait and hope for the best.

At around eleven o'clock that night he finally fell asleep in the warmth of memories of the previous evening and, he was pleased to think, with Jenny's perfume imbuing his bedding. Then at about 6.30 the next morning he was awakened by a buzzing from the old-style walkie-talkie system that he employed to keep in contact with his security guards. Sleepily he responded.

"Yes, Hart here. What is it?"

"Mr Hart, it's Tom. I'm on gate duty. I think you'd better come down here. There's something bad happened."

"I'm on my way," Hart said, rising from his bed as he did so. Throwing on his clothes he set out for the main gate at a trot. In a matter of minutes he was there and met by a pale-looking Tom who gestured mutely towards the ERA sign on its plinth. There was a naked body tied to the sign, a body which Hart instantly recognised. Jenny's corpse was covered in bruises and burn marks, her long hair had been shorn, and, to Hart's horror, he saw that her fingernails had been ripped out. He groaned and sank to his knees next to the lifeless figure. Tears came as he reached out to touch her hand, as if that could somehow rekindle a response in her.

"Bring something to wrap her in," he called to the guards, "and a knife so that we can cut her down."

He knelt before her amidst the ashes of his hopes of the previous day. When the guards arrived with a sheet and a knife, he held her in his arms while they cut the ropes that bound her to the sign and then lowered her gently onto the sheet and wrapped it around her. Waving away the guards' offer of help, and still in tears, he carried her back into Whipsnade for the last time, leaving behind the crudely written placard that had been placed at her feet. It was headed with an insignia comprising two interlinked Ps over a crucifix, and its crimson lettering spelled out a biblical passage which it ascribed to Romans 2:8. 'For those who are self-seeking and do not obey the truth, but obey unrighteousness, there will be wrath and fury.'

z z z

Life on Malvern Edge Farm did not prove to be an instant bucolic idyll. In the circumstances this was hardly surprising since the first news that her brother broke to Julie was that their father had died from flu-triggered pneumonia a couple of months earlier. Brian had tried to contact her at the time but with no success; Hart's replacement of her CommsTab had left her without a publically accessible identity on the standard networks. Since then her mother had reacted badly to her father's death and was now living alone in the bungalow, communicating very little with the world beyond her walls. On top of the emotional strain, this had left Brian running the farm virtually single-handed. Disease had seriously diminished local availability of farm labour so, although he could buy in help from a small group of estate employed peripatetic farm hands, this was intermittent, expensive and unpredictable. He was working long days and still not managing to keep on top of everything.

As if all this wasn't enough, he had a remarkable story to tell them about the Malvern area itself. As everywhere, when the epidemic took hold it brought with it food shortages, collapse of local government institutions, and, initially at least, small-scale criminality. Into the power vacuum that this created had stepped the unlikely figure of a Birmingham racketeer who had owned a country mansion in the area for many years. Bringing a group of hard men with him, he had imposed order by dint of ruthless elimination of opposition and the imposition on the rural community of the kind of protection rackets that he had successfully operated in the city. All businesses in the area, including the many farms, were obliged to pay what were euphemistically described as 'taxes'. Of course some refused, but after the adults and children of one stubbornly resistant farming family were murdered and their land appropriated, all the others recognised the grim reality of their predicament and capitulated.

The criminal boss, who had by now grandiosely renamed himself Lord Malvern, recruited additional young men locally and took complete control of the region. He asserted ownership of all land within his self-proclaimed boundaries and treated those working the farms as his tenants. This was the basis of the orderly countryside that Irene and Julie had noted as they approached the hills – a kind of crude feudal system in which the local lord ensured the safety of his tenants and, in return, extracted value from them. Any malicious invaders were met with force and either repelled or, more often, killed, while those simply in search of sustenance and shelter were put to work as modern-day landless peasants.

Needless to say, Brian and the other farmers resented this subjugation, the injustice of which was further underlined by the requirement that they address their principal exploiter as 'his Lordship'. But in the circumstances there was little that they could do. The reins of power were entirely in his hands, backed up by a monopoly of the means of violence and the forcible introduction of a distinctive Malvern currency which they were obliged to use in all everyday transactions. Any English pounds in their possession had to be exchanged for Malvern dollars through his Lordship's Estate Bank, pounds which he then used in trading beyond the Malvern boundaries wherever sterling still survived as legal tender. Unjust though all this was, insofar as it was ensuring a relatively stable environment in an increasingly unstable world, the population reluctantly accepted the new order as a necessary evil. At least, they reasoned, the desperate gangs that were elsewhere spreading across the English countryside gave the Malvern Estate a wide berth.

In these circumstances Irene and Julie had been fortunate not to run into any of Lord Malvern's men in the final stages of their journey. But there remained a problem in that as new arrivals they would be viewed as immigrants to be used as labour where and when they were required by the Estate. Brian thought that he could certainly retain Julie on the grounds that she was family and would be best employed working for him, so relieving pressure on the Estate's reservoir of farm workers. Lucy could be claimed as her daughter – the little girl was already treating Julie as her surrogate mother anyway – but Irene presented difficulties. They finally settled on identifying her as an aunt who, as family, would also be helping out on the farm. To their relief the Estate's agents accepted all their claims without demur.

The other immediate problem was food. Three additional mouths to feed was a challenge, however sparing their appetites. There were still supplies coming into the area, largely courtesy of profiteering criminal networks in the Midlands, although there were also some long-established trading relationships with more legitimate businesses in Bristol. On the farm, of course, they were able to develop their own sources of food above and beyond what they grew or raised for sale. Rabbits, once a pest, were now a welcome addition to their diet, and Brian had been encouraging the warrens rather than seeking to destroy them. Any food source that could be concealed from the prying eyes of the Estate's agents was doubly valuable, so a proportion of the farm's hens, ducks and turkeys were allowed to run wild thus ensuring that their egg production could not be monitored. The boys, now aided by Lucy, were given the task of tracking down the birds and collecting their eggs.

But Irene remained very much aware of the additional load that the new arrivals placed on the farm's limited resources, so she still nurtured the possibility of getting to Scotland and to Sarah, hazardous though that journey might prove. Even if she perished in the effort, at least there would be one less mouth to feed here. Brian and Jean insisted that the farm could support them all since they now had the much-needed additional help from the two extra adults, but Irene remained sceptical. She could see shortages arising further down the line, especially when winter came, a point she made to Julie one day some weeks after their arrival. They had spent the morning working on various tasks around the farm and now sat outside in the autumn sunshine, eating their meagre midday snack of home-baked bread and cheese.

"Yes, I know it will get hard," Julie agreed. "But at least we're accepted here and we're well out of the Homeland and the risk of the Work Camps."

Irene nodded. "That's true, I know. Even Lord Doo-Dah's crooked regime is preferable to that. But I worry about it getting worse."

Contemplating that possibility they relapsed into silence until, squinting against the sunshine, Irene asked, "Is that someone coming this way across the fields? On a horse?"

Julie looked in the direction that she pointed. "Yes it is. The agents checked us last week so it can't be one of them. Besides, they don't use horses."

As the figure drew nearer it resolved itself into a young man wearing an expensive-looking riding outfit.

"Good god!" Julie exclaimed. "It can't be."

Once in the yard the man dismounted, looped the horse's reins around the gatepost and walked towards them.

"Hello Jools," he said. "I heard you were back so thought I'd come and visit."

"Con! I had no idea you were still around. I thought you were working for your dad's firm in Bristol."

"Well, yes I am, but I have to come up here every so often to check in with the old man."

Julie turned to Irene. "This is Con," she said. "Conrad. We were at school together."

"Hello, I'm Irene. Pleased to meet you."

Conrad turned towards her. "My pleasure," he said, giving her a graceful bow as if meeting a dowager duchess at a refined garden party. "The local gossip says that you escaped the Homeland to get here."

"Yes, we did. Things were getting really scary over there," Julie said. "What's it like in Bristol?"

He shrugged. "It's so-so. You have to be careful where you go but it's not as bad as some places that I've heard about. I stay on the boat when I'm there and we keep it anchored offshore for safety."

"Not *The Cormorant?*" Julie asked.

"Yes, you remember her then?"

"Oh yes." She smiled at the memory. "I always thought that if you really wanted it named after a seabird it would have been better called *The Shag*, given what everyone used it for." She turned to Irene. "We went there to party in our teens. A lot of fun."

"Not much of a party boat now, I'm afraid," Conrad observed. "Marie's living there permanently with her husband Stuart. Marie's my sister," he added in an aside to Irene. Then, turning back to Julie, "You know that she got married?"

"Yes, she sent me some photos. A guy she met in Bristol, wasn't it? But why have they gone to live on the boat? There must be loads of room in your parents' house."

"If you've seen pictures I'm sure you can guess. You know what they're like around here. Ingrained racists. Locals didn't like the idea of her marrying a black guy, her being an heiress and all. So the two of them decided to leave. Can't say I blame them. It was quite nasty at times."

"That's awful," Julie said. "But I can well imagine. My dad would have been among them."

"Yes, I think he was, but very politely. They were all very polite. Load of shits that they are." He shook his head. "I only come here when I have to. But now you're here… well, that's different."

Julie smiled and, as Irene noted, blushed a little.

"It's really good to see you again, Con," she said. "Come and visit us any time."

"I will," he replied. "In fact, the reason I came over today was to find out if you wanted to go riding sometime. Like we used to."

"Lord, I've not been on a horse since… I don't know when… probably just before we went off to university."

"Don't worry, it's like riding a bike. You don't forget. And I've got a very gentle mare for you. How about I bring her over tomorrow and we'll give it a try?"

Julie did not have to think for long. "Yes, that would be fine. Let's do it."

"It's a date," he said. "I'll be here around this time tomorrow. OK?"

Julie nodded and, after bidding an elaborate farewell to Irene, Conrad mounted up and disappeared across the fields.

Irene looked at Julie and smiled broadly. "I see," she said. "An old flame then?"

"We went out for a couple of years in the sixth form," Julie replied. "He was my first properly serious boyfriend. We had all sorts of plans, but then I went to university in Southampton and he went to Durham. We tried to carry on for a while but you know the way of those things. It's a long way from Durham to Southampton and our lives just went in different directions. Then he came back to work for his dad's company and I left to be a journalist."

"What does the company do?"

"All sorts of import/export stuff. Some of it on the edge of legality I suspect. The family's very rich, or at least they were. The boat that he mentioned – *The Cormorant* – it's quite something."

"He seems… um …" Irene paused, not quite sure how best to put it, "… very upper class."

"You mean the way he speaks?" Julie nodded. "He got sent to a couple of expensive schools and was only dragged back here for the sixth form because his mother wanted him at home. It's all surface. He's a decent person underneath."

Irene was not so sure, but wary of allowing Julie to see what she really thought. After all, she had only briefly met the man. It was just that he had about him that public school aura of entitlement that she had encountered so often in her contact with government ministers and senior civil servants. Something that she had learned to distrust after years of bitter experience.

As he had promised Conrad returned the next day, riding one horse and leading another. Then, a couple of days later, he showed up inviting Julie to dine with his parents who, he said, had seen some of her reporting and were eager to meet her again. Julie rather doubted this claim since she was certain that they would have disapproved of her investigative work, but when Conrad said that she was expected to stay over for the night she quickly agreed. Thus began a pattern of her spending two or three nights a week in Conrad's company, mostly at his parents' house but sometimes at the farm. On the latter occasions Lucy moved in with Irene, the little girl clearly disconcerted by her temporary expulsion from Julie's bedroom. Conrad himself now spent less time in Bristol and, for all her misgivings, Irene had to admit that he appeared to be entirely serious about Julie and that she certainly seemed much happier.

All this meant that Irene was left more on her own, time that she frequently filled by thinking about her daughter and granddaughter. Caught up in these melancholy reflections one winter morning, she rescued Hart's CommsTab from the handlebar bag where it had remained since they reached the farm. A couple of hours on the charger restored it to life and, to her astonishment, when she switched it on it immediately displayed a text message from Hart, dated several weeks earlier. Brief and to the point, it read: 'How are you two doing? If you get this, please reply. Don't worry about the CommsTab being traced. That's no longer a problem.' Hastily Irene wrote a reply describing their flight from the Homeland and their present circumstances, then sent it off. A few seconds later the single word 'Delivered' flashed up. Now excited, she composed a message for Sarah which when dispatched also generated the 'Delivered' confirmation. Of course, the fact that one electronic device had managed to communicate with another did not mean that either of her messages would actually be read by anyone. But she could hope, and right now hope was something in short supply.

z z z

As so many had predicted for so long, the Korean peninsula had finally become a nuclear desert. Pyongyang itself, once a city of extraordinary skyscrapers, had been razed to the ground in a series of nuclear missile strikes. After the Democratic People's Republic had used the influenza crisis as an excuse to bomb Seoul, the world's nuclear powers had collectively concluded that the only way to stop further escalation was to blast the rogue state out of existence. This they had done with neither warning nor pity. Missiles had rained down on town and country alike, raising a vast cloud of radioactive dust which settled over everything and, carried on the prevailing winds, drifted across the sea towards Japan. The few survivors of the blasts and the firestorms that followed found themselves in a grey, ash-covered world, stranded without food and without a future. For them, in their protracted terrible suffering, death by Zeno would have been merciful.

7

For a couple of months after Jenny's funeral Hart maintained the monotonous rituals of his daily work. He checked security, he walked the boundaries, he attended futile meetings and he conducted one-sided conversations with the uncomprehending yak. Finally he concluded that he had to get away from Whipsnade, both from its memories and from its infuriating inhabitants. Jerry Rowlands tried hard to dissuade him, managing in the end to extract a promise that he would return. Hart did not feel that to be any great compromise. He had every intention of returning, if only to retrieve supplies and weapons from his secret caches. But for now he wanted nothing more than to be disconnected from everything that had happened here, to be alone and out on the road again.

Initially he headed south, thinking to work his way along the northern border of the Homeland and assess the situation there. Increasingly, however, he found himself drifting east. This was not unreasonable in as much as the border ran west–east. But slowly it dawned on him that what he really wanted to do was to see the PeePees' territory at first hand. This had always been his intention, he realised, he had just been unwilling to recognise it. How this related to Jenny's terrible fate was not something that he wanted to reflect upon, although he knew that it did so in some tangled way deep in his subconscious. Instead, he rationalised the whole enterprise in terms of discovering what she would have reported for them – the scale of the PeePees' army and the probable timing of its march west.

He settled on a final goal of the PeePees' notional seat of power, Chelmsford, and slowly he made his way towards the town. As he travelled he cultivated the appearance of a tramp, deliberately damaging and dirtying his clothing, allowing his beard and hair to grow unruly, and generally adopting the manner and speech of a frightened victim of society's collapse. Occasionally he encountered other travellers with whom he might briefly pass the time of day or, more often, walk by with a nervous nod of greeting. Only once before reaching the environs of Chelmsford did he encounter anyone of interest. This was an elderly man busy in his winter vegetable garden. Hart stopped by his fence, offering a greeting and an observation about the inevitability of hard work for gardeners. The man looked at him warily, then, deciding that he was probably harmless, leaned on his spade and enquired where he was heading.

"Nowhere in particular," Hart replied. "I'm just drifting really."

"Well, best be careful drifting in the direction that you're going," the gardener replied. "You'll be in PeePee country a few miles further on."

"PeePee?" Hart found playing ignorant a useful way of eliciting information.

"The Peculiar People," the man replied. "They started out as an apocalyptic sect but now they seem to be turning into an evangelical army."

"It's a strange name," Hart said. "Are they peculiar?"

The man laughed. "I think you'd probably say so but that's not the reason for the name. There was a nonconformist sect called that back in the nineteenth century and this new lot have stolen their identity. It comes from the King James version of the bible. Peculiar in the sense that we might say 'peculiar to' meaning 'belonging to' or 'distinctive of'. So, people peculiar to God." He paused looking blankly into the distance, then, shaking his head, smiled sheepishly and added: "Sorry, I used to be a teacher. You never miss the opportunity to display your erudition."

Hart returned the smile. "No, that's really interesting. So they think they're a chosen people?"

"They do indeed. Chosen to convert us all to the rightful way, I'm afraid, and with no compunction about how they do it. They're really dangerous. They've got a very charismatic leader and they're having a lot of success gathering desperate followers who want to guarantee their place in paradise before the final judgement arrives. So yes, if you're going that way, take care."

"Thank you, I will," Hart said, and raising a hand in farewell continued on his way.

Over the next two days he edged slowly towards Chelmsford, finding little in the way of shelter and so spending chilly nights outdoors in his bivvy bag. As a result he was looking very much the worse for wear, sufficient certainly to attract askance looks from those few he encountered on the road.

Before arriving at the town itself he came upon a large area of green parkland in which a considerable crowd was assembling. Some appeared to be wearing uniforms, dark shirts and trousers accompanied by a badged black cap for both men and women, while others moving among the crowd were clothed in what looked to Hart like a brown monk's habit, tied at the waist, and with a cowl. Round their necks hung a pendant which, when he got close enough to see it clearly, was all too familiar: the two intertwined letters P superimposed on a crucifix.

As he stood taking in the extraordinary scene, one of the brown-robed functionaries came up to him.

"Prophet's word be with you," he said, inclining his head in Hart's direction. "You have the look of a stranger in a strange land. Have you come to join us?"

"Um, yes," Hart said, doing his best to appear bashful, simple even, at being directly addressed in this way. "That's if you're the Peculiar People. You are, aren't you?"

"We are indeed. And always happy to welcome another into the fold." The man made a sweeping gesture across the crowd. "As you see, we have multitudes."

"What are they all doing here?" Hart asked.

"The Chosen One is going to address us. This is Hylands Park." He pointed to a white neo-classical villa in the distance. "The house is his residence, but shortly he'll be coming down here to walk among us and to speak."

Hart looked wide-eyed at the man. "Will it be all right if I wait to see him? Me being a stranger and all."

"Of course. You'll be very welcome. We are open to everyone. Just stay close to me and I'll make sure that you get to hear him. We who wear the robe..." he held out his arms as if to show his garb to best advantage, "... we are The Guardians. His special disciples and protectors."

Hart did his best to look suitably impressed at this self-important claim, while wondering if their protection of the Chosen One ran to torture and murder. Probably so, he thought. Apocalyptic religious fundamentalism had all too often proved to be a happy home for psychopaths. Still, this accidental contact might well prove useful.

"Thank you," he said. "What should I call you, sir?"

"We are all Brothers and Sisters," the man replied, "and I am Brother Lionel. You are?"

"John," Hart said, adding with a tentative smile, "Brother John."

"Praise be! It's a good biblical name, Brother John." Lionel took his arm. "Now, stick close to me and I'll make sure that you are near enough to see The Prophet when he speaks."

Which he did, subjecting Hart to a constant commentary on the PeePees' beliefs, both before and after the Chosen One had spoken. Hart noted that wherever their leader walked among the adoring crowd he was surrounded by a group of Guardians, the kind of men that at other times and in other places would have been wearing dark suits, sunglasses and earpieces. They were taking no chances with their white-robed leader even in the midst of his own people. As for the speech itself, it began with an invocation of the Zeno epidemic in a prophetic passage from the Book of Daniel – 'they shall place the abomination that maketh desolate' – then, after that, appeared to Hart to be no more than a series of rhetorical flourishes and non sequiturs. The crowd clearly thought differently, however, and enthusiastic cries of 'Praise Be' and 'Hallelujah' punctuated it throughout.

Once the prophet had retreated to his villa – no sackcloth and ashes here, Hart thought irreverently – Lionel proposed that Hart came home with him for that night and then, the next day, they would find him a place in one of the hostels that the PeePees had set up for newly arrived converts. Hart accepted with alacrity. Hopefully he could find out more about the PeePees' plans by playing the simpleton in need of guidance. Over a meal Lionel proved garrulous enough, but Hart did not learn much other than what little might be gleaned from a string of quotations from *Revelations* and assorted other biblical sources. By 10pm he was relieved to be shown the bedroom where he was to spend the night.

Left alone, he extracted his hunting knife and silenced pistol from his bag. He was not about to place any trust in the seemingly avuncular Brother Lionel so, when he did get into bed, he remained almost fully dressed and kept the knife and pistol close at hand. He lay back to rest, neither quite asleep nor fully awake, a skill that he had learned many years earlier in his security service training. Sure enough, at around 1am he heard the soft tread of bare feet on the landing outside his room and then the slow opening of the door. Hart lay still, hugging one of the pillows to his chest as might a child in need of comfort, concealing the pistol behind it. Lionel, wearing pyjamas, came into the room, glanced briefly at the apparently sleeping form and then began going through the contents of Hart's bag. He'll find nothing incriminating in there, Hart thought, taking a firmer grip on the gun. The search complete, Lionel walked across to the bed, sat down on its edge and placed a hand on Hart's thigh. Hart started as if suddenly awakened, then sat up, still clutching the pillow to his chest.

"It's all right, John," Lionel said. "I thought we might keep company with one another during the night."

"Did you?" Hart said, and then again more harshly, "Did you indeed?"

He pushed the pillow towards Lionel to repel him, ensured that it was wrapped tightly around the gun and squeezed the trigger. There was a dull thump and Lionel fell backwards off the bed, prostrate on the floor and gasping in shock. Hart stood over him and, recalling the dreadful circumstances of Jenny's death, pressed the pillow over Lionel's face and held it there until all movement ceased. He dragged the body over to the room's empty wardrobe, stuffed it in and closed the door. Then he sat down and listened carefully. Not a sound. If anybody had heard the muffled gunshot they would have thought it was someone dropping a heavy object or banging into some furniture. After collecting his possessions, Hart set about searching the house, beginning with Lionel's bedroom and working his way downstairs.

In Lionel's wardrobe he found an almost new Guardian's robe. He stood looking at it for a moment then folded it up and crammed it into his rucksack. He also took Lionel's PeePee pendant which was hanging on the back of a bedroom chair. Downstairs he discovered a wallet containing a quantity of PeePee currency and Lionel's identification papers, which he added to his haul. In a folder of documents he came across a letter instructing Lionel to join his section of the Holy Army at Wisbech on a day some five weeks hence, as well as a map which showed the Army's line of assembly stretching north from Chelmsford to Lincoln. Five weeks, Hart thought, I don't have long. Pocketing the letter and the map, he took what food remained in the kitchen then slipped out the back door into an untidy rear garden. In a small lean-to shed were stored a few rusty gardening implements and, Hart was pleased to discover, an old but functional bicycle. He wheeled it out, checked that the tyres were firm, and prepared to leave. It was now almost 3am.

Fortunately Lionel's house was on the west side of the town so Hart was quickly into countryside. He would be far from the PeePees by dawn and, all being well, should be back at Whipsnade before nightfall. As he cycled he reflected upon what had happened. He had never killed a man before so he tried to examine the sensation of having done so now. But it proved elusive. He couldn't quite grasp what it meant for him to have directly taken someone's life. Of course, while at the DSD he had been involved in activities which had led to others' deaths, but they had always been at a distance. This had been up close and personal. Yet he found that he had no distinctive feelings about it, neither sorrow nor guilt, nor even satisfaction. It had just been something that was necessary and he had done it efficiently enough. He knew now that, if he needed to, he would be able to kill again. But the more important lesson that he had learned from his visit to Chelmsford was quite how serious a threat were the PeePees and their Prophet. This gave him a renewed sense of purpose and so, as he pedalled onwards and dawn eased into the sky behind him, he began to formulate a plan.

z z z

It proved far too long a winter for so many people that year. A population weakened by cold, hunger and stress had little resistance to the flu when the virus came calling. Many died, while many more were closer to it than their friends and families would have wished. In the little Argyll community the two children had to be nursed through desperate fevers and, having avoided it for so long, Ali finally succumbed. She was six days bedridden and for a significant proportion of that time knew little or nothing of what went on around her. She was not left alone for a minute, Douglas and her father taking turns to sit with her as she oscillated between lucidity and incoherent rambling, between fever and fits of uncontrollable shivering. When at last she returned to the world of the living she lacked energy and stamina for several weeks, only slowly getting back to something like her old self.

She and Charlotte convalesced together, reading and playing games while tucked up on the sofa in front of the wood-burning stove. So cold had the winter been that their stock of seasoned wood was running low and, much to Duncan's disgust, they were threatened with the need to use freshly felled timber on the fire. Not that the two recovering patients were greatly concerned just as long as the logs kept appearing and they could keep warm. It was on such a fire-hugging day that Charlotte suddenly made an announcement.

"Auntie Ali, I want to be called Charley from now on."

"Why's that?" Ali asked. "Charlotte's a lovely name."

"Yes, it's OK, but it's very long. Yours gets shortened to Ali instead of Alison, and there's Rav and Kenny and Jimmy, and..."

At this point she ran out of examples, allowing Ali to intervene.

"But Douglas stays Douglas," she said.

The little girl looked at her conspiratorially. "I asked him about that," she whispered, "and he told me that it was because he didn't like to be called Doogie. But I have to keep that a secret."

"Yes, you'd better," Ali whispered in return. "All right, I'll call you Charley if that's what you really want. But you'd best explain to your mum and dad that it's your idea or they might tell me off."

Charlotte nodded. "I promise," she said, cuddling up to Ali and staring happily at the glowing logs.

Ali, too, looked deep into the fire and contemplated their situation. She was more or less better now, feeling guilty about still spending the days resting instead of doing her share of the work. Apart from the flu, they had survived the winter without facing any desperate crises. In preparation for what they now thought of as the inevitable move north, Jimmy and Kenny had made several trips to Poolewe. The Magic Wagon, as Charlotte-now-Charley had dubbed the lorry, proved remarkably reliable, and with various ingenious adaptations had allowed them to transport not just supplies and possessions to the relative safety of the far north-west, but also Murdina's cattle and sheep. They had bought the animals from her when she had moved in with her sister in the nearby port town of Oban. So there was now yet another deserted house in what had once been a viable crofting community. The flu, it would seem, was doing a better job of emptying this part of the Highlands than had the infamous Clearances.

Ali's sleepy ruminations on Scottish history were suddenly interrupted by the arrival of first her father, looking grim, closely followed by his dog, and then the rest of the group other than Jimmy and Kenny who were still away in the north. They gathered around the fire as Ali forced herself to sit up and pay attention.

"What's happened?" she asked.

Duncan, who had squeezed onto the sofa next to her, gestured towards Douglas. "Douglas has got some news," he said, putting an arm around Ali's shoulders.

"Not good news, I'm afraid," Douglas began. "Winter's been very bad further south, a lot of people starving around Glasgow, and with the first signs of easing weather the Reivers have started moving north again. I've spoken with some people who managed to stay one step ahead of them. It sounds like they're not just coming up the main route past Loch Lomond but also through Inveraray and, I guess, up the coast. I think it's time for us to move on."

"How long have we got?" Sarah asked.

"I simply don't know." Douglas frowned. "It's impossible to predict. Depends on how many there are and what they find to delay them along the way. But I think we have to assume the worst and leave as soon as practically possible."

Ali slipped her arm round her father's waist and leaned her head on his shoulder. This was what she had been dreading for months.

Meeting no disagreement, Douglas continued. "If you could all start getting organised as we've planned. I'll radio Jimmy and Kenny to see when they can get here. We should meet again this evening when I've had a chance to talk to them."

The group dispersed, leaving Ali and Duncan sitting forlornly on the sofa with Pike flopped out on his sheepskin rug in front of the fire.

"Please come, Dad. What's the point of staying here?" Ali was close to tears.

"We've been through all that, Alison. There's nothing to be gained by going over it again. I'm content here. I don't want to go traipsing off to the north at my time of life." He paused, staring absently at the sleeping dog. "I haven't mentioned it before sweetheart but I'm not in good health. I've probably not got long left anyway. So I'd rather stay."

Ali turned to him in disbelief. "You're just saying that. It's not true."

"I'm afraid it is. I have a tumour. Before all this happened they might have operated, perhaps got me a few more years. But there's no chance of that now. When it gets to be too much I'll know what to do."

"Oh god," Ali groaned. "Why didn't you tell me before?"

"No point in worrying you," he said. "Nothing you or anybody else could do about it."

Ali was unable to think of anything to say, certainly nothing that would persuade her father to change his mind. Sensing their unhappiness Pike came across and rested his chin on Duncan's leg, looking up at the two of them with mournful brown eyes. Idly scratching the dog's head Duncan murmured, "Good boy, Pike," then turned to Ali.

"Have you heard anything from your mother?"

Ali was surprised at the enquiry. Her parents had not parted on good terms when her mother had left for the USA with a new partner. Ali could not recall Duncan ever asking about her before.

"No," she replied. "Not since Zeno happened. They were in California. She was never very good at keeping in touch anyway. I did try to contact her when I was still in Edinburgh, but no response."

"I tried too when all this started. I wanted to make things better between us before... well, you know, before everything fell apart. I don't even know if she got the message."

Ali squeezed her father's hand and they sat in silence as the afternoon wore on until they were interrupted by Douglas bursting in, clearly irritated and swearing under his breath.

"You're still here. Good," he said, "they can't make it down here. Jimmy and Kenny, I mean. Something about Fort William. It's become a kind of fortress again. Last time they were travelling up it was already getting difficult. If they try now they think they'd lose the lorry and maybe their lives. But they believe they can safely meet us just north of there if we can make our way to them."

"Plan B then," Ali said. They had already discussed alternatives that might be managed on foot if they were forced to flee at short notice.

"Aye, and we'll need to keep well away from the main roads north in case of Reivers. It's the rough route up the east side of Loch Etive for us, then along the glen and onto the old West Highland Way at the Kingshouse."

"Should take you about three days to the Kingshouse from here," Duncan observed.

Ali smiled at him. "You might do it in that," she said, "but we've got young children and adults who aren't accustomed to hillwalking."

"Hah," Duncan replied, mock affronted. "I'd do it in two, but OK, for you lot I'll say four days then. It's not the bairns you'll have to worry about, it's the unfit grown-ups."

"At least four," Douglas said, then turning to Ali: "Alison, while I talk to the others could you go down the road and tell Shona what's happened? I don't know if she and the two boys will still want to come now, but if they do they're welcome and their ponies will be very handy."

"Right. I need to get out for a bit anyway. Too long in front of the fire." She stood up and went in search of her coat. "Come on, Pike. You like to visit the ponies, don't you?"

Much of the next day was spent in packing and, Shona proving willing to join them with her teenage sons, setting up saddlebags for the three Highland ponies. Ali worked even harder at these tasks than she might otherwise have done, partly to prove to herself that she was fit again, but more to take her mind off the imminent separation from her father.

They had their last communal meal that night, then Ali and Duncan were left alone in front of the fire. They talked for a while about memories, happy and sad, about what the future might bring, about their love for each other. Then they simply lapsed into silence, Ali with her head in her father's lap as she had so often lain as a child.

Douglas found them still there, both asleep, when he arose at six in the morning. Gently he squeezed Ali's shoulder to wake her and set about preparing breakfast. By eight o'clock the group were ready, ponies laden, weapons and rucksacks distributed among the adults. Ali and Duncan had said what they had to say the night before and had agreed to keep farewells short in the morning. She hugged her father, whispering "I love you" in his ear, then knelt down and cuddled Pike who had been nervously watching the travel preparations.

"You look after him, Pike," she said, the dog licking her face in response.

Then she turned away and joined the others as they set off, resisting the temptation to look back. Duncan and Pike watched them out of sight then retreated together into the empty house, its heavy silence a reminder of the finality of their parting.

That day Pike never strayed from Duncan's side, except occasionally to look down the road along which the group had disappeared as if expecting their return at any minute. Duncan tried to fall back into the daily routine that he had maintained for so long before the visitors had arrived, but it was difficult and he found himself constantly speculating about where they would have reached on their journey. On the day after their departure he tried once more to re-establish normality, but this time, at around midday, his efforts were interrupted by the unmistakeable sound of gunfire. Pike, always nervous of fireworks and thunder, retreated immediately to his favoured hiding place beneath Duncan's desk.

Fearing the worst, Duncan grabbed his shotgun and the automatic rifle that Douglas had left with him, carrying them upstairs to a window overlooking the drive. He opened the window and, taking care not to lean out too far, looked to left and right. There was a group of five armed men working their way along the road, one or two breaking off at each house to check it out. Some way down the road he could see what looked like a body lying in a front garden; perhaps that was the source of the gunfire. He pulled back inside the room's shadow hoping to make himself invisible to the Reivers out on the road. When they reached his front gate, two men turned up the drive towards him. Duncan thought for a moment, then with a muttered "What the hell" lifted the rifle to his shoulder. He fired a burst and both men fell to the ground. The three remaining in the road dived for cover behind the hedgerow and followed up with a fusillade of erratic shots that smashed into the glass of the windows and thudded against the front of the house. Then there was silence.

Duncan, who was crouching to one side of the window, snatched a glance outside. Immediately there was a shot and one edge of the window frame splintered. He was pinned down. Maybe he could wait them out, he thought. But then again, maybe not. There were three of them and they could surely outflank him. Perhaps if he made it downstairs he could simply ambush them when they broke in. But first, while he had his high vantage point he should try to lower the odds. What did he have to lose anyway? A few months more and a growing tumour? Taking the decision, he stood up in the window and fired repeatedly along the hedgerow. A scream suggested that at least one of his bullets had found its target, but then fire was returned and he was thrown backwards to the floor by what felt like a hammer blow to his chest. When he recovered from the initial shock he looked down to see blood spreading across his shirt. I must get downstairs, he told himself, be ready for them.

He made slow progress crawling down the stairs, slumping at last onto the hallway floor and still bleeding heavily from the wound in his chest. He could barely sit up. Leaning against the wall he did his best to think clearly in spite of an overpowering desire to close his eyes and sleep. Were they still out there? He tried to remember how many sources of gunfire there had been and how many of the Reivers he was certain he had hit, but numbers were increasingly slippery in his semi-conscious state. He still had the rifle, he realised, clutched in his right hand, its barrel lying across his legs. If he could raise it a little he could cover the front door from here. He tried to draw up his legs and the gun barrel with them, but the effort was too much and he sagged even further against the wall. Perhaps he just needed to rest a little before trying again.

When the quiet had extended from seconds into minutes Pike emerged from his hiding place and came in search of Duncan. Confronted with the supine figure he sniffed at the growing bloodstain and then at his master's mouth and nose. As he always did in the morning when he felt it was time to get up, he nuzzled Duncan in the neck and licked his face. Duncan stirred.

"Pike," he murmured. "Hello boy. It's not time to get up yet is it? I'm still sleepy." And he closed his eyes.

The two frozen figures resembled one of those old-fashioned, moralistic tableaux beloved of the Victorians: the man asleep and the dog standing by, the whole thing graced with a title like 'Man's Best Friend' or 'His Master's Guardian'. And so they remained until, suddenly, the dog's ears pricked up, he rose to his feet and began first to growl and then to bark. With a crash the front door flew open to reveal the figure of a man, one arm hanging limply at his side and the other pointing a pistol into the hallway. Pike barked even louder and more ferociously at the intruder who, with a shouted "Fucking dog," took aim at him. The sound of a shot bounced around the enclosed space as if seeking and failing to find a way out until, at last, its reverberations died away.

The Reiver staggered, the gun falling from his hand as he fell backwards out of the door. Duncan, still levelling the rifle resting across his raised legs, slipped to the floor, no longer able to prop himself against the wall. Once more he closed his eyes. In the returning silence the dog resumed his position by Duncan's head and lay down next to him, his nose close to the man's cheek. Feeling Pike's proximity, Duncan turned his head to look into the animal's eyes, a fixed stare which the dog returned.

"Good boy Pike, good boy," he murmured, trying vainly to lift a hand to scratch the dog's ears. "Pike, listen, you must find Alison. Go Pike. Look for Ali. Find Alison. Go. Go." His voice faded to nothing and his head rolled to one side, eyes closing. Time went by and Duncan showed no signs of life but still the dog sat by his side, moving only once to return with a battered grey toy rabbit, its stuffing long since extracted, which he laid carefully by the now cooling body. But the familiar toy could produce no response, no repetition of the games that they had so often played together. At last Pike stood up, nuzzled Duncan's face a final time and set off through the open door, his nose close to the ground. He headed down the drive that led from the house, past the bodies and out onto the main route through the glen where, with a single look back at his home of many years, he turned to the right, as Ali had a day earlier, and loped purposefully towards the mountains.

z z z

North Kolkata is the oldest part of West Bengal's capital city, its overcrowding, poverty, and general state of dilapidation making it an ideal location in which the Zeno virus could spread and mutate. In its midst lies Sonagachi, a warren of streets and alleys that had for years played host to countless brothels and sex workers. As one of the world's most infamous red-light districts the area had always been a magnet both for men of the city itself and for those visiting from elsewhere. When Zeno arrived, the constant play of physical intimacy in the brothels of Sonagachi served only to further propel the virus far and wide. Forty years earlier, interventions to limit the spread of another virus – HIV – among the sex workers and their customers had been at least partially effective. But Zeno proved to be an altogether more ferocious antagonist, and now the entire area, and a large part of the great city of Kolkata itself, had been transformed into a mausoleum of rotting bodies and rampant disease.

8

Like many a real feudal ruler before him, when times got hard Lord Malvern proved more than willing to grind the faces of the poor. In his case the poor included almost everybody who found themselves under his sway, as faced with growing shortages he and his men sought to extract ever more from their long-suffering victims. The folk of Malvern Edge Farm were no exception to this harsh discipline and, as a result, had suffered a demanding winter. They were constantly hungry, and if that were so for them with a farm to draw upon, who knows what it was like for people in the towns and villages. Or so Irene was thinking as she distributed silage to the cattle. She had always had misgivings about imposing on Brian's generosity. It was fair enough that he should support his sister, but Irene and Lucy were simply extra mouths to feed, hangers-on in all but name. While they did what they could to help around the farm, it was really not much compensation.

Irene had more than once aired these feelings to Julie who insisted that she was welcome. Still, Irene had noted how often Julie stayed with Conrad and, therefore, ate with his family, which was striking since as Julie freely admitted she did not get on well with Conrad's parents. Irene assumed that Julie was trying to ease pressure on the farm's meagre food supplies, as well as simply wanting to spend time with her rediscovered boyfriend. Now, with Malvern's thugs turning the screw yet further, Irene was sure that she should try to move on. She was still of the view that it would be best to go north to Scotland to find Sarah who, according to the last message that had reached Hart's CommsTab, had arrived at Duncan's home in Argyll. But Irene was at a loss to know how that long trip might be managed, although increasingly certain that she would have to somehow make the effort once spring had properly arrived.

These depressing thoughts reminded her that she had not checked the CommsTab for some time so, when her work with the cattle was finished, she retreated to her room and powered up the tablet. To her delight a beep indicated the presence of a video message, though her pleasure was ameliorated somewhat by the discovery that, rather than being from Sarah, it was from Jonathan Hart. She watched the video with growing concern, then sat on her bed staring absently into the distance. When she heard the sound of horses' hooves followed by the voices of Julie and Conrad, she went out onto the landing and called to them.

"Julie, Conrad. Have you got a moment?"

"Yes, OK," Julie shouted. "Just coming. What's up?"

When they arrived Irene set the tablet in front of them and said simply, "Watch this."

"What is it?" Julie asked, then as the video began and she saw who it was, exclaimed "Good heavens! It's from Hart."

"Who's Hart?" Conrad enquired.

"Just someone we know," Julie replied.

On the little screen Hart began to speak.

"Hello Irene and Julie. I hope you receive this. The Comms infrastructure still seems to be working so there's a good chance. The reason I'm messaging you is to give you a warning. It's about the Peculiar People. You perhaps heard of them while you were still in the Homeland."

"Who are the Peculiar People?" Conrad interjected.

"Just a crazy apocalyptic sect that's developed out in Essex," Julie responded, while Irene added, "He gets on to that next".

Hart was continuing. "I'm afraid they've become a much more serious proposition. I've seen their leader addressing a big meeting and I can understand why people find him so charismatic. The PeePees are now highly organised and they have grand ambitions. They've turned themselves into an evangelical army and they're planning to head west from East Anglia and convert the whole of central England. Their actual beliefs appear to me to be utterly confused, but circumstances have become so desperate that many people are willing to become zealots in support of any cause that promises them salvation. I can't stress too much how dangerous they are. If you're in their way you'll either have to hide, undergo forced conversion and join their army, or be tortured and killed."

Hart paused for a moment, staring at something off camera. When he turned back he looked desolate.

"I'm sorry," he continued. "That happened to someone I knew. It really is as bad as that. I know you will think you're a long way from the PeePees over there in Malvern. Don't believe it. They'll reach you. They're intending to start their advance within the next few weeks and they have a massive army of fanatics. My advice is to get out of their way while you can. You could retreat into Wales, I suppose, but I think they'll keep going until they reach the sea on the Welsh coast. You'd probably be all right down in the West Country south of Bristol, or perhaps up north beyond Derbyshire – if you can safely reach any of those places. But don't stay where you are. They'll overrun everything in their path like the proverbial plague of locusts. Sorry to be the bearer of such terrible news. I feel that I owe a lot to both of you so please, please act on this information as soon as you can. Good luck."

He remained looking into the camera for a few seconds then leaned forward and the video went dead. Julie turned aghast to her two companions.

"Oh shit," she said, burying her head in her hands.

"But how seriously should we take that?" Conrad asked, looking sceptical. "Who is he? Can he be trusted?"

"Oh, I think we should take it very seriously," Irene replied. "Before Zeno he used to be Director of the Domestic Security Division – one of the major intelligence agencies. He knows what he's talking about and he's not given to exaggeration."

"Yes," Julie added. "Along with Irene he was the main source for all my Zeno stories. If he says it's going to be bad you can be sure that it really will be."

Conrad still did not look entirely persuaded, but confronted with the women's shared conviction he clearly felt that there was not a lot that he could say. Finally he spoke up.

"It's all very well him saying you should get out of their way, but where? If you go south like he suggested, once past Bristol it would get really difficult. Down in Cornwall the Cornish nationalists expelled all the incomers, and when they fled into Devon and Somerset it caused no end of problems there. If you went north, well, the Midlands are very lawless. I wouldn't fancy your chances. It would be much tougher than the trip you did to get here."

Irene nodded. "Yes, I know. If I could find a way I'd go to Scotland, to where my daughter is up in the Highlands. Not much chance of the PeePees or anyone else going that far north. But, as you say, there are many dangers between here and there."

She lapsed into silence and looked glumly at Julie who was lost in thought.

"Con," Julie said at last. "I know we were going to stay here tonight but perhaps we should go and warn your parents about this."

"I don't think my dad will take much notice. You know what he's like. He thinks he's well in with Malvern's gang and rich enough to buy his way out of anything."

"Still," Julie was insistent. "You're off back to Bristol tomorrow morning so we wouldn't have much time unless we go over there tonight. Come on, let's go now."

Grumbling a little, Conrad hauled himself to his feet and headed for the door, Julie following just behind. As he disappeared she turned round and, with a grin, winked at Irene. "It'll be OK," she mouthed silently, and then she was gone.

That night Irene explained the situation to Brian and Jean. Though recognising the seriousness of the PeePees' threat they remained determined to stay.

"This is all we have," Brian said. "It's been my entire life. If we have to pretend to convert then that's what we'll do. There's nowhere for us to go that will be any better than staying here. They surely can't be worse than the present lot."

Irene was of the opinion that an army of religious fanatics could be a great deal worse than Malvern's iron hand, but she kept her thoughts to herself. There was no point falling out with her hosts and, anyway, she had no practical suggestions to make. Things were beginning to look hopeless.

It was almost lunchtime the next day when Julie returned and sought her out.

"What are you looking so happy about?" Irene asked, for Julie was smiling broadly.

"I think I've got us a plan," she said. "Last night I persuaded Con that we should get out of here. It took me half the night but I knew I'd win him over in the end. He's fed up working for his dad and making these increasingly dangerous runs between here and Bristol. He doesn't think the trading will last anyway and then his family will have no influence left with Malvern. So he was always going to be persuadable."

"That's all very well, Julie, but it doesn't solve the problem of where we go."

"Ah, this is the clever bit." Julie looked pleased with herself. "You remember us talking about *The Cormorant?*"

"Yes, I remember," Irene said. "The yacht. Conrad's sister is living on it."

"Right. It's a serious boat, and both Marie and Conrad are experienced at sailing it. Apparently Marie and her husband have had enough of hanging about in the bay down there and would be more than happy to sail off into the sunset. I've persuaded Conrad that we should take it to Scotland. Don't you see, it solves all the problems. We can get away from the PeePee threat, you can find Sarah, Marie just loves sailing, and the boat's big enough to take them and us and Lucy. It's a perfect plan."

Irene looked at her sceptically. "You really think that it's possible?"

Julie nodded. "Yes, I really do think that it is. Besides, what else can we do? At least this way we'll have a chance." Her face was alight with enthusiasm. "And Irene," she said, now very much the old Julie, "it'll be an adventure."

z z z

Rather to Ali's surprise, the little band of travellers made good progress on the first day of their long walk. The main challenge was a muddy climb across rough ground which took them over a pass, Lairig Dhoireann at around 600m, and then an even more muddy descent into Glen Kinglass. Having previously dismissed the easier route to the east as too close to the main road, they turned west along a track which followed the river down to Loch Etive. Here they met another track running up from the south which, as they could see from their vantage point concealed among some trees, led to a small group of buildings close by Ardmaddy Bay. After studying them through binoculars Douglas reported that he could detect no movement. Should they approach the main house? His concern was that if it was occupied, and they went as a group, its residents might take them for Reivers and so shoot first and ask questions afterwards. This conundrum was resolved by Shona.

"I know the family who stay there – went to school with one of them. How about me and the boys walk up the track? They'll recognise us."

"That's if the place hasn't already been raided," Ali pointed out.

Shona scoffed at the idea. "Och, it's no likely this far up a road to nowhere," she said. "Why would the Reivers bother?" And summoning her two boys she walked resolutely towards the buildings.

The group held their collective breath as she neared the house and called out.

"Are ye there, Moira? James? It's Shona here, and ma boys."

There was no reply. Finding the door unlocked, she disappeared into the house then emerged a few minutes later.

"It's all right," she shouted, waving them on. "The place is empty."

On that first day, then, they were saved the effort of making camp, instead distributing themselves throughout the house. Other than Ali, who was worrying about her father, they were all cheerful enough when they retired for the night. But the positive mood did not last. The next morning Ravi rose early and went for a stroll, returning to report that he had discovered a recently dug grave. It was marked by a wooden cross and a roughly painted sign which read simply 'Moira and her daughter Ròisin. Perished from the flu'. Of her husband James and their other child there was no trace. Confronted with that gloomy reminder of Zeno's perils, it was a much chastened group that set off north that morning.

Although there were no high passes to negotiate, the walking was rougher than it had been the previous day. The track soon ran out and while there was a notional path along the side of the loch, all too often it disappeared. Progress was slow, not helped by the fact that some of the adults were now suffering pain in long-unused muscles. The scenery was magnificent, had anyone been looking. Away to their right loomed the massive snow-capped bulk of Ben Starav while to their left the long wall of Beinn Trilleachan rose above the water. Sadly, none of the travellers was in a frame of mind to appreciate this natural spectacle. They simply trudged onwards, barely raising their eyes from the ground beneath their feet.

It was with considerable relief, therefore, that they finally reached the head of the loch where they were to camp for the night. After they had settled in, at six o'clock Douglas called the Poolewe pair on the radio, one of two prearranged daily time slots. The little radio's batteries had been sufficiently charged in the day's sunshine such that he did not need to recruit the willing children to take turns on its wind-up mechanism. When contact was made he explained to Jimmy that they would be at least another four days, probably five, an estimate which brought pained looks from those around him who were already nursing tired legs. An early night was welcome.

As they were having breakfast the next morning, Charley, who had wandered down towards the water's edge, suddenly cried out.

"Auntie Ali, Auntie Ali. Look."

She was pointing back the way they had come.

"It's Pike!" she announced and ran to the dog who was trotting steadily towards them, pink tongue lolling.

"Oh my god," Ali murmured to herself, following Charley to the oncoming animal.

The three of them met in a tangle of arms, licks and a vigorously wagging tail. Only when this initial greeting was over did Ali turn an anxious face to Douglas.

"You know what this means," she said. "Something's happened to my dad. I have to go back."

Douglas knelt down beside her and the now resting dog. "But…" he began.

"No buts. He needs help. That's why Pike's here."

Douglas shook his head. "Stop and think, Alison." He took hold of her shoulders and locked his eyes onto hers. "Pike would never leave him unless," he paused, seeking the right words and finally settling on being blunt, "unless he was dead."

"No, no." Ali was determined not to believe him. "I have to go anyway. I have to know what's happened."

Douglas continued to look at her intently and then, at last, released her from his gaze. "All right. I'll come with you," he said. Then, turning to the others who had gathered around them, "If you could all stay camped here, travelling light we can be there and back inside three days. If we're not back in four, then you should go on without us. We'll leave the radio so that you can make arrangements with Jimmy and Kenny."

"You can't do that," Ali protested. "They need you here."

"And I need to be with you," Douglas replied. "I'm certainly not letting you go off alone."

Sarah knelt down close to Ali and spoke softly in her ear. "You should both go, Ali. We'll be OK here. But you mustn't go by yourself. That's the last thing your dad would want."

The decision made, it took only half an hour to strip their rucksacks down to the minimum necessities and prepare to leave.

"Right, let's go," Ali said, decisively turning away from her friends and walking as quickly as she could down the loch-side path, followed by Douglas struggling to keep up. "C'mon Pike," she called.

The dog pricked up his ears, eyeing her receding back.

"Come on," she called again, this time louder.

Pike ran after her and Douglas, but when he reached them instead of simply keeping pace he ran past then sat down about twenty metres ahead, barking continuously as they approached.

"Stop it, Pike," Ali said as they drew level. "To heel!"

He allowed them to pass, remaining seated but turning to watch them as they pressed on. Then he did exactly the same as before, planting himself ahead and barking loudly. Ali swore in frustration, waving an arm to encourage him forward. Again he waited and watched, then once more he overtook them and sat down directly in their path. His barking became even more frantic, now intermixed with angry growls.

Douglas looked at Ali and shook his head in dismay. This time when they reached Pike, Ali sat down and put her arms around the dog who immediately stopped barking and rested his muzzle on her shoulder. Ali began to weep softly.

"You know what he's trying to tell you, don't you? About Duncan," Douglas asked.

"Yes, yes. I know. That he's gone." She was whispering between spasms of crying. "I can't do this, can I? It's desperately selfish. We all need to go on together today. Not wait about here for days on end."

Finally recovering herself, she stood up, fondled Pike's ears, and with a wan smile to Douglas started back to the camp, the dog now walking obediently beside her. Her friends, who had been transfixed by Pike's extraordinary performance, greeted Ali with hugs and words of comfort.

"I'm sorry," she said to them all. "That was stupid and unnecessary. We have to stay together, of course we do. It's the only way we'll survive."

The next few days would remain a blur for Ali, just fragments lingering in her memory. Mostly they were associated with her father. Passing the great pyramid face of Buachaille Etive Mor and looking across to the Kingshouse, she was overwhelmed by recollections of a holiday spent there with her parents when she was a young girl. This was before the hotel had been given its extensive makeover, when it was still a lovely eccentric building echoing its eighteenth-century self. She had been enchanted one morning when her father had called her to the bedroom window to see a family of pine martens who had taken up residence in the roof space. Now, as the group walked on, she realised that with Duncan she had visited so many of the places through which they were passing. They had climbed mountains in Glen Coe and walked together over the Devil's Staircase. And one lovely summer's day they had completed the final stage of the West Highland Way, from Kinlochleven to Fort William.

This time, unfortunately, the day was anything but lovely for that part of their journey. It was as dreich as only the West Highlands could be. When the band of refugees finally emerged from the Nevis Forest onto the flat of the glen floor they were chilled to the bone, having spent the entire day in gloom and drizzle. The great mass of Ben Nevis was barely visible when they crossed the river and chose a spot to camp close to the start of the Pony Track. The nearest Kenny and Jimmy were prepared to risk bringing the lorry was to the old North Face car park near Torlundy, and they had advised the group not to continue down Glen Nevis which would take them too near to the town. Instead, the plan was to follow the Pony Track up the Ben's shoulder and descend from there to the car park.

On the next morning, the seventh of their journey, by some miracle the weather had cleared and they could see their path winding up the mountainside. Once more this brought back memories for Ali. Her father had taken her up the track when she was thirteen and introduced her to the art of walking in crampons on the icy summit plateau. Today, as the tired group of travellers neared the halfway lochan, Ali looked at the zigzags leading up and away to the right and remembered vividly her sense of achievement when her father had perched her on the summit trig point and told her that she was now the highest person in Britain. Up there, she thought, the snow would still be lying, metres deep, frozen.

"Where are the snows of yesteryear?" she murmured to herself.

"Eh? What?" asked Sarah who was walking beside her.

"Oh nothing." Ali shook her head. "Just a line from an ancient poem that my dad liked."

Fortunately for the weary travellers, snow on their route was limited to patches at an altitude of 600m or so, after which they passed the lochan and began their descent towards the forest and Torlundy. Before reaching the trees Ali stopped to look back at the now distant splendour of the

North Face as, one by one, the others overtook her. On her own at last, with only Pike for company, she whispered, "Goodbye Dad – bless you," then turned and followed her friends.

When finally they reached the track that would take them into the car park, Charley was out in front leading her favourite of the ponies. In truth, it was more a case of the pony leading her as it plodded steadily forward at a pace of its own choosing, the rest of the group strung out behind. Suddenly they heard a cry from Charley.

"The Magic Wagon! It's here."

Leaving her pony to fend for itself, she ran towards the lorry and leapt into Kenny's arms as he stood by the vehicle, an automatic rifle casually slung over his shoulder.

"Kenny," she said. "We've come such a long way. And now you're here. I'm so happy to see you."

"And I'm happy to see you too, wee one." He hugged her then lowered her to the ground. "And all the rest of ye as well."

Jimmy was already walking out to meet the others as they came down the track, embracing each in turn, obviously hugely relieved that they had arrived safely. Eager to be on their way they made a final effort to load their baggage, themselves and the ponies onto the lorry. Ali volunteered to go in the rear with Pike and the ponies, where she was joined by Sarah, Charley and Hugh who were determined to keep her company, and by Shona who wanted to stay close to her animals. Ali insisted that Douglas remain up front, remembering how he and Jimmy had dealt with trouble together back in Northumberland, and all the rest squeezed into the compartment behind the cab. It was not going to be a comfortable journey.

Nor was it a short one. For the first hour or so Ali sat looking out through one of the ventilation slots that Kenny had made when he adapted the lorry for transporting animals. She could see only partial views of mountains and lochs as they rattled along, unable to get any precise sense of where they were. Then it began to get dark and she lay back on her mattress and dozed, Pike on one side and Charley on the other. At some point she must have fallen asleep because the next thing that she knew was the noise of the rear doors opening and Jimmy shouting.

"All out sleepyheads. We're here."

Ali clambered down and was immediately aware of the smell and sound of the sea. Blinking the sleep out of her eyes she realised that there was a full moon, its reflected light fractured and shimmering on the surface of Loch Ewe. She was half conscious of the ponies being walked off the lorry behind her and of doors opening and lamps being lit. But it was the sea that held her attention. She turned to her left, looking north along the line of the coast to where the loch met the open ocean. To the west lay the Outer Hebrides and beyond them nothing but the odd rock until you reached North America. She wondered about her mother somewhere across that huge expanse. Was she even still alive? Ali would probably never know. And she thought of her father and promised herself that she would make a good life here in spite of the dangers and travails that they would face. That's what he would have wanted from me, she thought, as she turned and made her way towards the lamp lit cottage that was to be her new home.

z z z

The young boy burrowed as deep as he could into the undergrowth at the edge of the clearing. He had been on the run for several days now, his parents dead from the flu, his sister forcibly taken into whoredom, his friends scattered and lost. He knew that he was somewhere on the fringes of the Talladega National Forest, one of Alabama's surviving reserves, but he was uncertain of precisely where. Earlier he had heard the hounds baying as they followed the scent of some other poor fugitive, as well as the sound of men on horseback. Now the hounds were silent and, amid much shouting, the horsemen arrived in the clearing dragging their hogtied victim. They were robed in white and wearing improbably pointed masks that covered their faces, the regalia of the recently revived and, in the wake of Zeno, now rampant Ku Klux Klan.

They put a noose around the neck of the elderly black man that they had captured then threw the rope over the branch of a tree and hauled him off the ground. Already exhausted from the chase, he did not kick and struggle for long. Disappointed not to derive more entertainment from the lynching, the Klan members consulted among themselves and finally rode away in the direction that they had come. The boy, trembling in his hiding place, watched them go, then emerged and stood staring up at the now dead man. He looked down at the black skin of his own arms, then back to that of the hanged man, and from somewhere he heard the disembodied voice of Billie Holiday, his father's favourite singer. 'Southern trees bear a strange fruit,' she began, and the boy ran, trying in vain to escape the terrible message of the voice in his head.

9

Rowlands, exasperated at Hart's insistence on leaving Whipsnade before the PeePees' advance, shifted restlessly in his seat, all the while scowling across the desk at his friend.

"Come on, Jonny," he demanded. "Why not stay and fight?"

Hart aimed a sympathetic half-smile in his direction. Then he sighed.

"Jerry, I've already told you why. You can't win."

"But we have a good supply of weapons and people who know how to use them," Rowlands insisted. "We can defend this place well enough to put anyone off. Even if they do come here, and they may not, we can make things so hard for them that they'll decide to move on to easier targets."

"Oh, they'll come here all right," Hart said, rubbing his eyes anxiously. "After the business with Jenny we'll be high on their list. And when they do, they'll want to destroy us for having the effrontery to put a spy in their midst."

"So, like I said, we'll fight them off."

At this Hart allowed his irritation to show, raising his voice. "There are too many of them, Jerry. How many times do I have to tell you? They'll just overrun the place by sheer weight of numbers. Remember, these are fanatics. I've seen them. They'll march straight into the guns if that's what's required by their prophet and they'll be happy to do so. For them martyrdom is a direct route to salvation." He shook his head, calmer now, resigned even. "You can't win," he said quietly.

Rowlands leaned his elbows on the desk and put his head in his hands. "I thought they were Christians," he muttered, then looking up at Hart, "whatever happened to 'Love thy neighbour' and all that shit?"

"Oh come on, Jerry." Hart smiled thinly. "You used to be some kind of Marxist. Remember 'Religion is the opiate of the people' – Marx knew how powerful a force religion can be."

"Yeah, but that was to maintain false consciousness, hide people's real circumstances from them, offer them consolation for the misery that they faced."

"And that's not what the PeePees are doing?" Hart asked. "They've got hundreds of thousands of people believing that the end days are here and that it's their god-given obligation to convert all those that they can and to punish those that refuse. Only when they've created a holy realm in England, or died trying, will they be guaranteed paradise. Zeno and starvation and lawlessness have made people willing to believe any crap that promises to save them, whatever the cost."

"They can't be that stupid," Rowlands protested.

"It's not a question of stupidity," Hart replied. "Think about it, Jerry. You studied history at university. Remember all the madness and the murders and the genocide that have been done in the name of religion." Hart stood up and began to roam agitatedly around the room. "Look at the Christian Crusades. Look at all those weird millenarian sects. Look at the English seventeenth-century witch-finders or the American witch-hunts. Look at the Catholic Inquisition, for fuck's sake."

His voice was rising as he became more angry. "And it's not just ancient history when we like to think that people were more superstitious. It's modern too. Remember last century's Bosnian genocide? Religion was a force in that along with ethnic hatred. What about Africa? Religion overlaid all sorts of tribal conflicts there. It fed the Troubles in Northern Ireland, fuelled the violence in Indian partition, set Sunni and Shia Muslims at each other's throats, and in this century it gave birth to all those Islamic jihadi movements." Hart was warming to his theme. "And what about the quasi-religions, the ideologies that motivated the Khmer Rouge in Cambodia or the Chinese cultural revolution? All these appalling events were grounded in the absolute belief of people in their misbegotten transcendental causes. Fuck religion, and all totalising belief systems like it. Throughout history they've done much more harm than good."

Hart collapsed back into his chair, exhausted by his tirade.

Rowlands looked at him, astonished. "Bloody hell, Jonny. I've never seen you so worked up about something. Not even back in our student days."

"Ah well," Hart said smiling sadly. "I've learned a lot about human gullibility since then, including my own, and especially in the last few years."

Rowlands gave him a quizzical look, was about to say something but then thought better of it. Instead, he drummed his fingers on the desk and stared past Hart at the wall behind him. Finally, when the silence became uncomfortable, he turned his attention to Hart once more.

"All right, what do you think we should do?" he asked.

"I think you should disperse. When I travelled down here from Nottingham I found a lot of empty houses and I'm sure there are many more now. Scatter your people in all directions and leave this place deserted. Then, when the PeePees have pushed on west you could return here if you wanted. Even if they leave behind a holding force, I doubt that it will be very big. They'll want maximum numbers when they reach the more populous areas." Hart paused, thinking, then continued. "Mind you, I don't know what chance you'd have in the long run. A lot will depend on whether they succeed in their campaign."

Rowlands looked sceptical. "I don't like it," he said. "I don't think we'd ever get all our people back together again."

"Would that be any great loss?" Hart asked. "It's not exactly a homogenous committed group of communards that you've got now." Conscious that Rowlands had a great deal of his ego invested in the ERA community, he added solicitously, "Maybe you could start again somewhere safer with more carefully chosen members?"

"Somewhere safer!" Rowlands laughed, though without humour. "Where would that be? I chose Whipsnade because it was such a promising location and I thought we could defend it. I'm not inclined to give it up just because of those religious maniacs."

Recognising that their discussion was going nowhere, Hart stood up. "It's up to you, of course. You know my views. Now I'm going for a walk in the park."

Rowlands nodded. "When will you leave?" he asked, clearly now resigned to the inevitable.

"In a day or two. I'm going to go south so I need to talk to those guys who are hoping to form a republican cell in the Homeland. I want to know what route they're going to take so I don't get tangled up with them."

He might have added, though he did not, that he also needed to acquire certain equipment from their growing arsenal. Instead, he said simply, "I'll see you before I go," and left Rowlands sitting disconsolately at his desk.

The park was a pleasant enough place in the evening sunshine and he could easily understand Rowlands' desire to stay. He would be inclined to do so himself were it not for the imminent arrival of the PeePees and, more important, the fact that he now felt that he had something specific to accomplish. He wandered down to the yaks' favoured grazing area and sat on his bench. The usual beast – his yak, as he thought of her – left the others to their feeding and lumbered over to visit him. She was now so tame that she all but pushed him over, lowering her head to be scratched and grunting contentedly.

"I'm afraid I'll be leaving soon, old girl," he murmured. "I hope you weather the storm that's coming."

With one final pat on her bony skull, Hart continued across the parkland until he reached a nondescript building with large double doors at the front and a smaller entrance to the side. He knocked firmly on the side door and, after a pause, it opened a little way and a man peered out.

"Well then, it's the important Mr Hart," he said, backing away to allow Hart to enter. "This is a rare treat."

"Don't take the piss, Geordie," Hart said with a grin. "I might take offence."

"Aye, that'll be the day, Jonathan. What can I do for you?"

They were standing in a large open area, once some kind of repair shop for the zoo, with workbenches around the perimeter and a variety of more substantial pieces of machinery scattered here and there. Several of the benches held weapons in various states of disassembly, while the surface on which Geordie had been working boasted a number of obscure electronic devices to which Hart could not even give a name. He picked up a small plastic box with two buttons on its surface and wires trailing from its rear. Turning it over in his hands he eyed it suspiciously.

"I'm going to need one of those explosive belts that you've been working on, Geordie, but with some minor adjustments."

Geordie took the box out of his hands. "Careful with that," he said. "You never know what it might do." He replaced it gently on the bench. "Minor adjustments, eh. What kind of minor adjustments?"

"You make them with a timer for detonation, don't you?" Hart enquired.

"Yes, and a tidy piece of work it is too."

"What I'd like," Hart continued, "is that, but with the addition of a dead man's switch."

"And what would that be for?" Geordie asked.

"Emergencies," Hart replied. "If I'm going to get captured it will allow me to take a lot of them with me. Not that I intend to get caught, but it's a fail-safe just in case."

The engineer gave him a hard look. "That's a bit of a desperate measure," he said.

"Desperate times, Geordie, desperate times. But can you do it?"

"Aye, it's easy enough." Geordie picked up another of the small devices that littered the bench, this one looking rather like a fat pen with a button on its top. "This is the sort of thing," he said, showing it to Hart. "It connects into the existing detonator. Once you enable it you have to keep holding this button down. Let it go, boom!"

"That's exactly what I need," Hart said, taking the device and examining it. "Could you set up a belt with this for me?"

"OK. If that's what you want. I'll fix it so you can power it down if you change your mind." He eyed Hart suspiciously. "You're sure about this? It's a dangerous bit of kit to carry around."

"Yes, I'm certain." Hart smiled at him. "It's only a backup in case of emergency."

"A backup – I see." Geordie sounded sceptical. "All right then. Come by around midday tomorrow and I'll have it for you. But don't you go blowing yourself up."

Agreeing to return the next day, Hart left the workshop and walked back to his chalet. Retrieving the letter and map that he had found in Lionel's house, he sat at his table and examined them again. Then he took down a much larger map from a shelf and spread it across the table. He knew from Lionel's documents the extent of the PeePee army's proposed front. What he didn't know was how far they might stray south of that front and what towns and cities were to be major targets. He presumed that they would want to steer clear of any entanglement with Homeland troops after their humiliation at Loughton. Hence his intention to move south himself and wait for them to pass by to his north. But how near dare he go to the Homeland border?

After much consideration he settled on heading for the area around Kings Langley which lay only just outside the Homeland. The PeePees would surely remain north of the small satellite towns like Hemel Hempstead and St Albans so he would be well placed to check on their progress. As to their principal goals, he could only speculate. Once they had moved on he planned to follow them in the hope that their intentions might become clearer, allowing him to decide only then on his best strategy. Satisfied at last that he had done what he could, Hart retired to bed and to a restless sleep constantly interrupted by bad dreams.

The next day he collected his modified explosive belt from Geordie, who warned him once again about its dangers, and then retrieved an automatic weapon, ammunition, and dried instant food supplies from one of his special caches. He carefully packed all this into his rucksack, adding his silenced pistol as well as the PeePee pendant and the Guardian robe that he had taken from Lionel's house. Then, bearing the last of his bottle of whisky, he sought out Rowlands in the early evening.

"I'm going to leave first thing tomorrow. Got some glasses?" he asked, laying the bottle on Rowlands' table and adding with a wry smile, "We can drink to the future."

Rowlands fetched two glasses and, after pouring the contents of the almost empty bottle into them, he took one and held it up to the light, eying the small quantity of golden spirit that it held. "That's probably about as much future as there'll be," he observed.

"Mmmmn," Hart nodded. "Perhaps so – tomorrow's the day the PeePees are scheduled to start their advance. Here's to it all going wrong." He raised his glass, clinked it against his friend's, and savoured the whisky.

They continued chatting for a while, mostly about the past since the present and the future had so little to recommend them. At last Hart stood up and embraced Rowlands.

"I'm sorry things have worked out this way, Jerry. I'm glad I came across you again after all these years. Maybe I'll find you after the PeePee crisis is over. Please hide somewhere. They'll be coming."

Rowlands nodded. "Perhaps I will. I'll decide with the others tomorrow. You take care of yourself."

After yet another restless night, at first light Hart arose, looked around the chalet for the last time trying to recall only its few happy memories, then strode unobserved out of the zoo's main entrance and disappeared down the road to the south.

z z z

In the heat of early evening four indistinct figures, two adults and two children, struggled up the steep forest path which led from Parque Lage onto the granite outcrop of the Corcovado. They emerged from the trees to discover that they were not alone. The viewing platform beneath the massive Cristo Redentor was crowded with others also seeking refuge from the chaos of the city below. The view of Rio de Janeiro from here was justly famed, a panorama running from the beaches in the south to the sprawl of streets and buildings and people, so many people, to the east and to the north. But it was not that familiar spectacle that had drawn these stunned observers. It was instead the radiance of the many fires that were raging throughout the city.

The destruction wrought by a series of flu epidemics had finally pushed Rio over the precipice of social disorder on which it had teetered for so many years. Vigilante groups, aided by an always violent police force no longer paid nor commanded, had set about destroying the favelas whose largely innocent residents they blamed for Rio's troubles, while the gangs who had so often controlled the favelas fought back and fought each other. Just as the poor had once spread their impromptu housing up Rio's forested hillsides, so now fire followed in their footsteps. Everywhere there was burning. The hushed group on the Corcovado clung together, at a loss to comprehend the scene of destruction that lay spread out before them, hoping and praying that Christ the Redeemer, beneath whose statue they sheltered, its arms outstretched in welcome, would indeed bring them redemption.

10

Irene was not much enjoying the experience of bouncing around in the back of a small, poorly sprung lorry, surrounded by sacks of root vegetables. At either side of the half-open rear sat two armed guards, apparently immune to the constant lurching as they watched the countryside go by. Lucy had managed to bury herself in among the sacks with only her head and shoulders visible, a position which held her small frame stable while the vehicle gave the impression of wilfully seeking out potholes. Julie and Irene, however, were too big for that solution and so were grimly hanging on to the rope handles provided for the purpose. Between impacts they were managing a sort of conversation.

"How far are we going in this boneshaker?" Irene asked.

"Only as far as Gloucester Docks," Julie replied. "After that it's a barge down the canal to Sharpness and then the River Severn. That should be a lot more comfortable. Con said that this road is in a really bad way because nobody does any maintenance any more. But they daren't go too slow because of the risk of hijackers."

"So this is the trip that he's been doing regularly," Irene said. "No wonder he's willing to sail to Scotland with us."

Julie laughed. "It's not just that. He's fed up with the whole set-up between his father and that shit Malvern. This stuff," – she gestured at the sacks around them – "this is food that's grown in the Malvern area but is sold on for a profit when it could be used to feed hungry folk back there. His father gets a cut but Malvern takes the lion's share. Con thinks that

Malvern will dispense with their services pretty soon – he needed their help at the beginning but it would be easy enough for him to take over the whole operation now, including their Bristol trading end."

"He who sups with the devil..." Irene observed drily. "Get involved with somebody like Malvern and pretty soon you're not much better yourself."

Julie frowned. "I know. I've been saying that to Con ever since we met up again. But he takes a survival-of-the-fittest line. Just do what you have to do, he says. Let the weak go to the wall."

"That's a harsh doctrine. I'd have thought that in the long run it's co-operation that will allow people to survive the Zeno crisis, not a war of all against all." Irene eyed the armed guards. "Still, I suppose I'm grateful to have those two here right now."

Unnoticed by the two women as they talked, the road surface had improved and now they could see out the back of the vehicle that they were no longer in countryside. One of the guards turned to them.

"Nearly there," he said. "The worst is over."

Which proved to be correct. The subsequent trip on a laden barge was comfortable and uneventful, although the machine guns mounted fore and aft were a constant reminder that this was anything but an idyllic waterborne holiday. At Avonmouth they transferred yet again, this time to a small boat which ferried them out to where *The Cormorant* awaited its passengers.

Irene had no idea what to expect, so when they arrived she was pleasantly surprised. Apart from looking remarkably picturesque silhouetted against the low sun, the boat proved to have extensive facilities. Given a tour by Marie, who was clearly very proud of her maritime home, Irene was taken aback to see how much could be packed into such a small space.

"She's a forty-footer," Marie explained. "Built back in the twentieth century in Scotland so we'll be taking her home. Of course, she's been refitted more than once since then. My dad bought her because he thought rich men should own yachts, but he was never really interested. And anyway she's not a yacht in the way that people think of them –

those big luxury boats or the slim-line ones that they see racing. She's a motorsailer, very sturdy and dependable. We'll be safe aboard her."

Irene was shown the saloon, the two cabins, the galley, the shower, and what she was to learn to call the head. She was duly impressed.

"What's the wood?" she asked, eyeing the polished surrounds of the saloon. "It's a gorgeous colour."

"It's mahogany. Lovely, isn't it?" Marie smiled at Irene, obviously pleased to have someone who appreciated her treasure. "For sleeping arrangements, Stuart and me are in the aft cabin. We can put Con, Julie and Lucy in the fore cabin, and you can have one of the settee berths in the saloon. I originally thought of putting Lucy in here," she added apologetically, "but then I realised that she'll probably have to go to bed before the rest of us."

"Oh no, I'll be fine," Irene insisted. "I'd sleep on deck if I had to, just to get to Scotland and find my daughter and granddaughter."

Marie laughed. "No need for that. I think it might be a bit chilly and damp up there. How old's your granddaughter?"

"She'll be nine soon. About a year older than Lucy."

"That one's a live wire, isn't she?" Marie said, nodding upwards towards the deck from whence giggles and the patter of feet could be heard. "That'll be Stuart playing some game with her. He's good with kids. We thought about having one but with the world in the state it's in, well, it hardly seems responsible."

Irene looked at her solicitously. "No, it would be difficult to justify, wouldn't it? Bringing some poor little mite into such a terrible situation. But maybe things will be different up in the Highlands."

"Maybe," Marie replied with a shrug. "Anyway, we've got to get there first. Let's sort out an evening meal and then you can tell me exactly where we need to go. As usual, my little brother was rather vague."

Once they had eaten and an overtired Lucy had been persuaded into her bunk, Marie lifted a large tablet out of its mounts by the wheel and carried it over to the dining table.

"Just let me get the charts up," she said to Irene, "and you can show me where we're going."

Irene pointed at the tablet. "Does that thing connect to the public network then?"

"It used to," Marie replied, "but that stopped working a while ago. The charts and information logs are all held locally so we're OK without the connection." She waved towards the helm where there were other screens and dials mounted. "The GPS systems are still functioning and we've got all sorts of radio. We'll be able to navigate without the network. Now Irene, here's the Scotland chart. Where should I zoom in to?"

Irene indicated the west coast north of Glasgow and then, as Marie zoomed the map, leaned over and swiped it towards Oban. "The nearest we can get to Duncan's house by water is to sail up Loch Etive. If we can get ashore here..." she pointed to a spot on the now much enlarged map "... then we can walk over the pass at the head of Glen Noe. It'll be about eight miles or so. I did it with Robin once when we spent a holiday at Duncan's. Do you think that's possible?"

Marie looked at the map for some time, zooming in and out and then consulting various other navigational sources.

"Yes, it looks OK," she said at last. "We'll need to get under a road bridge at Connel and some HT cables further on at Bonawe, so we'll have to lower the mast for both even if there's no longer any power in the cables. The information here is quite old and rising sea levels may have had an impact on the clearance since then. But with the mast down we'll be fine anyway. And there's a tidal race to deal with at the bridge: the Falls of Lora."

"Yes, I've seen that," Irene said. "It's very impressive. Lots of turbulence and white water when the tide runs. In the right conditions you can even get a standing wave. Looks a bit like a step in the water. When I saw it there were kayakers kind of surfing it."

"We'll have a close look when we get there. We can always wait until slack water if we have to." Marie looked again at the chart. "I'm more worried about the narrowness of the access. In fact, the whole of Loch Etive is fairly narrow. You're more open to attack in narrows than in the open sea and you've got nowhere to run to."

"We've got plenty of arms, sis," Conrad said. "We're not exactly defenceless."

"How come?" Julie asked.

"When the military withdrew to the Homeland, Dad struck a shady deal with some deserters. He thought there would be a good market for armaments as things got worse. I made sure that we got hold of some of them, and a lot of fuel too. As a result *The Cormorant* is a very well-found boat." Conrad looked pleased with himself. "We've even got a little rocket launcher. Ideal for seeing off pirates."

"Ignore him," Marie said, noticing the expressions on Irene's and Julie's faces. "Boys' toys. But it's true, we are well set up. Along with diesel for the hybrid motor we've got the most recent military batteries which we can top up by wind, solar, and hydro. We're pretty much self-contained." She looked around at her passengers. "Right then, I'm going to start plotting our course. Get some rest. We set sail first thing tomorrow."

Early next morning Irene was awakened by Marie arriving in the wheelhouse adjacent to her bunk.

"We're off, Irene. Stuart's dealing with the anchor up there. It's a lovely day if you fancy enjoying the view from on deck. We'll motor out into the Bristol Channel then hope to pick up a breeze."

They were under way by the time Irene had finished dressing, and when she went up on deck she found Stuart sitting on a hatch cover in the early morning sunshine. She sat down next to him.

"Morning," he said. "Look," pointing away to the west. "That's Cardiff. And over there, Weston-super-Mare. They look so normal from out here, don't they? Yet they're anything but." He paused then shook his head. "It's such a relief to be doing something at last, not just sitting back there wondering what terrible thing will happen next."

"What did you do before all this?" Irene asked.

"I was an electrical engineer," Stuart replied, staring thoughtfully into the distance. "Had a PhD and a decent job with a generating company until things went wrong. Then it was a question of 'last in, first out'. They're out of business now anyway."

Before Irene could respond, a small figure emerged from below and snuggled herself in between the two adults. Lucy beamed up at each of them in turn. "This is exciting," she said. "I think I like boats."

She had plenty of time to cultivate her new-found enthusiasm as they set the mainsail, rounded South Wales and headed north. Prevailing winds favoured them and they made good progress, only briefly encountering the rough conditions for which the Irish Sea was famed. This was still more than enough to afflict both Julie and Irene with seasickness, but Lucy seemed entirely immune and appointed herself Stuart's personal deckhand. Tethered to a safety line, she showed every sign of enjoying the pitch and roll of the boat and the crash of the waves as *The Cormorant* rode them. Fortunately, by the time they arrived at the northern reaches of the Irish Sea the weather had calmed, allowing the two erstwhile patients to come out on deck and breathe some fresh air. It was from there that they caught their first sight of Scotland as they passed between the Northern Irish coast and the Mull of Galloway.

Marie's desire to avoid narrows took them west into the open Atlantic to round Islay, but then they had no choice but to head into the constricted mouth of Loch Etive. Dunstaffnage Marina was crowded with boats when they passed but with no signs of activity. To their relief, slack water greeted them at the Falls of Lora where they had only to pause briefly to lower the tabernacle mast and then motor on beneath the bridge. In almost windless conditions they continued under power past the cable at Bonawe and then up the loch until they could drop anchor off the mouth of the River Noe. It was five days since they had left Bristol and in all that time they had seen only two boats under way, both of them distant and showing no inclination to make contact.

For what remained of the day Irene and Conrad sat on deck with binoculars trained on the Glen Noe farm and its group of outhouses. They detected no movement and after dark there were no lights to be seen anywhere along the shoreline, so Irene, Julie and Conrad resolved that on the following day they would walk up the glen and over the pass. At 8am Stuart ferried them ashore in *The Cormorant*'s inflatable, Lucy dissuaded from joining them by the promise of going fishing with Stuart.

The walk up to Lairig Noe was rough going. Irene recalled traces of a stalker's path from her previous visit but there was little sign of it now. Once over the pass, however, they found themselves on a good stony track and by early afternoon they were among Stronmilchan's deserted crofts as they neared Duncan's house. The two women prevailed upon Conrad to conceal the short-barrelled automatic rifle that he had insisted on slinging over his shoulder, and, grumbling, he hid it in his rucksack. They had no wish to give the impression that they were a threat, although they saw nobody before arriving at their destination. Irene knocked on the door and called out but there was no reply. When the door proved to be unlocked they ventured in to find a deserted, silent house. An upstairs window was broken and, as Conrad pointed out, there were what looked like bullet holes in the ceiling and in the wall opposite the window. There were also ominous brown stains in the downstairs hallway. At this sight Irene sighed deeply and, unable to hide her dismay, turned to the others.

"Something terrible has happened here," she said. "Maybe we should walk further down the road, see if we can find anybody?"

The next several houses were also deserted, their gardens neglected and overgrown. But then, a little further up the hillside, Julie spotted a column of smoke rising from a cottage chimney. Cautiously they approached, Irene calling out as they walked up the path.

"Hello. Is anybody there? We were looking for Duncan MacGregor but his house is empty."

At the mention of Duncan's name they caught a glimpse of movement behind a window and, seconds later, the front door opened and an elderly woman peered out.

"Who are ye?" she asked.

"I'm an old friend of Duncan's," Irene replied. "My daughter, Sarah, and her husband and my granddaughter were staying with him and Ali."

"I'm sorry, I've bad news for ye about Duncan then," the woman said. "He's dead. He was shot by Reivers, but not before he killed five of them. That saved the rest of us. A good man. We buried him in the graveyard by the kirk." Then, seeing Irene's desolate expression, she quickly added, "But that was after all the young folk had left. My niece Shona and her two laddies went with them."

"Do you know where they went?" Irene asked. "Sarah told me that there was some place they might go to further north."

"Aye, they went north. A couple of months ago, just before the Reivers came. They were aiming for – och, what's the name of the place?" She stared past them, eyes unfocused, thinking hard. "Poolewe, that's it. Where the Inverewe Gardens are. I went there once, years ago."

Irene beamed. "Yes, of course. I've been there too with Sarah. That's what she mentioned, visiting those gardens. Thank you so much. We'll try to find them there. But is there anything we can do for you?"

"No, I'm fine thanks. I've family away up the glen and they keep an eye out for me. I hope ye find your folk." She turned back into her cottage, murmuring as she went: "Awfy times, awfy times."

Although Irene was eager to return immediately to the boat, the other two persuaded her that it would be dark before they even got as far as the pass so they would be better making a meal and spending the night in Duncan's house. Irene found sleep elusive, in part because of her impatience to hurry on, but more because she was haunted by thoughts of Duncan's violent death so close to where she lay awake. As a result, she was up at first light chivvying the other two into reluctant action. It was a damp, grey Highland morning that accompanied them on their walk back, clouds sitting low over the peaks of the Cruachan range. Descending towards the farm at last, they could see Lucy waving and calling out on the *Cormorant*'s deck. As they learned later, she had spent the whole morning peering through the big tripod-mounted binoculars that she trained on the hillside down which they were to return.

Once both good and bad news had been imparted to the others, Irene sat down with Marie to plan their onward course while Stuart motored *The Cormorant* back down Loch Etive and towards the open sea. As they approached the narrows at Bonawe he suddenly called out.

"There's a small boat approaching us."

Those below rushed out on deck just as the visitor hailed them.

"I mean you no harm. I'm just out to check my creels. Where are you from?"

Stuart slowed the boat as Marie replied, "We've been away up the loch looking for someone, but originally we sailed out of Bristol."

"A long voyage, that. How are things down there?"

"Not good. It's chaos right across England. How are you managing here?"

"I stay in Taynuilt," the fisherman said. "We've lost a lot of folk to the flu and we've had Reivers through as well. But we're getting by."

In the midst of this exchange, Irene noticed out of the corner of her eye that Conrad was lying flat on the rear deck clutching what she assumed was the rocket launcher, which he was aiming at the fishing boat. She nudged Julie and, frowning, nodded in his direction. Julie swore under her breath and with seeming casualness strolled towards him. "Don't be stupid," she hissed. "He's on his own and he's no threat."

Meanwhile, the others having fallen silent the fisherman called out, "I'll be on with my work then – good luck," and with a wave continued up Loch Etive.

Marie and Irene returned to the charts as *The Cormorant* cruised on, Lucy at the wheel closely supervised by Stuart. Julie and Conrad disappeared into their cabin from whence raised voices were heard. Irene looked at Marie who shrugged apologetically. "He's a hothead. Always has been I'm afraid. Julie has a good effect on him, but..."

When they reached the Falls of Lora they were confronted with foaming white water as the tide retreated and the waters of Loch Etive plunged through the channel. Eyes shining, Marie took the helm and steered the accelerating boat through the deeps on the southern side of the turmoil and out into open water.

"That was fun," she said, as they set about raising the mast. "Now let's go north."

When visible through the periodic squalls and mist, the parade of mountains and sea lochs along the West Highland coast formed a spectacle far beyond that which any of them could have imagined. Irene was disappointed not to pass through the dramatic narrows separating Skye from the mainland, but Marie, whose authority as captain was unquestioned even by her brother, deemed it too risky and took *The Cormorant* around the west coast of the Isle. Unlike the earlier part of the voyage when Marie, Conrad and Stuart had alternated night watches at the helm to speed their progress, now in less haste they sought out sheltered inlets in which to anchor overnight. At last, rounding the northern tip of Skye they set course for the Rua Reidh Lighthouse after which, late one calm morning, they swung south into Loch Ewe.

Irene's excitement was tangible but tempered by the fear that they would again be disappointed. Once they had anchored off Poolewe village itself, Stuart rowed Irene and Julie ashore, remaining with the dinghy near the mouth of the river while they sought information in the village. Coming across a woman sitting while her small child played on a swing, they approached her tentatively. She smiled at them, clearly undisturbed by their arrival. Evidently there had been no trouble with Reivers this far north.

"That's a bonny boat you have there," she said, nodding towards the anchored *Cormorant*. "Come far?"

"From Bristol," Julie replied, returning the smile.

The woman whistled softly. "That *is* a long way," she said. "What brings you here?"

"I'm looking for my daughter and granddaughter," Irene answered. "We think they travelled here with a group of others from Argyll about two months ago."

The woman smiled again. "Oh aye," she said. "That'll be the folk that's settled out Cove way." She pointed up the loch toward the open sea. "You'll have passed a big wind turbine as you sailed in. That's where they stay."

Irene could barely contain herself. "And do they have children with them?"

"Yes," the woman said. "There are two teenage boys, and another younger dark-skinned laddie." She paused then smiled conspiratorially at Irene. "And there's a bonny wee girl. Charley she insists on being called though her mum keeps on with Charlotte. That's mebbe your granddaughter? I can see the family resemblance."

Irene let out a deep sigh of relief. "Oh yes, thank you, thank you so much." She turned to Julie and hugged her. "We've found them," she whispered. "At last."

An hour later and a few miles back down Loch Ewe, Ali was busy weeding her vegetable garden when she looked up to see the yacht that had earlier sailed up the loch now dropping anchor about eighty metres offshore. She squinted in its direction as three adults and a child climbed down into a dinghy. One of the figures looked familiar, she thought, and she stood up to get a better view. The dinghy started to move towards the jetty just below the cottage that she shared with Douglas and, as the white blobs resolved themselves into faces, recognition dawned. She turned towards the house next door and screamed.

"Sarah, Sarah. Come quick. Look!"

The door opened and Sarah and Charley emerged, curious to know what all the excitement was about. Ali, now incapable of articulating anything, pointed mutely towards the oncoming dinghy. Sarah looked, looked again, and began to run down to the jetty.

"What is it, Auntie Ali?" Charley asked.

"It's your granny," Ali said, and grabbing her by the hand, ran after Sarah.

By the time they reached the jetty the dinghy had arrived and Irene and Sarah were in each other's arms. When they disentangled themselves Irene knelt down in front of her granddaughter.

"Hello Charlotte," she said. "I've come such a long way to see you."

The girl looked at her wide-eyed and edged forward. "Granny?" she said tentatively, and then with more certainty, "Granny." She reached out to Irene and, as she was drawn into an embrace, whispered into her grandmother's ear, "But I'm Charley now."

z z z

For those who were still in a position to read or hear or, in a minority of cases, view the World Health Organization's final communique, its contents served only to confirm what they had already suspected. In the video Dr Kiara Nareshkumar, the Sri Lankan Director General, sat sober-faced looking directly into camera. This would be her organisation's last statement on the so-called English flu, she explained, since the WHO no longer possessed the resources to function effectively. She confirmed that the disease had attained pandemic proportions on a scale never before experienced in modern times, and that it was no longer even possible to provide an approximate estimate of deaths among those infected. Certainly the figure had passed the billion mark, a number almost beyond comprehension in a world population of just over eight billion. She further reported that although where they could still do so scientists were engaged in pursuit of an antidote to the Zeno effect, thus far that research had proved fruitless. She paused for what seemed like minutes, then looked desolately into camera and spoke for the last time. "That is all that the World Health Organization can do or say." She was almost whispering. "May your gods be with you."

11

All but three of the 'Coveys', as Lucy had named them, were gathered in Ali's garden, the adults chatting or just enjoying the midsummer gloaming, the children running amok, pleased to be up so late. Although the sun had only recently set it was nearly 10.30pm. Such are the summer pleasures of northern latitudes that it would remain light for at least another hour. There was enough breeze coming off the sea to turn the blades of the turbine on the hill behind them and, mercifully, to deter the midges. They were waiting for Jimmy, Kenny and Stuart to return from beyond Gairloch where they had been inspecting the failed power station on the River Kerry.

A bark from Pike, who had been dozing at Ali's feet, followed by the whine of an approaching motor alerted them to imminent arrivals. Minutes later, the four-seater open ATV came bouncing up the track, Jimmy driving in his customary boy-racer fashion while Kenny and Stuart hung on for their lives. The vehicle threw up gravel as it spun to a halt in front of Ali's cottage, its passengers dismounting with evident relief.

"I didn't know it was possible to come up this track that fast," Kenny grumbled as they joined the others.

"So, what's the news on the hydro plant?" Ali asked.

Kenny shook his head ruefully. "It's a bit of a mess," he said. "When it stopped working some silly bugger tried to fix it – zapped some circuits and himself. Maybe he knew how to change a plug and thought that qualified him as an electrician."

"But can it be fixed?" enquired Marie.

"Ask your husband," Kenny said, "he's the expert."

"Yes, it can be done," Stuart responded. "We might need to pirate some bits and pieces from elsewhere but we can make it work. The hydro element is fine. It's some of the electrics that need repair. Me and Kenny reckon we could sort it all out in, say, three or four days. Assuming we can find the stuff that we need, of course."

"Somebody knowledgeable must have adapted it to feed the local grid in the first place," Ravi said. "What happened?"

"The guy died in the really bad flu epidemic they had over in Gairloch last year," Jimmy replied, looking glum. "Took out over half of what little population was left. There's an awful lot of abandoned houses around the bay now."

The group fell silent at this reminder of the precariousness of post-Zeno life, an unwelcome thought at odds with the beauty of the summer evening that they had been enjoying.

Finally, Jimmy continued. "There's something else. To do with local politics. There's clearly a lot of tension between that guy Alasdair Fleming and some of the Gairloch people."

"Who's Fleming?" Irene asked.

Ali looked across at Douglas. "You tell her," she said. "You've had more to do with him than the rest of us."

Douglas grimaced. "For my sins, yes," he said. "Not a pleasant man. He's a major landowner around here and considers himself to be the laird and therefore the person who knows what's best for the area. He's widely disliked, but has too often been able to impose his will on the locals. It's been very hard trying to negotiate things with him. He resents us, sees us as a threat."

"And so he should," Ali said. "He does his best to obstruct whatever we do to encourage co-operation. He's a divide-and-rule man."

"Well," Jimmy said, "they certainly don't trust him over there. When we told them that we could probably fix the system they were a bit wary about having us do it. They think that because we 'belong' – their word – to Fleming then that would give him a way to take over the whole thing.

In the end I persuaded them that we were our own people, so they do want us to do the job. But I'm sure we'll get trouble from Fleming."

"Somebody should just shoot the bastard," Kenny added vehemently. "He did my family out of some money years ago. He's an evil wee shite."

"We can worry about him later," Jimmy responded, giving his partner a warning glance. "For now we have to find the stuff that Stuart and you need, then get the job done. We can probably get some spares across the loch at Aultbea. The old NATO ship refuelling dock has all sorts of kit and we could do with getting some more fuel anyway. Once the hydro's working again the Gairloch folk are willing for us to run power across to here on the existing lines, so that will be a good supplement to our own generating systems."

To avoid them having to travel back and forth every day in the ATV, Marie volunteered to sail them to Gairloch Harbour and moor *The Cormorant* there as a kind of temporary workers' accommodation. It was not far from the harbour to the power station and their local contact, who was eager to learn about the electrical installations, could transfer them and their equipment in a garron cart each day. As Marie confessed to Irene, she was more than happy to have an excuse to take the boat out. At least it allowed her to feel that she was contributing to the general good rather than simply sponging off everybody else's hard work. She and Stuart were still living on *The Cormorant* even though there were empty houses that could have been renovated for them. At heart, she said, she was just happier on the water.

This arrangement produced an unexpected bonus in that, while the two men were repairing the electrical systems, Marie befriended the family who operated a fishing boat moored next to her. Between them, and the owner of a second fishing boat that worked out of the harbour, they came to a provisional agreement to trade fish for vegetables as well as for other supplies and technical services, initially with the Cove group but in the longer run, Marie hoped, with the entire Poolewe community. As she pointed out to Ali and Douglas on her return, they needed to make the most of Inverewe Gardens, which boasted the richest soil in the area. Even back in its days as a National Trust for Scotland tourist attraction some of the gardens had been given over to growing vegetables. Now, with the NTS no more, the estate had in effect become an arable smallholding and, therefore, a major local asset.

This new-found co-operation with their neighbours to the south was all the more remarkable for exactly that: being new. Why hadn't the Poolewe and Gairloch communities already conjoined their resources? Kenny supplied the answer.

"Fleming, of course," he said. "The Gairloch people never trusted him, and for good reason. So although it's obvious to us that working together would be better for everyone, the history of relationships with him makes it impossible. He just tries to screw anybody he comes in contact with."

"So we should bypass him," Ali suggested. "Let's try to arrange a meeting of people from both settlements and sort out a way of collaborating. If we stick together there won't be much he can do."

"Good idea," Sarah said, adding with a mischievous grin, "and who was always the outstanding go-between for obtuse, uncooperative scientists?"

"Yes," said Douglas. "I think organising that definitely falls to you, Alison. With Kenny and Marie to help since they already have contacts."

Ali smiled sheepishly, clearly pleased to have the task. "OK," she said. "I'll start on it first thing tomorrow."

"Keep an eye out for Fleming's factor," Kenny warned her. "Long thin beanpole of a guy called Carter. He came across us when we were checking the power cables. Told us we were trespassing on Fleming's land, so we said we were just ensuring their safety. But he'll have told his boss and they'll know something's up. He's the only other person left living on the estate. Fleming's wife and kids left him years ago, and now even the keeper has chucked it in and gone back to stay with his family up Ullapool way."

Fortunately, Ali encountered neither Carter nor Fleming in the several weeks she then spent drumming up interest and persuading people to attend the meeting. As she confided to Douglas, she rather enjoyed the challenge set by those who had long since become disillusioned with any kind of public involvement. It was good to be using her diplomatic skills once more, and now in the service of a much more important cause than scientific liaison. This time, after all, their lives might depend on it.

By the time the day of the meeting finally arrived, Ali had managed to speak with almost all the survivors in Poolewe and Gairloch. Compared to the pre-Zeno population it was piteously few, but enough of them showed up on the day to make Inverewe Gardens' former café look moderately crowded. Wanting to ensure that there was no dominant position from which the meeting would be run, Ali had the tables and chairs scattered at random across the room. She seated herself off to the side, as one person among many, and began proceedings by pointing out that she had no special authority. She was simply trying to encourage discussion, reminding them that they were there to plan a better future for them all. To set things going she explained that Stuart and Kenny had agreed to take responsibility for maintaining and monitoring the Kerry Falls hydro system. They expected no payment for this, nor was there any question of charging for the electricity. It would be their first contribution to a programme of mutual aid.

"Mutual aid." Ali emphasised the phrase. "This is what we need if we are to survive. A determination to contribute whatever we can to the well-being of all." She paused and surveyed the room, noting several nodding heads as well as one or two sceptical expressions. "Some of you have told me that you feel doubtful about that, worried that there will be freeloaders who take what is given but offer nothing. That's possible, of course. But it can be dealt with if it arises and it's well worth the risk if it allows us to make the best use of our limited resources."

Just then she was interrupted by the crash of a door being flung open at the back of the room, causing the entire group to turn and look. It was Fleming, followed by the much taller figure of Carter. Fleming swaggered in, as small men with large egos are inclined to do, noisily taking a seat in a central position and waving blithely to Ali as if giving her permission to continue. Ignoring his condescension, Ali simply carried on as if nothing had happened, refusing him the pleasure of obliging her to recap the meeting for his benefit.

"So," she said, not even looking in Fleming's direction, "what we need to do today is map out some of the things that different people can contribute and how we can best organise a co-operative through which everything can be channelled."

There followed a somewhat uneasy silence during which people looked expectantly at each other. Finally Conrad piped up.

"Perhaps we need to appoint a leader, someone authoritative who can sort these things out?"

Fleming looked pleased at this, turning to check where the contribution came from and favouring Conrad with a smile. "I'd support that," he said. "After all, I've had many years' experience of leading this community, something I'd be willing to carry on with in these difficult times."

Julie shot Conrad an icy look and spoke: "I'm not at all sure that's a good idea. We need to be working together, not passing the responsibility to one person."

"I must say I agree with Julie," Irene added. "I used to work with people who thought that strong leadership was the solution to everything – politicians, civil servants, that sort of person. Frankly, it solved very little and generally made things worse. It's one of the reasons that the Zeno crisis got to be so bad in England."

"That may have been your experience down there," Fleming said haughtily, "but here my leadership has been very effective." He gazed around seeking confirmation, but found only people looking at their feet and fidgeting until a sotto voce comment floated across the room.

"Aye, effective at lining your own pockets."

There were some smiles and nods at this, leaving Fleming red-faced and angry. He stood up and tried to position himself at the nearest thing to a focal point in among the tables and chairs.

"Who said that?" he demanded.

No one responded, although Ali noticed Kenny smiling to himself, while most people defiantly met Fleming's gaze until his eyes passed on.

"All right," he continued, "if that's the way you want it." He turned to address Ali directly, his voice gaining in volume by the second. "I've had enough of you lot moving in and stirring up my people against me. You're not welcome. I own much of the land around here and I don't want any of you on it, running electricity, travelling over it, anything at all. If I find you trespassing I'll have you physically driven off the place. No, in fact I'll set the dogs on you. Then we'll see how you like living here."

By now he was virtually apoplectic with rage, his face turning a disturbing shade of puce.

"Is that understood?" he bellowed, loud enough to make the people immediately in front of him flinch.

The words hung in the air for what seemed like minutes but must only have been seconds. Then Stuart's calm voice filled the silence.

"I'm afraid not, Mr Fleming. I think you'll find that ownership of land has fallen into abeyance. There's no longer a functioning central government. I very much doubt if the land register records survive anywhere. And even if they did, there's no one to enforce any claims to legal ownership. Scottish land must now be counted as a collective resource for the people who live on it, a resource which they all share and draw upon. That's why Ali MacGregor used the word 'co-operative' earlier. That's what we're trying to do – create a situation in which we can all co-operate to ensure the best use of what we have. As one resident you're welcome to be part of that process. But if you're not prepared to accept the framework, then I'm afraid that you have no business here with us."

There followed a stunned silence in which even Fleming was rendered momentarily speechless. Then, directing a look of disgust at Stuart, he waved to Carter to follow him and strode through the tables towards the door.

"You'll regret that," he announced as he walked, adding, "uppity nigger."

He was almost level with Irene at this point and she leapt to her feet in front of him, stopping him in his tracks.

"What did you say?" she asked.

"Get out of my way, you stupid bitch," he shouted.

Irene, who was several inches the taller, stood her ground and leaned down towards him until her forehead and nose were almost touching his. She spoke quietly and with menace.

"You are an appalling, racist little man without an ounce of decency in you. If you ever come near me or my friends I shall make it my personal business to kick you so hard in the balls, assuming you have any, that you will never walk upright again."

Fleming, exploding with incoherent fury, reached out to grab her, but before he could do so Jimmy and Kenny, who had silently come up behind him, took an arm each and lifted him clear off the ground. Kicking and screaming hysterically like a small child in the depths of a tantrum, he found himself carried out of the door and deposited unceremoniously on the concrete outside. Carter, who had carefully avoided the fracas, rushed to his side and helped him up while Jimmy and Kenny returned to the meeting, grinning broadly and making a great show of brushing off their hands.

Fleming's humiliation seemed to release something in the assembled company and suddenly everyone was talking animatedly to everyone else. For the next hour or so, people traded information on what resources they had access to and what expertise they might offer to each other. Ali wandered around, listening in on the conversations, occasionally contributing, but mostly making notes as to who was proposing what. Then she sat down by herself and began to arrange what she had written into some kind of order. When she was satisfied that she had established a workable series of headings, she restarted the general discussion.

"That was really useful," she said. "We've learned a great deal about what we can do together. I've made a list of the things that you've all been talking about and provisionally attached some names for each topic. What I suggest we do is go away and, in these smaller groups, work out how we can co-operate in each area. Then, in a week's time say, we can come back and fit the pieces of the jigsaw together. How's that?"

Mostly there were nods and smiles, although some looked a little doubtful. Finally, one of the doubters, a Gairloch fisherman, voiced his concerns in the liltingly accented English of a native Gaelic speaker.

"That's aye well and good, but it's going to take an awful lot o' time. I've no got much o' that – the fishing takes it all."

One of two of the others nodded agreement whereupon Conrad, who had been sitting in grumpy silence since his earlier intervention, saw his opportunity.

"It's like I said before," he announced. "You need a leader to take all the information on board and sort out policies. You can't just leave it to busy people; they don't have the time or the expertise. A leader, taking advice of course, can decide on courses of action. If it were me, I'd set up markets through which we can trade products and expertise. It was free markets that made English society work so effectively before Zeno."

Ali looked at him, dumbfounded.

"You think England was working effectively? Effectively for whom?" she asked. "It was deeply divided and unequal, people were starving, obliged to resort to food banks, exploited by self-interested irresponsible employers even where they did have jobs. The long-promised economic miracle, where riches would cascade down through society, turned out to be an ideological delusion." She shook her head in despair. "All the deregulated markets did was make the rich richer and the poor poorer. Why do you think there were all those crises? Why was Scotland so keen to become independent in spite of the obvious economic risks? England may have worked for you and for your rich father, but it sure as hell didn't for most people. And all those so-called strong leaders that you admire, they did nothing to resolve the problem even when it was staring them in the face."

She stopped and took a deep breath. Her audience, transfixed by her evident passion, looked on and waited for her to continue.

"No," she said firmly. "Strong leaders and free markets are a recipe for disaster. What we need here is co-operation not competition, a willingness to help each other in common cause. That doesn't need a leader. What it needs is collective commitment. Human beings first dragged themselves up out of the mud by working together. It was only later that you got people trying to be better than the next person, wanting to put one over the others, to become more important, to become boss. If we're to survive we have to avoid that kind of thinking, find ways of living that don't reflect those destructive attitudes."

She smiled at the fisherman who had been worried about finding time for all this. "Yes, it will take up our time. But we can manage that. We can recognise that some people, like you, will have quite enough on their hands ensuring our basic survival and no time left for organising or helping out in other activities. But many of us will be able to share those tasks and it's vital that we do. That way we'll all have a real sense of being in this together. This…" she pointed out of the window, "this is *our* world now. Only we can make a success of it, not some disembodied agencies away in Inverness or Edinburgh or London. It's ours to make work for us." She paused for a moment. "Us," she repeated, and gestured again to the world outside. "We need to create a way of life in which all is for all."

Realising that she had been wandering among the tables and waving her arms as she spoke, Ali blushed and hastily sought out her chair, subsiding into it. A silence followed, which was at last interrupted by a tremulous voice. It was a very old woman who had been seated quietly in a corner for the whole afternoon.

"The lassie's right," she said. "As many of ye know, I'm ninety-one and I've lived in these parts all my life. I grew up at a time when the only way we could manage was by helping each other. Back then my family were crofters, like many of yours. We'd been thrown off our land to make way for the sheep and the deer and the forestry, left to eke out a living along the coast here. My grandad used to tell me about the old days, about the coming of the big landowners, about our betrayal by the lairds. He was proud that we had stayed here and survived, and he always said that the only way we managed to do it was by sharing the load with each other. They were hard times. I wouldnae want them back. But he was right about the sharing. And so is yon lassie."

This quiet speech seemed to put the seal on the afternoon's events for most of those present. It remained only to arrange the work of the small groups and agree to return in a week to pool the fruits of their discussions. As they left, many of the participants stopped to thank Ali for her efforts and to compliment her on the success of the meeting. But she was less sanguine about it given the confrontation with Fleming, and also worried that the intensity of her response to Conrad would sow divisions among the Coveys. To calm herself she arranged with Douglas that he would pick her up later in the ATV. In the meantime she was going to take a walk around what remained of Inverewe Gardens.

The grounds were still impressive even though they could no longer be cared for as once they were. Beyond the area now given over to vegetables she found herself in among a thriving riot of exotic shrubs and trees. The paths were partly overgrown but still negotiable, and finally she found her way to a tiny jetty in a sheltered bay. There she sat down, looking across the loch to the headland which was now her home. It's an awful long way from Forrest Road, she thought, as she drifted into contemplating all that she had left behind. Minutes went by and then her melancholic reflections were interrupted by the sound of someone coming down the path. Turning, she saw that it was Jimmy.

"May I?" he asked, indicating the space beside her.

"Yes, of course," she smiled. "I'm just recovering from the stresses of the afternoon."

"You did great," he said, settling himself next to her. "Couldn't have gone better really." Then he grinned. "Did I mebbe hear a bit of Kropotkin there? Mutual aid? All is for all? Sounds familiar."

Ali turned to him, beaming. "You know Kropotkin, then. My dad got me reading him when I was in my teens. He was determined to educate me in all kinds of political theory, including anarchism."

"Aye, I've read Kropotkin. And all the rest of them radicals too. I'd a grandad who'd been in the Party, one of the Red Clydesiders. He didn't much approve of the anarchists, mind. He'd have wanted you quoting 'From each according to his ability, to each according to his needs' rather than 'All is for all'. But the spirit's much the same. And right enough for us."

They stayed there for a while sharing memories of parents, grandparents and radical politics until it was time to walk back through the gardens to find Douglas and the ATV. As they passed the now deserted café, Ali nodded towards it saying, "Let's hope it works, then."

Jimmy smiled at her. "Don't worry," he said, "we'll make it work."

That night, after a hastily prepared meal, Ali and Douglas fell exhausted into bed. They had spent much of the evening going over the afternoon's events until Ali felt that she could no longer think clearly about any of it. It was with relief that she finally fell asleep, curled around Douglas's back.

It was still dark when she awoke, uncertain as to what had disturbed her until she heard a low growl from Pike whom she could just make out standing by the window, his nose in the air and his ears erect.

"Whisht Pike," she whispered. "You'll wake Douglas."

But Pike continued to growl until she got up to calm him. As she did so she realised that there was a faint glimmer visible through the curtains which, when she opened them a crack, resolved itself into the flicker of a fire. In haste she woke Douglas, threw on some clothes, and rushed outside just in time to see the faint shape of two figures, one very tall and one short, disappearing into the darkness. She cried out to Douglas who was immediately behind her.

"It's Sarah's house."

"Yes, I can see," he replied. "Go and wake them while I get the water pump."

As she ran shouting out a warning, she half registered the crackling noise of the fire and saw that flames were licking up the end wall of the house. When she reached the door and flung it open there was already movement within. Sarah, Hugh, Irene and a very sleepy Charley emerged, just as Jimmy and Kenny arrived running.

"We heard the shouting," Jimmy called out. "Is everyone OK?"

"Yes," Ali replied. "Douglas is fetching the pump. Can you go and help him?"

Fortunately, they were able to get the pump working before the flames had reached the timber of the gable end so it was a simple enough job to douse the fire. Although the stonework of the building was blackened, there was no serious damage other than to the group's sense of their own security. By now everyone had gathered around.

"I saw two people running away," Ali told them. "One tall, one small. It's obvious who it was."

Kenny was inspecting some charred material at the foot of the burned wall.

"There's a pile of flammable stuff here," he said, lifting a fragment and sniffing it. "It's been soaked in something. Paraffin maybe. Hard to tell. It's as well you spotted it before it properly took hold."

"It was Pike, not me," she said. "He woke me up. Must have heard or scented them."

Charley, who was next to the dog, bent down and put her arms around him. "Thank you Pike," she said, "you're a clever dog."

The sight of the little girl embracing the animal raised some smiles among the disconsolate group, and, as dawn began to steal into the eastern sky, they assembled in Ali's house to consider their next move. Obviously something had to be done, and quickly, or they would never sleep safely again. They were now effectively at war with Fleming, and with some reluctance all agreed that the fight had to be taken to him. Jimmy, Kenny, and Douglas volunteered themselves for this task as the three most accustomed to using weapons, planning to set out as soon as they could. Nobody was going to sleep now other than perhaps the children, so it was a tired and chastened set of adults who watched the three men drive off down the track towards Poolewe. Fleming's house lay in the woodlands close to Loch Maree, and this was where they intended to confront him.

All morning Ali restlessly switched from one job to another, unable to concentrate on any of them. She was worried about Douglas, of course, although having seen him and Jimmy deal with the lorry hijackers she had no doubt about their competence. She was also troubled that so early in their attempt to foster a harmonious community they found themselves caught up in violence. Would this always be the way of it? Had Zeno left them with nothing more than a desperate struggle to survive at any cost? Her hard-won optimism of the previous day dissolved minute by minute as she watched and waited for their return.

It was past eleven when she heard the sound of the ATV approaching. Jimmy was not driving with his usual bravado and, when they came to a gentle stop, it became apparent why. He and Kenny carefully helped Douglas out of the vehicle and, one on either side, supported him across to the house where they settled him on the sofa.

"He's been shot," Kenny explained. "We think it's only a flesh wound in the upper arm – the bullet went straight through. He's lost some blood though."

Ali called to Charley: "Run up and fetch Eleanor. Tell her to bring her first aid kit. Quickly!"

Charley sprinted off to find Eleanor who was the nearest thing to a doctor that they had. A few minutes later she arrived, careering down the track on her bike, emergency bag flapping around behind her. While she examined and cleaned up Douglas's wound, Kenny explained what had happened.

"We parked well out of sight of the house. Jimmy worked his way closer in the woodland and once he was in a position to cover us, me and Douglas walked up the driveway as if we were coming to have a peaceful discussion. We got about fifty metres away when the bastard opened fire with a rifle. No warning, no nothing. Douglas was hit and went down from the impact, so I grabbed him and dragged him in among the trees. I could hear shooting as we went, and it was only once both of us were under cover that I realised that what I'd heard was a burst of automatic fire from Jimmy. Then it was quiet for a while until there came a shout from inside the house. It was Carter. He said Fleming was dead and he was coming out unarmed with his hands up. I figured he was telling the truth since we would be in a position to kill him if it was a trap."

At this point Jimmy took up the story. "I shouted to Carter to keep walking down the drive until he was level with those two, then told him to get down on his knees and shuffle towards where they were hiding. Then we waited. Finally I decided it was probably safe to make it into the house and, right enough, Fleming was dead. I'd seen where his second shot had come from while Kenny was dragging Douglas into the woods, and I'd hit him with that first burst of fire. Lucky, really. Then we brought the ATV up to get Douglas back here."

"What did you do with Carter?" Sarah asked.

"We took him with us, dumped him in Poolewe, told him to leave and that if we ever came across him again he'd be dead, no questions asked." Jimmy grinned. "And we told everybody we met in the village what had happened and where Carter was. Last we saw of him he was running away as fast as his long legs would carry him."

Ali looked up from where she was holding Douglas's good hand while Eleanor worked on his other arm. "Won't he come back?" she asked.

"No chance," Kenny said. "He's a complete coward and I gave him some graphic details of what I'd do to him. We'll go over there tomorrow and check out the house. He won't be there, and there's an ATV to be had and likely quite a lot of food stashed away. I think we can say that the Fleming problem is solved."

For the remainder of the day Ali insisted that Douglas rested on the sofa, much to his initial disgust, although he had to concede that she was right when he stood up and immediately felt dizzy. Eleanor was sure that there was no bone fracture, although the bullet had caught some muscle as well as tearing flesh. She strapped his arm to minimise movement and left him with a supply of powerful painkillers. Around nine o'clock, Ali persuaded him to retreat to bed where, after taking several of the pills, he fell asleep.

The sun had dropped behind the hills when Ali took herself outside to keep company with Pike in the garden. She sat looking across the loch at *The Cormorant* riding at anchor, Stuart visible in the stern longlining for haddock. Ali was troubled. The satisfaction that she had felt after yesterday's meeting had given way to a diffuse sense of hopelessness, a conviction that it was all far too difficult and that their good intentions were doomed to fail. She was desperately aware that she could have lost Douglas today; a few inches to the side and the shot would have taken his heart. His support had become so important to her since those first hesitant encounters in Edinburgh. She couldn't begin to imagine how she might have dealt with his death. This was love, she conceded to herself, for the first time in her adult life.

She mused on that as the light faded, trying to raise her spirits by – what was the line from the old song? – yes, accentuating the positive. But the positive kept slipping away, leaving only dark thoughts of loss and failure. Then, her ruminations were interrupted by the sound of a door closing and footsteps coming towards her. It was Irene.

"I saw you sitting out here so thought I'd join you if that's OK?"

"That's fine," Ali said. "I was just thinking about everything that's happened over the past few weeks."

"Mmmmn. Been eventful hasn't it," Irene observed. "How's Douglas?"

"He seems to be all right. Asleep and dosed with painkillers. I'm only just taking in how close that was to killing him. I don't know what I would have done."

Irene reached across and squeezed her arm. "But it didn't, did it. So be happy about that and stop entertaining terrible what-ifs."

Ali nodded. "I know," she said. Then, after a pause, "Do you ever think of how all this began for us? That day when we met at the National Gallery and you gave me the message for Sarah. Seems so long ago."

"Sometimes. Mostly to recognise that if we had known then what we know now we might have acted very differently."

Ali sighed. "But I don't suppose it would have had much effect," she said. "We'd still be caught in this impossible situation with so little to hope for. We failed. Well, I certainly did. If I'd gone public back at the beginning at least the Scottish government would have been obliged to do something earlier than they did."

Irene looked at her quizzically. "You think you're a failure?" she asked.

Ali nodded mutely.

"No, I'm not having that, Ali," Irene said firmly. "You couldn't have done anything to stop Zeno and does it occur to you that none of us would be here were it not for you? You got all these people together and organised them, first to go to your father's place and then to move on to here. It's you that kept them going. Without you this settlement wouldn't exist. Me and the others on *The Cormorant* would have had no safe haven to flee to. And now, after what you did yesterday and over the past weeks, we're going to be able to build a bigger community, make ourselves safer, create something worth having in the midst of all the death and destruction. If that's failure, I don't know what success would look like."

Ali looked at her friend, her eyes moist with held-back tears. "You really think so?" she asked.

"Of course. And you have to think so too because we all need you. You're our inspiration, Ali, and I'm afraid you're stuck with it."

She reached across and took Ali's hand in her own. Darkness was edging its way over the loch in front of them, broken only by a solitary riding light on the anchored boat rising and falling in the gentle swell. Hold onto the light in the dark, Ali told herself, hold onto the promise of a future. And sharing that hope, the two women gazed off into the still of the Highland night.

12

Some five hundred miles to the south, England is burning. The PeePees have discovered the cleansing joy of flames and they are leaving a trail of fire in their wake. Also in their wake is Jonathan Hart, tracking them by the terrible destruction that they are wreaking across the land. He sees the burnt-out buildings, the bodies, the PeePee symbols roughly painted on doors to mark their passing and to signal the forcible conversion of yet another poor soul. Hart is all but overwhelmed by despair at the horrors of which human beings are capable. 'Man's inhumanity to man' doesn't even begin to cover it, he thinks. But he knows what he has to do. Perhaps he has always known.

Remaining hidden in an empty house near Kings Langley, he waits until he is certain that the PeePee army has swept by to his north. Only then does he emerge, first working his way back to Whipsnade. The park is deserted. The buildings around the main entrance have been burned, but most of the rest – including his chalet – have been ransacked but left standing. He finds no bodies so presumes that Rowlands and the others have gone into hiding. Nor does he find the yaks. No doubt slaughtered for food, he thinks sadly, hoping that his yak might at least have met a speedy end. His hidden caches are still intact, allowing him to replenish supplies before moving on in pursuit of the marching hordes. After resting for a night in Whipsnade, he continues west.

This takes him not too far to the north of Oxford and, for reasons that are not entirely clear to him, he diverts a little from his cross-country route to visit the city. A kind of sentimental journey, he thinks, a farewell, an opportunity to recall a happier past. In the event it proves anything but a nostalgic encounter. Oxford is laid waste, now resembling one of those famous war photographs where the crazily leaning remains of buildings look like so many broken teeth. The ancient colleges have been razed, burnt out, and, in some cases, blown up, while over everything hangs the putrid odour of death. There are occasional movements among the ruins but Hart does not stay to discover who or what causes them. If there are survivors then, like him, they are doing their best to avoid each other.

From Oxford he turns north-west, knowing that sooner or later the core of the PeePee army will target Birmingham as the largest city in the region, and there he will find the Prophet. Along the way he picks up snippets of information from the few people that he meets who are willing to talk. In Banbury he strikes lucky, coming across a man who has succeeded in hiding himself and his family and who, after the uniformed main force had continued on its way, had seen the Prophet pass through in a horse-drawn carriage surrounded by a band of brown-robed Guardians. Feigning loyalty to the cause, the man had asked one of the ragtag band of converts in their train where they were headed and had been told that there is to be a great rally, addressed by the Prophet, in the grounds of Warwick Castle.

Hart covers the intervening twenty miles as quickly as he can, determined to reach the castle well before the rally. Once in the area he makes a surreptitious reconnaissance late one evening. Preparations are under way. A huge banner hangs across the entrance to the grounds announcing 'My God is a Consuming Fire', while a large open space close to the river is evidently to be the location for the rally itself, scheduled for two days hence. Hart goes into hiding then, and on the day of the rally dresses himself in Lionel's robe and hangs the PeePee pendant around his neck. Beneath the robe he is wearing the explosive belt and a holster for his pistol. He has cut through the robe's voluminous pockets so that when, monk-like, he thrusts his hands into them, as he has seen so many of the Guardians do, he can reach his weapon on one side and the dead man's switch on the other. Thus prepared, he sets out for the castle grounds.

Crowds are already gathering, some perhaps out of curiosity, but most out of misguided faith. As he walks Hart becomes aware that they make way for him or, rather, for his robe. To be a Guardian clearly commands respect and those around him are careful not to catch his eye, looking away or at the ground if he glances in their direction. So much fear, Hart thinks, what an extraordinary weapon it is. All these people, frightened of what awaits them, hoping and believing that there is another happier life to be had beyond the grave if only they follow the Word of the Prophet. As he wanders, a sense of revulsion grows in Hart, a loathing not directed at the desperate men and women around him, but at those who are playing on that despair for their own terrible ends.

Then, his train of thought is interrupted by a susurration that flows through the crowd like a ripple spreading out on the surface of a pool. Look, look, he is among us, the ripple says, and the faithful turn, searching to left and to right, wanting only a sight of the One. Hart also searches, at last locating a movement, a surge in the mass of disciples where a block of brown advances through them. In the midst of this protective cordon is a figure robed in white, supported on some kind of litter which elevates him above the heads of all the rest. He raises his hands, blessing those around him as the Guardians convey him towards a stage which stands in the midst of the arena.

Hart now begins to force his way through the mass of the faithful, the authority of his robe silencing any resistance. I have to get to them before they reach the dais, he thinks, and presses ever forward. The nearer he approaches to the Prophet's entourage, the more dense becomes the crowd and the more he has to struggle to make progress. But at last he reaches the outer edge of the brown-robed barrier where he slows almost to a halt. One or two of the Guardians look in his direction, puzzled perhaps that they do not recognise him. To them he murmurs, "Prophet's word be with you," to which they reply, "And with you, brother, and with you," turning their attention elsewhere as they seek out potential threats. Slowly he inches his way in among them, his hands now deep within his cloak, one gripping the pistol, the other, as he has rehearsed so often, priming the explosive belt and its dead man's switch. Now the Guardians ignore him, for he is to all intents and purposes one of them, a protector of the faith. It is not his face that they see. It is only his robe.

They are nearing their destination now, readying themselves to deliver the Prophet onto the platform from whence he will preach his sermon. Hart eases himself closer to the litter, ignoring the muttered imprecations of those he pushes out of the way. Here the crowd is at its densest, confining the Guardians' protective circle into a smaller and smaller space, compressing it such that Hart finds himself at last adjacent to the litter. He looks up at the Prophet. Just another madman on the make, he thinks, with a gift for oratory and an overweening desire for power.

The crowd is so tightly packed now that he can barely move his arms, but slowly he eases the pistol out of his gown, clutching it firmly in his right hand. Then he edges his arm upwards until it is free to level the gun. As he does so the Prophet catches sight of the weapon and for a split second he and Hart look at one another, the Prophet with growing astonishment and, finally, comprehension. Then Hart squeezes the trigger and the Prophet's head explodes, bone and brain and flesh spraying onto those surrounding him. There follows a frozen moment and then, as one, the Guardians fall upon Hart like hyenas onto a corpse. He disappears beneath a writhing mass of bodies. His task is fulfilled. His final thoughts as he releases the button on the dead man's switch are of Rosemary and of Jenny and of all the many millions of the dead.

EPILOGUE

It is a pleasant autumn afternoon of blue skies, warming sunshine and a scattering of fluffy clouds. An elderly woman is walking up the open hillside, each step taken with deliberation. It is not decrepitude that demands slowness of her. She walks as she does to enjoy the smell of the sea air, to feel the breeze on her face, and, above all, to think and to remember. Her long dark hair is now streaked liberally with white, or, as she confesses to herself when catching sight of it in the mirror, more accurately described as white streaked with black. Today it is tied into a ponytail, foiling the wind's desire to whip it back and forth across her face. She has vivid green eyes, as striking still as they were in her youth. She is sixty-seven years old.

Before reaching the brow of the hill where the wind turbines stand in silhouette, she turns to admire the view. Immediately below is her own house and those of her friends and their families. Beyond that, out on the sea loch, she can see a muddle of small sailing dinghies, criss-crossing each other at frightening speed. Lucy is teaching the children to sail, a vital skill in a world where harvesting the sea has become so important. Missing from view is the customary sight of the anchored *Cormorant*. Marie and Stuart are away on one of their regular voyages. Every few years Marie becomes restless, even now that she is nearing seventy, and they sail off for a month or more. On their first such voyage they dropped Conrad in Bristol so that he could return to the family home. He and Julie had suffered a none-too-friendly break-up and, given his distaste for the community's politics, there was nothing left to keep him in the

Highlands. Subsequently, Marie and Stuart have several times cruised the entire British coastline, returning with news of pockets of survivors scattered here and there. On this occasion they have been more ambitious, setting sail for Scandinavia where there are rumoured to be communities in the fiords.

Turning away from the loch, Ali calls to her dog who is busy eyeing the grazing sheep.

"Skye, Skye, come on. We're going."

The dog turns to see her continuing up the hill and follows obediently, constantly running circles around her. Skye, named for her Uncle Bill's dog of long ago, is a brown-and-white Border Collie with amber eyes, once the runt of a litter bullied by the other puppies and kept from his mother's teats. Ali bottle-fed him, and as far as he is concerned she is now his entire family. He knows where they are going today for this is a regular walking route. Up and over they climb, turning north towards the open ocean. Below them to the right there is a track running along the shore of Loch Ewe which would lead them to their destination, but she and Skye much prefer to walk across the low hills.

After a little more than a mile they are descending towards the Atlantic, aiming for a promontory beneath which the waves foam and break on the rocks. The rough track leads up to this spot from the right and there is a scattering of boulders where the track ends. Skye runs in among them, hoping for rabbits to chase but finding none. When Ali catches up she slows almost to a halt, looking around her. At this distance it is clear that the boulders have not gathered here by geological accident, nor have they been marked only by the sea-spray and the wind. Each has a flat sanded surface on which are engraved names and dates. Ali walks directly towards one of the less weathered rocks which reads simply: 'Douglas MacIntyre, 1991–2063'.

She stands before the memorial for some time, unseeing eyes fixed upon it. She had, she supposed, always expected Douglas to die before her. He was nine years her senior, after all. But it had still been a shock and had left a great chasm in her life. They had never had children, not by decision but by biological fiat. She did and did not regret that. It would certainly have added a new dimension to their lives, but it was not something that had seriously damaged the happiness that they shared. Besides, Ali had so many children by proxy. First, Charley and Lucy and that generation, and now their children and those of others. As the community's moving force she has come to be seen as some kind of mother to them all, although it is a designation that she would reject if anyone dared press it upon her. As she always maintains, she has been nothing more than a determined enabler. The fact that there is now a Wester Ross region, comprised of collaborating co-operatives from Ullapool in the north to Lochcarron in the south, is, she insists, merely something for which she has been the fortunate midwife.

At last she moves away from Douglas, walking among the stones, looking from one to another. Here is Jimmy, irrepressible Jimmy, with whom she has spent many an evening arguing political philosophy. He died in the only really devastating flu epidemic that they have experienced over all these years, as did Shona and one of her sons. Ali had been at a loss to understand how the virus reached them since there were so few travellers who might import it from elsewhere. But Sarah corrected her, pointing out that many of them could well be harbouring a mild and therefore unnoticed variant which, in lethal Zeno fashion, would suddenly mutate into something much more dangerous.

Ali continues onward, all the time getting closer to the sea. She is almost at the rear of the little forest of boulders now, and here she comes upon Irene. It pleases Ali to recall that Irene lived to see their plans for mutual aid come to fruition, for she and Julie had proved formidable campaigners for the cause, travelling up and down the coastline encouraging an ethos of collectivism. As she told Ali, Irene felt that she owed some recompense to the world after what she had come to think of as a misbegotten career in science and government.

Only one boulder remains beyond Irene's, this one the most weathered of all. Ali traces its blurred inscription with her fingertips. 'Pike' it reads, then below: 'in company with the spirit of Duncan MacGregor'. She smiles at the thought of Pike and her father reunited in the cosmic dust, something that Duncan believed to be the ultimate fate of all things. He would have approved of this entirely secular burial ground and would have been happy to be no more or less important than the dog. Ali pats the stone. "Good boy, Pike," she murmurs, then walks the final few paces to the ocean's edge.

The waves are much noisier here, rolling constantly onto the rocks just below. Ali sits down on a familiar flat stone, Skye beside her, and for a while watches the unpredictable flow of the turbulent blue-green water around and among the channels that the ocean has eaten into the land. Then she reaches into her knapsack and retrieves an old paperback book, its pages yellow and brittle. She dips into it seemingly at random, looking up every so often, turning her face to the sunshine, staring out at the vast vanishing horizon. After a while, a figure walks through the boulders behind her and calls out.

"I thought I'd find you here."

This is Charley, no longer the little girl who worshipped her Auntie Ali, but now a woman in her forties and with two children of her own.

"Your mum not with you today?" Ali asks.

"No." Charley smiles ruefully. "She's got herself worked up about the prospect of yet another breakthrough. She's in the lab with Dad. I expect it will turn out much like all the others."

"But she does keep trying," Ali observes. "It was always her great virtue, her determination. And it may yet pay off."

"Maybe," Charley says as she sits down. Then she continues, obviously excited. "I came looking for you because we've had a radio message from Marie and Stuart. They've come across a Norwegian community which sounds rather similar to ours. They have expertise that we don't, and vice versa, so we may be able to trade with them. They have several good ocean-going boats too."

Ali smiles. "As long as they're not Vikings. Wouldn't want all that looting and pillaging again."

Charley gives her a look. "Sometimes," she says, "I'm not entirely sure whether you're joking or not."

At this, Ali laughs out loud. "Yes, I could always fool you with a straight face when you were little. You used to get angry with me and go away in a huff."

Charley shakes her head, mock offended. Then, seeing Ali's book, asks what she is reading. Ali hands her the book.

"*Earth Abides*," Charley reads out. "By George R. Stewart. It looks very old."

"It is," Ali replies. "My father gave it to me. Well, he wrapped it up and buried it in the bottom of my backpack when we left his house to come north. I didn't know it was there. Didn't find it until we'd been here a while. Have a look inside. He wrote a message."

Charley looks and reads the message aloud: "Alison. You might find this interesting, perhaps even useful. Love, Dad." She turns to Ali. "And did you?" she asks.

"Interesting, certainly. Useful, I'm not so sure. It's a novel about trying to survive in a world in which most people have been almost instantaneously killed by a virus. First published in 1949. It's very much a product of its time. So many of its attitudes sound old-fashioned now."

She retrieves the book from Charley, handling it almost reverentially, and opens it to the page recording its printing history. She shows Charley the date.

"See, this edition is from 1965. My dad must have bought it second-hand somewhere. Although the cover says it costs five shillings, it has 'two and six' scrawled on it in pencil. That's the old British money, before the 1970s. Shillings and pence. A crazy system – Dad explained it to me once. The 'two and six' is half the five shillings."

Charley takes the book back, her attention drawn to a single biblical quotation from Ecclesiastes in the middle of the page opposite the printing history. She reads it out.

"Men go and come, but earth abides."

"Yes," Ali says. "The book ends with that line too. I guess it's the main theme. Human beings are transient but the planet will continue regardless. At the end of the book people are surviving in a kind of tribal society. Over-population has been curtailed by the disease, but at the cost of much of what people think of as civilisation. I think we're probably doing a bit better than them."

"Oh, I hope so," Charley says. "Out there" – she waves in the direction of the ocean – "there could be all sorts of survivors."

Ali nods. "Uh-huh," she says. "Who knows what's out there?"

She does not add, although both of them are thinking this, that once or twice in recent years they have heard the distant sound of aeroplanes above the clouds. Not the whine of jets, but the thrum of propellers. Someone, somewhere, still has access to technology beyond anything that they have here in Wester Ross.

Charley returns the book to her. "I'll have to have a read of that," she says.

"Of course," Ali replies, although she knows that reading is no longer something that much occupies the younger generations. The elders have carefully assembled all the books that they can recover into a library, but as time goes by it receives less and less use.

Charley stands up. "I've got to get back," she says. "The kids will be in from their sailing lessons shortly. See you later."

Once Charley has gone, Ali rests a hand on Skye's warm back and gazes at length into the clear Atlantic water. The sea has calmed while they were talking. It no longer batters the rocks but is now lapping tenderly against them. She watches the seaweed turning this way and that beneath the surface and she pictures all the life that the ocean supports: creatures too tiny for her to see; exotic crustaceans crawling across the seabed; fish of every shape, size, and colour; and, out in the deep ocean, the dolphins, the sharks, the whales, perhaps – she smiles to herself – perhaps even the massive sea-monsters of mythology.

She raises her eyes from the water, gets to her feet then turns and looks back at the land. Although they are not visible from here, she knows where to picture the great mountains that surround her Highland home. She whispers the names to herself, relishing their Gaelic beauty. Over there, to the east, the majestic An Teallach. To the south-east, hard by Loch Maree, Slioch. To the south, the giants of Torridon: Beinn Eighe, Liathach, Beinn Alligin. These mountains, she knows, are composed of some of the oldest rock in the country, rock that has endured many hundreds of millions of years. Against that ancient backdrop human beings have been little more than the tiniest flicker of light. A flicker that has shone brightly, to be sure, but a flicker nonetheless. As the inscription in her book says, men will indeed go and come. Perhaps they are going now, tumbling into the darkness of a passing age. But, she is certain, the earth itself will abide. And for Ali today, that is enough.

Acknowledgements

I am grateful to all those who read drafts for me, offering criticism, suggestions and encouragement: David Anderson, Kristyn Gorton, Tatiana Heise, Gail Murden, Phil Stanworth, Jamie Tudor, Olwen Tudor, as well as several members of Olwen's reading group.

I am grateful to Tom Halstead who corrected my outdated laboratory equipment terminology, and to John Illingworth who advised with regard to yachts and maritime matters. Needless to say, any surviving errors are my responsibility.

I am also indebted to Sophie Bristow for meticulous copy-editing, and to Lauren Bailey, Emily Castledine, Rosie Lowe, Fern Bushnell and no doubt others unnamed at Troubador, who eased me through the publication process.

Laura Spinney's splendid study of the 1918 flu pandemic, *Pale Rider: The Spanish Flu of 1918 and How it Changed the World* (Jonathan Cape, 2017) is fascinating and frightening in equal measure, and proved to be a constant source of stimulation and useful information.

For a novel whose characters are forced to traverse so many regions of the UK, a word on geography is appropriate. I have tried to ensure that overall geographical features are accurately represented. So, for example, the route followed by Ali's group as they trek through the mountains from Stronmilchan to Torlundy is real enough. But I have taken liberties with specific locations, which are often entirely invented, such as Malvern Edge Farm, Duncan's home in Stronmilchan, or Fleming's house by Loch Maree.

Lastly, I am grateful for the constant companionship of Azul, who nagged me to go for walks in the mountains when I spent too long writing, and who is the inspiration for the character of Pike.